River Rouge

"John Jeffire's brilliant new novel *River Rouge* takes readers on a riveting journey into the 'heart of darkness' of Henry Ford's dream and the gritty beginnings of America's working class nightmare. Jeffire's rich early history of Detroit includes a breathtaking story that will keep readers on the edges of their seats as the novel travels through early Detroit gangster culture, the exploitation of immigrant workers at The Rouge, and a wild plot twist that involves DIA Muralist Diego Rivera and his radical artist wife Frida Kahlo. *River Rouge* is an engaging novel that brings Detroit's history and the true grit of Detroit's working class struggles together in one of the finest novels to be written to date about The Motor City. Jeffire's poetic sensibilities weave an exquisite tale that readers will not soon forget."

—**M.L. Liebler**, author of *Wide Awake in Someone Else's Dream*

"John Jeffire's *River Rouge* is a wild ride through Depression-era Detroit, bringing to life such diverse local and international legends as Diego Rivera and the Purple Gang, the Rouge Plant and Harry Bennett, all bound together by a humble Armenian immigrant just trying to survive. Jeffire pumps passion and life into history here with the punchy dialogue and wit that only a Detroiter can bring to this material."

—**Jim Daniels**, author of *Eight Mile High*

"John Jeffire's *River Rouge* bristles with energy."

—**Anca Vlasopolos**, author of *The New Bedford Samurai*

"John Jeffire combines the notorious Purple Gang and Diego Rivera, creator of the iconic *Detroit Industry* mural, to make art from art. With grab-hold wit Jeffire pulls the workers off the DIA wall and into the fires of his prose. Jeffire summons the images, idioms and cadences of bootleggers and extortionists. Even the infamous union-buster Harry Bennett shows up. Jeffire grabs hold all the levers of industry to create a gripping story that makes so much sense you're certain it's all true."

—**Joy Gaines-Friedler**, author of *Dutiful Heart*

River Rouge by John Jeffire

Copyright © 2014 by John Jeffire

All rights reserved. No part of this book may be reproduced or transmitted in any form or by any means, electronic or mechanical, including photocopying, recording or by any information storage or retrieval system, without written permission by the author, except in brief quotations within a review.

ISBN 978-0-615-31724-3

Cover image credit, Diego Rivera mural (used with permission):
Detroit Industry, North Wall (detail)
    Fresco, 1932-1933
    Diego Rivera (Mexican, 1886-1957)
    Gift of Edsel B. Ford
    Detroit Institute of Arts

Cover design: Larry Hennessee.

The author owes great thanks to many people for their support and guidance. Specifically, Mariela Griffor for the Spanish translations and Arthur Stepanian for the Armenian. Also, the historians at the Detroit Institute of Arts for helping with historical accuracy when imagination could not fill the gaps. Wonderful friend and colleague Matthew Brown, for seeing when I was no longer able. And Konnie, for listening when there was no one else.

This book is fiction. Any resemblance between its characters and actual people, living or dead, is merely coincidental. In the case of historical figures, their portrayal is purely the product of the author's imagination.

Printed in the United States of America

*for Konnie—
my cup of wine
overflowing*

Part One

This was winter—misery, and slightly less misery. Every night for three weeks they ventured out and the hours blurred in the hum of January wind rushing through the Grand Trunk Railroad yard across the river from Canada. Watchless, they measured time by feeling, but all they felt now was the bone burning cold. Even with two pairs of wool socks, Haik's toes were numb inside his pigskin boots and he forced himself to scrunch them and lightly kick his heels together to keep his feet alive. He waited, huddled with his older brother Vahram and neighborhood friends Gee-Gee and Orlin. His hands had again frozen inside the unlined pockets of his jacket, so he lifted them out, cupped them dumbly over his mouth, and exhaled the moist warmth from his lungs to buy his fingers a moment of sensation. The rusted steel hull of the Ford flatbed offered a thin layer of protection, but icy hunger twisted in their stomachs, impossible to ignore, impossible to thaw.

"Goddamn, it's cold."

"Colder'n a witch's tit."

"How you know how cold a witch's tit is?"

"Least I felt a tit. You ain't felt nothing but your own crank."

"Get bent, piker. I done more than felt a tit. I…"

"Your sister's tit don't count, loverboy."

"Don't you say nothing about my…."

"Shhhh. Shuddup, guys. Not lonk now."

Vahram sat shotgun, looking out into the frozen dark. Most people, the Americans, said he spoke funny, with an accent, but Haik spoke the same way and it was less funny than their parents, who had escaped from Armenia with their young children and could speak only timid scraps of English, so humiliated they barely opened their mouths in public.

Aveli lav e Americayi mech kich ma anoti allank kan Hayastani mech meradz, his father would tell his sons, *Better to be a little hungry in America than dead in Armenia,* and both boys nodded. They were small when they fled their homeland, but they could still hear their wailing aunts and cousins raped and pistol whipped by the Turks, picture uncles and a grandfather bayoneted in the village streets, their severed heads left in a pile near the church. The boys were raised to respect their father, but it was getting harder to listen to his dusty lectures about stealing and honor and living a holy life. None of that bought food. And here in America they had known full bellies in their time running with the Purple Gang, but that time was over, finished, behind them forever. In some way,

Haik thought as the cold bit into him, it was better to have never been full than to have known it and then returned to hunger. Hunger was a madness, a disease whose only cure was these nights making war against the icy world.

A little hungry in America. Every morning, each member of the family got a slice of bread with butter and a glass of milk. At night, they split a piece of ham or a chicken breast plus another slice of bread and butter, and took half an apple or pear from the three their father brought home from work at the A & P. Their bellies ached, so the only answer was raiding the trainyards. In sleep, Haik sometimes wrestled in hunger and memories of Armenia. Wrestling with his brother and cousins, swimming and carrying huge rocks at the river, growing stronger by the day. Vahram, with whom he shared a small upstairs bedroom overlooking a new river, the gray Detroit, was always the one to wake him and calm him, telling him not to worry, they'd go soon, lurk in the frozen dark and take what was needed to survive. *I don't give two shits for badiv—our sisters need to eat,* Vahram would say, using the Armenian word for *honor,* whenever Haik questioned their trainyard runs.

Vahram was always right. Always, he knew the best thing to do. Haik did not like to think it, but Vahram was more his father than the graying, slump shouldered man who always had a lecture but never enough money in his pocket or food on his table. He did not like to think this way, but America was not a place for respect. Yes, their father had delivered the entire family from certain death in Armenia, quieted their fears in the stink and coughing of the dark bowels of a ship headed to America, but now, once delivered, he seemed empty of dreams or anything resembling strength. Even the bastard bow tied teacher they had known and hated in school, Mr. Tulloch, had more power than their father.

School. They had traveled to America in the dank hull of an oceanliner, rats crawling over them in the darkness, the stink of hundreds of other immigrants wedged into every scrap of inescapable space. They arrived in Detroit, a swarming city of jobs and every color of skin imaginable, their new life of promise ready to begin. After a year helping their father unload fruit, fish, and vegetables in Eastern Market, their father decided they needed to learn, so they ended up at the Bishop Ungraded School in Paradise Valley on Winder Street, an unruly, three-story madhouse. It was actually two schools, one for "academic" students, which Orlin and Gee-Gee attended, and the other, well, for anyone else. This was where Vahram and Haik were placed.

Mayhem ruled Bishop. So unlike the schools in Armenia, where silence and work were required or discipline came with a cane, Bishop was a carnival of lunatics and lawless flesh and bone weapons. "Shtarkers," the Jews at the school called themselves, strongarm toughs. There was Sam "Gorilla" Davis, the "bug" with his wormy lips and slit, nearly touching eyes, little as a girl but lethal; the Keywells, Harry and Phil, tall and thin but unsmiling and always looking right through you; little Mikey Selik, quick with a grin and slick with his words, the first to instigate blood but always avoiding shedding any himself; Harry Milman, beefy and belligerent and willing to attack even when there was no threat or provocation and fueled by a hatred of Italians; and Ziggy Selbin, the slight one whose head was topped with greasy blond hair and always tilted like he wanted to ask you a question.

Their first day was an adventure. Shouting and laughing ruled their floor of the school. The bespectacled principal brought Vahram and Haik to their room, where all eyes seemed to mock them. They sat down quietly, arms at their sides. Mr. Tulloch, bow-tied and sporting a thin mustache, approached them.

"You geniuses speak any English? Huh? You speak English."

He was practically shouting.

"Yes," Vahram offered, and the others all laughed.

"Shut up and work," Tulloch commanded, but the laughter did not cease. Selik grinned and Gorilla Davis would not take his eyes off them.

"'Yes,' well that's a glorious start. Now here's the lay of the land. Are you following me? Good. You're in here with the lowest of the low, loons, goons, misfits, and socially unacceptable incorrigibles. You keep quiet, though, do some work, and you might learn enough to not end up in jail for the rest of your life. Understood?"

Haik did not understand what Tulloch said, but Vahram nodded as if he did. Haik knew the word "work" so he figured the teacher was demanding that both boys work and not cause trouble. Tulloch's one front top tooth was yellowy brown and his oily hair did not camouflage the scabs on his scalp. He opened a book on their desk and, with a bit of pointing and gabbing, instucted them to begin writing English letters. The symbols were mysteries. Haik and Vahram tried to draw them as best they could. It was pointless but Tulloch seemed to approve and retreated to his teacher's desk.

"Who's you twos?"

Milman sat a row over. He was already growing a mustache. Vahram bowed his head while Haik remained silent.

"You's ain't I-tal-yins, is you?"

Vahram gave a look to Haik that assured him he would handle the situation.

"No, no Ital-yoon."

The others began laughing. Tulloch slapped a yardstick loudly on his desk and commanded them all to shut up. They complied and tried to look like they were working until their first break time.

On break out in the yard, Selbin and Gorilla Davis confronted them. Davis' mouth was open, his puffed lower lip jutting out.

"Where you from?" asked Selbin, his voice high and whiney.

"We? He and me, we from Armenia."

"Nar-neen-ya?"

They could barely make out what Davis was saying.

"Armenia. Yes. Our country name Armenia."

"Nut nigh-na pwace id nat?"

Davis peered at them, his slit-eyes narrowing even more, as if accusing them of something. Haik always deferred to Vahram, who searched for an answer.

"Hello. We Vahram and Haik. We from Armenia."

"Nat not what ni assed nu. Nu nink I'm stupit? Nu nink nat?"

There was an unreasonable challenge in his voice. He was a good half foot shorter than Vahram and even Haik looked down at him. Something began to burn in his narrow eyes. What did he want from them?

He attacked. He shot fist after fist up at Vahram, who stepped back in defense, narrowly avoiding the blows. Vahram was a strong wrestler, and he threw Davis aside, which ratcheted up his anger.

"Nu naffin' at me?"

He squinted at Haik, who had not laughed or even moved. What was going on here? What had Vahram said to ignite this fury? This was a school? Where was Mr. Tulloch?

Before he could grasp the situation, Davis was on him, landing a stone-like fist to his jaw, followed by another to his eye. Vahram moved to step in, but the tiny ape landed another shot to Haik's nose, exploding it with blood. Vahram jumped on Davis' back and drove him to the ground, smothering the whirlwind of rage. He maneuvered Davis to his back and pinned arms down with his knees, but as he cocked his arm to deliver a clean blow, Milman and the Keywells descended on him, raining boots and punches.

Haik thought they would die right there on the playground. Vahram rolled off of Davis and shielded his head from the avalanche of punches and kicks. Davis rose and was immediately at Haik, a lunatic beast, his eyes widening as he hammered away at Haik's head and body. Selik and Selbin joined Davis, kicking at Haik's ribs, while Milman and the Keywells continued to focus their onslaught against Vahram, who was fending them off and inflicting damage on his opponents despite the odds. And then, without explanation, the tide turned.

"Get off 'em."

A tall, thick-chested black boy waded into the fray, landing a shot to Selbin's cheek and grabbing Davis around the waist and lifting him off of Haik in one swift motion. A large-nosed, dark-skinned boy took Vahram's side and landed a blindside fist to Milman's face. The battle royale continued, the other students all crowding around, forming a wall of shouting, cheering gawkers.

After a furious minute, the scene calmed, all the boys panting, bloody, staring each other down, fists still cocked. Selik (who had avoided any actual fighting) and Selbin held Davis around the waist, trying to neutralize him as he struggled against the chains of their arms. The standstill iced the entire yard.

"Okay, okay, break it up hooligans! You heard me…."

Tulloch pushed through the crowd followed by several other teachers.

"You gonna be sorry you stepped in, nigger. You too, dago. You ain't nothing but a nigger that eats spaghetti," threatened Milman, spewing blood from a split lip.

"Shut up, Harold. You others, let's go, show's over, everyone back inside."

"Harold! He just called you Harold," beamed Selik, and Milman burst into a new frenzy, launching haymakers in Tulloch's direction. Two teachers rushed to Tulloch's rescue and began to administer a beating as severe as the one inflicted on Haik and Vahram. Milman would not stop, though, and Selik and Selbin had to pin Davis to the ground to keep him from leaping to Milman's aid.

"Welcome to the Bishop Ungraded School," smirked Tulloch as he smoothed his hair against his blistered scalp. "Take a minute and get cleaned up, and then right back inside. Understand?"

Haik did not comprehend the words, but he nodded and wiped the still-trickling blood from his nose. This was a place of learning? He backed against the brick wall behind him, fearful of an unseen punch catching him. Vahram still stood in his fighting stance, watching as the teachers beat Milman while the defeated shtarkers looked on. The entire war had lasted no more than five minutes, but the end had not come quick enough for Haik and Vahram, who now sensed what their relatives felt when the Turks invaded their village and opened the slaughter.

"Don't worry 'bout them," the black boy intoned. "Name's Orlin. Orlin Crutchfield. They do that to everybody who new."

The boy extended a hand, which Haik took. Again, he could not grasp what was being said, but he sensed it was not threatening. Why he had helped them against the mob, he wasn't certain, but he was grateful.

"Thank you, very good thank you," said Vahram. "I name Vahram. This my brother, Haik."

He shook hands with both Orlin and the darker boy who completed their foursome.

"Glad to meet you guys," said the fourth fighter, who could pass for Armenian but spoke with another accent. "I'm Luigi. Friends call me Gee-Gee."

"Them guys," the black boy, Orlin, continued, "especially the little bug, they just want trouble. They Jews. Crazy men. Stay way from them."

"Yeah, everyone says they're 'purple,' like rotten meat. They give you anymore problems, we'll be around," added Gee-Gee.

Haik and Vahram brushed themselves off and righted their twisted, bloodied shirts. They looked at each other. Drenched in blood, they had their first real American friends.

Despite their efforts to learn, the boys soon realized Bishop was nothing more than a den of violence and physical punishment. Milman and Davis were never seen on the grounds after that day, followed by the Keywells a week later, and one by one the worst of the toughs disappeared. In the classroom, the survivors were given assignments, words to write down, numbers to add, and supposedly taught "careers" in carpentry and mechanics, but Mr. Tulloch spent more of his time cuffing kids in the back of the head and pulling their ears than actually teaching anything. During breaks, Vahram proved himself with his fists and wrestling; in one playground scrap, he broke a boy's arm. Haik was more timid, but Vahram coached him and during breaks he and Orlin and Gee-Gee wrestled and did "play fighting," imitating their favorite boxers like Stanley Ketchel, Jack Johnson, Ad Wolgast, and Jack Dempsey in open-hand championship matches. They hated the school, but they learned what they needed to survive.

One day as they walked home from Bishop, Haik and Vahram saw the whole crew, Milman, Davis, the Keywells, Selbin and Selik, at a sidewalk fruit stand with a heavily muscled older man in a suit standing by, looking on as if he were evaluating them. Milman was arguing with the stand owner, an unshaven old Italian in dirty breeches.

"…and Mr. Ray here was just trying to help you run your business is all, that's it. All you had to do was pay him a little money and a bunch a bugs wouldn't come and visit you. But you I-tal-yins, that's how's you show respect…."

As Milman argued and pointed in the man's chest, the others circled around and began to take pieces of fruit and throw them at each other. When the old man turned to stop one of them, Milman grabbed a bushel basket of apples that sat in front of his wooden vending cart and threw it out into the street. When the old man turned to see what the thick chested thug had done, Selbin, Selik, Davis and the Keywell boys all put their backs into the back end of the cart and tipped it over, sending more apples, cherries, peaches, and other fruits spilling onto the sidewalk.

"Mr. Bernstein was trying to be real fair with you, but just like a I-tal-yin you wouldn't be fair with him. What kinda person is you, anyway?"

Milman took out a knife. Harry Keywell produced a sawed-off baseball bat. They closed in on the old man, smiling, their mentor looking on with approval.

Vahram grabbed Haik by the arm and guided him back around the corner. They would take a longer way home.

Although Milman and his crew no longer showed up for school, Bishop was no less dangerous. Haik learned to speak English with more confidence and to fight even better. One day a man approached him after seeing him beat a much larger boy during recess. He could use a man like Haik, he said, and Haik liked that word, "man."

"My name's Goldberg, real easy to remember," said the suited stranger with big ears, who smiled and pointed to a gold upper front tooth. "The deal's simple: Do what I tell you's, and if you ever get caught, you ain't never heard of no Mr. Pinchas Goldberg, and you don't know nothing from nothing about nothing. Hell, you guineas don't even speak no English, you see? So, you wanna make a little jack? I need me some little shtarkers with strong backs."

And that's where life in America really began. Since 1917, the Damon Act supposedly made alcohol illegal in Michigan, and in 1920 the Volstead Act spread the ban to the whole country. But booze flowed in Detroit. Plenty of it. Everywhere, especially in alley garages and warehouses throughout the city, brewers made sure no one went thirsty. Before long, Haik, Vahram, Orlin, and Gee-Gee would walk to the bank of the Detroit River, where they would meet Goldberg. Long after midnight, they would row a longboat from a cove just off Riopelle Street not far from Belle Isle to a makeshift dock on a tiny island not much bigger than the boat itself and meet Mr. Goldberg's Canadian bootleggers, who motored to the drop-off in a sleek boat with a powerful engine. The smiling Canucks watched as the boys loaded the wooden cases packed in straw onto their longboat. It was mostly easy. Goldberg held a lantern on shore to guide their furious rowing against the swift current. Once on land they'd load the cases onto the truck that was already almost full with stacked wooden crates and cover everything with a tarp. All the boys would hop into the back of the rig, laughing and swearing and recalling the evening's journey, imitating the funny accent of the Canucks.

The trip to their final destination always included one detour. Before heading to the Sugar House on Oakland Avenue, Goldberg stopped at a small garage in Highland Park where the boys would unload at least four cases of goods.

"Now, here's another little bit a business. Don't you's never mention the little stop we just made. Just between alla us, got it? You don't mention shit or shinola to the Bernsteins or none a the other Purples, see?"

The boys nodded. What did they care if they made a quick stop before the main delivery? Goldberg paid them like he said; they wouldn't open their mouths to anyone. And nothing was suspected at the Sugar House, which was always the same. The tartly sweet smell of sugar beets brewing somewhere in another part of the warehouse, Mr. Goldberg slipping in the side service entrance before the loading door was lifted and the truck was pulled inside, where a group of well-dressed men was always at a table playing cards, smoking, and drinking whiskey. Mr. Ray Bernstein, the stout, threatening man who had hired Milman and crew to terrorize the downtown vendors, or one of his brothers, Joe, Isadore, or Abe, gave them each a dollar and every so often a bottle of product. This was the home of the Purple Gang.

Treasure, pure treasure. The dollars they received from the Bernsteins and Mr. Goldberg could buy sausage from Kowalewski Meats or bread for a week for the whole family, and it was worth every sleepless night and every strand of muscle they burned into the oars until the tip of the boat ground hard onto the muddy shore. They sometimes even had enough money left over to buy their sisters Ovsanna and Arkina shoes or new underwear. The Bernsteins and Goldberg liked them and treated them with something resembling respect, a thing they had never experienced in America. America finally seemed like a place worth living in.

One day after a successful run, Goldberg took the boys aside before heading to the Purple Gang headquarters for the final delivery.

"Okay, you's passed the test, regular members of the Jewish Navy. You done like I told you, didn't steal nothing, kept your kissers shut. Hell, you palooks could be real live full-blooded Purple material some day. Now here's a promise: if you little pikers play your cards right and don't take no wooden nickels, I might just have some real work for you in the future. Courtesy of the Bernsteins," Mr. Goldberg assured them with a wink, then added without a smile, "but, you don't go nowheres near that river without permission, 'cause, well, let's just say the Bernsteins wouldn't like that."

They knew what he meant. They read the newspapers and looked at the pictures of the bodies turning up in the streets, riddled in bullets, and no one ever saw anything—they knew the consequences of knowing too much about the Purples' business. This was America. But unlike Armenia, where the Turkish army marched into town with guns and bayonets, too many to take on and hope to survive, here you could fight back and have a chance. The enemy was everywhere—their teachers, the beat cops in the lower East side, most of whom looked the other way when guns cracked and bodies slumped on the sidewalks, the warrior clans of Jews and Italians on either side of Hastings or the Irish in Corktown or the Poles in Hamtramck or Mexicans in Mexicantown that claimed their own little slum kingdoms. But at least they could fight back. And every single one of those dollars that found their way into their hands was reason to keep fighting.

They kept up with school, but Vahram learned the most by pouring over newspapers he collected from the sidewalk, scanning the pictures to piece together the story the words described, and deciphering what the street signs said, the names made out of symbols that looked nothing like what they had known in Armenia. Once Vahram had figured out the new alphabet, he taught Haik. But it was never enough for Mr. Tulloch, who always wore a red bow tie and found a reason to "discipline" them several times daily before they were allowed to flee. One afternoon, Tulloch called Vahram to the chalkboard and commanded him to spell a word called "ignoramus," a word they had never heard before, and added with a smile "that is, if you think you can," and Vahram, who was not as tall as the teacher but whose muscled forearms and thick neck spoke with new authority, said his last words ever in an American school.

"Maybe I spelling this words: you a big ass-hole."

Vahram and Haik had never defied their teacher—their culture forbade it. But Vahram knew when he was being made the butt of some new cruelty and his pride would not endure it. Tulloch stood speechless and the room froze. He then found his discipline rod and strode to Vahram, who stood up from his desk and gripped down steady with mouth set and fists balled. The teacher raised his rod but Vahram dug in on the chalky floor, flashed his teeth, hands cocked. And then the strangest thing happened, something Haik could not explain but he somehow understood. Tulloch stopped cold, lowered his whipping stick, and then rushed with his lip quivering from the room, his face as red as his bow tie. Within a minute, both Vahram and Haik were led roughly from the room by two men who smelled of old beer and sweat and they never returned to school.

At home, their father silently shook his head, looking down at the bare floor of their tenement house, and their mother, a work-worn woman of her country, said nothing as she patted her husband's shoulders, which seemed to slump even closer to the earth with a burden they could not see.

"Badiv," he muttered, *honor*, and Haik didn't know if the old man meant that Vahram had protected or harmed the family's honor. Vahram, like their mother and sisters, said nothing. He busied himself working on a radio he was building to sell to a neighbor. Maybe his older brother was ashamed or maybe he was just tired of listening to tired words spoken from a dusty, useless world that no longer existed.

In Detroit, the Purple Gang's guns and fast cars and mountains of money ruled everything. Milman and company were joined by two "yorkies," shtarkers from New York, the Siamese twins Eddie Fletcher and Abe Axler. They were both small, hell, Fletcher had fought pro in New York as a featherweight, but there was a cold distance in their black eyes that sent a clear warning about crossing them. No matter how tough any of them might be, though, all of them worked for the Bernsteins. The business of the Purples had grown from shaking down street vendors to using the Oakland Sugar House to front their booze enterprise, and they were at the glorious point they couldn't sell their product fast enough. And they were as smart as they were ruthless. Brewing booze wasn't how to best turn a profit. No, the Bernsteins figured out that it made more sense to let others make the hooch and then to steal it from them—why go through all the messy parts? They let stiffs smuggle good uncut Canadian whiskey across the Detroit River and then hijacked the bootleggers, gunning them down on the spot if any resistance were offered. Guns and empty consciences made them rich.

At the warehouse, Axler and Fletcher became their mentors, introducing them to yet another phase of the operation, cutting. In a back room, stacks of whiskey crates sat unopened, and next to it tables where empty bottles were lined up in rows like crystal soldiers. Overhead, two large metal troughs were suspended from the low ceiling and several copper spigots descended from each. Two older, rough looking men took turns watching over them, Mr. Selbin, whom they all called "Yonkell the Polack," and Isadore Swartz, a bulldog of a man whose crazy blue eyes and constant snarl burned instant fear into Haik and Vahram.

"Okay, monkeys, looky here and learn something," said Fletcher, his black eyes darting to each of the boys. "This is where we fix up our own little version of Canadian whiskey. You see, the regular stuff is too strong, so we, we doctor it up a bit, make it go twice as far. Here, see this bottle? See this little paper tag on the top? You peel that back and pop the lid, like this, and then you pour the whole bottle into the top a this here tub, like this, see? You do that with twenty, thirty bottles, then you set these empties under all these nozzles here. You following me? Next, you put these siphons in each a the bottles, and you turn on the nozzle and fill the bottle half-way with whiskey. Got it? We don't waste not one fucking drop of whiskey, you understand? Once you got a case of half filled whiskey bottles, you take it over to this other tub and you do the same thing all over, but this tub you fill up with water. You top off all the bottles till they're full and that's the whole shebang. Put the caps back in, put the little tag back over the cap, and then stack the crates over there. You got it?"

The boys all nodded.

"And don't none a you's get any idea about gettin' light fingers with no bottles," added Axler, who always seemed to be smiling even when nothing was funny. "Last pikers who lifted some bottles, well, they ain't around to talk about it no more, kapeesh? Huh? For Christ's sakes, at least nod or something if you understand, huh?"

They nodded.

"And don't you be sampling the goods, neither," Fletcher advised. "You need a clear head to do this job right. We'll pay you good, so don't muck this up, understand?"

They nodded again and went to work cutting.

"And last thing," Fletcher added. "We got old Yonkell the Polack and Mr. Swartz to watch the whole operation and keep an eye on you's. Don't drop the ball when old Izzy is on watch. He don't like mistakes and he don't take well to foolin' around. You all got it?"

Vahram and Haik understood the sick brilliance of what the Purples were doing. They, along with several former classmates from Bishop, were now junior Purples, too young to be driving trucks or carrying guns or handling money, but they were on their way. And they did as told. No stealing any product. No drinking any product while they were cutting. Do as Yonkell and Swartz said and never ever get on Swartz's bad side. And they were paid well, sometimes with a big juicy ham or a few pounds of bacon wrapped in waxed paper and a burlap sack thrown in the kitty. Most important, Fletcher and Axler took a liking to them. Whatever those two did in the streets when they were on a mission, they treated the boys like little kings and their life was good because of the Purples.

"We're gonna be branchin' off into some other businesses, so the Bernsteins are gonna need some new bodies on the streets," Fletcher announced one day in the cutting room. He nodded at Vahram and Haik. "You kids, you're what, how the hell old are you's?"

"I nineteen, he seventeen," Vahram offered.

"Okay, young enough. You, seventeen, that's good. You get pinched by the blues you don't do no time. Very good. And you, gorilla boy, we can use you in some other ways. Like I said, the Bernsteins are going into the dry-cleaning business. They appreciate a clean suit, but, you know, all them chemicals and machines they use, the buildings have a tendency to burn down if you don't protect them, if you's know what I mean."

They both nodded. Neither Haik nor Vahram knew anything about the cleaning business, but they soon learned what Fletcher was talking about. His turf was along Hastings from Jefferson north to Mack. The street was teeming with businesses, butcher shops, shoe repair, haberdashers, watch makers and jewelers, fruit and vegetable markets, and a fair share of laundries and dyers shops. Their parents never questioned where they went at night or why they didn't come home until the sun was breaking over the neighborhood because they always brought home some food or a few leathery dollar bills.

On their first mission, Fletcher and Axler picked the boys up at just past two in the morning and drove them to a shop off Larned, clueing them in on their mission along the way. They pulled into the alley behind the cleaner's with the headlights off. Fletcher put an index finger to his lips to indicate silence and quietly exited the car, with the boys following. He paced to the trunk and lugged out two metal five-gallon gas cans. Vahram stepped in and easily lifted the cans and awaited orders. Axler found two boxes of wooden matches, a hammer, a towel, and a baseball bat, and set his tools next to the back service door, where Vahram followed and placed the cans. Fletcher stacked some crates from a nearby garbage heap and whispered some last minute instructions.

"Okay, this is it, palooks. Won't be no cops around—I took care a that, but we don't want no extra noise or commotion, see? Just stick to what I told ya's. Hate, or whatever the hell your name is, you're smallest so you're goin' over through the transom as soon as we yank them bars off. You'll need the bat in case they got dogs inside. They didn't last we checked, but you never know. Then you just unlock the door from the inside and your brother come through and you get things done lickety-split. This shouldn't take no more than a couple minutes, you got it?"

Both boys nodded.

"Okay, Axe, here we go. I'll back up and you get that chain rigged up to the bumper. Monkey boy, you climb up them crates and hook up the other end of the chain to the bars over the transom. I'll jimmy 'em up and then watch out, them bars gonna come flying off."

Vahram scaled the boxes and ran one end of the thick chain through the first bar of the grate and handed the end down to Fletcher, who hooked it with a C link. Axler, a tiny, elf-like man, secured the other end of the chain to the back bumper. Fletcher smiled and hopped back into the car, then gunned the engine. The transom grating came clanking out into the alley.

"You see that? That was something!"

"Ha! Damn good show, bub!"

Fletcher was quite proud of his work, but if being quiet was at all a factor, the mission was in trouble. Axler scaled the stacked crates and motioned for Vahram to hand him the towel and hammer. He placed the towel over the hammer head and gave the window a swift blow. The broken glass clattered to the floor inside, but no barking erupted on the other side of the door. Axler cleared the glass out of the window frame with the hammer and set the towel down on the ledge before descending.

"Christ's sake, let's go! I'll hand ya the bat when you're up there."

Haik climbed the crates, then paused for the smiling Axler to hand him the bat. Nerves flared in every inch of his skin. He boosted himself up with his elbows and dug his shoes into the door and wormed his way up onto the transom ledge, the towel protecting him from ragged bottom edge of sharded glass. He shimmied up to the ledge and squirmed over, crashing to the floor below, the bat leaving his hands and clattering on the cement floor. His shoulder and side hurt from the fall, but within split seconds nerves captured him and he felt nothing. He was being too loud and Fletcher and Axler would be angry. As he pushed away from the floor to right himself, his hands pressed into small knives of shattered glass on the ground and he felt his skin punctured by the tiny blades but remained silent, one of Fletcher's first rules. Crouching down in the pile of glass and brushing the shards from his palms, he looked up—there was a light on somewhere up towards the front of the store and he could make out the outlines of machines and racks of shirts and dresses and suits and big tubs of clothing. It smelled like chemicals, clean yet noxious chemicals, dizzying to breathe.

Movement—was it a car that passed before the plate picture window in front, or was there someone inside? Dogs—Axler had mentioned dogs before they left, so he snatched the bat and peered more deeply into the shadowy silence.

One quick rap on the door. Haik sparked alive. The door behind him. Unlock the door. He was losing time and had to get his transmission in gear. He fumbled at the slide bolts all along the door and then turned the handle.

"Jesus H. Christ, what the hell you doin' in there? Gimme that fuckin' bat. Dogs woulda ate your dumb ass by now if they was in there. Now get to work!" spat Fletcher in a hurried whisper.

Haik could barely make out the outlines of his accomplices, but Vahram breezed past him with one gas can and box of matches. Fletcher snatched the bat from Haik and Axler struggled to hand off the other can of gas and box of matches. The instructions were simple. Start at the back of the store, and douse anything made out of cloth with gas, making your way to the front. Leave enough gas so that at the front counter you could drench all the papers and manager's desk and chairs. Once the gas was gone, ditch the cans. Hit the first match and let the gas go to work. Get back lickety split because the fire could take quickly, and then keep retreating, lighting matches along the path you took in and stay out of the way of the flames.

They were at the front of the store holding empty cans before they knew it. Haik looked at Vahram, who was already holding one of his matches. He nodded to Haik to move back out of the office area. He scratched the match against the box and tossed it at the front desk. The small torch had not even set down when the front of the store burst into a blinding flash of light. Haik raised his arms to shield his face and felt the scorching blast blistering his face and forearms. He opened his eyes and the entire front of the store flashed ablaze, shots of flame punching out toward him, pushing him backwards, the heat already burning through every part of him like he had no clothes on at all. He stumbled backwards and tripped over something on the floor. The heat was so intense he began to crawl on his hands and knees toward the rear door, anything to inch closer to escape, the flames seemingly biting his ass and shoe soles. He stopped for a second—his matches, where were his matches?—but Vahram grabbed him by the arm and yanked him to his feet like he was a mere child. How was Vahram still standing? How had he made his way out of the blast furnace of the office? Smoke billowed at him and began to beat him in the race to the back door, swirling around him and clogging his lungs in the sprint to escape. The flames seemed to roll on wheels along the floor, attacking anything made of cloth, leaping to the ceiling and speeding ever more quickly to pass Vahram and Haik in their scramble to safety.

"Le's go, le's go!" shouted Vahram above the clamor of the inferno. The flames must have hit some chemicals, because an explosion fired out in all directions and the floor quaked, knocking both boys off their feet. Chunks of ceiling fell about Haik, spitting spark and kicking up more black smoke that swirled about him. Just ahead he could make out the open frame of the backdoor and Vahram's black silhouette surging toward it. His legs were now heavy and his lungs burned for one clean breath of air, his whole body pouring sweat and his brain fluttering in and out of focus. His vision began to double and triple and his lungs clog with oily vapors. He wasn't sure he would make it.

But Vahram was there to pull him up and forward. He grasped Haik's shirt collar and dragged him ahead.

"Get the hell out here! What the hell you doin'? C'mon, c'mon, let's go!" shouted Fletcher, poking his arm through the door frame like reaching into a pirhana tank to retrieve a dropped quarter. He grabbed Haik by the arm and pulled him free of the giant blast furnace the cleaning shop had become. The outside air felt like winter gusting over him, and his eyes streamed tears to clear out the layer of soot that coated them. Haik took in some air and then hacked it out, his seared lungs unable to take the strain, fighting to find oxygen like he was underwater. A few feet away, Vahram heaved on all fours on the alley pavement, struggling for breath.

"Get in! Get in! We gotta scram. Now!"

Axler had the engine running and the back door open. Vahram found his feet and lifted Haik up, dragged him to the car. He tossed his younger brother into the back then collapsed awkwardly on top of him. Axler cranked the engine into gear and gunned off down the alley, the chain and grate rattling and spitting spark behind them. The "twins" could not stop laughing, punching each other on the arm, slapping each other's legs, euphoric at the mayhem they had just unleashed.

"Damn! You see that thing go up! Woooo, goddamn, I tell you's, what a sight!"

Fletcher could not control his giddiness over incinerating the cleaning shop. After hacking and digging at their eyes until they watered and cleared, Haik and Vahram slowly recovered their lungs and their breathing settled although the smell of burning chemicals and soot was seared into their nostrils. After they rolled out of the alley, Axler flashed on his headlights and headed back to the Sugar House, cackling and shouting the entire trip, oblivious to the skipping, clanking souvenir chained to the bumper.

"Ha! Burnt up like a tinderbox! Pooom! Up she goes! Maybe I gave you's a little too much gas. And next time, we'll have you's start up front and walk all the way to the back before we have you light the matches. Live and learn. Christ, you little pugs almost got deep-fried!

Toasted! Goddamn! Goddamn that was a doozie! Wait'll I tell the Bernsteins!"

"Hey, wait," Fletcher broke in. "Where the gas cans? You two pukes left the cans inside."

"Gonna hafta take it outta your pay," chimed Axler, and the the two yorkies exploded in cackles.

Haik looked over at Vahram, blinking, eyes on fire but his vision slowly returning.

They were now paid arsonists.

At the Milaflores Hotel, Haik and Vahram learned all they needed to know about the Purple Gang.

They woke late each morning after torching a laundry, smelling of gas and smoke. Their mother said nothing as she brought them clean clothes and gathered the filthy ones to wash. Their sisters Arkina and Ovsanna, though, were curious, and they asked questions. Where do you go at night? Why do you smell like a pot-bellied stove full of coal? Where does all your money come from? "Usica kezi chi veraberir," Vahram would tell them, *it's none of your business*, and the matter was left at that.

Setting fires became a nightly ritual, but during the day there was time to kill, so they often found themselves with Fletcher and Axler and some of the other senior Purples, including Harry "Two Gun" Altman, also known as "The Indian" because of his dark complexion and stoic lack of expression. While Fletcher and Axler were quick talkers with dead eyes and violence-sharpened minds, Altman appeared completely detached from the world around him. His eyes were empty. He might look directly at you and say something, but part of him was gone, completely missing, unaware of your existence. If you spoke to him, he might simply look at you blankly and say nothing—it was his way of telling you to shut up. And when he sent that message, it was best to heed it.

On the second floor at the Milaflores, the Purples had set up their latest temporary field office. While the Sugar House on Oakland Avenue was their headquarters, the gang ran small fly by night street operations in various hotels across the city, renting rooms to store guns, booze, money, and paperwork to keep the few cops who would actually stand up to them in the dark about their real business. As brutal as their operations might be, they were also very calculated, and several "brains" like Jack Wolfe, an accountant and numbers wizard, were hired to keep track of the books to make it look like they were simply running a sugar mill but, more importantly, to ensure that theft was not just minimized, but an impossibility. The Bernsteins killed whomever they wanted, but more often than not it was someone with whom they had a provable beef, namely someone who was trying to take a cut of their business without asking. They could be generous when the mood took them, but their generosity should never be taken for carelessness or a lack of attention to economics.

At the Milaflores one late afternoon, the boys were waiting for a torch run, hanging out while Fletcher, Axler, Altman, and their local bookkeeper, Earl Passman, killed time playing cards and drinking. On rare occasion, the boys were allowed to drink with the senior Purples—this was not one of them. Mostly, they waited to be sent on sandwich runs, and they could order their own stacked ham sandwiches with fresh swiss cheese and spicy mustard and huge sour pickles and a quart of fresh milk. Arson was easier on a full belly.

"Here, look here, tomorrow in the fourth, we're laying down on Sweet Konnie," mused Fletcher as he circled something on his folded newspaper.

"You don't say?" said Axler. "So, you had a chat with Rooney the Bear's jockey, huh?"

"More than a chat," smiled Fletcher. "He'll be pullin' the reins down the homestretch. I told him, that whip better be up his ass or, well, he better know how to swim without no arms and legs. This one's gonna pay off big."

"How much we in for?"

"I've got the figures right here," intoned Passman, a bespectacled, dapper young man who looked like he might be a college student. "Sweet Konnie's running, let's see, four to one. We'll lay down five grand 30 minutes before she hits the gates. That's 15 grand in pure profit, gentlemen. One race, and we're all sitting pretty. Not bad for a couple minutes' work."

Fletcher and Axler clinked glasses. Altman sat mute and drained a glassful of whisky in one gulp, his eyes for some unknown reason fixing on Passman. Axler dealt a new hand and everyone but Altman picked up their cards and assessed their next wager.

"Whattaya mean, 'a few minutes work?'" deadpanned Altman, his eyes still on Passman, who arranged his cards.

"What's that?" Passman said absently, looking at his hand one last time and tossing a few dollars into the center of the table. Altman fixed him in his gaze and did not let go.

"You heard me. You said the race is a few minutes work. I wanna know what you mean by that."

"What do I mean? What else can I mean?" Passman laughed, the intellectual's smirk on his face. "I mean that the whole race is over before you know it and we've got ourselves a nice return on our investment. It's quite a tidy business venture. We're all dancing like sheiks come the end of the fourth tomorrow. That's not too hard to understand, is it?"

Altman looked at Passman without blinking.

"No, it's not hard to understand. I understand. But you act like nobody done nothing till the race starts. Fletch, he talked to the jockies, he put hisself out there. Ax, he's carrying the dough to the track and picking up the pay-off and bringing it back to the Bernsteins. Me, I'm gonna pay the little shithead jockey a reminder just before race time and visit the trainers and owners and all the little fucks at the pay-out window and make sure they don't got a problem with nothing. That's a lotta time, not a couple minutes. It's real work. It's doing real things, Passman. It's not sitting at a desk with a pencil and a stack a paper. What the hell exactly you do anyways, huh?"

The bookkeeper smiled uneasily, rearranging his cards. Fletcher and Axler smiled, too, but in enjoyment of Passman's discomfort. Haik and Vahram just observed, waiting out the time before they could go to work, hoping Altman or Fletcher soon got hungry. Usually, they enjoyed the banter of the older hoods even though they were not allowed to join in their gambling, but this was going beyond the usual needling. Haik and Vahram were ready to run down to the front desk or the corner drugstore or tobacco shop to pick up food or cigars or cigarettes. Haik knew Altman's reputation for conflict, and he hoped they would send him on an errand so he didn't have to witness the tension.

"Harry, all I said was that this was a nice set up. I certainly didn't mean it to sound like nobody did anything to expedite the whole venture or to minimize anyone's contribution, nor did I imply that I did anything more than anyone else. In fact, the whole enterprise is contingent on a number of factors and players all doing their part. It's a team effort, each man making an invaluable contribution to the success of the whole. That's all I said, nothing more. Look, can we just play cards?"

Altman didn't budge.

"Answer my question, Passman. So what the fuck exactly you do? Huh? *That* was my question. Do you understand what that question means? What you do? I wanna know. What exactly do you do that's so goddamn important?"

Passman shifted in his chair, adjusted his glasses and tie. He was proud of his mental ability, though, and he wasn't going to let Altman bully him.

"What do I do? Here, I'll explain it to you, Harry. I do plenty. You see all those book and ledgers on that desk over there? Hmmm? Can you? Huh? You see them, Harry? Those are called books, and they're where all the brainwork takes place. Brainwork. No, not shooting a gun or doling out beatings, but it's work, work that the Bernsteins need done. You understand that? The Bernsteins, your bosses, the people you work for, want this work done. The brainwork. The thinking part. That's what I do. You do your part, I do mine. Plain and simple."

Altman put his cards down on the table.

"What I understand, Passman, is that you're always walking around like you're some kinda big timer. You think you're better than everybody because you can do this, that, and the next thing with your numbers and write it all down nice and fancy in those books like nothing could get done without you. You think you're so damn smart. You think you're better than me, don't you? Huh? Answer my question. Do you think you're better than me?"

There was no hint of humor in Altman's inflectionless voice, only a very tangible sense of threat. Passman refused to look at him, which seemed to only intensify Altman's gaze.

"Whatever you say, Harry. Here, Ax, I'll take two."

Axler tossed him his cards. Haik looked at Vahram—where exactly was all this headed?

"No, Passman, it's not whatever I say. It's what you say. Now answer my question. Do you think you're better'n me? Huh?"

Passman shifted in his chair again and cleared his throat.

"You want an answer, Harry? Okay, here's an answer. You're better than I am. A real genius. A mountain of intellect. Nothing could ever get done unless you did it. That good enough for you?"

Altman rose from his chair and sidled up to Passman, who continued to look at his cards as if Altman did not exist. Altman hovered over him, then took the frail man's jaw in his hand and twisted his head so that he had to look at him.

"No, that's not good enough. I don't like your answer. Fact, I don't like anything about you, Passman. You're nothing but a little worm with a pencil."

Passman reached to pry Altman's hand off but he could not budge it. His cheeks smooshed, his eyes bulged, and his face reddened as Altman tightened his grip. Axler smiled, filling Altman's empty glass with whiskey, approving of the entertainment, but Fletcher had seen enough.

"Harry, for Christ's sake, let'm go. Here, cool it down, siddown and have some more hooch. You damn near drank this whole bottle yourself. You Indians get feisty when you don't get enough fire water in your gullet," smiled Fletcher. Altman was as feared a Purple strongarm as any, Killer Burke, Abe "Angel Face" Kaminsky, "Abie the Agent" Zussman, or H.F., Harry Fleisher, all included, and he could drink, too, more than anyone the boys had ever seen. And the more he drank, the more he seemed to simmer—the danger was letting him reach the point he boiled over.

Altman released his grip but stood over Passman. The bookkeeper cowered, rubbing his face, which was imprinted by the mark of Altman's fingers. Altman lifted his glass immediately and drained it, looking at Passman the entire time. His black eyes glowed.

"I'm outta here. I got a few errands to look after."

Altman turned away and Passman slumped back in his chair, breathing deeply, his shoulders relaxing, his face a mixture of fear, humiliation, and anger.

"What the hell, Harry, that balls up the game," whined Axler.

"Let'm go," countered Fletcher. "The three of us can still play. The Indian's on the warpath. Ain't that right, Harry?"

Altman said nothing. He stepped into the walk-in closet to fetch his coat. Without pause, Passman rushed to the door, closed it, turned the skeleton key, and removed it, holding it up like a sports trophy, beaming at Fletcher and Axler, a winner's smirk stretching across his still-red face. A few seconds passed, and then the door handle rattled.

"What the hell?"

"How's the weather in there, Indian?" laughed Passman. Fletcher and Axler roared in approval, and even Haik and Vahram could not help but smile. Altman, one of the most feared murderers in Detroit, was now locked inside a walk-in closet.

"Hey Harry, make sure my coat's okay, will ya?" shouted Axler. Fletcher and Passman threw some gasoline on the situation with a few extra loud laughs.

"Open this fucking door."

"Sorry, can't hear you, Harry. You say something?"

"Harry, ain't you supposed to be at the track? Quit horsin' around and get to work. Ain't no horses in that closet, are there?"

"Who the hell got the key? I want outta here or I'm gonna start blasting."

Passman was enjoying the intellectual's revenge, and he would milk his victory for all it was worth and keep the joke cooking. He stepped to the closet door, then, looking back at everyone else with a wink, knocked on the door.

"Telegram for Mr. Altman. I say, I've got a telegram for Mr. Altman." Passman looked at the others, covering his mouth, enjoying every second of Altman's humiliation.

"I ain't laughing, Passman, you little fuck. Open the damn door."

"It's a message from Sweet Konnie. She says she needs you to show up at the track as soon as possible to see who's the bigger horse's ass."

The room broke into cackles. Passman stood in front of the door, bent double in laughter, then knocked again.

"I ain't laughing, asshole. My rod is out. Open…"

"Sweet Konnie says she needs a great big kiss, Harry, she…."

One, two, three shots blew through the door. Splinters flew in all directions and everyone in the room instinctively hit the floor. Everyone but Passman, who staggered backwards as if he had just been clocked with a thunderous haymaker, a look of total incomprehension seizing his face.

"I said open the fucking door!"

Haik toppled off his chair at the first gunshot and hit the floor. He looked up to see Passman collapse backwards to the carpet, his glasses flipping from his face. He was gazing blankly up at the ceiling, his mouth open, a trickle of blood streaming from the corner of his mouth.

"Jesus Christ, Harry, put the gun down!" Fletcher shouted as he crouched behind Passman's accountant's desk.

"I want outta this closet! Now!"

"Jesus H. Christ," said Axler, who huddled behind Fletcher. Passman was now sputtering up blood.

"Harry, we'll let you out. Just put the damn gun down."

"I want out!"

"We'll let you out, but not till you put the gun away."

"You'll let me out if I put the rod away?"

"Yes, yes, we'll let you out. Just holster the damn gun."

"Okay, it's away."

"You sure?"

"Open the damn door or the rod is coming back out!"

Fletcher whispered over his shoulder to Axler.

"The key, right there, on the ground. Get the damn key. Crawl over there and unlock the door. Now!"

Axler was no longer smiling. The key lay next to Passman's body, which had begun to convulse. Axler slid on his belly and retrieved the key, then squirmed over to the wall next to the closet door.

"Harry, it's me, Ax. You hear me? I'm gonna unlock the door for you. I got the key from Passman. It's right here in my hand, but I ain't gonna unlock nothing till that gun is away. That gun in the holster?"

"Yeah, but it's coming out again if that door don't open."

"I'm opening the door. You hear me? Keep the gun down. I got the key in my hand and I'm gonna put it in the door and unlock it. You understand?"

"Yeah."

"The gun's away?"

"Open the fucking door or I'm gonna blow this whole place to shit!"

"Okay, okay, here goes, the key is going in the door."

Axler propped up on his knees and reached to the lock with the key, inserted it, and turned. Altman turned the handle on the other side and burst from the closet, his gun drawn.

"Where is he? Huh? Where's that little four-eyed fuck?"

Vahram pointed to the body on the floor. Passman's eyes were glued to the ceiling, the blood still streaming from his mouth, but his chest heaved upward and his lungs gurgled. Altman looked down, his face still revealing no emotion.

"You fucking shot him," accused Fletcher, but nothing registered on Altman's face.

"Yeah? Served him right," Altman muttered. "I said to let me out."

"Whatta we do?" Axler broke in, looking to Fletcher.

"We gotta clear out. Now. We gotta pack everything up and clear out." Fletcher motioned to Haik and Vahram, and then to Passman's body. "You two, get him outta here. We gotta get all these books together and get all the heat out."

Haik looked at Vahram—what were they supposed to do?

"Where do we take him?" asked Vahram. Fletcher looked at him blankly.

"Where the fuck do I care? Anywhere. Just get him out. Out in the alley. Pitch him out in the alley."

"The alley?"

"What word didn't you understand? Carry him out in the alley and get your asses back up here and help us pack. Move it!"

Vahram didn't have to be told twice. He motioned to Haik to grab Passman's feet as he gathered the bleeding man under the arms. They lifted in unison and staggered to the door, which Fletcher had opened for them. Altman stood absentmindedly reloading his gun while Fletcher began to stuff a satchel with all of Passman's books and Axler retreated to a back bedroom to collect their weapons.

"C'mon, c'mon," urged Vahram. Haik tried not to look down at Passman, who continued to rasp and gurgle. They banged out the door and down the stairwell to ground level and staggered out the alley exit into the open air.

"Here, just put him here."

Haik could not wait to let go of Passman's legs. He released, and the dying man's heels clacked on the cement. Vahram attempted to be gentle as he set the baggage of Passman's upper body down. For a split second, the accountant's vacant eyes locked on Haik's before the rest of his body was dumped to the pavement. The boys looked at each other, then sprinted back inside and up the stairs to help the others pack.

The end came swiftly. Fires continued to destroy the laundries, and Haik and Vahram, after nearly killing themselves, grew quite good at their job. Too good. Fletcher and Axler were busy with their numbers at the track and Fletcher was starting to manage fighters, so they decided to farm Haik and Vahram out to another set of shtarkers so they could concentrate on their other ventures.

"You two's will still be the matches, but we got a few new wheels to get you to the ballgame and back. Not much older than you's, Jewish boys, real fine young men. Now, listen good, I'm counting on you to break'm in right, show'm the ropes. They been doing some other odds and ends for us, so the fire thing is all new to 'em. In fact, we got you a little job coming up shouldn't be no trouble at all. Understood?"

They nodded at Fletcher, ready to do as told. They were to meet the new wheels just outside the Ten Forty Club on Wayne at exactly 10 p.m., quite early for their usual rendezvous. They waited outside the Cass Theater, looking at discarded newspapers, checking out sports scores and scanning the theater posters to see what was playing inside, then walked up the cobblestone sidewalk to the club. It was hopping, with music jumping out into the street and well-dressed men and women entering, laughing, enjoying the merriment. After a group of revelers passed inspection by the front door security mugs, Haik did a double take. Leaning against the wall just past the glowing entrance were two unmistakeable faces: Milman and Davis.

They both stood smoking, their coats an attempt to look dressed up but the fabric was thick, coarse wool, and the dwarfish Davis' coat was ridiculous, the sleeves too long and the shoulders drooping off his tiny frame.

"It's them," Haik whispered.

"I know. Don't say nothing. We just act like we don't know nothing, like we ain't never seen them before. You understand? We never met these two never in our lives. Pull your hat down over your eyes, yeah, like this, and just act like you ain't never seen them. Got it?"

Vahram tapped Haik on the shoulder and they set out, approaching their nemeses with an air of indifference.

"You guys need matches?" This was their code to let the wheels know who their firebugs would be.

"Natches? We non't need no nat…," Davis shot in, as if he had been provoked.

"Gorilla, shut the hell up, huh?" Milman cut in. "Yeah, we need two matches. You holding?"

"Sure thing," Vahram replied.

"Good, let's go for a little ride. We'll show you pukes our wheels."

Milman grabbed Davis by the shoulder and headed around the building to the side parking lot and led them to a '25 Flint B-40 touring car. Before they all hopped in, Davis grabbed Milman by the arm, his lower lip jutting out.

"Ni nanna dwive!"

"What? You? No, you ain't drivin'. I seen you drive before. You're buggy."

"Ni nanna dwive! N'im nolner nan noo."

"Yeah, you might be older, but you can't even see over the steering wheel."

Davis straightened his tiny arms, defiant, ready to defend his right to drive.

"Okay, Gorilla, okay. You win. You can drive over to Little Harry's. Just a stone's throw from our hit, and I gotta meet Ziggy over there anyways. We can kill a little time before we head over. Go ahead. But just this one time and don't ask no more. I do all the driving after that. Got it?"

The little man smiled and looked at Haik and Vahram as if he had just proved something, then ran around to the driver's side, a giddy-up in his midget stride. Haik and Vahram climbed into the back, finding a place for their legs next to the five gallon gas cans and other implements of their trade. The drive to Little Harry's was, well, eventful. Davis did not know how to drive, specifically shift gears, stop at caution signs, or turn without nearly running every car on the street onto the sidewalk or into pedestrians anywhere near their vehicle.

"'Toopid nears!" Davis shouted as he nearly careened into the car next to him.

"It ain't the fucking gears, Sam, look what the hell you're doin'!" Milman countered, grabbing at the wheel to jerk the vehicle away from another certain collision.

"'Toopid nears!"

"Jesus Christ!"

"'Toopid nears!"

"That's it, pull over. Now, pull over. I mean it. No way you're driving no more."

"Nit not me, Hawwy, hit na 'toopid nears!"

Davis drove the car up onto the sidewalk, hitting a kielbasa stand, driving the cart into the front of a shoe repair shop, then stamped the brake through the floor, almost sending the whole crew through the front windshield. All four catapulted backward, then heaved a sigh of relief to still be alive and in one piece.

"'Toopid nears!"

"Shut the fuck up, Gorilla! Now get the hell outta the way, I'm driving. Open the door, move it. Goddamn bug! Christ, I need a drink."

Milman physically kicked Davis out of the driver's side door, sending him out onto the sidewalk. The kielbasa cart owner rushed over to Davis for an explanation for his ruined cart, but the diminutive brawler rose and instinctively clubbed him upside the head with his drawn pistol, sending him to the pavement. The shoe repairman rushed from inside his store, but Davis leveled his gun at him, freezing him in his tracks.

"Gorilla, get in here! Now! Put the damn gun down! Let's go!"

Milman was the only person on earth Davis would listen to. Everything inside Davis wanted to pull the trigger, the veins in his neck flaring, but he resisted, stuffed the pistol back into his coat, and ran to the passenger side of the Flint. The shoe repairman stood frozen, not wanting to move or in any way provoke Davis.

"Nit wudda 'toopid nears, noo nat-hole!" he shouted at the cobbler.

With that send off, Davis jumped in on the passenger side, Milman gunned into reverse, and they wheeled back on the road toward Little Harry's.

Little Harry's was a redbrick castle on Jefferson Avenue, and from the second story windows one could behold the wide Detroit River and Canada in their full glory. Haik had heard that some famous French people built it as a house to actually live in, but now it was the hotspot along the river, and mayors to millionaires to police chiefs to bootleggers and regular darbs all made it a point to sample its wares. The foursome walked up the long sidewalk under a green canvas canopy to the front steps, where they were met by securitymen who looked like they had studied charm at the Bishop school at one time. They knew Milman and Davis and let them in and, in an unexpected act of kindness, Milman signaled the gatekeepers to allow Haik and Vahram in as well.

"Wait, wait, wait, I almost forgot to ask," Milman started. "You two, you's ain't I-tal-yins, is you?"

It was the same question he first asked them back at the Bishop school.

"No, we ain't no I-tal-yoons," Vahram shot in. "We, we're Germans."

"Krauts, huh? You pretty dark for Krauts. Better'n I-tal-yins, though. Anyways, you two limp dicks can hang around downstairs here for a bit. Me and the Gorilla, we got business upstairs. You sit tight here where we can find you 'cause we still got action tonight. We'll be down, I don't know, in an hour, so be right here when we's come down."

He motioned for Davis to follow him and they headed off to the wide, carpeted stairway. Haik absorbed the surroundings. Thick carpet everywhere. Big fancy drapes over all the windows. Live jazz playing somewhere off in another part of the house. Men in tuxedos and fine coats and dames in slinky silk dresses and jewelry hanging off everything. The women moved like Theda Bara and Norma Talmadge, beautiful, movie theater beautiful, perfect and soft and glowing. What he wouldn't do to one day touch a woman like that.

"Quit staring," Vahram hissed as he punched Haik to life. "You gonna get a king size crankshaft. Here, let's go over there."

He led Haik through the crowd to a green table with dressed up bigwigs all about. They were throwing dice and a man in a bowtie at the far end of the table was saying things and acting like he was in charge. They threw dice at the Bishop school, but it was against the wall or the stone stairs or a curb, not on a fancy table with its own carpeting. Haik looked up, mesmerized by the chandeliers. He thought places like this only existed in movies, in faraway places that no one could ever really go.

"You two, gineas, move it out. Your kind is over there."

A man the size of Primo Carnera motioned Haik and Vahram over to the bar. Haik looked down at his own frayed clothes and then over at the spit shined and shimmery gamblers. He and Vahram moved to the bar.

Boombas of beer filled the oak counter and a rougher crowd gathered there, laughing loudly and lifting their mugs. The beer looked good, sweaty and glistening like liquid gold. Haik thought it would be grand to take hold of a boomba handle and clink it against the other raised mugs, to smile and feel a sense of oneness with the merrymakers.

"...How much? Name your price, chief. Name it."

At a table off in the corner, a wiry man with dirty blond hair stood over a bowtied older gentleman sitting at a table with compatriots enjoying their beer. His head was cocked oddly as he spoke—it was Ziggy Selbin, one of the toughs from the Bishop school. He was pointing at the man's ring, which glittered in the shadows of the bar area.

"No, I not sell. My ring, I keep. Very good thank you."

"What kind of gibberish is that? Huh? I said I'll pay you whatever you want for the ring. I want that damn ring. Look here, how much?"

Selbin pulled out his billfold and showed the man, a Pole or Hungy, a wad of green. The man raised his hand and smiled as if to politely say thanks-but-no-thanks.

"No, please, was my father ring. Cannot sell. From old country. You understand, please. Very good thank you."

Selbin's face began to redden, and his head tilted at an even odder angle. He wanted the ring no matter what. He looked away from the table for a split second, then drew his pistol from a side holster and swiftly clubbed the seated older man upside the head. His victim had no time to defend himself from the blow and he careened sideways from his chair onto the floor. His tablemates made a motion to rise, but Selbin waved the gun at them and smiled. They raised their hands in surrender and settled back into their seats.

"So you had to make this difficult, didn't you? Dumb Hungy-fuck."

Selbin leaned down over the downed man, whose head was spilling blood onto the hardwood floor. He kept his pistol trained on the table of stunned friends and with his free hand grasped the ring and pulled. Nothing doing. He twisted and pulled, but the ring wouldn't budge.

"Ziggy, what the hell you doing now?"

Primo Carnera, the security thug, stood with his hands on his hips. The tone in his voice said this was not the first time he asked this question. A crowd of rubberneckers was beginning to gather, which was not good for the festive mood.

"This guy's bein' an asshole," replied Selbin, still working to take the ring from the unconscious man's finger.

"First, put the gun away. That's right, put it away. Now, Zig, you know the rules. You were already on a short leash before you even walked in tonight. You're gonna hafta go. People don't come here to be beat on."

"What? This guy's bein' an asshole and I'm the one who's gotta leave?"

"No arguments, Zig, and that's final. Let's go. Leave now and we got no problems."

"Yeah, yeah, I'm on my way. Gimme a second."

Even with his gun packed away and two hands to work on freeing the ring, he could not budge his coveted treasure. Exasperated, he rolled up his pantleg to reveal a scabbard, and he drew out a thick bladed knife.

"Ziggy, what'd I just…"

"I said gimme a damn second."

What Haik next witnessed nearly made him pass out. Selbin grasped the bleeding man's ring finger and began to quickly saw through it. This was going to take too long, so once his blade had carved through the skin and a short ways into the bone, he pressed down and lifted up on the digit until the bone snapped and the knife severed the finger completely. Selbin smiled, holding the bloody digit, removed the ring with a tug, tossed the remains on the man's chest, and rose with a satisfied grin.

"Don't know why he had to make it so difficult. So what you think a my new ring?"

Carnera looked at Selbin, shook his head, grabbed him by the arm, and led him roughly from the bar area through the hushed crowd to the front door. Haik looked at Vahram, who shrugged and said nothing. They only carried knives, lashed to their ankles under their pantlegs—pistols were too expensive, and, ultimately, if you owned one in their business you would use it, and relieving hunger, not committing murder, was their goal. The friends of the unconscious man gathered round him, looking at Selbin as he was escorted out, applying handkerchiefs to their wounded friend's head and maimed hand. One of them wrapped the finger in his hanky—what did he think could be done with it?

A clamor then arose from upstairs. Haik felt like a spectator at a circus and each of the three rings demanded his attention at once—if he looked away too long, something amazing would be missed. He turned to the stairwell in time to see Gorilla Davis tumbling down like a human bowling ball, with Milman shuffling after him.

"Lay off the little guy!" shouted Milman as Davis hit the landing with a thud. Davis looked up, shook his head vigorously from side to side, determined his surroundings, then scraped himself off the floor and tugged his sleeves to their clown-like length as if nothing had happened. Milman hit the landing out of breath, followed by a crew of security goons, where he was met by Canera and another small troop of strongarms. The place hushed, with gamblers and drinkers and musicians now focusing their attention on the spreading commotion. The fingerless man's friends had propped him up, his head streaming blood, dazed, obviously unaware of the severity of his condition. A dapper little man with a pencil mustache arrived on the scene and took charge.

"Out, all a yous, out," he commanded.

"I just told the girl to polish the little guy's knob…."

"I'm not listening. We already sent Ziggy packing. You're out too. All you Purples. Out."

Milman began to reach inside his coat, at which point Carnera interceded, and he was joined by two others in apprehending their would-be triggerman. Davis kicked at the big man, but three other bouncers were on him and rushed him out the door.

"You don't know what the sam hell you're doin'," Milman seethed, trying to shake off his captors.

"Oh, I know exactly what I'm doing," countered the manager. "The Bernsteins've already been called. They know what you rats done tonight and they're not happy. They gave the word to send you packing. We run a clean business here and you just cost us a number a customers…"

"I didn't…"

"Are you buggy? You're bad for business, all a yous. You're out. For good."

"You're gonna pay for…."

"Only person gonna pay is you, shitbird, and your little pal the orangutan if you keep it up. You hear me? You know whose hooch we sell here? Purple hooch. Bernstein hooch. And now we're gonna sell a boatload less of it because people are scared to come in here and deal with you dumb-ass animals. The Bernsteins ain't happy with you, Milman. Just talked to Joe Bernstein two days ago about you cuckoos causing problems. You two and Selbin are on some thin ice. Now take your kike rear ends outta here and keep it quiet. Or maybe I can make another call to Joe right now and watch all you fall through the ice."

Milman struggled until the threat of calling Joe Bernstein registered. He did whatever he pleased in the city—as long as the Bernsteins approved or didn't find out. This incident, though, was now very public, witnesses, too many ears, too many eyes. It couldn't be denied or talked or murdered away.

"Okay, okay, we're out. No more phone calls. I take the little guy and we go. No more calls to the Bernsteins, right?"

"I'll think it over."

The manager slapped him lightly on the cheek, sending a clear, humiliating message. Milman's lip curled, but drawing the ire of the Bernsteins kept his mouth closed and any further thoughts of reaching for his gun tucked away.

Outside, Milman fumed. Selbin had already disappeared into the darkness, leaving Haik and Vahram paired off against Milman and Davis.

"Where were you two? Huh?" Milman's eyes darted between Vahram and Haik.

"Where you think we were? We were right there," Vahram offered.

"Oh, you were right there, huh? No shit. Yeah, I know you were right there, that's my point. What I'm askin' is why the hell didn't you step in?"

"Step in and doing what? Making more trouble? What you want us to do?"

"Not sit there like a couple dames, that's for sure."

"'Toopid names!"

Both Milman and Davis carried heat, but Vahram wasn't backing down. Haik would follow his brother's lead, trusting that he knew what he was doing, but they were outgunned.

"We come to work. Not cause no troubles. We do what Mr. Fletcher says, that's it. He didn't say cut nobody's finger off or go to no speakeasy and get kicked out and make trouble for the Bernsteins. Why we not working?"

Milman's lip curled.

"Hey, I let you two matches come in the club and it wasn't to stand around oilin' your crankshafts. I'm runnin' this here mission tonight and what I say goes. If you're Purple, you stick by Purple. You…"

"We come to work, not make no troubles. Let's just shut up and go, huh?"

Milman was not used to being challenged.

"Listen here, you ain't in charge, I am…"

"Noo non't nalk nat way nah nim!"

Davis stepped forward to confront Vahram, but Vahram squared, ready, and Milman grabbed his minion by the shoulder and pulled him back. Vahram feared nothing, not even the threat of guns. Haik would have to take on Davis and Vahram the heavier, beefier Milman. The key to defeating the puny bug in a fistfight was keeping him at a distance and using the length of his arms with jabs, and if he closed the distance smothering him with the wrestling he and his brother learned in Armenia, the type of wrestling that focused on attacking a limb or joint and—if necessary—eliminating it. But if a gun was pulled, he had to rush him quickly and keep the barrel pointed somewhere away from himself. His stomach climbed into his throat.

"Okay, okay, enough. Listen here, you two, there's something about you I ain't liked since we first run into you, and I still don't like you. You ain't no Germans—my gut says I-tal-yins. One day, we're gonna settle this, but it ain't today. We do the job like we're supposed to. That's it."

"Fine," Vahram said, his eyes not leaving Milman's. "Let's quit wasting time and just go."

Milman sized Vahram up, then motioned everyone forward. They paced to the Flint, Milman seething the whole way, blaming the manager, whom he suspected of being Italian, with Davis senselessly punctuating his rants with indecipherable gibberish. Vahram and Haik followed in silence, keeping a distance. A battle loomed, sometime, somewhere, but they had work first, serious work. Once in the car, all talking ceased. As they pulled out onto Jefferson and headed toward Chene, tension sat in the car like a fifth hoodlum. Haik preferred the ranting and raving—the silence was unsettling. They turned right on Atwater and trolled slowly along the row of warehouses and stores overlooking the dark river.

"Okay," Milman whispered, "there it is."

The street was poorly lit, with a few security lights burning, the moon and random passing ships providing a bit of additional visibility. Milman pulled into a side alley and crept to the backside of the row of buildings. They parked before a two story structure.

"Lots a clothes in there. Now here's the deal. You gotta soak the upstairs too. Come down, hit the first floor, light it up, then we take off. We'll be right here waitin', engine hot. Got it?"

"We done this before. Just have the engine ready," countered Vahram.

"I said the car would be ready, didn't I?"

Silence. Something was not right, but what that might be was a mystery. They all exited and gathered their bats, matches, and other goods. The five gallon cans were filled to the brim, but they felt like nothing. Haik's nerves flared. Vahram, smart Vahram, took him by the shoulder as they readied for the assault.

"Don't worry, little brother," he whispered. Haik breathed deeply. Vahram smiled. "These two up to no good, but I won't get us hurt. Believe me. Stay close by and we're good. You got it?"

Haik nodded.

"I'll take the upstairs and you do the downstairs. Keep your ears open and listen for each other. Understand? We meet at the back door. Have your knife ready when we meet. Good?"

Haik nodded.

The back door was secured with three padlocks welded right into the frame, so Milman produced a large set of metal cutters and snipped through them. Davis swung a sledge and knocked off the door handle and then bashed in the dead bolt.

"There you go. Get to work. You better have your asses down here fast. We ain't waitin' all night."

Vahram looked at Milman then nodded at Haik to follow him inside. It was dark, with the revolving racks of clothing looking like myriad people lined up on the sidewalk outside a soup kitchen. They were experts at their craft now, but this was their first go at a two-story target. They only drenched the fronts of the buildings now—once the flames started, the clothes and chemicals took over. Vahram took the lead.

"Okay," he whispered, "you got the bottom floor. I take the upstairs. Anything wrong, you yell for me. We meet here by the back door, knives out. Okay?"

Haik nodded.

The stairwell to the upstairs sat next to the rear entrance, so Vahram hustled up the steps with his gas can and faded into the darkness, his footsteps creaking on the upper wooden floor tracing his progress to the front of the building. Haik sped past the conveyer racks of clothing to the entrance. Halfway to the reception area he stopped—some type of clanking was coming from the back door. Time was short; he had a job to do and he had to motor quickly, so he put the curious noise away. A musty, fetid smell hung in the air from somewhere, but he couldn't place it and jogged ahead, the gas sloshing in the metal can. The entrance way was a mess, papers and balled up clothing here and there, a fitting area off to one side with a wrap-around curtain, two desks and a sewing machine table on the other. He looked out the picture window into the deserted street—no cops, no one at all.

He winced—with a thud he was down on the ground, his gas can clanking to the cement floor. A dog. A big dog. Haik instinctively covered his face and throat but he felt the fangs cut through his jacket sleeve into his forearm flesh. He kicked and flailed and created some space between himself and the beast, whose snapping teeth flashed and flared in the dull moonlight.

"Vahram!"

He was supposed to be quiet, but his brother's name flew from his mouth out of reflex. The world boiled into instinct. His bat was still in his hand. He flailed his free arm and then swung and the bat connected with the beast's frothing maw, but it snapped so close to his face its hot, sour spittle covered his cheek. He scuttled backwards, fleeing the animal's next screeching advance, swinging the club back and forth to hold it at bay, his heart tommy-gunning in his chest. His adversary crept forward, its eyes sparking, guttural snarls seething from somewhere within. Haik's back hit the counter—he was out of escape room. The beast knew it had cornered its prey and hunkered down, its jaw snapping, feinting, sizing up an opening. It was tethered on a thick chain—that's why it had not attacked when the back door was busted open.

Haik reached slowly to his pantleg, searching for his knife. Time evaporated. His coat sleeve was saturated in blood. The dog leapt, an ignorant missle of muscle and hate, bulling past the swatting club, intent on tearing out Haik's throat. He caught it around the neck in a headlock and rolled it to the side, trying to smother its crazed writhing. It kept biting, clamping down on the air, twisting its head to squirm from Haik's grasp, fighting savagely to taste his blood again. He held tight, throwing a leg over the beast's body, pinching it between his legs, trying to smother its ferocity with Armenian wrestling. The dog would stop at nothing, and he couldn't seem to cinch the headlock tight enough around its neck. Both combatants became tangled in the chain. The dog squirmed and snapped until Haik was belly to belly with his opponent, his ear tucked tightly to its head to avoid the ripping teeth. He squeezed but the dog was crazy with hate, snarling, groaning madly, its fevered breath singeing the back of his neck.

At once, the dog let out a wounded yip, then another. It spastically convulsed, yipped again, then disappeared in his arms. He refused to let go—the dog's mouth was inches from his neck, and even though it was no longer moving, he could not trust that it would not resume its mission to kill him.

"Haik, Haik, leggo."

Vahram. Vahram was next to him, but Haik's face was still buried in the beast's fetid fur.

"Leggo. Leggo, he's dead. We gotta move. The upstairs is already soaked, I just didn't light it. Le's go."

Haik released the limp dog's neck and unwound himself from the chain. He looked up to see Vahram, his knife drawn, blood glistening on the blade, his eyes urgent. He had no time to say thank you—it was match time and they had to move. Vahram grabbed the shoulder of his coat and pulled him to his feet. Haik was light-headed, the adrenaline coursing so swiftly through him that he felt weightless.

"Head to the back. I'll soak the front here. Go!"

Haik recovered his bearings. His forearm throbbed and spat pain. Vahram was already pouring gas on all the papers and desks and furniture in the reception area. He had to move.

At the rear of the building, he turned to see the front of the shop blaze to life. A small black mass grew before him—it was Vahram sprinting toward the back door, knife in hand. He reached the back and automatically swung up the stairwell.

"Be right down. Have that door open and your knife ready."

Haik watched Vahram fly up the stairs. He turned and pushed against the back door. It didn't budge. He shouldered it again—nothing doing. The fire from the front of the store was bolting toward him. He tried the door again. Nothing. Vahram returned, his eyes with a wild, unfamiliar look on them. Haik retreated a few feet and flew into it. It buckled a bit, but was nowhere near opening.

Haik looked to Vahram.

"Here, together."

The fire was roiling closer to them, the heat causing them to sweat. Vahram motioned to Haik to throw his weight in with him. They both backed up and then charged the escape route, smashing into the door. The door was locked from the outside—someone had wedged something in the old padlock latches, as good as slapping on new locks.

"Sheet! We got no time. Up the stairs."

Vahram grabbed Haik's jacket and pulled him up the stairs. The path was clogged in thick black smoke, causing their eyes to burn and tear. Haik pulled his coat up over his mouth so he could breathe. At the top of the stairs, their path forward to the front windows was already enveloped in fire and toxic fumes. They were trapped. The heat tore into them. Haik looked to his brother, whose arm covered his mouth, his face glowing before the leaping flames. He was frozen in the unbearable heat. This was it, their death, agony, unescapable pain, total annihilation.

"Here!"

Vahram pointed to a window behind them. Haik was ready to give into the smoke, his vision and consciousness fading. Again, Vahram grabbed his arm and dragged him along. He staggered forward and kicked through the glass, nearly falling out of the opening. Haik caught him and pulled him back, almost toppling out himself. They were on their last breaths, but they at least had a way out. Vahram stood in the open window frame and took Haik under the arm and lifted him upward next to him, squeezing him into the opening.

"We gonna jump."

Before Haik could process Vahram's words, the blast. The chemicals ignited into a timebomb explosion. The boys were blown out of the second floor window with massive force, two immigrant angels catapulted burning through the black air.

And so life with the Purples ended. It took the boys over a month to recover from their wounds, their mother and sisters nursing them back to health, their father silently shaking his head as he passed the upstairs bedroom they shared. Vahram broke both his legs upon landing along with some ribs. Haik broke an ankle and his good forearm; the opposite forearm was a criss-crossed mangle of stitches needed to repair the flesh torn apart by the dog. Their skin was scorched, scraped, and split, but they were alive.

The moments after the explosion, though, were pure misery. Milman and Davis were nowhere to be found. They had driven a metal rod through all the padlock shackle mounts, sealing the boys in—the intent was murder. With the freeing explosion, the boys were airborne, their legs sprinting weightless through the night sky, blasted from the window frame as if shot from a howitzer. They collided with the earth, bones snapping, their bodies rebounding off the cold turf at the river's edge. Haik was out for some space of time. He was awoken by firetrucks grinding to the blazing wreck of the laundry, the fire spreading to the adjoining buildings. Whether his head was scrambled from the concussion of the explosion or the carwreck collision with the ground, his vision blurred in double and triple images against the underworld tsunami of fire. He and his brother had always fled the scene before the fires had reached their zenith. Their creation was amazing. Beautiful and hypnotizing. He watched until his head grew heavy, the flames dancing and flaring and kicking up against the blackness.

When he awoke, Vahram was lying perhaps twenty feet away from him, belly down and motionless. They had been blown far enough away from the fire to elicit no attention—two more piles of rubbish off in the shadows. The ground was cold. His skull had already exploded and was filling up again with gasoline, creating immense pressure. He reached to the back of his head and felt the crispy, scorched stubble on his stinging scalp. He ached. Everywhere. He tried to prop himself up on his forearms, but they burst to life, causing him to curse. His right forearm was caked in blood that formed a plaster with the shredded remains of his coat and shirt sleeve. The left forearm throbbed and he could not make a fist with his hand because his fingers were so swollen. How to get up? He dug his elbows under his chest and drew his legs up to his gut to begin the process of rising, but his right ankle blew up when he tried to take his feet.

"Haik…"

He had never heard his brother's voice sound weak. Vahram was struggling to raise his head, the side of his face caked in dried blood and dirt and blades of withered grass. Haik crawled on his knees to his brother's side.

"I can't walk."

Haik surveyed Vahram's damage. The back of his jacket and shirt was burned away, leaving his flesh red, blistered, and pussing.

"You gotta get help."

"I can't walk, my ankle…."

"Dammit, Haik, you got to. My legs, my legs is broken. I, I can't move."

Haik looked toward Vahram's feet. His left leg was crooked out sideways at the middle, his pantleg painted in blood. In all Haik's memory, he could not think of a time when his older brother could not physically conquer any person or challenge. For him to admit he was hurt, the pain had to be unimaginable.

"Okay," Haik returned. "I'm going. Don't go nowhere."

Vahram gave him a darting look. Haik braced himself. He would have to stand. He pushed up off his knees onto his good foot and steadied himself. One. Two. Three. He pushed off his good foot and stood. A butcher knife shot up from his heel into his damaged ankle and through his shin as he transferred weight to his damaged wheel. The pain brought him to attention but was tolerable. He would have to walk all the way home and see if he could find someone with a car to retrieve his brother.

After three blocks agony gave way to anger. To hell with Milman and Davis. To hell with Goldberg. Hell, to hell with all the Purples, the Bernsteins included. Where were they now? Vahram was suffering and needed help, a doctor, a ride home, but no one was there. The brothers did everything asked of them. More. The ankle ached and sparked. The sidewalks were coming alive and he was drawing glares. It dawned on him what a sight he must be. His clothes were smoke blackened. His arm a bloody mess. He limped like a wounded soldier. He must have looked like some kind of scorched monster.

"Hey! Hey!"

A flatbed Model-T truck was trolling past. Haik glanced over but did not stop shuffling forward.

"Haik! Haik, that you?"

Haik looked more intently.

"It's me, Luigi. Gee-Gee, from Bishop. You okay, man?"

Haik recognized his old pal from his school days.

"You okay, old man? Here, hop in."

Haik tried to explain what had happened as they drove to retrieve Vahram. They found him face down in the dirt at the river's edge, little whisps of smoke still emanating from the cleaning building. It was horrible lifting him into the bed. Vahram made no sound, but the strain on his face screamed the pain he was in. Once home, their mother cried out at the condition of her two sons. A home doctor was called in to set all the broken bones and stitch the open cuts. Their burned butts and backs felt like they had been stretched bareskinned across the top of the pot-belly stove at full glow in the middle of winter. Vahram had to lay on his stomach until the long bones in his legs had healed enough to bear weight. He walked like a man trying to cross the Detroit River when the melting ice was paperthin. But neither boy would give in. They had to heal quickly because they had to eat.

All the money they had made working for Mr. Goldberg and the Bernsteins ran out as they were just about fully recovered. They had to work again. Fast. The Purples were done with them and they had no desire to work for anyone who employed backstabbing rats like Millman and Davis anyways. So they made their own gang, but they kept it small: Vahram, Haik, Gee-Gee, Orlin, and little Antonio, whom they called Toe, Gee-Gee's younger brother. And they took to the railyards, busting boxcars, stealing whatever they could eat, drink, or sell.

The boys sat still, impatient for a train, and the truck fell silent. Vahram knew more than all the boys in the truck combined, and when he gave an order it was followed. He could sense things, where they needed to be and what they must do. Even though no one had a cigarette or a pint of whiskey—their supplies of everything that made these winter nights bearable all run out—Haik could feel warmth seeping into him, even into his dead feet. His mended ankle ached. He stopped tapping his heels and let his toes relax in the tips of his worn boots.

Haik dreamed.

He saw Vahram as his city's Al Capone and himself as his brother's right arm, driving a yacht up the Detroit River into Lake St. Clair to entertain Al Jolson and Rudi Vallee and Norma Schearer and Janet Gaynor and whomever else they saw on theater marquees while hired saps delivered all the hooch they could stomach and fancy ham and roast beef sandwiches so thick your mouth could hardly fit around them. Maybe he'd gather up the kids from the old neighborhood and hire them as waiters and go-to boys, doing jobs like he had done for Fletcher and Axler. He'd give them all a tux and make sure they had haircuts and cleaned themselves up and then they'd get to live on the boats and keep them tidy when he and Vahram weren't throwing parties. They'd have dependable jobs keeping the boat running and washing cars and keeping everything in order, and they would eat, all they wanted, whatever they wanted, hot dogs with onions and mustard and steaks dripping with fatty juice and sweet rolls and all the milk they wanted. He'd tip them a buck here and there, tell them good job, keep up the good work, everything's tip top, and they would respect him back by doing whatever they could to impress him.

Yeah, he decided, he'd wait out the misery until his ticket was punched.

"No, not lonk now, boys. Lissen."

In the distance, a train whistle.

Four months had passed since Haik and the others last set foot in this particular yard, Grand Trunk property, and they all knew and remembered and said nothing. Little Toe, Antonio, Luigi's kid brother, used to always go with them, the youngest, and it was an adventure then, fun, a game. Their father did not approve of stealing, preferring to work seven days a week stocking produce at the local A & P to provide what he could for his wife and four children, but everything the boys hoisted from the trains their families needed, the food or car parts that could be traded or sold for food. No matter what their father said about *aznvutune*, honesty, and Christian ways, he never refused the loaves of bread they brought home.

Most than the food, though, their trips to the trainyard filled them with a sense of mission since their Purple days had ended. Gee-Gee, dependable Luigi, would rumble up to the boxcar they had chosen like a pack of wolves singling out the weakest member of the herd, Vahram would burst out the side door and leap up into the bed of Mr. Leoni's truck, swing the fifteen pound sledge to break off the lock, Haik and Orlin were already sliding back the heavy car door to reveal their booty. They lifted armfuls of hams, bricks of cheese, crates of tomatoes or sparkplugs, anything of value, until it was no longer wise to delay escape. Toe, little Tony, crazy little Antonio, was look-out, a special job they told him, a good job for the youngest, too small to carry much, a special member of their army. "I see them!" he would yell, his eyes wild with fear and excitement as if he'd seen a legion of the Kaiser's army or Talat Pasha's black bearded murderers, his tiny arms flapping and his curly black hair blown back from his forehead as he beelined to the truck.

But Toe was the one who was robbed that day last summer. They were furiously unloading tires, the oily rubber smell burning their nostrils in the July heat, and they had nearly four complete sets thrown onto the flatbed before they noticed their tiny look-out was gone. And then the screaming. Little Toe came running out from between two distant cars, trying to pull his pants up, his eyes wide not with excitement but animal terror. When he was halfway between the boxcars and the truck, they saw three bulls, railroad guards, appear. The superior smiles on their faces were visible even in the dark, hazy distance, one even pointing and doubling over in laughter.

"C'mon, c'mon, the engine's hot," Gee-Gee shouted, and Vahram, Haik, and Orlin knelt at the edge of the truck bed to gather Toe in as the rusted Ford lurched forward. Toe scrambled toward them, his eyes crazy. Haik noticed how the bulls did not even attempt to pursue them but rather kept their distance and laughed and clapped their hands and hooted. The truck nosed ahead to the back gate, which they had clipped the lock off of. With Vahram gripping him about the waist so he could stretch out even further, Orlin leaned over the edge and snatched the running boy under his extended arm and pulled. Haik caught him under the other arm and they gathered him in unison. Toe screamed, pulling air into his lungs to immediately punch it out into another ear splitting squall.

Haik knew why the boy was out of control. His pants were about his knees as he clutched at Vahram and Orlin, and Haik saw the rivulets of blood streaming from his private area. But down there, where his boy parts were supposed to be—nothing. Gone. Nothing.

And now, a lifetime later, he still shuddered at the thought. They sat in the frigid yard without Toe, freezing, ready, no longer anticipating a game but rather the serious, violent business of survival.

"Here go."

The belching train neared and the clanking, straining sounds of wheel on rail grew shrill and piercing. Vahram made sure they were ready. As the oldest, he was in charge, but he was also strongest, able to swing the sledge like it was a mere hand mallot. Haik remembered how two summers before they found a large solid concrete ball that workers were going to mount on a pillar outside some rich mug's house being built near Grosse Pointe. Haik, Orlin, and Gee-Gee were having trouble pushing it along the ground, but Vahram dug his arms underneath it, and in one motion hoisted it upon his shoulders. *Look*, he said with a laugh, *from now on you call me Atlas*, and he carried the boulder-like ball for miles, all the way to their backyard, where it was still kept as a family heirloom. From that day on, their father called Vahram *zoravor mart e*, or *strong man*, and the name stuck. How his body was layered with such muscle with so little fuel, Haik could only guess. He would be content with just half his brother's strength. Even now, with his limp and stiff leg, Vahram was the strongest person any of the boys knew.

Vahram still carried the sledge and a blade strapped to his ankle, but since the episode with Toe the rest now held something to mete out pain as well: Haik an axhandle along with his knife, Orlin a tapered two by four with nails clawing out on the far wide end, and Gee-Gee a tipless butcher's knife found in the alley behind Kowalewski Meats. At the yard in Hamtramck just a month before, they had used the axhandle and two by four (the flat side, not the lethal clawed one) on an overconfident bull with a blackjack. Crack-crack, a double blow to the side of the head, then another across the back of the neck. They left their attacker disoriented and bleeding, crawling in the dirt, searching for his railroad cap. It was not revenge, not payback for little Toe, but it was a sort of justice and it felt right. Haik could still feel the power in his hands after his axhandle had landed its blow, and the pleasing concussion sped into him like a jolt of electricity from an exposed battery wire.

"There, right there. That one we take."

Same plan as always, but Vahram spoke to alert them and calm them at the same time. Unlike the last summer's mission here, they were out of sight of the station house and its glowing overhead light, hidden between stacks of wooden palettes. Their eyes had completely adjusted to the dark like small nocturnal scavengers. This is what soldiers must feel like, thought Haik, just before leaping out of their trenches to attack an enemy stronghold. He liked the feeling. It was better than torching a dead laundry. At the railyards, their opponent moved and was manned with bulls who carried weapons. This work made him alive.

"Okay, now, le's go."

Gee-Gee turned the engine over, the sound drowned out by the squeal of train wheel on rail grinding to a halt and railroad ties groaning under the immense tonnage of sliding steel. He shifted into drive. The old gears ground defiantly, but within seconds they were sidling up to the train, the truck engine's panting lost under the churning pump of the locomotive and the rattling of the boxcars. The engineer was applying the brakes, steel on steel whining in the temples, and Vahram opened the shotgun side door and swung to the bed of the truck as it bumped alongside the train. A burst of bladed winter air brought Haik to life and he shifted over to take Vahram's spot, Orlin pushing along beside him. Just before both train and Ford stopped in unison, Vahram flashed the sledge, a chink and flare of metal spark signaling his success at busting the lock open.

"Move, move, quick."

Vahram used the butt end of the hammer to lift the newly freed door latch and tugged the hand grip on the massive door. Haik pushed against the door frame, and when enough of a gap had been created, Orlin leaped into the bed of the boxcar and heaved his shoulder into the door, shoving it wide open. The frozen breath of the four filled the air.

"Go, go, le's go!"

Haik joined Orlin in the boxcar, grabbing into the crates stacked to the ceiling of the car. The procedure was simple. Grab and grab and grab and hand what you've grabbed down to Gee-Gee and Vahram waiting below on the flatbed. Don't stay too long—keep the truck engine running and gun it out of the stationyard after a minute or two of plunder. No stops, a circuitous route back to the Pehlivanian house, quickly unload, and when the shadow of danger had safely passed, assess the spoils in the warmth of the Pehlivanian living room, divy them up, then survive and dream until the next mission.

"Oh my God! Oh, my loving God!"

Vahram had pried opened one of the crates.

"You see this? Oh my God!"

Vahram crouched over the packing straw, where the polished wooden top of a radio caught the moonlight.

"God be damned, Kolster 6D TRF receiver, oak finish cabinet, three dials, bee-yoo-tiful inlay, just needs batteries…" Vahram was lost in his own world. "…jazz, champ-een-ship boxing, you name it, this baby deliver it right into your God be damned living room clear as bell. No way we selling this one. We get rid of that damn homemade piece of…."

"Hey, Louis Armstrong, we got work to do," urged Gee-Gee in a low tone, but Vahram was lost in a haze of sound and glamour and Jack Dempsey and flappers kicking up the Charleston. His weakness was radio. He had constructed his own with tubes, coils, a horn speaker, an antenna, and filaments and powered it with an old Ford Model T battery. The whole Pehlivanian family had heard everything from President Calvin Coolidge to Wendell Hall and his ukulele. Vahram was proud to bring his family joy, to be the one they needed to experience something good in life, and this new radio would rain light into their lives. Gee-Gee took one more crate from the hands of Orlin while Haik stood ready to hand another to his older brother, but still Vahram sat mesmerized. Haik was angry now—didn't Vahram always say to wait until they were back safely in their cramped living room before they thought of crowbarring the lid off a crate?

"Soooo, like ray-di-uhs, does ya?"

The new voice was low and cracked with whiskey and cigarettes and from a different place, a land called South, wherever that country was, where everybody talked in this snakey, lethal way. But who did the voice belong to? Haik saw both Gee-Gee and Vahram looking up, somewhere above him, directly over his head. A bull. He hadn't even heard the footsteps on the roof he'd been so consumed in his work and irritated with his brother.

"Well, ain't gonna be goin' nowheres with them there ray-di-uhs. Fact, y'all in a whole heap a trouble. Only place all y'all be goin' is the hoosegaw."

They couldn't be caught. That was never in the plan. Whatever was about to happen did not include going off to jail or the rail house for a beating or giving up. Never. Not after what happened to Toe. Haik looked over to Orlin. He was lowering himself slowly, reaching over to where he had leaned his two by four against the side of the boxcar. Orlin raised his other hand and put an index finger to his lips to signal quiet, and Haik began to follow suit, crouching, creeping silently toward his axhandle. They would fight. They would bring the bull down and then escape no matter what.

"Le's go!"

Vahram shouted, then an explosion buckled Haik's knees. Confusion. He saw Vahram's shadowy figure launch backward in the truck bed onto his radio crate before both he and his treasure toppled overboard onto the frozen ground. In a split second Orlin swung to the door frame and scaled upward along the jamb, then unleashed his club at an unseen target overhead. On the truckbed, Gee-Gee cursed, ducked, and covered his head.

Haik stood motionless, iced to the organs. He saw everything at once. A dim outline now lying on the ground where his brother had fallen and the radio crashed in glassy ruin. A dark cloud, the bull, plummeted before him with flailing arms and legs swimming in the ocean of night, then thudded to the frozen earth. Orlin let go of the door jamb, feet clumping down onto the boxcar floor, and then catapulted onto the just-fallen shadow on the ground below, the nails of his weapon reflecting fierce, speeding blades of light from the distant station house.

Haik awoke. He did not remember jumping from the boxcar, but he found himself kneeling on the ground, holding Vahram's head, supporting it with his hands and feeling the warm wetness of blood covering them and seeping into his pantleg. *Zoravor mart e*, thought Haik, *zoravor mart e*. The radio lay in pieces around them.

"Move! Move! Christ amighty, we gotta move!"

Gee-Gee was shouting at Haik, who could register nothing. Orlin stood over him, impatient, his hand outstretched. The still body of the fallen bull was slumped on the ground no more than ten feet from him, his pistol a few feet farther, still wafting smoke.

"C'mon, let's get'm in the truck."

Haik awoke again. He and Orlin shoveled their arms under Vahram and began to lift. Haik struggled, like he had too much whiskey and was floating inside a cloud of breathy mist, weightless and without strength. Besides the jumbled voices of Gee-Gee and Orlin, he could hear nothing. The next thing he knew he was sitting in the cab next to Gee-Gee and Orlin was propping Vahram against his shoulder and slamming the door shut.

"I'll ride in back," Orlin shouted into the cab. "Go. Let's get the hell out. Now. Go!"

The truck rumbled over the stationyard toward the splintery gap in the fence. Haik held Vahram against him. Blood seeped onto his chest and from what seemed a long way away he could hear the rasping sound of his brother's shallow breaths.

They pulled Vahram from the cab of the truck, his blood already freezing into a thick plaster against his head, his muscled, once powerful arms limply falling from his body as they carried him into the Pehlivanian living room. His mother was the only one awake, as she always was, waiting for her two boys to come home safely. Her scream brought their two sisters, who covered their mouths, unable to make a sound. Their father, still groggy from sleep, appeared last, his worn face registering nothing any stronger than disappointment. This is why they had left Armenia, to avoid slaughter, but death trailed them across the world like an Ottoman wolf. Vahram was dead. Haik was only 18 that night, but he knew the first chance he got, he would leave the city, especially if he had a family of his own, whenever and however that would happen. He would find a place and he would it make his and protect it from uninvited outsiders and thieves and brutes without respect. He would kill for it and never feel remorse.

The first step toward founding this new sanctuary came when word spread through the neighborhood that Ford was opening up a hire, something about a car to replace the Model T to be made at the new plant on the Rouge River over in Dearborn. Haik's father offered to pay their neighbor Mr. Meadows to take Haik to the plant so his son, his only remaining son, could find an honest job with a timeclock and bosses, an honest job that would not end in death. Mr. Meadows was Mr. Meadows, though, and the money was refused, but the next day Haik turned the crank on the front grill of the Irishman's Flivver and climbed into the back and took his place with three local men who had already started work at the Rouge Plant. The car smelled of sweat and oil. Haik said nothing as the black Ford jostled its way toward Dearborn into the unknown.

Less than twenty minutes later, the plant came into view, and Haik was alive. He had heard plenty about it, how it was a hundred times the size of the factory in Highland Park, as big as a whole country by itself, but he and his friends had stayed away because Ford property was always well-guarded and so many of his neighbors worked there and they didn't want to cause anyone trouble. There was nobility in their crimes, and the whole point of their raids on the railyards was to help everyone they knew who was starving or freezing, not to create problems.

His eyes swelled as he gazed at the plant. It looked like the entire planet could fit inside the main building in front of him. All around, smoke belched out of mountainous stacks and trailed off into the sky and became the sky itself. Gigantic conveyers criss-crossed before water towers and in the distance a fleet of ships as long as city blocks camped beneath the iron arms of loading cranes. My God, there was even a railroad, the boxcars appearing to be little more than toys beside the colossal assembly building. Fences surrounded everything, and on the other side buses chuffed in all directions, stopping at the entrance to pick up more men streaming to work and transport them to their stations. His father could haul all the tomatoes and lettuce and apples he wanted for pennies at the A & P—here was a place for men, Ford men who were not embarrassed by how they spoke or afraid of the new ways of a new country, making automobiles and trucks and whatever else could be powered by oil and gasoline. More than anything, he wanted to be on the other side of those fences, fading into the clouds of bodies headed for work, real work that earned you Ford money.

He was jarred from his awe by Mr. Meadows' Flivver creaking to a halt and the older men jostling out, grabbing their containers of coffee and sacks of food. A black ocean of cars flooded all around him and men moved in schools toward the entrance in front of the massive main factory. Was it real? His world, the world of his neighborhood and the railyards and beggars and hobos and shtarkers and drugstore cowboys and conmen, all of it shrunk into nothingness. Here was a place that could not be equaled in size or power or importance anywhere else in the world and he had not even stepped inside yet.

"You wait 'ere," said Mr. Meadows, a tall Scots-Irishman with clear blue eyes and a long face lined deeply from chin to forehead. His hair was gray but the hard leanness of his body and spark in his eyes made him appear a much younger man. He did not whisper, but his voice was soft and slow and calming, as if he thought speaking any louder might harm his listener. "Stand right 'ere by the Fliv 'till I come fer you. I'll need a quick word w'me boss."

Haik did as told. Deep into his hollow stomach, he wanted to finally be free of boxcar busting and nightly raids and arson and summer river rows to fill his gut with a little more bread and milk. How many times had they come up empty and returned home with only a box of coal chunks gathered from what had fallen off the side of the coalcar? It was just enough to burn for heat and cooking, and his family was blankly grateful but all hope for some fullness in their bellies was stamped out, unspoken bleakness left in their eyes. The reality was that the thrill and purpose of breaking open a boxcar was now, along with Vahram, dead. The Purples still ruled the streets, but they were as good as enemies now, especially since goons like Milman, Selbin, and Davis were running up the ranks.

Haik had crossed his line. He could not go back to the railyards or the laundries or the Sugar House. Every day, he thought of Vahram, the powerful dreamer running wires to a battery, totally absorbed in the world of electricity and radios and everything they had ever heard of men like Thomas Edison and the Dodge brothers and Henry Ford and the other kings of the world and how they mounted thrones through sheer will power and imagination and never let anyone hold them down. That world was not theirs but these stories of great men made it seem like it could be. Vahram saw a path to it every time he built or repaired a radio, a vague trail opening outward from the hazy, polluted misery called the present to a mysterious yet gleaming place off in the distance.

For the first time, here at the Rouge Plant, Haik could see it too.

"You're in luck, lad. Me boss will have a word w'you. We're all kinda new 'ere, comin' over from 'ighland Park and everything being so new, so things still ain't settled in quite yet. But you're in luck today, boy, some poor fool stoo-pit enough to be sick and that's one thin Mr. 'enry Ford don't abide. Now, y'lissena me. From 'ere on out, you're name is 'ank, not 'ay-ik. And yer last name, it ain't Pe-lee-van-yoon. Me boss, he don't take kindly to darkies a no kind, but he tolerates I-tal-yoons joos' fine. So, when he takes y'in, yer name is 'ank, uh, oh, le' see, Pah-lee-ni, yes, 'ank Pelini. Y'unnerstan'? When you're on Mr. Ford's proberdy, you're 'ank Pelini. And y'call me boss *Mr.* 'oarseman, y'know, just like it sounds, 'orse-Man."

Mr. Meadows' eyes sparked and he made a motion with his fingers on the hood of the Flivver like the legs of a horse galloping. Haik felt comfort in Mr. Meadows' presence. He was honest. He worked, he helped whom he could, he told you straight out what he thought in a kind manner no matter how unkind his message, and you accepted it. When he held a celebration at his house, it was not only the Irish from Corktown who were invited, but anyone he knew, whites, blacks, Italians, Poles, Germans, Hungies, Jews, Greeks, Armenians. Haik had last been to the Meadows' house just over two years ago for the funeral of Mr. Meadows' son-in-law, who was crushed at the old Ford factory in Highland Park when a stack of Model-T doors toppled over on top of him. The whole neighborhood showed up to help the Meadows mourn and eat and drink and sing and heal in the Irish way. If there was a man to be trusted in Detroit, it was Mr. Liam Meadows.

The day of the funeral, what Haik remembered most was the young woman who cried and held a baby in her arms. Even with her face concealed behind a black veil, her blue eyes gleamed, and against the cloth of her black dress her skin was white as the china you saw in the windows at J.L. Hudson's on Woodward Avenue. The way she held the baby and stood so strong as the casket was lowered into the ground at the cemetery amazed Haik. Lucille, her name was Lucille. Later, at the Meadows' house, she spoke with everyone, the veil gone from her face, her eyes sad but more blazing than before. Haik stood with his parents and Vahram and his two young sisters and they made their way to her to offer condolences. Even though Haik's father could only bow his head and say, "Surry, we surry you," she accepted his clipped words with great warmth and took each family member by the hand. Haik could still feel the soft heat of that small white hand in his own. He wanted to take her up right there just as she took up the baby that would never know its own father. This woman, he thought, was someone who could need him and he could make her life right despite all that was wrong. He wanted her then, to protect her, to never die for her or allow a mountain of steel to fall on him so her new son could depend on someone, a man, a real man to be there as a father even if the true father would never have the chance. The infatuation passed when he returned home, but the image of that Irish princess was safe in his memory.

"Mr. 'oarseman, this be 'ank Pelini, a good I-tal-yoon boy from the old neighborhood. His father be a good man and friend t'me, and I promise him to see what could be done fer his boy here. He'll work hard and give yeh an honest eight hour day and then some. He won't fuss none and make no mistake he's strong as a country mule, he is. He'll need'm some teachin' but we all did when we first come to."

Mr. Hoarseman was a rainy-eyed man whose face melted at the edges. He wore wire-rimmed spectacles and a vest with a pocket watch and chain, and on his jacket lapel was a kind of important looking badge with a star on it, like he might be some sort of policeman despite the fact he looked so completely unthreatening. Although he appeared to have been ladled into his expensive clothes and wingtipped shoes, he had a kind of unspoken, unphysical power and he knew it, his hair carefully greased and parted sharply on the left side of his narrow head.

"Well, he better work hard, that's all I've got to say. There's no place here for lay-abouts and lolly-gaggers. Mr. Ford wants a solid automobile made and made fast, no two ways about it, and we're going to need more young strong backs to build those cars. Now, Pelini, yes, you boy, look at me when I talk to you, Christ, does he speak any English?"

"Aye, yes, he speak 'imself some fine English. He's a wee bit shy now an'en. 'ank, soon, y'can speak to the man, it's okay."

Haik came to and nodded.

"Well, he better get over that and quick. You, boy,…"

"Yes, sir, Mr. Hoarseman." Haik would not miss another cue to speak.

"…hmmm, that's good, couldn't even tell you were a dago if I wasn't looking right directly at you. You're going to come with me and we're going to process you. Do you have any papers? Some sort of identification?"

"Ah.…"

"Poor boy, his family's kind of backwards to the times. Ain't a one of them got nothin' but their nat-ral-ah-zashoon papers and his papa don't let them leave the house. Thinks they're magic, y'know."

Mr. Meadows formed a knowing smile, which Mr. Hoarseman returned.

"And how, Meadows, no need to say more. These monkeys come here straight out of the wine fields. What on God's green earth would be done with them if they weren't strong enough to turn a wrench? Okay, son, Pelini, you come with me, we'll fill out your papers and get you what you came here for, some nice honest work and a day's pay for a day's labor."

"Okay, I'll be off. Can't be late to punch me clock. 'ank, you show 'em 'ow yeh can work."

Haik looked to Mr. Meadows, who smiled and nodded, and that was it, he was on his way. He followed Mr. Hoarseman to a place of desks and smartly dressed, clean women and typewriters clicking away and papers being handed here and there and telephones ringing and so many people talking at once he couldn't hear anything. It was a new world within a new world. He hesitated before he signed the first form. What was he supposed to do? Hieroglyphs filled the paper, the alphabet he pretended to learn at the Bishop School. Hoarseman looked at him intently and smiled, then pointed to a flat line on the first paper—this is where he was supposed to put his name. But how did you make a name you did not know how to spell? He had to move fast. He knew "Hank Pelini" had an "H" and a "P" but the rest, what to do with the rest? He saw signatures before—he had seen his own naturalization papers—so he knew it was mostly scribbling. With a very unsteady, childish hand, he made a "H" and followed it with scribbles, and then the "P," followed by more scribbles on the first document, and then on each document where the smirking Mr. Hoarseman pointed.

He remembered Vahram and their teacher Mr. Tulloch and the word "ignoramus." He scribbled away until all the scribbling was done. Hoarseman seemed to grow large as a boxcar as he watched Haik labor.

"Now, I'll have Higgins here take you to your first station. Take him to disassembly for now—we're getting backed up there and Stephens needs an extra hand. And you, Pelini, let me make something very clear to you. In my book, you're one step up from a nigra, and that's a hell a lot of steps down from an Irishman or Englishman or even a golldamned Kraut or a bohunk. And my book rules, and as far as you're concerned I am Henry Golldamned Ford. You'll get fifteen minutes for lunch and fifteen minutes for dinner, depending on your shift, but don't let that fool you. No beating the gums or butt time. No smoking, ever, when you're on the clock or inside any building. When you're not eating or pissing you're building the finest automobiles on the planet the fastest they can be made. You work hard and keep your nose clean and above all don't let me hear about you running afoul of Harry Bennett and the Service Department, because guaranteed that's the last anyone will ever hear of you. Who knows, you hit on the sixes here and somewhere on down the line, praise the Lord and Mr. Henry Ford, you might even make something of yourself and, heaven's sakes, dirt dumb as you are, become a real live bona fide American."

The world took shape. Haik worked hard each day at River Rouge and most nights visited the Meadows' house for dinner and drifted off into drunken dreams in Lucille's presence. Those dreams followed him home, home to the room he used to share with Vahram, now his room, and in those dreams Lucille was right next to him at night, soft and fragrant and warm and the hand touching him was hers. It started that morning when the men, all piled into George Bozouki's Model-T, awaited Mr. Meadows. Like clockwork each day for the past year when it wasn't his turn to drive, he emerged from the battered, wood-sided house, the ever-present grin on his face.

"A blessed mornin' to yeh, gents."

They all said hello and Griff Slater climbed into the back to give Mr. Meadows the honored shotgun seat next to George—although outwardly he never did anything to ask for or demand it, Mr. Meadows was respected without question. As the gears of the weathered car were ground into reverse, a voice called from the house.

"Father, your supper."

The girl, the woman from the funeral of Seamus Lynch, the beautiful widow who carried the young child with such strength and grace, was at the window with a lunch pail and bottle of milk. Her hair burst in fiery waves of perfect, angelic curls and her teeth were straight and white. It was morning and she wore a long robe and slippers, but she looked as if she could walk right down Jefferson Avenue right at this very moment and stop the electric trolley cars in both directions.

"Ah, thank you, darlin'. And Lu, have y'met the Pe-lee-van-yoon boy, young 'ay-ik? Son, this be me eldest daughter, Lucille."

Haik was in a cloud, heat swirling inside him, his nerves flaring in a thousand eruptions.

"Pleased to meet you, Haik. I'm Lu."

Her voice tugged him back to earth, reached deep inside him, down to the place where the boiler room of his manhood surged to life, so long shut down by his hunger, his anger at his hunger, and his lonely foreignness. He bore it well when Vahram was alive, because they were brothers, a team, blood joined by blood against anything that opposed them, and Vahram could keep his mind and thoughts busy with talk of boxcars and radio shows and moving pictures, but now in this brotherless world Haik's own inadequacy was in every mirror and storefront window and shiny new car he passed.

"Thank you. I, I mean, hello, good morning."

Haik could feel the other men grinning at him and he could not deny his own awkwardness. When had he really talked to a woman before? Not a girl, not someone at the schoolyard or the church they went to each Sunday, not his mother or his two little sisters. A woman, a real woman, a dame who had a child and had already made her way into the world. About two years before he died, Vahram made headway into the world of females, and sometimes he would walk home from church not with the family but Yeva Manoogian, a girl whose black hair shimmered like a freshly waxed Studebaker Big Six touring car and whose eyes were an inescapable green, so rich set against her deep olive skin that one could not help but stare at their radiance. Vahram even traded a lamb shank, a fifty pound bag of flower, and two headlights to Mr. Assadoorian for a fine, thin wool suit that Mrs. Pehlivanian tailored to fit Vahram so he could, with all the proper permissions granted, go visit Yeva.

When he would come home at night into their room humming "Somebody Loves You After All" or "Indian Love Call," Haik always questioned him about Yeva and what they had been doing that evening. Vahram would return a quiet laugh and tell him, *In a little while, you'll know what I was doing.* Haik would press on, asking what Yeva looked like, what she was wearing, what they talked about, what he said when she said something—when the time came for him to take a girl, he wanted to know how those things worked, all the little parts that were now a mystery to him, what you did, what you said, where you were allowed to touch her and when and what it felt like.

One thing from their talks he always remembered. When he asked Vahram how he knew what to talk about with a girl like Yeva, he explained it all.

"You know, I think about what I can say the night before," he lectured. "I imagine everything in my head, maybe a movie picture like, I don't know, *The Covered Wagon* or maybe *The Hunchback of Notre Dame*, or maybe an actor like Lon Chaney, I don't know, whatever, it don't really matter. In my mind, I hear me and Yeva having this whole talking, what I say, what she say back, how she look, her smile, her hair, how she smell, and you know, the next night when I meet her, it all come true. And even if it don't, it's okay, because I still can remember that talking in my head from the night before and I can always bring up whatever I was talking about in my dreams and know that I'll know what to say. It can't go wrong."

It made no sense to Haik, but everything Vahram said he stored away until it was needed later and he could understand it because, one way or another, what Vahram said always ended up being true.

"Well, we best be movin' along, girl. Thank y', Lu. Help yer mother today."

"I will, papa."

She smiled at her father and shot one quick glance into the backseat at Haik. He felt it like lightning, his whole body incinerating as if it had been pitched into a blast furnace at the Rouge. He watched her walk back up the wooden steps of the porch, glance back at the car with another slight smile, and withdraw into the old house. He quaked. He needed to climb out of the car and move, run, throw himself about, free himself from the cramped quarters wedged between the the older men. He had watched her with her back turned, his eyes tracing the fabric of the robe as it covered her behind. He knew he should not look, that he should force his mind onto work or baseball or anything but Lucille Meadows' chassis, especially with her father right there in the front seat, but it was stuck. He began to throb and grow and he glanced at the other men to see if they somehow detected what was happening to him inside his trousers, but they had begun to talk of unrest at the plant and something about yoon-yins, whatever that was. Haik looked out at the different cars passing by in the street, all headed somewhere, and he tried to go with those cars, to Eastern Market, the small island off Riopelle, the Bernstein warehouse on Oakland, Belle Isle, anywhere but here in this car, but his mind stayed stuck on Lu, Lucille Meadows, only on her.

The car rolled down the drive and into the street, and as it lurched forward Haik's mind flooded with the creamy perfection of Lucille's face. He burned and tingled and pulsed everywhere. He had never been with a woman before, in that way, the way he felt pulled at this very minute, but somehow he could picture himself with her, touching her, being touched by her, and it was real, as good and real as a glass of cold milk flowing down into his stomach after a bottomless night of hunger.

He looked again at his drive mates, and they continued to talk above the din of the Flivver's engine. Had Mr. Meadows noticed Haik's interest in his daughter? Haik's mind fogged. He wanted to be at work so he could occupy himself, pour himself into physical labor, but he couldn't get out of the car with a smokestack bursting out of his pants. It was agony. The car lumbered ahead, and with each bump in the pocked road he felt a combination of death and sweet friction, and his mind locked in a blind dilemma, wishing he could be rid of his waking dreams and at the same time completely given over to them. His hardness reached unbearable tightness, the rollicking ride bumping and rubbing him in ways he felt powerless to escape, and he shifted in the backseat and quickly adjusted himself so that he did not feel so much godawful ecstacy.

He was still hard when they reached the plant, but thank the Lord above the smokestack didn't belch in the Flivver and he had a disaster of a spill to explain. He made one last trouser shift before climbing out and hurried to his station, anxious to work.

At the Rouge, he advanced quickly. That first day, he was taken to the disassembly building, where damaged and abandoned cars were brought and stripped down for salvageable parts. Haik soon learned that Henry Ford was more than a creator—he was a wizard who never wasted anything that he could possess, repossess, shape, reshape, sell and resell. Everything, old tires, chassis and frames, glass, even upholstery, were carefully torn apart to be reused in some way in building a new car. Even the crates used to ship parts were carefully broken down and used to frame car seats. What came from Ford returned to Ford and made money for Ford again.

Here, Haik was noticed. On his first shift, he was partnered with a balding, unshaven man who needed a major scrubbing with lye and steel wool. The bald man was to remove the tires from the vehicle and stack them, and then Haik would hustle the tires outside and throw them into the back of a huge flatbed as he tore out the seats and unhinged doors. Haik did not like to sit still—his mind was often filled with pictures of Lu Meadows, and he wanted to pour himself into labor as quickly and as strenuously as he could. After his first paycheck, he was eating well, sometimes a whole baked chicken by himself for dinner, and his strength grew so that he could work at an athlete's pace. As soon as a tire came off, he ran it right out to the flatbed, and dashed back for more, piling up doors, bolts, washers, pins, seatbacks and bottoms, anything salvageable.

"What's your hurry?" the bald man seethed.

"No hurry," Haik returned, sensing his partner's resentment.

He did not come all this way to waste time, and he wasn't going to be harassed by a stinking bald man who eyed him sharply, trying to send some kind of message or secret threat. Haik refused to pay him any attention. Mr. Hoarseman said that they were there to make the best car the fastest it could be made, so Haik just applied that idea in reverse to the disassembly process—he would tear apart even the worst car as fast as it could be destroyed, carefully preserving every nut and bolt and gear that could be saved. As the work continued, the bald man grew frustrated, sweating profusely, which kicked up the level of his stench. He began cursing and striking the tires with a wrench.

"Here," Haik offered, and they switched jobs.

Haik could strip the tires off a car before the bald man could get his second tire out to the truck. Soon, he was taking the tires off and running them out to the truck himself along with his other tasks. Two days later, the bald man was nowhere to be seen.

Within weeks, Haik could take apart an entire Model T by himself if he had to. His overseer, Mr. Stephens, watched him closely and one day even Mr. Hoarseman came by to watch him work.

"You're on the trolley now, Pelini, you're a big six," mused Hoarseman with a smile, comparing Haik to a six-cylinder engine, the most powerful around. When had anyone ever told him he was good at something? Vahram told him *good job* every now and then in their boxcar days and it lit a fuse in him to work harder, to grab quicker, to steal more important items. Mr. Goldberg the whiskey bootlegger told him he would make a good Purple Gang member one day—he liked hearing that. And Fletcher and Axler knew he and Vahram could be trusted with any task from fetching a sandwich to incinerating a building, but that partnership ended bitterly. Even if he didn't like or trust Mr. Hoarseman, he still revved up at hearing his approval.

Haik could carry things all day long and never need a break—radiators, doors, seats, tires, headlights, crankshafts, you name it, he would take it apart and stack it and be back for more. It was almost like he was Charlie Gehringer of the Tigers out on the diamond at Navin Field clobbering the ball and making game-saving catches—this was his gift, and when people like Hoarseman or Stephens watched, he rose to the occasion.

There was no other place Haik wanted to be. At the end of the week, the armored pay truck would arrive and Haik and the others, sweaty, happily exhausted, would receive their pay, five dollars a day, at least double what anyone else in the city was making, and only eight hour shifts, while the saps at General Motors had to put in 12 hours, six days a week. One custom he didn't understand was giving one dollar every pay day to a Stetson hatted man with a scar across his nose from the Service Department for what he called "insurance," but he went along with it because everyone else did and he wanted no trouble.

One evening after punch out, his pockets full and savoring the day's events, Haik stopped dead in his tracks when he saw Orlin Crutchfield getting off a bus in a worker parking lot. There was no hesitation. Their days boxcar busting bonded them like war veterans. After Vahram's death, they laid low, afraid of more trouble if they were seen together and the loss of their leader an uspoken wall between them. When the chance to go to River Rouge arrived, Haik had quietly grown apart from all he had known.

"Hey, you! Hey, Orlin, over here!"

Orlin swung around, bewildered to hear his name called, then smiled broadly.

"Sweet Jesus! Haik! My Lord, Haik Pehlivanian!"

A knot twisted in Haik's gut—he was not Haik Pehlivanian here, he was Hank Pelini. He hadn't seen Orlin in, what, almost a year. Fear, anger, shame, and uncertainty had kept them apart since their last boxcar bust. The two met inside the fences and embraced. Orlin was now even taller, thicker, a full-grown man.

"Hey, look at you, big cheese Ford worker! How's life, old man?"

"Doin' ducky for a Negro. Can't complain. Still livin' in Paradise Valley, just off Hastings, got my own digs with my older brother and his family. How you been? Been a long time, brother. How you living?"

Haik looked into Orlin's eyes. One more time, he could see Vahram, feel him bleeding in his arms as Luigi drove the truck from the trainyard. He could see Orlin swing his weapon and the bull lying on ground, no longer moving. They believed that breaking into trains gave them power, but they learned how small they were and how their hunger, their frozen bones, their survival meant nothing to anyone but themselves. Report Vahram's death, and it was Haik, Orlin, and Luigi who went to jail, especially if the bull stayed down. Living like they did, America wanted them one of three ways, dead, chained to an assembly line, or in prison. River Rouge was their refuge from the past and their only path to a livable, survivable future.

The night after Vahram passed, after all the wailing and mourning, they drove Luigi's truck north on Mound Road until all they saw were pine trees shagged in snow. There, near a stand of birches, they took picks and shovels and battered the frozen ground until it cracked and gave up its insides. Six feet. Haik and Orlin and Luigi knew they had to mine six feet. They raged at the earth until they had made a hole deep enough to jump into. They took turns in the grave, digging and hacking until ground level was at Orlin's brow. Sweating, they shoveled deep enough no animal would claw up its contents. They retrieved the stiff bundle from the back of the truck and passed it down into the hole and began to cover it over. As they packed the clods of earth over Vahram, Haik wanted to crawl back into the hole with him, his brother, his teacher, his protector. They stepped on the clods to pack them down until a small mound had formed and no more dirt was left to pile on.

Haik looked at Orlin, a flesh and bone ghost from his past.

"Oh man, this is the life. Everything is Jake, Orlin. How about for you? Where they got you?"

"I'm over in the glass house. Laminating glass. About a month ago they let go ten guys at glass and I got called over from the foundry. Been there ever since. You believe that? Windshields, door windows, you name it. Make me as much jack as the white workers. Only Negro on the floor. You believe that?"

"We both making tracks here. Hey, one thing…around the plant, I need you to call me Hank. Long story, but you see me or anybody asks, I'm Hank Pelini."

"Hank Pelini? You bringing spaghetti in your lunch pail, too? Shit, least I get to keep my name."

They laughed and turned toward their cars.

"Hey, you hear anything about Gee-Gee?"

"Man, you ain't heard? Hell, old Luigi a member of Detroit's finest now. Wearin' himself a badge."

"Luigi's a cop?"

"Oh yeah, so watch your I-talian ass," Orlin chuckled. "Don't see him much. Hell, last time I talk to him was maybe, I don't know, months ago. He's doin' fine. Livin' over in Dearborn off Greenfield."

"And little Toe?"

Orlin stopped and looked off into the parking lot.

"He's doin' his own thing. Don't nobody know what he up to. Ain't seen him, and Luigi don't talk about him, so I don't bring it up."

Haik looked down, and then quickly changed the subject, telling him about Mr. Meadows and catching him up on his sisters and parents. They laughed and talked and agreed to meet the next payday after work at a black and tan juice joint just up the highway from the plant where blacks and whites were allowed to sit together and all the police and Prohibition men had been warned to leave Henry Ford's people alone.

When Haik came home on pay day, he made a point of counting his money at the kitchen table in front of his parents and sisters. Maybe it was cruel, but he wanted to show them where he now stood in the world and, maybe, just a little, let his father know that he was the real man in the house now. Yes, he would obey his father, it was tradition, but he made the old immigrant look at all the money he brought home. He made more in a week than his father made in three; if the roof leaked, it was Haik who went to the hardware store to buy the tar and shingles and nails to fix it, and if the girls, Arkina and Ovsanna, needed shoes it was Haik who took them to Hudson's. Sometimes he'd stop at the

Greek bakery on the way home and bring fresh baklava to his sisters, who squealed in delight. They counted on him, not their father or mother, and he liked the feeling of being needed.

His father embraced Haik, an old, awkward man attempting to hold his growing, powerful son. He told him he was proud of what he was doing, and Haik could not help but feel guiltily superior to the man who had brought him into the world.

The best turn in his life, though, came with Lucille. After two months at the Rouge, Mr. Meadows began to insist that Haik come to his house for dinner at least twice a week after work. They would go into the back yard and wash at the spigot with soap and fresh towels. Haik would toss a ball to Lucille's young son, Charles, now a boy of five, and wrestle with him in the grass. Inside, the whole Meadows clan was there, Mr. Meadows, his stout wife, his teenage daughters Emily and Cassie and son Liam (whom they called Junior), who was only a year younger than Haik and already working at General Motors, their little grandson Charles, but most of all, his oldest daughter, Lucille.

At first, she sat across from Haik, a curious smile barely visible on her face, and they would eat corned beef, cabbage, red-skinned potatoes and carrots and drink creamy reddish beer Mr. Meadows brewed in his basement. They laughed, all of them, and Haik tried not to seem like he was looking at Lucille, but he couldn't be sure his efforts were working. Lucille had married Seamus Lynch young and was still only 23 but had lived so much life. And she was a worker, answering phones and running the switchboard at Hudson's while her mother watched the boy. Haik could not imagine a more beautiful woman. She was slender and her skin white and clear, her red hair radiating a tempting warmth.

Haik was now 20 but he felt twice as old. He was a man. His belly now full, he labored like a steam drill. He had seen his uncles and grandfather and older brother die; he had fought in the schoolyard and learned to sleep with hunger twisting in his bowels. He was nearly beaten to death, blown up, and burned to a crisp. He had run with the Purples and raided the yards. But he was still here. With his job at River Rouge and his pocket full of jack each Friday, he was a man, as much a man as any in Detroit.

After several weeks of eating across from Lucille, Mr. Meadows welcomed Haik in after they washed up and the only open chair was right next to her. Haik stopped for a moment, unsure, jarred from a routine he had come to know and take comfort in. He forced himself forward and it seemed all eyes were on him as he pulled out the chair next to Lu and sat down. He could feel her next to him, a kind of heat that made that side of his body start to sweat and tingle. She joked with her family members, teased Haik by calling him Hank, the fine I-talian boy, and they all laughed together.

It was torture. He could smell her, a light scent of flowers or fresh soap or both, and when her arm or sleeve of her dress brushed against him his blood began to flow in mad rushes, filling him up inside his trousers; he had even begun to adjust himself in his underdrawers before coming to the table in anticipation of the torment to come, making sure the impending crowbar was at least positioned in such a way that it caused minimal discomfort or detection. The fine red beer Mr. Meadows brewed helped take the edge off, and by the end of dinner he was standing at an appropriately softer level of one-eyed attention.

One evening as Mr. Meadows was leading Haik to the door after they had finished their last beer, he put his arm over Haik's shoulder and took him onto to the front porch.

"'ay-ik, yer a fine lad. Yeh work hard."

"Thank you, sir."

He owed Mr. Meadows his life for bringing him down to the plant that day, and he owed him more than his life for letting him sit in Lu's presence at dinner and treating him like family and sharing his food.

"Y'know, Lucille, she's a fine lass. It's hard on her, with a little one an' all, but she's a fine woman. Can cook, clean, she holds a job, a fine mother to her boy."

Haik listened and looked out into the deserted street. He didn't need to be told any of that. There wasn't a keener woman in all of Detroit. Lucille was his dream, something that moved him in ways he had never been moved before, and anyone who didn't feel that way about her, well, he was a damn fool. Haik looked at Mr. Meadows, who gazed off into the distance.

"Y'never plan on somethin' happening like a 'usband dyin' so young. Yeh can't. It's not natural. And somes, they thinks because a woman been married once and she give birth to another man's baby, well, she ain' no good after."

It was true. Some might think Lu spoiled or tarnished, a bruised apple only a starving man would bite. And a boy like Haik, with his funny name and dark features, people would judge him as a backwards fool, a hopeless gutter crawler fit only to clean toilets and sniff around other men's castoffs. But Haik was learning from Mr. Meadows, how he always seemed to get along with everyone at the Rouge, mingling with black as well as white and boss as well as co-worker and lackey. Lucille was no charity girl, cashing in with any man she met, opening the vault between her legs in hopes of winning a new husband the easiest way possible. Haik remembered seeing Seamus Lynch in the neighborhood back in the day. Blond, muscled forearms, always smiling—he could not hate Seamus Lynch for loving Lu and being with her first. He must have had some sense and goodness in him. Seamus was first with Lu, but if he had anything to say about it, Haik would be last. Facing what she had, suffering, having fought on and raised a child, no, that just made Haik's desire to protect her more concrete and unmovable.

"Lu, she ain't seen no one since her 'usband die. No sir, she stayed put here at 'ome, work her job, look after her boy, 'elp her family at the house. What I'm sayin' t'yeh, 'a-yik, is sometime if yeh like, Lucille would like for yeh to take her out sometime, maybe for a walk, maybe to the river or somewheres, maybe for dinner sometime out someplace and not 'ere at the house. You'd have me blessing. Would yeh think on that?"

Out. Out with Lu. Haik would go out with Lu? He did not have to ponder. He did not have to consider. He had Mr. Meadows' approval to see Lucille, to be with her in a way that was more than a dinner guest. What exactly he would do with that blessing, though, was not clear to him. What was he supposed to do? Ask Mr. Meadows to ask Lucille if she'd like to go for a walk with him? Ask her himself? When? Where? A walk—where to? For how long? What would they talk about? Who would talk first?

"Mr. Meadows, I'll do it. Tomorrow night. After dinner. If that's okay."

He looked at Mr. Meadows, who smiled and nodded. And with that, his first date was made.

That night, he barely slept, and he found himself doing what Vahram had talked about, seeing himself with Lu, walking with her, talking about cars and work and pictures he wanted to see. In this moving picture in his mind, he was confident, smiling, walking about with an elegant, Valentino-like gait, ever mindful of his mesmerizing guest, who hung on his every word. And she was beautiful, her red hair pulled up in the back and wearing a lacey white summer dress and ribboned sun hat. But the movie was too real, and it only made his impossible tension worse, causing him to roll and thrash in his bed until the sun began to rise and it was time to wake for work. It would be a long day.

After work, worn senseless with a lack of sleep and a hard day's labor at the Rouge, he washed at the spigot in the Meadows' backyard and then had dinner with them, quietly eating his Irish stew. Before he knew it, dinner was over and plates were being cleared by Lu's younger sisters.

"A nice night it is," broke in Mr. Meadows. "Very com-fort-able on the porch."

Haik looked at him, his mind hibernating. It then clicked that Mr. Meadows was setting the table for him with Lu, and he should pick up the lead and ask Lu to accompany him to the porch. He looked for Lu, who had stood and was now stacking plates to be cleared from the table. Did she know what her father was doing? Had they worked this out between themselves ahead of time? He studied her, the ever-present slight smile forming at the corners of her mouth.

"Would you…," Haik started, trying to find the exact words, unable to retrieve this scene from the movie that played in his mind the entire previous night and into this morning.

"Yes, Haik?" Lu offered, still stacking dishes, that slight smile both devious and irresistible.

"Your father, he said it's nice out, on the porch. Would you like to go out there?"

He fumbled, Valentino with two left feet, tripping over his own tongue.

"Well, the table still has a bit…."

"Nonsense," shot in Mrs. Meadows, her wide face creased with authority.

"You young'uns go off. We'll get this cleaned up lickety-split."

"It's not…," Lu started.

"I said go."

And that was it, no further argument. Haik stood, weightless, looking down at the table. He looked up for a split second at Lu, who smiled, catching him in her eyes and holding him there. Haik followed Lu through the screen door to the porch, where they stood side by side at the railing. Night had already fallen, the moon set in the sky above them, throwing down pieces of light that sparked in Lu's eyes.

"Lovely night."

Lu's words settled into Haik's mind. They were part of the soft moonlight and the dark street and the lights coming from somewhere over by the river. Now, maybe now, he could fall asleep, right there on the porch. Here was contentment, this woman, this place, this moment alone with her.

"Would you, would you like to take a walk sometime? You know, go someplace?"

Haik was completely at peace with himself and the situation, as if awake in his own dream. Had he not been so drained of energy, he might now be nervous, but he held no such power and wanted no such power. He was a strong young man capable of immense physical feats, yet here with this woman standing quietly in the moonlight he had no substance or weight.

"That would be nice, Haik."

He breathed in her words, soft and melodic. *Nice*. Yes, it would be nice, the two of them, walking, together, a couple.

"How about now?" The words walked right out of him, without warning, in no rush but not waiting if there was no need to wait. "I, I mean, if you're not busy."

"Why, I can't say I have any immediate engagements at the moment. Certainly, let's walk. It'll do good for the digestion."

He finally looked at her, the moon glinting off her eyes, her smile waking him, energizing him. They turned to each other at the same time. She hooked her arm through Haik's and her warmth immediately seized him. She was smiling and he smiled back. He led her down the front steps and out into the open air of the neighborhood. Who would have imagined that a simple walk down a hazy street with a beautiful woman could be the most important moment in a person's life?

That very Friday after work Haik went home to wash and Ritz up in Vahram's old suit, the one he traded for with Mr. Assadorian. Vahram used to let Haik try it on when he first got it, but it was too big and it hung from him like a clown's clothes, and he joined Vahram in laughing at how foolish he looked. Now, he had no choice and would have to wear it, but maybe his mother could take it in and mend it in spots so it fit.

His mind swam—when he had enough money, he'd get some new glad rags of his own. Yes, he'd seen the perfect vest and tie and wide pleated pants with suspenders and a pair of gleaming leather wingtips behind the plateglass window at Hudson's—it wouldn't be long before he had the money, and he'd buy them, but for now Vahram's old suit would have to do.

He pulled on the pants and started to do up his fly, but as he got to the top button, he marvelled at how snug they were. He'd have to use a belt to cover up the undone button—he couldn't risk popping it. Even Vahram's dress shirt seemed to have shrunk, and Haik could not fasten the top neck button; oh well, the tie would cover that up. And the jacket, forget it. What on earth had happened to these clothes? He pulled it on but he knew if he rolled his shoulders forward with any force he'd rip out the back; he'd bring the jacket, but just drape it over his arm as a decoration. How had everything shrunk?

He stepped out of his room and studied himself in the hallway mirror. Now that he could eat more than once or twice a day, his frame had filled out. His neck had thickened, his back widened, and his chest become broad and full. The work at Rouge had built knots and bulges of muscle in his arms and back. He stared at himself with a newfound, proud amazement—he was an Armenian George Hackenschmidt. He had thought of women many times before, and Lu exclusively for the past several months, but with hunger eating at his belly day after day, the thought of physical contact was at best an empty, tormenting distraction, something to be destroyed and crushed in his mind. Now, though, those feelings and cravings to touch and smell and taste a woman possessed a vivid, viable life inside Haik.

It was time. He was a man, a sheik, and now he would find a way to make this beautiful woman his own.

And so it went, quiet walks and then simple, chaste dinners, until one night after a meal they visited the old Beer Garden near the Belle Isle Bridge. The president, someone named Herbert Hoover, another wet blanket, made sure there was no real beer in public, just the kid piss legal near beer, but they really didn't need any alcohol to feel good when they were together. They laughed and danced to Dixieland music in the clean summer darkness, and he was the proudest man in Detroit that night. He swirled her around in the open night air and she was light as a child. She smelled of flowers and her eyes dazzled in the reflection of the strings of lights surrounding the garden, her fiery red lipstick and nail polish making her luminous skin even more white. Everyone looked at the couple, the dark man and the fair woman, and that's what they were, a couple, a man dressed as sharp as John Barrymore and a beautiful dame swooning in his arms, a real Clara Bow, his own sheba.

When the band slowed down and played "Three O'Clock in the Morning" they waltzed beneath the clear, star-specked sky looking into each other's eyes. She had taught him to dance and there was so much more he wanted to learn from her. They left the garden early, and ventured to a speakeasy that served the best uncut Canadian whiskey and champagne. They laughed and talked and listened to a jazz band play Bessie Smith and Fanny Brice tunes. They took the dance floor for the song "Chicago," and roared with the crowd when the black singer wailed "Dee-troit, Dee-troit, that toddlin' town!"

Soon, Haik could see a pleasant exhaustion set in on Lucille. When was the last time she had been out for an entire evening of food and music and dancing and drinks? Haik offered his hand, she accepted, and they walked back toward the Meadows' neighborhood, taking a slow, moonfilled route along the river.

"Anushas."

"What? What's that?"

"It's Armenian."

"So what does it mean?"

"My beautiful one."

She lingered under the radiant moon. Haik felt a power now, a kind of control he had never felt before. This feeling, it was good. His mind swooned. The booze swam in his skin and played jazz in his veins. He had listened to the older guys at the Rouge during meal breaks, and he stored away some of the little phrases he heard them say when they described their moments of conquest.

"Cash or check?" he murmured to her, and he saw her teeth catch the soft light.

"Oh Haik! You behave now. I think I might have had a little too much of the giggle water," she cooed, the slightest trace of Irish lilt in her voice.

"Oh, applesauce," he teased.

He stopped in the cool night air and looked into her, his hands on her hips, feeling the sweet, soft flesh beneath her loose dress.

"Well, let's go for cash," she said impishly, and soon his lips were tasting hers. Electricity flooded him. He kissed her, and in his first kiss he learned that he knew how to kiss and he wanted more. All the months he had dreamed of her and the light flirting of the last few weeks made the smoldering torch inside him unbearable. They kissed until their kisses could no longer fill their need for each other.

Haik found himself laying his suit jacket in the grass where he and Lucille resumed their hunt. She smiled at him, stroking his hair, running the backs of her hands across his cheeks. What happened in the next thirty minutes convinced Haik that he must make this woman his wife.

It happened fast. With Orlin as best man and Haik's sister Arkina, now 16 with dark beauty beginning to blossom on her thin frame, as maid of honor, Mr. Meadows gave Lucille away to Haik in marriage in September of 1929. Mr. Meadows smiled broadly; Haik's parents, on the other hand, had hoped for an Armenian bride for their only remaining son. In Armenia, their father festively pointed out that Arshile Jafaryan, a neighbor, had only daughters, servile and polite and pretty as morning flowers, and Vahram soon understood that a marriage had been arranged for him, a marriage only escaped by escape from Armenia itself. With the wound of Vahram's death still seeping blood, though, they did not put up much protest over Haik's choice of an Irish widow who already had another man's child.

The newlyweds moved into the Pehlivanian house, wedging into the room Haik had shared with Vahram. Little Charlie slept in Vahram's old bed and Lu and Haik shared his—it was cozy, at times too cozy. Lu called Charlie their little fire extinguisher when his light sleeping kept them chaste and quiet, and Haik mostly laughed, but they were happy and together and would make do. One month later, though, Black Tuesday hit and something called the stock markets crashed or fell down. Haik did not understand. He bought food and when he could flowers for Lu, not stocks, and he didn't even use a bank. His money was hidden in a hole in his old mattress; no one, not even Lu, knew about his money.

So why, suddenly, was everyone poor? There were the same amount of people, the same amount of houses, the same amount of cars, the same trolleys and streets and stores, but now everyone was instantly in the gutter. Nothing changed for his family—they had always been in this condition. So how could all the big eggs end up in the flusher? The Penobscot Building just went up on Griswold Street, 45 stories above the earth and lost up in the sky itself, the Fisher Building and its theater were the talk of West Grand Boulevard, the Guardian Building was set to open, and they had just built and rebuilt the Ambassador Bridge a mile across the river to Canada and back—how could there be no money? Why not just make more money on a big paper press and send it out to all the banks across the country? At work, they were now building the new Model A, more cars and better cars than ever, so how could the world suddenly be bald and broken?

"It's not me and yeh that's got no money now," explained Mr. Meadows on the drive to the plant one morning. "We always had nothin'. No, now it's the big darbs, the ones with the millions. The same ones built all them buildin's and bought all them cars. Damn fools done decide they want to share our misery. Well, they be welcome to join us."

It still made no sense. On the radio, President Hoover told the country that "prosperity was just around the corner," but he didn't seem to know what street he was on or where the corners were located. In no time, the squeeze hit the Rouge. More of Harry Bennett's heavy-knuckled snoops in the Service Department looked over everyone's shoulders. They were bimbos, salted hoods and hard guys fresh out of the clink, along with pink faced, heavy chested college boys who played football or wrestled, and a smattering of smash-faced palookas whose luck had run out in the prize ring and who had no other skill to offer the world but the willingness to unleash their gnarled fists. They didn't build cars, they didn't process ore, they didn't run a drill press, they didn't laminate glass, they didn't grind metal, but here they were, making the same amount of money as the men who did the real labor and collecting their "insurance" fee each week.

And what was happening to the workers? Haik first noticed that Joe Stanton was no longer operating the conveyer at the disassembly line. Then he was stunned to see what he thought was a new driver on the worker bus from the lot. No, it was not a new driver, but the same old Tommy Gilman, only with a foolish amount of black dye drenched into his hair.

"What's eating you, geezer? The old lady got an itch for younger daddies now?" jibed George Bozouki, slapping Tommy on the shoulder with a laugh.

"Beat it!" snapped Tommy. "Don't give a damn about the old lady—I'm protecting my job, y'hear? You get your head out of the Ouzo long enough you'd splash a little tar too, Greek."

"Oh, dry up, Tommy," complained George, put off by Gilman's inability to take a little friendly ribbing.

"You dry up, yourself. Word's out, Greek, you're old, you're done. All the hayburners gettin' the heave ho. A jalopy like you better wise up and get on the trolley."

There was a hint of threat in Tommy's voice. Mr. Bozouki was a short, barrel-chested man with muscled forearms and strands of white hair gliding in and out of thick waves of black and gray. He laughed again at Tommy, but Haik felt a warm pit in his own stomach.

A week later, when they trekked out to the car after shift, George broke them the news.

"This is it for me, boys. End of the line. I won't be needing no ride tomorrow."

"What yeh mean?" asked Mr. Meadows.

Bozouki was shaken, and he couldn't bring his eyes to meet Mr. Meadows.

"Hoarseman come by a half hour before shift end. He said no hard feelings, but he had to give me the bum's rush. Too old, he said. And not to feel bad, because I'd be having company soon enough."

Bozouki looked hard at Mr. Meadows.

On the ride back after they had dropped off Bozouki and Slater, Haik asked Mr. Meadows to stop at the pharmacy and he'd get him some black dye. Mr. Meadows just laughed.

"When I put dye in me 'air to keep a job it's a job I ain' doin' no more," he sighed, the ever-present grin on his face barely visible. "I'm strong as any man half me age and I know automobile makin' good as any man in Detroit. Color a me hair don't change that, 'aik."

In the middle of February, though, Hoarseman's axe fell again, square on Mr. Meadows. He was the real McCoy, working for Henry Ford for 25 years, all the way back to the old Mack Avenue days when everyone owned horses and nobody knew who the hell Henry Ford was or had any interest in gas powered buggies. It wasn't on the level. You couldn't just deep six a man like Mr. Meadows. Haik felt the same anger he did after the railyard bulls had done Little Toe, and he could feel his old ax handle gripped tightly in his fingers.

"Chinless puke. I could break his crummy neck easy as pie," fumed Haik on the ride home.

Taking a pipewrench and delivering a quick shot to the back of Hoarseman's head just before the close of shift wouldn't be any harder than taking a two-by-four to the skull of a railyard bull.

"Naw, 'aik. Yeh promise me, yeh don't lay a mitt on the man. Ain't no need for that. 'oarseman, he ain't the real problem. It go 'igher than that. The whole shebang gone rotten. 'oarseman, he just a drop a oil in the engine, no more. We work these machines, these tools, and then we become them, all our parts made a metal, ready to be replaced, no more, no less. You replace a belt or a gasket, you replace a man. Don't make no difference to the big darbs."

Mr. Meadows was usually easy to understand, but now he lost Haik. The promise to not hurt Hoarseman, that was clear, and he would abide his elder. But how could this man be so calm? So empty of anger? So free of desire to harm someone who had harmed him? And he talked of men and machine parts in the same breath, as if they were the same thing. All Haik could do was listen.

"'aik, I'm gonna give yeh the Fliv," he said as they sat in the drive of his home. "Yeh got Lu and Charlie to feed and yeh got to get to the plant. It ain't fancy, but it'll get yeh where yeh needs to be."

"I can't take your wheels."

Haik looked out at the Meadows' front porch. He took the man's food, his daughter, and now he was supposed to take his car. No, he couldn't take any more.

"Yeh ain't takin'm, son, I'm givin'm. That's final. Please don' disrespect me, son."

There was no threat in his voice, only fact.

"What're you gonna do?"

"Oh, they be talking of relief I hear, emergency money. Goverment 'scrip, they call it. But that don't suit me none, though. I'm still young an' I can do a fair day's work. Maybe I'll bootleg me beer from the basement," he laughed, looking straight ahead. "Liam's doin' fine at GM and he'll help with money. But there's trouble brewing. Mark me words. Yeh already seen wha' they doin' las' month. All them men been let go, they meet on Woodward Avenue to let the world know what been 'appenin', and the coppers and Harry Bennett goes at'm, all fer wha'? Wantin' a job? Wantin' t'feed their families? It gonna get worse afore it get better, son. Anyways, here yeh be, take it. She's all yers, son. Tell Lu not to worry none. You come by with Charlie for supper on Sunday, like always."

He smiled at Haik, put a hand to the young man's shoulder, and then opened the driver's side door to the Fliv and walked to his front door, his pace slow and measured as always but now somehow defeated.

That night, Haik paced back and forth over the splintered kitchen floor at his parents' house. He broke the news to Lu as she cooked after she asked why he had the Fliv and where her father was. Her eyes momentarily showed panic, but she then returned to cooking, methodically stirring the stew simmering on the stove. Unable to stay still, Haik bounded upstairs to Vahram's bed and took out his wads of hidden money. He counted out $100, more than the old car was worth, replaced the remainder of his stash, shuffled down the stairs and out the door past Lu without a word, then drove to the Meadows home. Mrs. Meadows answered the door, a downcast look on her face.

"Evening, Hay-ik. You okay, son?" she asked. He could not speak. He took her hand, placed the money in it, and sprinted back down the walk to the car. Mr. Meadows would never take his money, so it was best to do this quickly and without words. He would face Mr. Meadows' wrath another night, but tonight he was going to take Haik's money whether he wanted it or not.

Now it was just Haik and Griff Slater who made the trip to the Rouge, alternating each morning in almost empty vehicles that were much too quiet. Griff was a simple man, younger than Mr. Bozouki and Mr. Meadows but at least ten years older than Haik, a family man with two sons and three daughters. Griff had a glassy, wandering eye and said next to nothing. Some thought he was touched in the brain, which he might have been, but he was dependable and never missed his turn to drive and that was really all that mattered.

A week after Mr. Meadows was released, Haik showed up at disassembly fifteen minutes early as usual and took in the daily lay of the land, going to the bathroom before shift began so he did not interrupt work once he took over. The air was cold and he felt an uneasiness come over him again as it had every morning since he had paid Mr. Meadows for the Fliv. That night, Lu was in tears when he came home and demanded that he take her and Charlie to see her parents, so he drove back again. Mr. Meadows did not mention the money Haik had left with his wife, but he eyed Haik with an uncustomary seriousness that hinted at reprimand. When Lu asked what he would do, Mr. Meadows just smiled and said he'd be fine, he had some money, he came to this country with no job and no jack and he would find work again. Besides, Junior still had his job and they'd make do. Lu told him that she and Haik and Charlie could move back and pay them rent and help them out, but he wouldn't hear of it.

"Yeh have yer own life, girl, and I'm no baby. Yeh stay with yer 'usband and child where yeh belong. Yer parents be fine and that's that."

Haik was mystified by the exchange. Lu didn't discuss moving to the Meadows house with him and Charlie and paying anybody rent. Not that he would have objected to the idea—he already thought of giving part of his salary to Lu's parents until her father could find work again, and he was going to suggest that Lu give her paycheck from Hudson's to them as an alternative and his money could continue to go to Lu and Charlie and his sisters. Lu was upset and her words were spur of the moment, but the fact that she fired out the idea of moving without talking to him first knotted his temples. He was the man in her life, not her father but her husband, and her first allegiance had to be to him. In a matter like this, they should talk about things first, and as the man he should be the one to bring it up and make the offer. That was tradition, and she had broken it, leaving him mute and powerless. For the first time since he'd known her, he felt a distance creep between himself and Lu.

So that morning he again poured over what Lu had said to her father, how she talked as if she was in charge of what they did and how they spent their money. Haik was not so traditional that he wanted a slave or handservant for a wife like in the old country, but he didn't want anyone, even Lu, to think he could be disrespected or silenced or passed over like a child. Maybe he should have spoken up, not in front of Mr. Meadows, but when they got home later that night. He admitted he did not have the best schooling in the world, but he was not stupid and did not need to be spoken for. The matter gnashed inside and would not let him sleep as he lay spooned around Lu, smelling her rose-scented hair and resting his arm on her tender hip.

"Pelini, a word with you," piped Higgins, breaking the tightening rope in Haik's mind as he readied to tear into his first vehicle of the day. "Mr. Hoarseman says we're gonna move you over to stamping. They've been slowing down on one of the lines and he needs a bohunk to set it straight. You're the sparkplug he's countin' on."

Haik nodded. He had long grown tired of repeating the same brainless tasks hour after hour, day after day, week after week in disassembly. It had gotten to the point that someone would have to physically put a hand on his shoulder to alert him for his supper break. Away from the line, he talked a bit with his shiftmates, felt the same clockwork need to crap as he finished off his last sandwich, used the john, then quickly fell back into his trance of labor until the end of the day. The early joy and gratitude he felt for his job were still there, but not when he was actually in the plant. It was good money, the best actually, but it ground on him by the minute. He was paid to work, though, not be happy, so he buried his thoughts and went back to the line.

At stamping, plate metals were shaped into car roofs, bumpers, fenders, you name it, depending on what line you were on, and then all the pieces were hooked onto overhead chains and sent one by one in a river to the main assembly line to be bolted or screwed or welded onto a car frame. Haik wandered behind Higgins, oblivious to the titanic clanking presses smashing steel as easily as a child shapes mudpies. He understood how amazing this operation was, but he was no longer awed or impressed. It was all just work, and too much anger was building in him now, anger over Mr. Meadows and Mr. Bozouki, anger over the possible disrespect of Lu, the old anger over Vahram and his uncles and cousins turning to dust. A new job would help, something to reignite his mind, but he no longer owed anyone around here awe or politeness or respect.

"The operation is simple, really. Reilly over there controls the rate the plates are fed to you. The press stamps and cuts the plates into car door shells, leaving some excess metal to clear away. You just take the shells off the press and hook 'em on these conveyers so's they can go to grind and trim, and extra metal scraps, you put'm in these bins and these two niggers will cart 'em off to reprocess 'em."

Higgins pointed to two black men who could have been father and son. They said nothing but looked at him intently, their silence speaking volumes.

The job took no more brainpower than disassembly. Once Haik figured out the best place to grab the shell and how to swing his weight to lift it up, he powered into the job. In this entire complex, Haik thought, all the real thinking had already been done years ago by somebody else. It took great brain power to design a press, to calculate gauges and tensile strengths of metals, to figure angles and temperatures and pressures. All that was left now was the stupid manual repetition of men like Haik and the others on the floor, who were themselves but flesh and blood pistons and levers.

It wasn't an hour before Haik began to pull ahead of the crew that gathered the leftover metal and tossed it for scrap to be reprocessed. Haik would lift the door shell and stack, then wait what seemed like a minute while the two scrappers cleared away the leftover metal pieces and put them in the bins. He then made a deal with the other two—he would move over to help the weakest of them, a narrow shouldered older man, and the stronger of them, a young Irish looking kid, would take Haik's place in hopes that the process would even out. And it did, with Haik and the strong kid working in silent tandem. Talk was not allowed on the job, and there were always enough hardguys wandering around looking over your shoulder to make sure you toed the line.

After two hours, though, Higgins returned with an oversized, slack-jawed follower, an immense man who still looked as though he had yet to shave, sporting slicked-back hair and a smirky college-boy grin. He was obviously a member of Harry Bennett's Service Department, a hired goon whose job was to incite fear in workers.

"Wait, wait, wait," bellowed Higgins. "What gives here?"

Haik looked at the strong Irish boy, then at the weak narrow shouldered man, who bowed his head and refused eye contact with Higgins and his sidekick.

"Pelini, when I left you was totin' doors and Murray and Freddie were on scrap. Why the changeroo?"

"Well…," began Haik.

"Yeah, you got somethin' to say?" smiled the giant.

Haik felt the old anger rise inside him. At this moment, he did not care for Higgins or his blubbery shadow, but he had to be wary. They were up to something with their questions, and they were not workers, his kin in labor, but an enemy that preyed in the shadows, feeding on people like him and Mr. Meadows.

"It worked better this way, changing the jobs," said Haik blankly.

"But that's not your place, sonny, decidin' who does what," snapped Higgins, suddenly a bold man as he hid in the giant's silhouette.

"Well, ask anybody here, Reilly or them two guys. Things worked better, faster, when we switched."

Haik nodded at Reilly and the others, at which point the giant sensed an opening.

"I think Mr. Higgins just said you ain't the boss, guinea," smirked Goliath, and he planted a thick, sausage finger into Haik's chest hard enough to push him a step backwards.

Haik looked away. He knew where this was headed, from the big boy's confident king-of-the-playground smirk to Higgins' lack of intervention. So be it. This was to be a show, an example of how the law worked for everyone to witness and take stock of. Here, Haik was to be sacrificed in the name of order and doing exactly as told without thinking, even if thinking made things better. Thinking was not a worker's place; he was to do as told or else. Haik looked at Higgins and the giant. He would not play along, donning the role of the disobedient worker who meekly assumed his place. No, he was done. His family had run from Armenia, but today he was not going to run from this windbag and his shiny faced walrus.

"You ain't gotta push me," Haik returned in an even, controlled voice. He returned to his first days in America, the days when he and Vahram would fight every afternoon at school until no one dared look at them let alone taunt them for fear of the savage beating these skinny, crazy-talking, dark-skinned wildmen promised to dole out. He had survived too much to cower. He was no longer skinny, no longer a stickman, and he was not afraid.

"No, I don't gotta push you, but maybe I want to."

Before Haik could prepare himself, a cannonball slammed into the side of his head and he was sprawled on the workroom floor. The giant flopped down on top of him. Another blow catapulted toward his face but he rolled to one side and the behemoth avalanched toward him, missing his target by inches. Haik moved on instinct, clutching onto this fancy suited zeppelin. This man-boy was bigger, stronger, heavier. He had no chance in a test of brute power. What Haik did know was wrestling, though, Armenian wrestling, the attacking of limbs and joints and not the whole man, especially a very large man lying smotheringly on top of him. He would have to find a weakness and attack it with all his strength.

The giant rose up on his knees over Haik and brought another fist onto him, but Haik curled at the last second and the blow glanced off the crown of his head, dazing him. He gripped onto the monster's clothing. He could absorb two or three more of those shots before he was totally helpless. He would isolate a limb, one limb, and put his entire body against just that one limb. The giant grappled with Haik, grabbing for position, until he held him down with one hand by gripping at his shirt collar.

Split seconds flew like tommy-gun rounds. Haik clutched the railroad-tie thick wrist with both his hands, like gripping a baseball bat, and drove the limb up and across so that the giant's own arm acted as a shield from any potential blow. The giant adjusted, trying to find leverage so that he could punch again with his free arm and land another wrecking ball blow to Haik's skull, at which point Haik released with one hand and grabbed up and over the giant's back, catching enough of his greasy shorthairs to pull the block-like head down into his chest.

Haik could hear the monster panting, refueling, the hot breaths scorching his chest, sweat from his forehead soaking into Haik's shirt—he had to move quickly.

The big boy released Haik's shirt collar, but Haik maintained control of his wrist and then let loose of the shorthairs gripped in his other hand. He reached overtop the giant's shoulder and under his armpit until he could lock his grip onto his own other wrist—this is what he and Vahram called the Ararat Armlock. With the lock secured, he arched his back with all his might and drove off his heels until he began to tip the behemoth forward, never releasing the captured arm. Once the mass of boyish muscle was tipped to the side, Haik continued to raise the Ararat Armlock and force the giant's wrist behind his humped, whale-like back. He was nowhere near as strong as the monster, and his head was light from the concussion of blows he had taken, but now the battle was between his two arms, two legs, and entire body and the whale's one elbow and shoulder joint.

For a split second, Haik weighed the possibility of releasing the smirking, bloated boy, showing compassion in victory, but then the whale began to struggle and the rage he had been trying to control shot through him and overpowered his senses. He exhaled and then arched fully onto his near shoulder, belly thrusting to the ceiling, heels digging into the concrete, and forced the armlock behind Goliath's back with all the hate and strength he possessed.

Snap.

Haik continued to rotate the gorilla's wrist up and back, but he felt the resistance of the joint disappear like a door toppling off its hinges and heard the pained shriek of his foe. The gorilla tumbled over onto his own back and began kicking and screaming in a combination of shock and spastic agony. Haik lay on his back panting, but a few of the involuntary kicks caught him and brought him back to his senses. The ceiling above flashed in blue and green flares and his vision blurred in and out of focus.

"You did it, man! My blazes, you did it!"

Haik squinted and, with great effort, forced the face of Murray into focus. The young Irishman beamed and offered him a hand up. Haik accepted, and as he gathered his feet under him the work area swirled and tremored, causing him to struggle to find his balance. The Irish boy held him steady, and by this time a crowd had gathered.

Crowds were not good. Workers collected around the beached walrus, who still writhed and whimpered on the workroom floor, which meant that there were jobs not being done and therefore cars not being made. It was different if a gear or bearing wore out or a belt jammed or broke and they had to wait for a mechanic to come repair the glitch before they could get the line moving again—no, this was a human delay, a shutdown they had caused, something that couldn't be blamed on a machine. Mechanical errors were expected; human errors were not.

"Okay, okay ladies, break it up, break it up."

It was Higgins, who must have fled when the fight went sour for his man, but he was now accompanied by a troop of eight or more bimbos, who were not as large as the walrus but older, rougher, more deadly looking. Two of them locked onto Haik's arms and he had no more power left to resist. Two others scooped up the simpering, disgraced leviathan, who wailed and gripped his damaged arm, and led him away while the remaining henchmen began to shove and shoo the gawking workers back to their stations.

"What the fuck is going on here?"

A short, squatty man in a tailored wool suit, neat bow tie, and glossy patent leather shoes appeared, flanked by two more towering goons. The regiment of hoodlums straightened up at this small man's arrival.

"Here, sir, here's your problem," offered Higgins, pointing to Haik.

"This dinky wop?" smiled the well-tailored Napoleon, who sported the nose of someone who had spent some time in the prize ring. "What's the name, dago?"

"Haik…ah Hank, Hank Pelini," gasped Haik, still catching his breath, his chest pumping hard, his head throbbing and contracting in flooding, stinging pulses.

"Pe-lee-ni," repeated Napoleon, flourishing a comic Italian accent as he sized up the captured man before him. He then glanced over at the crippled walrus. "I tell you what, Pelini, you finish up the day's work without incident and I'll have a couple of the boys meet up with you at quitting time. We need to have a little chat."

Haik said nothing. His wobbling mind began to piece together what awaited him. It was not good. At punch out, he would be met by two bimbos, not peachy faced kids like the broken winged ape-boy. No, these would be real toughs, and they would escort him to a sedan that contained two more thugs and drive him someplace behind the electrical plant, force him out of the car, and the four of them would use fists, bats, pipes, whatever fit their mood, to make sure he never caused Mr. Henry Ford a problem again. He knew the stories, "accidents" that happened throughout the plant, accidents that signaled the end of a career or worse. "Fell down some stairs" meant "complained too much" or "talked about workers uniting." The language of Henry Ford was getting easier to understand.

The goons released their grip and Haik had to catch himself to keep from dropping to the floor.

"Thank you," Haik murmured dumbly, resting his hands on his weakened knees, and Napoleon smiled slightly.

"Let's go, boys," the commander announced, scanning the scene one more time, making sure everyone was back at their stations. "Show's over for today, gents. The Service Department better not get another call here, period, or they'll be hell to pay. You got work to do, and I suggest you do it, double time, you're already behind for today. Okay, boys, we're done here."

"Yes, Mr. Bennett," the regiment mumbled in unison, and off they marched, puffed and violent-eyed, trailing dutifully behind their general. The workers returned to their posts, most unable to keep from smiling.

The presses again lurched to life, churning and firing, and only now was Haik aware of the magnificent din they created. It was as if he was seeing the machinery for the first time, the incredible struts, arms, gears, pistons, and joints. What god could have envisioned such things let alone created them? He felt as if he were hovering a few feet above the ground, a bodiless eye observing all. He had to step out. Catching his breath, he stood up and staggered to the nearest exit.

Haik pushed the service door open and the bitter winter air slapped him back to earth. He could taste the iron flavor of blood in his mouth, and the heavy tightness on the side of his face told him he must already be swelling rapidly. He found a bank of snow huddled against the outside wall and crouched down, scooped up a wet handful, packed it flat, and pressed it against the side of his face. The snow both soothed and burned, so he pressed it harder against the skin of his face until it froze a handsized piece of his head. He gathered more snow and reapplied it to more sections of his face until the injured side of his head was dumb with numbness.

He looked up and surveyed his surroundings. Conveyers crisscrossed and spiderwebbed the sky in all directions, carrying rivers of coal to anywhere it could be burned into power. As he took in the conveyers, his mind began to form ideas. He could leave the plant now, just walk back to the worker lot, rest low and concealed in his car and wait for Griff Slater to arrive, explain to Griff that he was now the last Ford man left from their original crew and he'd be on his own from here on out. Once Griff had been dropped off, he would walk into the back door of his home and his mother and Lu would panic and cry at the sight of him and he would take his cue from Mr. Meadows and reassure them, laugh it off, tell everyone they'd be fine, hell, you should see what the other guy looks like.

The next day, though, what would he do? No one was hiring, nowhere, nobody, nothing. But maybe this was where some old connections might come in handy. Maybe he could visit the old Bernstein warehouse on Oakland Avenue, knock at that bay door and drop to his knees and beg for work, maybe even locate Mr. Goldberg, remind him of the old rumrunner days on the river. Maybe the Bernsteins could forgive the run-in with Millman and Davis and let him run with the Purple boys again—half his head was probably already purple with swelling and they'd get a kick out of it. Hell, Fletcher always liked him—maybe he had some torch jobs or some drops at the track he could take care of.

"Hey, Pelini, there you are. Why don't you come back in? We can use you, old man."

The strong Irish boy, what was his name, Murray, or was he Freddie, leaned out the service door. Haik raised up slowly, threw his snowpack to the ground and stumbled to the open door. When he stepped inside he almost went blind—the artificial light of the factory seeming to have lost all power of illumination. He detected a human sound momentarily top the steady humming and churning of the machinery and his eyes could now make out the dark figures of workers at their stations pumping fists into the air and waving. They were cheering. For the first time in his life, Haik felt what it was like to be cheered. It hurt to smile, but he did, and then returned to work.

He continued his shift, deciding to accept his fate at the hands of the Service Department. His head and body throbbed, but lifting the door shells and hooking them to the conveyor helped him focus on something other than his own possible, no probable, misfortune to come. If anything, he was calm, almost serenely energized as he grabbed, lifted, hooked, and returned. The press could not stamp fast enough and the conveyer could not feed the sheet metal quickly enough. Work, brainless repetitive work, was medicine for his misery.

Sure enough, at about ten minutes before punch out, two thick-necked toughs strolled to Haik's station and wordlessly observed him toil. He glanced at them only once, but he noticed Murray and Freddie peering at them apprehensively. Haik was no martyr—the only true martyrs had turned to dust in the villages of Armenia years ago—but he wanted to tell Murray and Freddie to rest easy, no one would drop a nickel on them, they hadn't done anything, he would take the long walk on the short pier alone.

After punching out, Haik gathered his coat and hat, nodding at the new shift members filing in, receiving a few slaps on the back from those who had seen him conquer the giant, and then the darker of the two bimbos nodded at him to follow. Should he run? Crazy thoughts tottered through his mind. Once outside, he could bust from the goons and run to a conveyer belt, jump in and ride the coal heap to freedom. No, the belts led to furnaces—hell, maybe burning up quickly was better than bleeding out after a beat down. He was tired. He was tired from work and tired from fighting and tired from thinking so much about things he could not understand or change even if he did. His sleep was fitful, and he could never seem to fully recharge his body. If he ran from Bennett's thugs, they would track him down like a dog and there was no question what his fate would be then—there was no place to hide at River Rouge.

Haik walked single file between the men to a car parked outside, a Model A Tudor, not too different than what he had imagined earlier. He climbed into the back and the door slammed shut, sealing him in. His senses came alive and all his nerves hummed. If these were to be his last living memories, he wanted to fill himself with all that could be captured. He saw the gray masses of his free shiftmates herding toward the busses and to the nearest exits, their frozen breath rising in opaque clouds mixing with bluish tufts of fresh cigarettes lit by those tired enough to risk being fired. The sky overhead was colored a pinkish, yellowish hue by the sulfur billowing from the massive smokestacks, streaked here and there with faded blues and oranges. He could hear the Tudor turn over, the transmission clank snugly into gear, and the voices of workers joking and shouting, suddenly energized by their release from laborious captivity. One of the toughs lit a cigarette and Haik savored the sudden aroma of the burned match and tobacco and allowed his mind to drift in the blue haze of smoke gathering under the roof of the car. Smoking was forbidden at the Rouge, but Bennett's men played by their own set of rules.

Reality intruded on his sensual dream as the Tudor ground to a halt just off Schaeffer Road and the latch of his door was lifted.

This was it.

The dark hood nodded Haik toward the entranceway of the building ahead of them, above which a painted sign announced the inevitable: Service Department. The beaten side of Haik's face now felt as if it had bloated into a kind of swollen deadness that did not hurt so much as merely feel heavy, like he had to consciously keep that side of his head from slumping over onto his shoulder. He climbed from the backseat, adjusted his coat, and set himself to meet his fate.

Once inside, the dark mug strolled ahead while his partner held Haik by the arm in an area that, in the daytime, must have been staffed by a number of secretaries. He suddenly wished some females were here, a sympathetic feminine face he could make eye contact with, a womanly presence that would look with pity on him and remember him so that, if there were any scrap of kindness in fate, perhaps one day she could tell Lu of his last moments and confirm exactly what had happened to him. There were so many ways for a body to disappear here. The murky Rouge River lay just outside. No one would bother scouring its soupy depths looking for a cement-shoed body. A person could be chopped, ground, pressed, floated down a coal chute and then funneled into a gargantuan incinerator—disappearing was not a problem at all.

As Haik imagined the many ways he could exit the earth, he was shoved from behind past the empty desks and chairs and dark offices and brought to a dimly lit stairwell leading to a blackened basement landing below. He walked down the stairs, his hands on the clammy walls for support, fearful he might be kicked from behind and sent cascading headfirst into the abyss. He reached bottom, though, and was guided to a large inner office, where behind a great oak desk sat the dapper, pug-nosed Napoleon who had summoned him.

"Boy, that's shaping up as one hell of a shiner," beamed Bonaparte. "Here, here, pull up a chair, let this man take a load off his dogs. Pelini, isn't it? Get Mr. Pelini here a chair."

Haik noticed that he was surrounded by a troop of hatted men, all shapes but large, each one projecting a kind of unspoken, indifferent viciousness. The dark complected man, probably because he had brought Haik here, pulled up a straight backed wooden chair and gestured for Haik to take a seat, which he did even though, at this point, he would have preferred to remain on his feet.

"Here, seein' how you didn't get a chance to see a doc, let me offer a little medication."

Pug-nose produced a bottle of Canadian whiskey, two tall water glasses, and a pistol, which he placed on the desk in front of him. He filled both glasses with a generous shot. Haik buzzed eerily inside—here it comes, he thought, it's here. A drink, a bullet, an exit.

"Make mine a double."

Haik was startled to hear the sound of his own voice, and could not remember consciously making the decision to speak. What was he thinking? A man about to die should not make demands or provoke a crueler death than what surely awaited. Even dumber than brawling on the workroom floor of Mr. Henry Ford was rapping a hungry bear on the snout while slathered in trout blood.

"Well, I'll be a son-of-a-bitch!" laughed puggy. "'Make mine a double.' I'll be goddamned! You palooks hear that? 'Make mine a double,' he says! Christ almighty, I like you, Pelini. You got heart. You got a set of balls. Harry Bennett's the name. You just earned yourself a double."

Bennett filled Haik's glass just short of the rim, lifted his own, tilted it in salute, and drained it. Haik reached slowly, unsure of exactly what was happening. He raised his glass and took in the searing, mediciney aroma, and then put the rim to his lips. He allowed a short burst to pass over his tongue and slip down his throat, feeling it burn where the inside of his mouth was cut, and then followed it with a more healthy swallow. When had he last had whiskey? Real whiskey, not the watered down, caramel colored fraud served in speakeasies? The power of the amber elixir suddenly made him aware of how much pain he must be in as its tranquilizing effect hit him hard, making him raise the glass in an Ararat Armbar until the last hot drop had vanished.

"Hank, if you don't mind me calling you Hank, let me be honest here. What you did today in the stamping plant was stupid. Very stupid. Totally unacceptable. The fighting part, hey, I used to box, I was in the Navy, men will be men, shit yes, but you fight on your own time, not Mr. Ford's. You gotta problem with another fella, you meet him in the lot after you both punch out and settle your differences—*after* your shift is over. Now, normally, this would be it for you, done, no more job for you, out in the street you go, the bank is closed...."

The whiskey spun Haik hotly in its wheelhouse. They could kill him now and he would almost be grateful. If he were dead, he would never again be hungry or see hunger in the pale faces of his sisters and parents. He would never again die in the death of a brother. He would never again feel the breath of poverty heaving down his back as he tore into pieces of automobiles under the metallic music of despair. He would never have to look into the eyes of a man like Liam Meadows after he'd had his job and all his dignity stripped away. He would never be bludgeoned in the side of his head or grapple on his back on a factory floor like a misfit schoolboy. Death would be the end of all good he had ever known, lying in bed with Lu after Charlie was soundly asleep, feeling her warm wetness and pure roundness under the covers, but it would also be the death of all unpleasantness he had ever known, which, overall, seemed to be the heavier of the two loads in his life.

"…any idea who that tubalard was you put into the soup line?"

Haik became aware of being asked a question, and because he had no idea what that question was, he covered his bases and nodded a half yes, half no reply.

"Here, let's give you a refill, 'a double,' and then we'll get to brass tacks. That big fella was Gustavus Schmidthacker. Yes, Gus Schmidthacker, the All-America defensive tackle. Dumb as cement. Couldn't even pretend he was a college student after one year of college ball. Was just about to make the Chicago Bears last year but made some poor decisions with his off the field time and the people he decided to call his friends…."

Bennett filled Haik's glass again and poured himself a good measure as well. Haik looked over at one of the filing cabinets and noticed a red and white bullseye target painted on the side and a number of holes pocked into it. None of this made any sense. Just kill him, or let him get drunk enough he felt nothing, but no need to lecture about football and guts and ships and hackers and bears. Bennett's men looked bored, perhaps a bit bitter at being left out of all the uncut whiskey. To hell with them. All of them, Harry Bennett included. Haik wouldn't even be here if there was no such thing as a "Service Department." He'd be dropping Griff Slater off at his house and looking forward to washing up at the kitchen sink before a hot meal, wrestling with Charlie, teasing his sisters, kissing Lu into tomorrow.

"…thought old Gus was going to work out for us here in Detroit, I really did. I'd given him a couple chores and he performed admirably. Until today, that is. Now tell me, and here's where I get to the point, and you better be fucking honest with me, Pelini, straight down the assembly line, did you get lucky today with big Gus or do you have a talent for, ah, neutralizing people?"

Haik's fog was beginning to clear a bit. Was there a hint of admiration in Harry Bennett's question? Was he impressed that a lean, bulldog dago iceberg could sink an oversized titanic like Schmidthacker? Bennett looked right at Haik as he placed his hand on the pistol he had set on his desk at the beginning of the meeting.

"I can break your arms," Haik blurted too quickly, still unclear how these words were coming out of his mouth.

When he drank hard liquor, he became blunt as a lead pipe. Immediately, as if on cue, Bennett's men stood and their hands reached into their jackets, but Bennett raised a deflecting hand and smiled.

"Ah, Hank, my friend, would you care to clarify that?"

"Clare-fry?"

"Clarify…ah, clear up. Explain what you just said to me, about breaking my arms."

"Oh, no, not you, Mr. Bennett, I don't mean hurt *you*. Not *you*, like *your* arms. Never, no. I just mean, if I had to, you know, I know how to do what I done today again if I had to. If somebody tried to hurt me, or my family, well, then, yes, then I could do like what I done today to Shitkicker."

"Shitkicker! You hear that? Shitkicker! This wop fractures me! Now that's the answer I was looking for," cackled Bennett. He paused and summed Haik up. "So, Hank, here's the lay of the land. You're going to be switching jobs. You are now officially a member of the Service Department. You took a member out, fair and square, and now you take his place. On paper, it's the same pay, but off the page, trust me, you're gonna be way better off. First of all, you ain't gonna be dry-humping a machine all day. Second, you're gonna have a chance to move around, both at the Rouge and, well, let's say other places of business interest. You're gonna be somebody, Hank, somebody with some class and some clout. Nobody fucks with the Service Department. Nobody. Our job is to help Mr. Ford in all ways possible and to keep this company up and running and pumping on all cylinders. You with me?"

Haik nodded. His shoulders loosened in relief. He was not going to die, not yet, not today, not here at least. He was not going to be beaten any worse. He still had a job, a paycheck, a way to feed his family. All things considered, the lumped up face, the throbbing pain, the day was turning out to be a success.

"…certain elements are threatening this country. Yes, there's a depression, but nobody wants to admit it's due to laziness. Like Mr. Ford says, and it's true, 100% true, there are plenty of jobs for people willing to work…."

Haik pictured the shame on George Bozouki's face when he informed them he was done at the Rouge and heard the strong, honorable lies Mr. Meadows told when speaking of what the future held for him. These were not lazy men. No, laziness had nothing to do with why they no longer had jobs.

"...unions. Mr. Ford is very clear—he knows what's best for his workers. He's like a goddamned father to them, for Christ's sake. He pays them more than anyone else in the world. He educates them, feeds them, helps them so they can help their families and raise their goddamned children the proper way. Shit, he even hires niggers for the love of God. We don't need any son-of-a-bitching union commies to start spreading their poison on Ford property. You want a union, go work at Chrysler or General Fucking Motors or move to fucking Russia. Hell, Higgins had his suspicions about you after your man Meadows quit...."

Quit? *Quit?* What was Bennett talking about, quit? Mr. Meadows never quit a damn thing in his life. Mr. Liam Meadows would have worked for half the money he was making just to keep his job.

"...but you checked out, Pelini, just a hard working wop, not a communist agitator. So, we're copacetic. Any questions from you?"

Bennett folded his fingers together and looked at his new hired hand, pleased with their conversation. Haik had a thousand questions. Why did you just lie about Mr. Meadows? Why the hell was I attacked today? Can I have just five minutes alone in a quiet room with that bastard Higgins? What the hell is a communist? Can I take the rest of that bottle home with me? Does Lu really think she can order me around like another son? Is that what she thinks of me as, a son, an older brother to Charlie? Is there a heaven, and if so, how soon after I get there can I see Vahram?

"So, what exactly do I do? I mean, what exactly is my job?"

"Hah-hah-hah," chuckled Harry Bennett, pleased at so simple a question. "Pelini, you come in tomorrow at the regular time and we'll get you up to speed. Basically, our job is to fight against everything that's wrong in the world today: unionizers, communists, belly achers, candy asses, rabble rousers, un-American cry-babies, welchers, anybody with a hand out who doesn't want to work for an honest living. Too many damn Reuthers out there. And we keep all those sons-a-bitches the hell out of the Ford Motor Company, the finest automobile company on the goddamned planet. Now, boys, get this wop the hell outta here."

Bennett waved his hand and began talking to the two thugs closest to him, as if Haik was no longer there and had never existed. The dark mug who had brought Haik in put a hand on his shoulder and nodded, and within seconds he was back in the Tudor heading back to the worker lot.

When he arrived, he saw Griff Slater contentedly waiting by the gate, crouched against the fence eating an apple. He climbed out of the car and waved to Griff.

"Boy, that sure looks like it hurts," Griff observed, chomping loudly, a small rivulet of apple juice dripping from the corner of his mouth.

"A little bit," Haik explained.

He held out a hand and helped Griff to his feet. They walked to the Fliv and got in, and not a word about the condition of his face or his new job was exchanged the rest of the way home.

Haik Pehlivanian could not hate a man more. The problems with Lu, what happened to Mr. Meadows, the evil boiling inside him, all could be traced to Cam Lister.

He met Lister the first morning he reported to the Service Department. He bid Griff Slater goodbye in the parking lot and was met at the gate by a leathercoated man in a brown felt fedora.

"Pelini? They said look for an ugly mug with half his head beat in—that's gotta be you. Name's Lister. You're with me today, Bennett's orders," he said, maneuvering a toothpick in his mouth.

He was taller than Haik, but his age was not clear. He could have been as young as Haik, but his face was pocked, as if it had once been covered in boiling sores that scabbed over, and a welted scar under his jawline on the left side of his face and another that crossed his right cheek made him look as old as Haik's father. His skin was so white it almost glowed with an eerie, deadish quality. When he spoke, Haik could see that his lower teeth were ringed in a kind of black, stone-like slag, and his upper teeth sported patches of brown stain. Apart from his looks, there was something about his twitchy manner, the way he rolled the toothpick in his mouth, that made him unlikable and, worse, untrustable.

Haik thought about his "ugly mug," and self-consciously wanted to tilt his herringbone Brooklyn cap over to shelter that side of his face. That morning before he left to pick up Griff, he looked in the mirror on his dresser and saw how his left eye was nearly shut, ringed in a puffy bluish black, and his cheek bone was lost in a bloat of blood trapped under his skin. He *was* ugly.

The night before, when he brought the Fliv to rest in the drive, he took a moment to close his eyes and compose himself. He didn't want a scene, especially since, despite his appearance, everything actually turned out so well. He tried to enter his house quietly, but when he walked into the kitchen and his mother and Lu looked up and saw his face, their mouths both opened wide in choked silence. Lu dropped her paring knife and ran to him, touching the good side of his face while her other hand hovered an inch away from the swollen, purple-blue injured side.

Sit, sit, sit, she cried, running to the sink to wet a cloth and then pushing outside to gather some snow to wrap in the cloth. *Oh my God, oh my God, who did this to you? What happened?*

In her worry, he felt her love for him and he loved her back, forgetting his anger. His head did hurt, but now, dry-mouthed and the whiskey worn off and so many thoughts in his head, he was more tired than anything. Charlie came running down and his mouth opened wide.

Dad, he said, and Haik loved him every time he said that word, *dad, are you okay?* Charlie looked scared, so Haik brushed aside the ice to gather him in his arms. He told the shortest version of the story he could, reenacting the fight with the behemoth in comical, wide-eyed gestures, finally getting Charlie and Lu to laugh as he described the mountain of flesh falling on top of him like a crashing marshmallow Empire State Building, the great creation in New York City he had heard about on the radio, over 100 stories tall. Later that night, Haik had to sleep with his back to Lu because he could not bear to rest that side of his face on his pillow, so she curled around him and rested her thin white arm lightly across his side.

"First thing, Pelini, is we'll see what Bennett can do to get you outta that Fliv. You can't be a SD man and drive a crate a shit like that," Lister quipped, casting a thumb over his back towards the Fliv as he led Haik to his own car, a jazzed up 5-window Deuce coupe with chrome, red-rimmed hubs.

So, this is how SD men rolled. My God, what Haik would do to own one of those babies.

They drove to the Service Department office, and inside clacking away at their typewriters were the secretaries Haik had imagined the day before. But even they had a kind of hardness about them, an impenetrable coldness, and they did not look up when Lister and Haik entered.

"Mornin', beautiful ladies," smiled Lister, causing the women to look up only momentarily before returning to their work. "Mr. Bennett here yet?"

"Downstairs," one secretary answered, and Lister looked a bit put off by their unwillingness to give him eye contact.

He went to a wall of mailboxes and retrieved an envelope from one of the cubbies, and then signaled Haik to return to the car.

"Just a little business before business," Lister said, settling behind the wheel of the coupe.

He opened the envelope to reveal a thick helping of green bills. He took out the stack and made a point of fluttering his fingers through it for Haik's entertainment.

"Just finished a little chore for Mr. Bennett. You think this is a lot of clams? Huh? Lemme tell you, this ain't the berries, not even close. This here's chump change. Here, here's ten bucks, a little piece of the pie, I'm giving it to you because this ain't shit to me. I'd just wipe my ass with it and give it a good flush, so a sap like you is better off with it. Go ahead, find yourself a Jane tonight and give her a few extra strokes from Cam Lister," he lectured, stuffing the money into the front pocket of Haik's shirt.

Haik didn't like Lister's pasty hands touching his body or his clothes, but ten dollars, ten damn dollars?!? Almost half a week's salary and he hadn't even started work yet! But what were these "chores" Lister was talking about? How on earth did someone just find himself with an envelope stuffed with money and acting like it was no big deal?

"Now, we're heading to Mr. Bennett's office. You keep your trap shut. You say yes sir, no sir, and if he says go shit in the corner or pound your monkey you do it, and you do it fast. Got it? For some reason, he seen something in you he liked and you're in, but let me tell you, you muck around and just as quick as you got in you're gonna be out. Mr. Bennett's as hard-boiled as they come. He done some things, let's just say, it's best not to know nothing about. You pike him, you're history. I seen it happen many a time. Got me?"

Haik nodded. It was pretty straight forward as far as he could tell. Whatever he was going to end up doing, he had to do it right and do it fast. But if he wasn't making cars, what exactly would he be doing? He had stayed away from the Service Department whenever he entered the plant. He paid his dollar of "insurance" to whomever was walking the SD beat without question. Is that what he would do, shake down workers? Things were so clear they were completely unclear. Instead of going in through the upstairs offices again, Lister led him to the back of the building where they approached a back stairwell into the basement. As they set to descend the stairs, the door at the bottom opened and through it emerged Harry Bennett, who held the door for a thin, wiry older man with gray hair and sharp, birdlike features.

"Right this way, Mr. Ford," beamed Bennett, an air of gentlemanly politeness threading his every word, again sporting a dapper bow tie.

"Why thank you, Harry," the old man returned, and Haik froze.

It was *him*, the man, the person who created this entire universe he now circulated in. It couldn't be but it was…Henry Ford! The one and only Henry Ford! *The* Henry Ford, ruler of all worth ruling in the world.

"…sometimes wish Edsel was more of a man like you, Harry. For the life of me, I can't understand his thinking sometimes. You know what he wants to do now? Do you? He wants to pay some Mexican communist $10,000 to come to the Institute and paint up the garden court walls. Ten thousand dollars! Can you fathom that? Do you know how many cars you can build for $10,000? Do you know how much profit you can generate from a $10,000 investment? And he wants this man to paint pictures on a wall, for goodness sakes. What is that going to accomplish? It's $10,000 he'll never see again. For the life of me, Harry, I just can't understand the boy's thinking."

"I can't say as I understand it, either, Mr. Ford," interjected Bennett, using his free hand to motion the old man up the stairs.

"Valentiner and Richardson are bending his ear with their hands out, same old story. They've convinced him he's an art lover…phsssh. The boy's always complaining about how the workers are treated, as if we don't do enough for them already. If he feels so sorry for them, why doesn't he take his $10,000 and buy them all tickets to a matinee for goodness sake!"

"I'm with you, Mr. Ford. I never understood these fancy ar-teests and their scribbling. That bullseye down in my office? That's my idea of art," offered Bennett, and both he and Ford began to cackle.

"My word, Harry, thank goodness I have you. I don't know what I'd do without you to talk sense with."

Ford put his clawlike hand affectionately on Bennett's shoulder, and Bennett helped him the rest of the way up the stairs.

"Well, looks like we've got visitors," beamed Bennett.

"Good morning, Mr. Ford, Mr. Bennett," chimed Lister, shooting a darting glance at Haik.

"Ah, good morning, Mr. Ford and Mr. Bennett. Good morning," rasped Haik, still in awe of being in such a giant's presence.

"One of the new hands, Mr. Ford," declared Bennett, and he slugged Haik on the shoulder. "Look, he's already shed blood for you. Some union goon tried to pull a fast one in the stamping plant yesterday and Hank here showed him what's what."

The old man sized up Haik, admiring his bruised and swollen face. This was his art, the art of the practical, the art of flesh and bone and reality, of pain and progress that could be observed and measured and proven and turned into labor and profit. His eyes poured quickly over his subject, taking in all the detail of color and disfigurement in Haik's wounds, and Haik stood self-consciously, unsure of what he should do, careful of anything that would upset the demagogue before him.

"Now see, that's what I like to hear. Someone who will make a stand and do what's right, no matter what the cost to his own person. We need more men like this young man. And your name is?" inquired Ford.

"Ah, Pelini, sir, Hank Pelini."

"Oh, Italian. Your people ruled the world at one time," he observed with satisfaction, then smiled slightly. "But now I do."

"Now ain't that the truth!" piped up Bennett, and he and Lister began to bellow in laughter and Haik joined in, followed by the master joke-teller himself.

Something was funny, although he did not know exactly what. Haik had never ruled his neighborhood let alone the world, and neither had anyone else in his family, for that matter. He sensed he was being made fun of, but he would not allow himself to feel offended by such a great man.

"Well, off to Fairlane. I'll bid you gentleman good-day. I've got to talk with Mead Bricker about another speed up on the line. You'd be amazed how much profit can be generated by just one half second more of efficiency."

"Everything you do amazes me," said Bennett. "Do you want me to drive you there personally, Mr. Ford?"

"No, thank you, Harry, I've got my driver. Well then, I'm off. We'll see you later in the day," said Ford amiably, and away he went to his waiting car and driver. Haik, Bennett, and Lister watched in silence as he approached the vehicle and the chauffeur opened his door, eyes averted, and drove his master off to his next destination.

"There's one giant of a man," mused Bennett. "Now, let's take care of some business of our own."

The three men retreated back down the stairs and entered Bennett's office through a door Haik had not noticed the day before. He could appreciate the décor a bit more today—rich paneled walls, some photos of Bennett with various important looking people, including Mr. Ford. Without a word, Bennett marched across the office and went through a third door, with the other two following. They entered what appeared to be some kind of pitch black tunnel, the air musty and cold. Haik was third in line and could not see a thing. He took one cautious step after another, afraid he might step into some kind of hole or into a wall. He could hear the footsteps of Bennett and Lister echoing lightly ahead of him and he did his best to keep pace. He lost all track of time and distance as he trekked in the clammy darkness. Where were they going? Why all the secrecy? He felt reasonably safe—there was no reason to kill him, not after Bennett had spoken so kindly about him in front of Mr. Ford, but he still felt a slight trepidation.

Off to the right, a light flicked on and Haik could make out Lister's silhouette bobbing in front of him and then disappearing off into the light. Once he neared the source of the light, he could make out another room, a kind of storage room, where before him sat every type of gun he could imagine. On one wall, shotguns were aligned and under them boxes of ammo. On the other wall were an assortment of machine guns (Thompsons, choppers with the big drum magazine, the kind Haik remembered from the Bernstein Sugar House on Oakland and all of Fletcher and Axler's hotel hideouts) and pistols of every shape and size with more ammo in neatly stacked crates. Here and there were stacks of baseball bats, pipes, billy clubs, blackjacks, knives, hammers, shovels, strands of rope of all thickness, picks, axes, you name it.

"This is where we outfit you for the job," mused Bennett matter-of-factly. "What's your choice?"

Haik wasn't one for guns. Knives, sure, he still had his strapped to his calf from his Purple days, and bats, he swung one in the boxcar busting days, but in his mind if you carried a gun, eventually you would have to use it, and somebody had to die, either you or the guy you were pointing it at. Bats, clubs, ax handles, you could send your message and adjust the level of damage you inflicted—from death to a simple broken bone. But guns, no, as Haik had already learned, that was another story altogether.

"Ahh...," Haik stammered.

"Don't tell me you never used a piece before," said Bennett, a mixture of disbelief and disgust mixed in his voice. "Lemme tell you right now, you cocksucking dago, I just went out on a limb for you with Mr. Ford, *Mr. Henry Ford*. Don't make me regret that. Now, Lister, let's get this dumb-ass square. Here, get him, let's see, let's get him one of these, a nice little Colt Detective Special, double action, it'll do him just fine. Set him up with a shoulder holster and a half dozen boxes of shells. What else, what else, I want you to keep a baseball bat, shovel, and rope in your car at all times…"

"Boss, about the car," interjected Lister.

"What? This asshole has a car, doesn't he?" questioned Bennett, obviously becoming irritated.

Haik stood frozen. There was a time to say funny things that Bennett might find amusing, but there was a time to keep the kisser closed and this was definitely one of them.

"Well, if you could call it that. It's a Flivver, sir, looks like something some hick from West Virginia jacked up so he could go bang his cousin down the road," explained Lister, seeming to relish Haik's utter ridicule.

"My God, shit, okay, take him over to the garage later, have him turn in the Fliv and pick him out something usable. Nothing too nice— he ain't really proved a damn thing yet and we don't want him drawing attention. Classy but none too fancy. Alright, that should do it for now. Get him to the range to learn how to use his heat. We are going to be *very* busy in the next couple of weeks and I'm gonna need all hands on deck, understand?"

"Yes, Mr. Bennett," both Lister and Haik chimed in unison, and that was it, he was one step closer to becoming a full-fledged SD man.

Once back above ground, Lister drove Haik to get his Fliv and led him to the reclamations garage, where he began another little tour.

"This," Lister explained, interjecting laughter here and there, "is where cars end up that are, shall we say, acquired by the SD. Some people, well, heh, they just can't seem to keep track of their automobiles or, in some cases, heh-heh, let's just say where they end up they don't need a car no more."

The garage was immense, filled with at least a couple hundred rigs of all make and model, a good many not even Fords, Chryslers and Dodges and Packards, with room for plenty more. Lister greeted the mechanics and guards and, with a hand to his chin, evaluated the pickings for Haik.

"Here, here we go, this is you, Pelini, right here," smiled Lister, pointing to a Whippet 98 Sedan. "I can tell you from experience, this here's a real struggle buggy—you get yourself a doll in that backseat and even a wet blanket like you's makin' whoopee before you know it. The garage boys, they fix these things up inside so you got a little extra giddy-up under the hood. And don't worry it's a Whippet, like Mr. Bennett'll be sore at you. No, we don't always want the Ford name attached to everything, if you know what I mean."

Haik didn't know what Lister meant, but that was it, he was now the proud owner of a 1928 sedan. Sure, it had seen a few years of wear, but it was a damn sight better than what Haik was used to. Man, he couldn't wait until the end of the day when Griff Slater came out looking for the beat down tinlizzy and he directed him instead to the little beauty now before him. What would Lu say when he pulled into the drive? She'd be worried that some stranger was ready to heist the house, and then he'd bust out and take her and Charlie for a nice spin. Oh, they'd be impressed, and how. This was a piece of the new life he had earned, earned with his own muscle and willpower, and damn straight he was ready to start living it.

"Now, this is what we're gonna do," Lister told him. "You leave your new wheels out in the lot and we're gonna get to your first assignment. You been where, disassembly, the stamping plant, so we're gonna find you a new place to camp out. Let's see, we got some need for eyes in Building B, the glass house…"

"How about the glass house," chimed Haik, knowing that Orlin worked there.

"Yeah? The glass shop? Kinda boring over there, but, what the hay, why not, we'll start you over there. Now, your job is simple: you watch those sons-a-bitches like your life depends on it, because you know what, make no mistake, it sure as shit does. Things get balled up there, then your life gets balled up and maybe that nice new car of yours comes back to the garage without a driver. These line bastards are paid to work, and they better. No smoking and joking, no grab ass, just work. And nothing leaves the house. Not a hammer, not a nail, not a piece of toilet paper, not a goddamned thing. These guys get light fingers—you find somebody with light fingers, you take a ball pene hammer and you smash the living fuck outta those fingers and make so them fingers can't grab nothing don't belong to 'em ever again, you see? And you keep an ear out, too. You hear even a peep about unions, you lickety-spit it back to me with some names and we'll take it from there. What else, what else? Yeah, there's other little jobs you can do, too," counseled Lister with a wink and Haik took it all in, a bit uncomprehending but getting the general gist of his teacher's message.

Lister said that Haik could collect a little "service tax" if he wanted, maybe a dollar a week from each man in his section, a sort of insurance policy you could call it. If anyone refused to pay, well, just remember the little can of heat he had gotten at Bennett's office. If the mood struck, you could play a little numbers with the boys, take that dollar a week, throw it into a kitty, pick a winner on Friday, and he gets half the take and you pocket half for organizing the whole she-bang. Haik liked the sound of that second one—it sounded more fair, less greedy. And there would be other jobs, special assignments Lister called them, that took place off the Rouge grounds. It could be anything, standing guard at a party or a pow-wow of the honchos, driving some politicians here or there, delivering some hooch or some Dumb Doras to Mr. Bennett's pals, and, Lister's personal favorite, crashing parties, all kinds of parties, commie meetings, union gatherings, you name it.

They drove over to glass and Haik was amazed anew by what he saw. One whole outside wall seemed to be made just of glass, and when they entered he stood beneath a ceiling filled with giant windows through which fresh daylight poured. How could a building be made of glass and not fall down or break? Only a magician like Henry Ford could create such an illusion. Lister walked Haik around the floor, showing him the areas where the men ate, the bathrooms, the basic set-up of the operation. They also visited some pods of workers, with Lister introducing him as the new eyeball for the Service Department reporting directly to Mr. Harry Bennett. The men said nothing, most giving Haik a wary, unwelcoming look before heading back to their stations. Haik looked intently for Orlin, wishing to surprise him with a playful sock to the gut and warm embrace, but Lister offered a caution.

"The main thing, Pelini, is these fucks ain't your friends. You got one friend in the world right now, Mr. Harry Bennett, and that's all you ever gonna need. These clowns, they come and go, but long as there's a Ford Motor Company, Mr. Bennett's your first, last, and only friend. You wanna be friends with one of these saps, well, it interferes with business. You may have to drop a nickel on him, maybe even take him out for a ride one night, but because he's your friend, you can't do it or you stop to think about things. And you ain't being paid to think about nothing. That don't go. That will just not go, my friend."

Haik pondered Lister's words. He had no friends, no one, only Mr. Bennett. As he considered this thought, they turned a corner around a massive glass furnace and there he saw Orlin, stoking the furnace, sweat pouring from his dark skin. As Lister began talking again, Haik and Orlin made eye contact, and Haik could see a smile begin to form on Orlin's face and his mouth ready itself to shout out a greeting. Before Orlin could speak, Haik swiftly put his index finger to his lips and then quickly sliced it across his throat in the universal sign language gesture to immediately stop. Orlin caught the message, and Haik could detect a kind of hurt in his eyes, but he had to keep following Lister. In a last attempt to communicate, Haik gave a wink with his unswollen eye and flashed a quick thumbs up and rounded another corner.

They returned to Lister's car and the next stop was a woody area in Ecorse near the river. Here, Lister showed Haik how to fire his pistol, field dress it, and keep it in general running order. Haik aimed at trees and felt the powerful surge from his hand up through his forearm into his shoulder each time he fired. His arms had been muscled by all the time disassembling and lifting and twisting and pulling and shoving and, to his surprise, the gun felt more like a toy in his hand than a tool for human death. But the sound, the chesty crack, took him back to the Grand Trunk Rail yard. Each round, he returned, frozen in time until he pulled the trigger again. Between shots, he was holding Vahram in his arms, feeling his brother's blood soak into the arms of his coat. With each squeeze of the trigger, he knew he never wanted to use the gun in real life.

"Not bad for your first time, but you got a long way to go before I'd want you at my back crashin' a party. You got a close quarters weapon, Pelini. Me, look at this beaut, a Walther PKK with nickel finish, just minted in '31. I'll blow your ass to kingdom come from halfway down a city block," Lister smiled, proudly displaying his glinting weapon and baring his corroded teeth. "The thing is, you only flash this when you got to. We got plenty of other tools of this trade, so this is strictly end of the line. Look at some of these birds I used to run with. Shapiro, Nigger Joe, Ziggy Selbin, geez, all of 'em, all dead now. Hijackin' smuggled hooch, runnin' with the Purple Gang, tryin' to impress every hoofer and Jane out there with their big mouths. Real big cheeses with little brains and now where are they, gettin' blow jobs from worms. Me? Two years in the clink and I got smart, Pelini. Caught on with Mr. Bennett and now it's the bee's knees. I'll never see a cell again no matter what I do. Cops'll never touch Mr. Bennett and they sure as hell will never touch Mr. Henry Ford. You got it lucky now, Pelini, so you count your blessings. Oh yeah, and, on a personal note, don't never fuck with me, never. I only say that once."

Haik returned Lister's gaze and did not look down. Maybe Lister had a better gun, but man to man Haik would break him in half. His time with the Purples had been a great teacher. Even though he was out of their circuit, he had survived their training with the scars to prove it. And he probably got out at the right time. Word still spread on their escapades, and the blood was flowing even more freely, even Purple blood. The Collingwood Massacre, bodies finding the pavement all over the city, even killing each other, compassionless Irving Shapiro and smirk-faced Ziggy Selbin and others gunned down and dead without having lived anywhere near a full life. Hell, Selbin was only 19 when he was filled with holes coming out his own front door over on 12th Street, and the back of Shapiro's head was literally blown off when he was "taken for a cruise" by his fellow Purples. Haik was not afraid of Cam Lister, but what exactly was he getting himself into? Hadn't he left the Bernsteins and torching buildings and boxcar busting to go straight and avoid following in Vahram's footsteps, leaving their father sonless? Wasn't he married now to a beautiful woman with a young son to raise? Lister was talking about using the gun and other tools of this new trade—wasn't that what Haik had decided to *avoid* on this new, life-protecting path shown to him by Mr. Meadows?

Lister smiled as he drove them back to Haik's new wheels and Haik looked at his cratered, bone white profile. He was helping Haik in giving him these facts about how to survive as a SD man, driving him here and there, showing him how to use a pistol, but he was no friend and Haik would never mistake him for one.

They drove together to the worker lot and Haik took the Fliv back to the reclamations garage to change it out for the Whippet. The day had flown by, and he was glad to finally be out of Lister's grip. He waved good-bye out of courtesy and then he got behind the wheel of his new ride, smiling and drumming the steering wheel. He gunned over to his lot and parked, and then began to search out Griff Slater, finding him at the gate and telling him to hold tight, he'd be right back.

First on Haik's agenda was finding Orlin to talk, to explain everything, to make sure there was no misunderstanding. He ran to the next gate over where Orlin usually parked, hoping he hadn't already gone to his car. Haik paced and rubbed his hands together, patting himself every now and then under his right breast where his new pistol was holstered. He was about to head back to get Griff when he saw Orlin approaching.

"Orlin!" he shouted but received a wary look in return.

"You know me?" questioned Orlin.

"C'mon, man, you know I know you. That's why I'm here. I got to explain what's happening."

"You can start by explaining what the Sam hell happened to your face," Orlin said, wincing as he took in his friend's pummeled visage.

"Oh yeah, well, that's part of it. Had a little tussle yesterday. Long to short, I get pinched by some SD goons and next thing I know I'm in the damn Service Department."

"SD man, huh? Shit, you be careful with that load. Maybe we need to do us some practice fighting like back when we was kids, get you in rumble shape."

Haik thought back to their childhood and "practice fighting." When was the last time he thought of those treasured times, the hours spent reenacting big prize fights they had heard about or listened to live on the radio, Jack Johnson against Jim Jeffries (with, of course, Orlin getting to be Johnson), Jimmy Wilde versus Jack Sharkey, Ad Wolgast the Michigan Wildcat against Battling Nelson, Bob Fitzsimmons and Benny Leonard and Sam Langford and Stanley Ketchell and Joe Gans and others. Those were good times, open-handed brawling out on the streets or in the grassy parks, just having fun, no one getting hurt but feeling like they were the center of the squared circle in fights to determine the best man in the world, sparring and slapping away and wrestling about. Sometimes they'd get out of hand, landing a blow with a closed fist, but it was all in good physical fun and it readied them for life with the Purples and busting boxcars in the yards.

"I know, I know, it's not like I had a choice. I might just need some sparring if I'm gonna survive. Hey, let's meet down at Dolgovich's in Hamtramck. I just got to drop a pal off and I'll see you there."

Orlin nodded, and Haik was off to pick up Griff, a definite lift in his step. Old Slater would drop in his drawers when Haik introduced him to the new wheels. Again, he found Griff waiting contentedly at the fence.

"C'mon, old boy, I got a surprise for you. Step this way, Mr. Rockefeller," Haik laughed, and Griff, blank-faced, followed him up to the Whippet.

"Get in, my good man, we're puttin' on the Ritz from here on out," Haik declared, opening the passenger door.

"Jeezum Crow," Griff whispered. "What you doin'? This ain't your ride."

"Oh, my good chap, it certainly is," Haik teased. "Now you get your ass in or you don't got no way home."

Griff did as instructed, a dumb grin filling his face, the wandering eye traversing every square inch of Haik's new automobile. Haik told the triumphant tale of meeting Mr. Henry Ford himself and of his new job, which he could only describe as a "policeman" without it sounding like something to be ashamed of.

He drove proudly, a new man, a man of importance, dropping Griff off and making his way back to Hamtramck to Dolgovich's, a friendly black and tan where everyone, black or white, gentile or Jew, Hungy or Slav or Pole could find a seat and order a drink. Above was a small market, but below, behind a storage area, was a nice sized basement speakeasy. All you had to do was knock and say *Is the sheik of Araby home* and you were in. Haik found Orlin at a back table, picking up two bottles of Stroh's beer before joining him.

"Well, look who's here, Mr. Al Capone. Except you ain't 'scarface,' more like 'smashface'," jibed Orlin.

"Real funny, you're a regular Buster Keaton, except you been near that blast furnace too long. Kind of well done in the brain, brother," returned Haik.

They clinked their bottles and savored a good long tip.

"So, who uglied you up and what you doin' struttin' round the glass house today, high-hatting me like you don't know me?" leveled Orlin.

"Long story," Haik began. "And I'm sorry, man, I didn't mean to be no pill. I'm not even sure how everything's happened these last 24 hours. Yesterday, this bimbo come into the stamping plant, where I just got moved, and I swear, he's at least two hundred fifty pounds, six foot and then some, and he starts to put the pinch on everybody. You should have seen that little asshole Higgins, walking around like he's Jack Dempsey with this oversize palooka standing behind him. I don't remember exactly what happen, but next thing I know, this pug ends up clobbering me, and I mean hard, and we end up on the floor. Well, thank the good Lord above I get ahold of his one arm, because I snapped it good, the old Ararat armlock. If I didn't, you'd be at my funeral right now instead of drinking my goddamn beer, you cheap bastard."

They both laughed, but Orlin pressed on.

"So keep going. How exactly you get to be walkin' round like J. Edgar Hoover?"

"You won't believe what I been through, Orlin. I been in Harry Bennett's office, I seen Henry Ford himself today, I...."

"Hey, friend, how many beers you have before you walk in here? You expect me to believe all that shit?"

"Believe this," Haik offered, and pulled back his jacket to reveal the revolver holstered beneath.

Orlin did a double take. They finished their beer in silence, and Haik took him out to have a gander at his new ride.

"Pretty damn nifty. Yes, indeed," Orlin marveled.

"So, you coming over Sunday for dinner?" Haik asked.

It had been tradition since they had met up at the Rouge to gather on Sundays for large dinners at Haik's parents. Everyone was invited, and often the Meadows brought their clan over, bringing along food and beer and no one, no matter how tight everything was, how poor everyone was, left a Sunday dinner at the Pehlivanian's feeling hungry.

"Oh yeah, I plan on being there. And...there's something I want to talk to you about."

Orlin looked down. He was a large man, a good head taller than Haik, but at times you might mistake him for a poet.

"Go ahead."

"Well, it's kinda personal," Orlin offered, treading lightly. Haik had never seen him so serious.

"C'mon, you can talk about anything with me, you know that. You need some money?"

"No, no, no, nothing like that. Something...something else."

Orlin looked off at some cars in the lot, straining to find his words.

"Shit, man, speak up," encouraged Haik, puzzled at what his friend was getting at. They had been through too much together—there were no walls between them.

"Haik, lemme just come out with it. Your sister. I love your sister, Arkina. I want, I... I wanna marry her."

They stood next to the Whippet for a split second of silence, both looking into each other's eyes, wordlessly digesting what had just been said. Orlin had always gotten along with his entire family—Vahram when he was leading their gang, and both his sisters, Arkina and Ovsanna, and his parents. Yes, he had been best man with Kina at the wedding, and they ate and drank and danced together. In the backyard on Sundays, Orlin pushed Kina on the tire swing that hung from the backyard oak tree, and he was always making sure she had dessert and a full glass of water or milk. She was a woman now, Haik realized, although to him she was always just his little sister, a child to be protected and provided for. How had he not seen it?

"You wanna middle aisle my *sister*?" asked Haik, astonished. "God damn, Orlin. You already ask her?"

"In the books. She feel the same way I do, man. Fact, it was her idea."

Orlin looked for a read of Haik's face. They had been friends for many years, but this was different, this was a big step, and there were a lot of issues involved, not the least of which was skin color. Black and white did not marry. Hell, Armenian and non-Armenian was bad enough, as he had experienced with Lu. But Haik was at least kind of white or close to it. Orlin, though, almost glowed blue in mid-summer. No way would anyone accept him marrying Arkina. Whites would hate her, even to the point of attacking Orlin if they were ever seen together in the wrong neighborhood. Haik loved Orlin like a brother, but what Haik thought didn't matter if the rest of the world was filled with hate. No, this was not a good idea.

Haik looked Orlin straight in the eye.

"Well then, you black-ass son-of-a-bitch, let's head back inside and get us another beer."

Easy money carries a price. Even somebody with barely any schooling knew this, and Haik Pehlivanian certainly knew this, just as well as Vahram knew radios, but he felt trapped. He told himself he was *trapped*, and the more he listened to that voice the more he believed it and the more firmly he obeyed its command to take the easy SD money flowing his way.

He obeyed as he went to work each day in his new car, obeyed as he collected up the lottery money from the glass house workers each week, obeyed when he made a big deal out of the drawing and saw the smiles and tense anticipation on the faces of the men and let one of them pick the name out of his hat to show how honest the numbers game was. He obeyed when he made runs of booze out to the Green Lantern Club in Ecorse, popped the fake trunk bottom out of his car to reveal shiny bottles of Old Log Cabin whiskey, and delivered the goods to tuxedoed, soft-skinned men and their gold-digging dames awaiting inside. They'd slip him a bottle and a 5, 10, even a 20 dollar tip, and he'd gratefully pocket it and bring the actual cash payment back to the Service Department on Schaefer Road, every dollar accounted for. He walked the rows at the glass house and smiled at the workers while at the same time looking for any signs of theft or laziness. But he was still one of them at heart, he told himself, and he shared the lottery money and never took more than his share. He did not rule by threat or violence, and to him this justified, even made him feel deserving of, his easy money as a SD man.

When he first rolled into the drive in the new Whippet, Lu was at the door and peeked her head out cautiously. That morning before Haik drove off to the Rouge, Lu whispered *be careful* and kissed his bruised face, trepidation in her eyes. He understood. She had already lost one husband and now here he was, bruised and puffed-faced like a washed up prize fighter. Later in the day, a strange car was in her driveway, and she looked warily for some explanation. Then Haik emerged, beaming as wide as his swollen face would allow, and yelled for her to get Charlie and come on down for a spin. Lu and Charlie appeared on the porch, a quizzical half smile on Lu's face and utter joy on the boy's.

"Don't be late, trolley's leaving," shouted Haik, and Charlie broke free of Lu's grasp and climbed into the new auto.

Lu walked more slowly, still trying to fathom what she was seeing before her.

"What…what is this?" she asked, gesturing at the Whippet.

"This? Baby, this set a wheels is now officially *ours*," Haik boasted, and then looked anxiously at Lu. "So what you think?"

"What do I think? I…," she stammered, obviously shocked to see such a vehicle in her young husband's possession.

"You don't gotta think nothing. All you got to do is get in this beaut and go for a ride with me. C'mon, Charlie's waiting."

"But, dinner…"

"To hell with dinner, I'm buying dinner for anybody who gets in this here car with me."

Lu climbed slowly into the passenger side and they were off. Haik waved to neighbors who eyed the car from their porches and put a little extra weight on the gas pedal. He was somebody in this set of wheels. Charlie laughed and Haik pulled him up into the front seat and had him take the wheel while he sat on his dad's lap. Lu looked on, but

Haik would not be denied today. He took them down Hastings Street and parked on the main drag. They went to the Attaboy Club, located above a delicatessen. Its walls were festooned with colorful paintings of spiffy flappers hoofing it up. Lu voiced if this was an appropriate place for a young boy and Haik told her to relax, not to be a bluenose, they were here to celebrate.

  He ordered steaks for each of them, beer for the grown-ups and a Vernor's cooler for the boy. They ate and Haik regaled Charlie with a blow-by-blow description of his meeting with Henry Ford, king of the entire Ford Motor Company. He explained some, *some*, of what Bennett and Lister told him. Some, well, was just better off not said. In fact, before he left Orlin in the parking lot at Dolgovich's, he looked around before unstrapping his holster and new pistol and placed them in the trunk so he wouldn't be armed when he got home. Lu would worry if she knew everything and there were things that were just not necessary for her to know. Why ruin a perfect evening over silly details like a gun he would never use?

  Haik's life was good, the bee's knees, patrolling the glass house and a job here and there, until the night he made a run to the Deutsches Haus at Mack Avenue and Maxwell. After he made the delivery of hooch, he was given a black leather bag, like a doctor's bag. He took the bag to the drop off and handed it to Mr. Bennett's second, Cutty, who looked inside the leather satchel, smiled, thanked Haik, and called him a good boy before releasing him.

  As he walked to his car, tired, eager to drive home, a Ford 3-Window Coupe and a '31 Model A Roadster dashed up and several men jumped out. Before he could even think to draw, they were on him, beating him to the ground, striking him with clubs or axe handles from so many angles he could only cover his head and bring his knees up to protect his man parts. Someone stripped him of his gun, then his arms and legs were bound, followed by a burlap bag slipped over his head and tied off. He was held down by at least two men sitting down on him, and he lay on the frozen, snowy ground, blind and immobile. Before he knew it, his body was lifted and then flung into the trunk of one of the two cars. What was happening? His mind flared in all directions. Who were these men? He had no jack on him, so they could beat him all they wanted and it wouldn't pay off. He did everything he was supposed to, was on time for pick-up and delivery both, no stops, no monkey business, everything accounted for. Hell, he didn't even get a tip this night, just straight business with no beefs from anyone.

He lay in the trunk, shaking as much from fear as the cold, and took the shock of bumps in the road as the car rolled into the unknown. At least the money was delivered—he had done his job. If he was in trouble, it was not with Mr. Bennett or the Service Department. Despite the icebox environment of the trunk, he sweated underneath the scratchy hood, struggling against the thick hemp rope lashed about his hands and arms and legs.

They drove maybe five minutes when he felt the car roll from pavement to backroad, gravel popping beneath the tires. At least fifteen minutes passed when they rolled into a wide turn and the vehicle slowed. When they stopped and the trunk was opened, someone untied his legs and several hands pulled him out and began shoving him, walking him to an unseen destination. He smelled the river through the thick burlap. The voices around him were hushed and quick, but he could soon detect an echo as he was brought inside some kind of garage or large shack, where he was pushed down into a chair and his ankles tied to the chair's legs. The sack was untied and removed from his head, and his eyes were met squarely by the blinding beams of an automobile's headlights.

"What'd'jou do wit it?"

A low, apelike voice emanated from somewhere off to his left. He knew the accent—Polack, a goon from Hamtramck. Above the beams, he could see cigarette smoke, the breath of his kidnappers, and the vapors from the car's grill drifting off into the upper beams of the building and he could make out a hayloft above.

"With what?" Haik countered, only to receive a slap across the face.

"Don't play stupid. Somebody awreddy squeeled on you, piker. Said you was gonna line your own pocket wit some of tonight's dough."

Haik's mind raced. What was there to tell? He didn't have any money except his own traveling money and the little emergency stash he kept hidden in the Whippet. He'd never skim a dime from a drop, never, so whoever was asking the questions was not someone who knew him. Who squawked on him? He didn't tell anybody anything about what he was doing or where he was going tonight. That morning, Lister had given him his route for the evening, he spent some time at the glass house, he did his job at the Deutsches Haus, and that was it, end of story, nothing to report. How did these people know he was on a run and handling cash?

He squinted in the burning headlights but surveyed as much of his surroundings as he could, trying to not make it obvious he was looking. From the smell of hay and animal shit, he figured they were in a barn or some type of farm garage. Beyond that, his mind balled up, uncertain why he was even here or who these pugs were or what their intentions might be. Whoever they were, he was completely at their mercy.

"Check his hands," came another voice, and a man with a bandana across his face crossed into the headlights and grabbed Haik's hands, turning them up and inspecting them before disappearing back into the shadows.

"Clean. No black."

"You sure?" another voice chimed in.

"Yeah. If he had his hants on the grub inna bag da polish woulda tagged 'im good. He ain't put his hant in nat bag. Lucky fer'im. He's clean."

Haik squinted in the lightning beams of the headlights. What the hell was this about? He never so much as looked in any bag he collected let alone put a finger in. Counting money was for other people, the secretaries, Mr. Bennett, Cutty or sometimes a partner assigned by Mr. Bennett who went with him on his run and did the counting in Haik's car, whoever, other people's money didn't interest him and he never opened anything. Sure, he might get curious, that was human nature, but he received his pay and then some and he made a point of not knowing too much, especially how much money he was hauling. All his deliveries, solo and chaperoned, had gone without a hitch. Nobody had anything on him.

"Pat him down. Mick says his ride was empty, but he could have put the dough in a pocket. Skin him."

Two men emerged from the shadows and frisked him, emptying out his pockets, removing his billfold, taking off his shoes and shaking them out. He could see one of the shadows take his money from his fold and throw the empty leather on the ground.

"This guy's worse than a nigger," laughed the man who had rifled the wallet. "Two stinkin' dollars. He ain't got nothing."

"So, who pocket the clams?" came the first interrogator.

Haik breathed deeply. There wasn't anything to say or explain, but he'd have to answer.

"Didn't nobody pocket nothing."

A hand shot from the darkness and caught him square on the jaw and he tumbled over, chair and all, unable to break his fall.

"Bullshit. I tink I know who it was. I tink it was Lister. Cam Lister. He's a filty bucket a scum, nat one. It was Lister, wu'nit?"

"Lister? I don't know nobody name Lister," Haik spat, and a foot caught him in the gut as he lay on the ground, puncturing the air from his lungs. Someone lifted him back upright into the chair. He finally heaved in a breath of air, the muscles in his stomach burning as if with hunger.

"Ba-loney. Just tell us da troot. Just tell us it was Lister," came the bodiless Polack voice.

And then, there it was. Icy steel jutted into the back of Haik's neck, a barrel jabbing him right where the skull connected to the top of the spine. And then the unmistakable *click* of a pistol hammer being cocked into position.

"Last chance to dance, wop. Lister got da money, right?"

Haik's mind fumbled. Tell them what they want to hear. Shut up. Tell them. Just say it, Y*eah, it was Lister.* Shut up. Just keep your mouth shut. You don't know anything, so just stick with that. Lu. Charlie. Tell them what they want to hear. Vahram. Orlin and Arkina. Shut up. Tell them. Shut up. Dammit, just tell them.

"I don't know no Lister."

His life stopped. The beams of the headlights froze in midair. Finally, he heard the hammer eased back into resting position. The bag was quickly placed back over his head and the world went dark again. He legs were untied from the chair and he was stood up and jostled back out of the barn, lifted, and thrown into the frozen trunk of the car.

The drive in the trunk rattled and banged him about, but this time his legs were free and he had a little more control over his body. The sound of gravel was soon replaced by pavement. In what felt like seconds, the car slowed down to a halt and cool air hit him when the trunk popped open. Hands came from all angles and grabbed, lifting him, then heaved him to the snowy earth. He heard a heavy thunk on the grass behind him as the engines idled. Then, peculiarly, he felt a presence draw near to him as he lay spent on the ground. He heard breathing and then smelled a decayed, rotten odor, followed by a hand patting him lightly on his cheek through the burlap. Within seconds, the sound of car doors slamming was followed by engines revving, gears shifting, and then tires peeling away into the night.

Haik lay there. He was exhausted, more exhausted than the day he tangled with Gus Schmidthacker. This was a different kind of depletion, though, a kind that was not so much in his body but his mind and his thoughts and his whole being. Was it real? Had he really been picked up? The stinging in his jaw and the searing pain in his ribs confirmed everything. But why? For what? What had he done? What was this about stolen money and shoe polish and somebody squealing on him? Was this going to get to Bennett? Cutty would have to back him up—he took the money right from Haik's hands, looked in the bag, and told him good job. He could verify Haik had taken nothing, not one thing, not a damn penny. That is, if Cutty was on the level and not in on the barn party.

He struggled with the ropes on his hands and twisted his body and legs against their power. He must have wiggled and flexed and kicked for at least an hour. Half his body would freeze against the winter earth and he'd rotate over and fight his binds, panting so hard that rough fibers from the burlap bag fell off into his mouth and scratched and stuck to his sweating forehead. Once he had twisted a wrist free, he went to work and ripped the bag from his head. The air was cold and sweet. He groped along the earth behind him and found his gun, which had been thrown on the ground and was now empty but undamaged, firing pin untouched. Why would his kidnappers leave his weapon? Nothing about this night made any sense.

He collected himself, brushed off his soiled clothes, and headed stiffly back to his car. How would he explain this one to Lu? She had not forgotten the beating that landed him this job, and here he was again, banged up and beaten down. What would happen in the morning? Would Lister be waiting for him at the gate, ready to take him for a little visit to Mr. Bennett? Would *Bennett* think he pocketed any of the money? Fear coiled through him, quickened his breathing, motivating him to reload his gun once he was safe inside his car, turn the engine over and hear his wheels rolling.

He wasn't ready to go home, to explain everything, to answer questions he himself had no answers to. He would drive. Van Dyke past Forest Lawn Cemetery, to McNichols, hard left, up to Mound, over some railroad tracks, past more factories and foundries and plants and tool and die shops and breweries supposedly only brewing "near beer" everyone ridiculed, then out, out, the hell out of the city. He had no idea where he was going. His mind needed to retrace everything that had happened to him. Picking up the hooch, packing it under the false floor in his trunk, walking up to the Deutsches Haus, the giant white stone illuminating the quickly darkening sky, the beautiful massive pillars rising into the night, talking briefly with his contacts and helping carry the stock inside, grabbing the bag, walking back to his car and meeting Cutty at the park. Where was the glitch? Who knew where he'd be making the hand off?

He drove into the dark. He knew this terrain. Unpaved road, pocked with ruts and trees and shadows and more trees. What was drawing him deeper into the wilderness? Light was now beginning to appear faintly in the distance—what was it, three or four in the morning now? The further he drove, he began to recognize his surroundings, a clearing here, farmland there, an occasional house. He slowed down. He knew where he was.

There, just over there, in the grasp of the headlights, next to the stand of birches, there, right there was where Vahram was buried.

He veered to the edge of the road and let the Whippet roll to a halt. He turned off the engine and sat for a moment, looking out into the snowy woods, the icy trunks of the birch trees taking on an almost holy glow. He opened his door and stepped out into the cool air, which felt clean on his face and in his lungs. His latest set of battle wounds were nothing, nothing at all in this tranquil spot. What would he tell Vahram now? Face to face, how would he explain the craziness of the world he had been taken from? He would try to explain what it was like to work an official job with paperwork, bosses, and a timeclock. He would tell his older brother that he began with pure intentions. He started out as a faithful worker on the line and then moved up to, well, however it was that you described his new position. A strong-arm. A goon. A paid fist. A shtarker. Whatever he now was, he was trying to be a good man. He would make it work out. He would never use his gun. He would never beat an innocent worker. He was a good husband to Lu. He would raise Charlie as his own and then he and Lu would give him brothers and sisters. He was caring for their parents, Meadows and Pehlivanians alike, and making sure their sisters married good men like Orlin and lived properly.

And all was good until...until what? He got beat up, broke someone's shoulder, was handed a gun and some money and a new car and...kidnapped. What was this mess? What would Vahram say?

Not lonk now.

Haik stood in the glowing forest. A slight winter breeze was threading through the branches. He had heard Vahram's voice. Somewhere, somewhere close by, close enough to touch, Vahram was there. Behind that tree? In the wind itself? He was here, but where? He always saw the gold lining, the opportunity to come, the chance to make life better with each chance he took. So what exactly was Vahram now telling him out here on this deserted road in the wilderness?

Haik looked about. Off into the stand of birches, Vahram's body rested, but somehow Vahram was free, not contained by the earth, here next to Haik and all around him. The rise in the earth was no more than twenty feet away, buy Haik would step no further. Not now. He wasn't ready. The wounds were still open, still bleeding, still painful. This was as close as he'd come since the day they buried him, but he still couldn't make those last few steps. Not yet. Not until he could tell Vahram something good about his life, something settled and permanent so he would not have to worry about his little brother. Vahram would understand. He was not only all about Haik in the trees and snow and wind, he was inside Haik, in his mind and his bones and blood.

Haik turned back to the car and the road and let the slight breeze touch his skin. He closed his eyes. Nothing. He opened them and they were now adjusted to the faint light floating about him. Off in the distance, on the other side of the road, he saw something, a road marker or a sign. To give his mind something new to fill its space, he walked toward it. His feet trod over the rutted, uneven dirt and he stood before a hand-painted sign. *Land for Sell or rent*. Underneath the scribbly writing was a crude arrow. Haik looked up and saw the dark silhouette of a house in the distance with a light on. He began walking.

The house was nice. Old, in need of some new siding here and there, a coat of paint, but nice. He climbed the porch, the old stairs whining, and took a moment before knocking on the front door. He could hear rustling in the house and saw a face peer out at him from one of the front windows. A long pause followed, and then Haik heard the locks of the front door being turned. The door cracked to reveal two chain locks still secured, behind which an old woman peered out. To say her faced was lined would not be accurate. Haik could not find one single part of her weathered skin that was not cracked, creased, or crowfooted.

"Yes?" she creaked softly, a fearful look in her eyes.

"Yes, ma'am, I was out driving, and I, I saw the sign you have out front," explained Haik, nodding back towards the road.

"Yes?" she repeated, no change in her voice.

"Well, I, uh, I'm interested in this land, your land, your house, whatever it is on your sign out there that you're selling."

The weathered face continued to size Haik up.

"Sign? Oh, the sign. I put that sign out," she said with no further explanation. Haik stood puzzled, unsure exactly how he was supposed to respond.

"Well, are you selling some land?"

"Yes, I'm selling land. What the sign says, doesn't it?"

"Well, yes, it does. Can I, can we, can we talk about the land?"

The woman continued to frame Haik with her watery, ancient eyes.

"You're not a member of the Purple Gang, are you?" she questioned directly, her mouth crinkling tightly into a hundred more creases.

"Me? The Purple Gang? Oh, no, no way, ma'am," Haik laughed. It was not a lie—his Purple days were behind him. "I, I work for Henry Ford at the Rouge Plant. I'm just a worker, ma'am, a Ford worker."

Haik wondered if he betrayed the least suspicion of lying. And his appearance—he had to look suspicious, cut and bruised and dirty. The woman continued to watch him, and then the door closed. He was about to turn away and trek defeated back to the car when he heard the chain locks being slid and the door creak open. The old woman, hunched and dwarfish, beckoned Haik in with a withered hand. Haik entered and followed her into the kitchen. The house felt like the country, the rooms a bit small but he could tell the frame was sturdy, and the floor was solid and in good repair, as were the tightly planked walls. The woman gestured for him to sit at the kitchen table.

"Kind of early," she said, a hint of wariness in her voice.

"Oh, I worked the late shift today and I couldn't sleep, so I decided to take a little drive to settle down," Haik lied.

"My name's Gertrude Branch. You looking to buy my land?"

"Well, Mrs. Branch, yes, I want to see if it's possible. I live in the city now at my parents' with my wife and our son, plus my two younger sisters, and it's, it's very crowded. I'd like my son and, and my future children, I want them to be in the country. You know, where it's clean and they can breathe."

"So you got you a little one. How old?"

"Charlie, he's eight now."

"And no brothers or sisters? My word."

"We're working on it. But I'd rather wait until we've got some room."

"Eight years is a long time to wait, son."

Haik didn't want to go into the whole story and explain that he was not really Charlie's father and that Charlie had been born before he even met Lu. It was nobody's business and off the point he was trying to get at with Gertrude Branch.

"So, you're selling this place?" Haik asked, changing the subject. "How much land do you have? And, if I might ask, ma'am, what are you asking?"

"Would you like some coffee, Mr...." Gertrude Branch asked, still probing him.

"My name is Haik, Mrs. Branch, and yes, I'd love some coffee."

She poured two cups and pointed to a sugar bowl and small cream pot on the table.

"Haik? What kinda name is that?"

"Oh, it's a Armenian name. I was born in Armenia."

"Never heard of no such place."

"Most people ain't. But the land. How much do you have?"

"I got me five acres here. We, my husband Leo and me, we had us thirty acres but we sold most of it off already, little bits at a time. Leo, he died last month. I got kids in Indiana and one in California. The one in California, he says if I sell this place off I can come live with him, help him watch over the grandkids and cook for him and his wife, keep the house clean. I think I'm ready. It's too much for me here now without Leo. I'm out here all by my lonesome and I don't drive. Neighbor takes me to the store down the road a piece once a week but then that's it, I'm alone here, me and two dogs and some cats out in the barn. Got me a three hole outhouse out back, the barn with a old truck in it, running water here in the kitchen, nice big stove heats up the whole house in the winter, a deep well and a strong pump, big fireplace in the parlor made out of rocks and stones from the creek out back. I don't bargain with nobody. I want $2,000 for the whole thing, not one dime less. You pay me $240 down payment and you can pay me off $40 dollars a month till you done paid the full amount. Take you 'bout three years and then some. I don't want me no interest, just that $40 every month. You don't make a payment, I get the land back. If I die, you pay my son in California what's left under the same terms. No negotiating. Those are my terms."

Haik looked about. He did some math in his head: he brought home $25 a week, $100 a month straight pay, plus what he, ah, acquired other ways, sometimes $50 a month, sometimes as much as an extra $110 in his best month. He was stashing away more inside Vahram's mattress, at least $350 just sitting there—even if he had a bad month or two, he could weather it and then some and still keep up with the payments. He could buy groceries, wait, he'd have to spend more for gas, one clam could get him 12 gallons, he'd drive, what, 35 miles give or take one way, he could do that, just leave earlier, no more Griff Slater to share the rides with, sure, so he'd be driving every day now, not alternating. And he'd keep helping his parents and the Meadows.

His head swam in dollars and addition signs and big numbers and small numbers and more big numbers. He could see Lu cooking cabbage from a garden she tended right outside the door and roasting some quail he shot out in the woods behind the house. He saw Charlie racing through the house and upstairs to his own room, or walking with Haik out in the woods, hunting deer or fishing down at the creek, quietly sharing time together in a place so unlike the city he grew up in. He could see Lu with babies in her arms out in the parlor and Orlin and Arkina and Ovsanna on couches laughing and talking and drinking tea and eating baklava and cakes Lu baked. He could see all of this, very clearly, and the phantom images in his head brought a slight smile to his face.

"Mrs. Branch, just make me this deal. Please, don't sell this land to no one until I come back later today. If everything checks out, I'll have the down payment right here with me, straight cash. Just please make me that promise."

The old woman sipped her coffee and looked around at her home. She had spent the last 52 years here, raised children, tended a husband, cooked meals, watched grandkids, loved her dogs and cats. She was in no hurry.

"Well, if you got the money, I'll need at least a week to get my belongings situated and make the arrangements with my son and...."

"Mrs. Branch, take two weeks, take as much time as you need. I'm not in no rush. Like I said, if all the figures work out, I'll be back and we can talk about all that tonight. All I ask is you hold onto my offer until I come back. If I don't show up tonight by, say, 7 o'clock and you get another bid, you sell your place, no hard feelings, and take the first train to California. My blessings would be on you, Mrs. Branch. Deal?"

Mrs. Branch looked around, her worn eyes caught in visions of a past in this house that now only she was the the sole keeper of. Haik let her look, drinking his coffee, which he was grateful was so strong because he had not slept and he would not be able to sleep until some time later that night.

"Deal," Mrs. Branch whispered, her eyes watering, looking off into the parlor and beyond.

An idea came to Haik as he rumbled back to the city after his meeting with Mrs. Gertrude Branch. He had a few dollars in the stash he kept tucked under his carseat, pinched in one of the coils, and, luckily, the goons who had jumped him the night before didn't find them. Once back in Detroit, he stopped off in Greektown and bought several slices of baklava, eating one with a cup of coffee, his breakfast, and having the rest of the sticky treats wrapped in wax paper and placed in a small white box. He had to report for work already—he didn't have any time to go home, and he certainly didn't have any time to explain to Lu what had happened to him in the last twelve hours and why he had failed to show up home at night for the first time in his marriage.

If everything fell right, he'd have more than an explanation for Lu—he'd have the best present he had ever imagined giving anyone in his life.

Hygiene was a personal forte. He always brushed his teeth, threw on some aftershave even when money was tight (he'd go without breakfast for a week just to have some aftershave around) and no matter how poor he ever was he was never dirty, but he had neither the opportunity nor the temperament right now to be overly concerned with all that. He looked at himself in the mirror: a mouse under one eye, dried blood caked in his nostrils. He gingerly washed up his face and hands in the bakery bathroom, gargled with some soapy water and rinsed several times, and headed in to the Rouge, still formulating his plan.

His number one concern was Harry Bennett. If Mr. Bennett thought Haik pocketed some of his cash, he was done, finished, end of the line. No explaining, no pleading, no running, no second chances, no escape. Haik accepted this. If his number was up, he'd make sure it was cashed directly and bring nobody else into the mix and keep it as far away from his family as possible. He took his pistol from his holster, placed it in his coat pocket for the quickest possible access, and headed straight to the Service Department. Once there, he breathed deeply, grabbed his white box of baklava, and headed to the front door. He would get his answers directly from the source.

"Good morning, ladies, is, ah, Mr. Bennett in yet?"

One older secretary looked up and smiled in recognition.

"Downstairs, Mr. Pelini," she answered. "Were you out playing football this morning?"

"Football?"

She looked him up and down, and he looked down at his clothes: grass stains, a few strands of straw adorning his pants and jacket.

"Oh, sorry, this, this, well, I had some early morning duty out in Ecorse. On a farm."

She smiled at him, and he smiled back and strode quickly to the stairwell, where he placed his box of baklava between his legs and gave himself a good brushing off.

After skipping quickly down the steps, he took another deep breath, slipped his right hand in his pocket and felt his gun, close range its specialty, tucked his box of baklava under his right arm, and knocked with his left.

"Yeah," came a voice from within.

"Pelini here," he piped up.

He could hear movement and mumbling within.

"Whattaya want?"

"I have something for Mr. Bennett."

"Okay, c'mon in," a voice commanded.

As usual, Harry Bennett was impeccably dressed and several of his usual boys, Mickey Gellinger, Otto Franks, Zabriskie, and one other guy he didn't know, were inside. They eyed Haik, but he could detect no immediate sense of danger from them.

"Whattaya need, Pelini, we're gettin' a wiggle on here in about two seconds," said Bennett impatiently.

He did not make eye contact, but instead examined some papers on his desk.

"Ah, here, Mr. Bennett. My wife thought you might like some of these. In appreciation for the job and all," Haik said, stepping forward and setting the box on Bennett's desk.

He raised his eyebrows, shot a glance at Haik, and opened the box.

"Well, ain't that sweet. What a dame. What we got here? Hmm, some kind of pastry shit. Boys, help yourselves. Now, Pelini, you're gonna have to beat it because I've got a meeting to attend," announced Bennett, and the look he gave Haik meant leave, now, right now.

However, as he grabbed his hat and reached for his coat, he stopped in midstream.

"Wait, just one second, Pelini, now that I think of it, I do need a word with you," smiled Bennett, still not looking up.

Haik placed his right hand back into his jacket pocket, finding his revolver handle.

"Yes, Mr. Bennett?"

"Pelini, in about a week or so, I think I got the perfect job for you. We got some painter comin' in here, some guy who's, I don't know, gonna do some painting for the Fords. He's gonna need someone to show him around, drive him places, give him the lay of the land. I can't give this job to just any stiff. You seem to get along with folks, know how to talk polite, be a gentleman, all that jazz. So I think you're gonna be my man on this one. When the time gets near, I'll have Lister send you over, so be on the lookout. And by the way, what the hell happened to your face again?"

Haik self-consciously touched his cheek.

"On second thought, I don't wanna know. But when that new job comes around, you can't be looking like goddamn Harry Greb. And here, here's $20, get yourself some new threads, for Christ's sake, those make you look like you been milking cows. Now scram."

Haik loosened the grip on the pistol, accepted the money, let out a breath, and nodded in acknowledgement to Bennett. He did a quick about face and exited the office, hopped up the stairs and out the building to his car. He was free.

Once inside the safe confines of the Whippet, he exhaled fully and placed his gun back in the shoulder holster. If Bennett thought he had double crossed him or pocketed some money, he would have been well aware of it by now and Haik would have never left his office in one piece.

So what exactly was the deal? Cutty had not ratted him out to Bennett, and yet there Haik was last night, laying on the stinking ground in some garage or barn, blinded by a set of headlights, punched and kicked and scared shitless with the barrel of a gun to his head. Fatigue was starting to hit him, but he was surging with questions about who had taken him for the ride and what they were really trying to get from him. All he could do for the time being was head to the worker lot and get ready to report to the glass house.

After parking, he made his way to the gate with some other workers. Surprisingly, he saw Lister pacing inside, smoking a cigarette. By now, if Lister wanted to see him, he just stopped by the glass house to check in or to give him fresh assignments. Meeting him right at the gate, something had to be fairly urgent.

"Hey, hey, there you are. How goes it?" Lister intoned, a bit too friendly.

"Oh, I been better, but I been worse too."

Haik eyed Lister, trying to decipher his motive.

"Says you. Geez Louise, Pelini, what the hell happen to you? You look like you just took a walk in a shitstorm."

Haik looked down at his attire. His pant legs were stained with dirt from the barn, and his shoes were smudged and muddy. He no doubt was sporting a heavy shadow on his face, the gift of being an Armenian of shaving age. There had to be a shiner on the side of his face. Yes, no question, he probably was a sight.

"Heh-heh, old lady kick you out, old boy? Jesus Jenny, and looks like somebody put the boots to you again. Look at your jaw."

Haik felt again the blow that had knocked him to the barn floor and the kick that had done a number to his ribs. His fatigue had helped him forget, but now the pain was front row and center.

"Long story. A long night."

"Everything okay? The delivery didn't get balled up, did it?"

What did Lister care about the delivery? It wasn't his gig or his money. And if something went wrong with the drop, Cutty would have already been on the horn to both Bennett and Lister. Lister was playing dumb and doing a very bad job of it.

"No, the delivery was jake. Cutty got the loot. Just somebody invited me to a party I really didn't want to go to when the deal was done. No big deal."

Lister smiled and his corroded teeth shown in all their festering glory. He put a hand up to Haik's chin and leaned in, as if to examine his wound, and whistled in admiration. As he exhaled, a stale odor of rot struck Haik right between the eyes. The stench was unmistakeable. Cam Lister was in the barn last night and had given him the pat to his cheek as he lay bound in the snow.

"I tell you what, Pelini, you been working real hard lately. Some of the SD boys, nobody's home between the ears. One way or another, they fuck up. They get carried away with the physical part of the job, hurt somebody beyond the point of hurtin' 'em, or the money, well, the money causes them to make some bad decisions. You, I'm convinced more than ever now that you're a loyal SD man, somebody who'd go to the wall for me. You say you had a rough one, hey, no questions asked, anybody asks me, I'll say Hank Pelini was home in bed last night checking his wife's oil, God as my witness. Right now, though, you earned yourself a little down time. Mr. Bennett has given me the authority to reward men, and right now I'm giving you the rest of the day off. Enjoy, pal. Go home, get cleaned up, and get some rest. Don't do nothing I wouldn't do."

Lister extended his hand, and Haik reluctantly took it. They shook and Haik watched Lister head off toward his wheels. He felt for the handle of his pistol. In the movie in his mind, he pulled it out, aimed directly into Cam Lister's back, snapped off several quick rounds, and Lister lurched forward and tumbled to the ground. It felt good, like justice, like he had rid his world of a disease. But he couldn't use his heat here, of all places, not here, on Ford property against a fellow SD man, one with seniority.

He turned, suddenly very tired and wanting to be at home with Lu and Charlie. Cam Lister was a bastard. He had always known that, but now this bastard's ways were leaving cuts and bruises on his body. And for what? What the hell did Lister have to gain by putting the boots to Haik and putting on a kidnapping? What was the damn point? So Lister now thought Haik was a "loyal" SD man. But that was the thing, all Haik had proven the night before was his loyalty to Cam Lister, not the Service Department. Lister didn't run the SD, so what he thought didn't mean piss all. Unless maybe it was Bennett himself who put Lister up to the dance in the barn. But Harry Bennett was a busy man, too busy to concern himself with a pawn like Haik. The whole episode made no sense, and yet it had happened.

Haik drove home, the wheels in his head turning and spinning. When he approached the driveway, Lu was already on the porch and running out to meet him.

"My Lord, Haik, where on earth have you been?"

Where was he supposed to start? How could he explain being abducted? Being punched and kicked? Did she really need to know he recently had a gun to the back of his head? She hugged him and then looked up into his face, seeing the swelling on his jaw and his closed eye.

"Not again, Haik, not again. What on earth did they do to you this time?"

"I don't know," he said quietly. "I don't even know who it was. I'm okay, though. It won't happen again, anushas."

"Won't happen again? It just *did* happen again. And I know about the gun. You carry a gun now and it doesn't make you any safer. Haik, you're in more danger than ever, more than in the trainyards or with the Purples. Does that make any sense? I don't know what they've got you doing over there, but whatever it is it's not worth your life. Charlie and I need you, Haik. We don't have anything else. Charlie lost one father—he can't lose another."

He looked away. What was he supposed to say? He couldn't justify what he was doing with the SD. He couldn't say he he had to work for Harry Bennett because Lu was an expensive woman to please who had to put on the Ritz every night. No, he knew that she would have been just as happy with the straight workman's salary he used to bring home. She never complained. She didn't demand silk dresses or perfume from Paris or champagne every Saturday or ever at all. Mr. Meadows had raised her properly and she was straight and true. She was right—he shouldn't be staying out all night and not coming home to his family, even if it wasn't his fault. Lu should not have to worry about where he was and what was happening to him.

But that's exactly why Haik had to tell her about Mrs. Gertrude Branch.

"Lu, honey, I ain't gonna argue. You're right, I know you're right, but I got something more important to work out with you. Listen, listen to me now, how would you and Charlie like to move? Into a new house? A big house, on a lot of land, with running water and enough room to raise a big family?"

He waited for her expression, but she was still looking over his injured face.

"A house? Haik, what do you mean, a house? Where? What are you talking about?"

They had mentioned a dream, a distant dream of a place of their own, but they had both agreed they didn't have the money now and there was too much uncertainty in their lives and in everyone else's lives to make any moves. The whole country was a rickety ladder. You had a job one day, you were on the street the next. Until this Depression thing passed, any move was a dangerous one.

"C'mon, let's go inside. Let me get cleaned up and I'll tell you."

In the kitchen, his mother looked at him and only nodded her head in alarmed disapproval; she was done spilling tears over sons who refused to live safely like their father. After he washed and Lu made him a sandwich, Haik talked, speaking excitedly about meeting Mrs. Branch and revealing all the financial particulars. He couldn't say anything about the down payment and the stash of money he was hiding, but the $40 a month was a cinch. Could he really be discussing this with his wife? Buying his own house, his own land, something that belonged to him and him alone and over which he would be sole decision maker, his own little refuge where he made the laws, where he was no less than a Henry Ford? It didn't matter how long it had been since he slept, because now he had something he wanted, for his wife and son, something he wanted for them to make them happy and proud and protected. No sooner had Lu voiced her doubts, they were in the car together heading north to the Branch property.

Along the way, Haik pointed out the beauty of the landscape and Lu appeared to be pleased, the slight smile he loved returning to the corners of her mouth. Mound Road was unpaved and full of bumps and chuckholes, but he plotted as gentle a course as he could, easing off the gas when the road got rough, gliding left or right to avoid trouble. He would do all he could to make this the paradise they planned for their future.

In the distance, Haik spotted the stand of birches that held Vahram's body and then the Branch house off on the other side. In the daylight, he could see it needed some paint but the roof showed no signs of buckling or sagging. All the windows appeared stocked with uncracked panes. He was not dreaming last night. It was a damn nice place.

"Well, there she is," he announced, and glanced over at Lu, whose face was hard to read. "What you think?"

"It, it looks nice," she said noncommittally. What was she thinking? Why wasn't she bouncing in her seat and clapping her hands together? Uneasy, he steered onto the gravel entrance up to the front of the house, and he could see Mrs. Branch peek out at them from one of the front windows. Haik got out of the car and waved, and then opened Lu's door. He was quick to point out that the stairs up to the porch were solid, as was the porch itself, no squeaky boards or rotting wood. Mrs. Branch opened the door and motioned them inside.

It was March now, a typical Michigan winter in its biting frigidness, but the kitchen was warm and homey and smelled of bread. Mrs. Branch was welcoming and gracious, and Haik could swear he saw Lu softening. They talked terms of a possible purchase, Lu grabbing Haik's hand when the down payment was mentioned, and then they toured the house, going upstairs, finding rooms enough to fix up four bedrooms (even though two of them would be small, they would be no smaller than what Haik and Lu now shared with Charlie). Lu let a small smile escape every now and then, and Haik felt his mood lighten. They went outside and toured the outhouse and barn, taking their time, wandering back to the woods behind the house, finding the creek Mrs. Branch had mentioned the night before. Winter birds sang in the bare arms of the dark trees. It was beautiful.

"Well?"

"Well, it's nice. But what about the money, love? Forty dollars a month…it's a lot. And this down payment, good Lord, we don't have that."

"Forty dollars a month ain't nothing," Haik countered, his blood heating. "If it gives you what you want and makes the people you love happy, it could be a hundred dollars a day and it'd still be worth it. And the down payment, I got ideas. I got ways to come up with that kinda dough."

"Ways that don't involve that gun?"

He looked at her. Here he was ready to deliver the greatest gift she could ever ask for, and all she could do was talk about something that didn't matter.

"They ain't got nothing to do with no gun. I promise. That gun, it's just a big show. I get my jack and I ain't never used the gun. In fact, I got me the exact amount needed right here in my pocket."

Haik patted his coat pocket. Lu looked at him in silence.

They walked back to the house and sat down once more with Mrs. Branch. They held hands and looked into each other's eyes. Before they rose to go, Haik handed Mrs. Branch the wad of bills for the deposit and agreed to come back the next week to sign a deed to the house. She gave him a handwritten letter acknowledging receipt of the downpayment. Haik and Lucille Pehlivanian now owned their very own house in the country.

They shared a quick kiss in the car and Haik rolled triumphantly back to the city. It was done. He'd made it happen. Finally, he had done something good. He would take a hundred more beatings to do something as good as this again. Within two weeks, he and Lu and Charlie moved out on a Saturday and both of their families came along with Mr. Bozouki and Griff Slater and Orlin and two of Orlin's sisters and a younger brother. They ate and laughed and the women fixed the place up, and he even brought the solid cement ball Vahram had carried to their backyard so many years ago. It was good.

Everything was tough all over for everyone, but no one could be jealous of Haik and Lu and their sudden good fortune. Griff, George, Orlin, and Mr. Meadows knew how hard he worked, his own parents and sisters were grateful to have a living male child still left in the family, the Meadows all knew how much he loved Lu and Charlie and took care of their every need. Everyone knew the pain Lu had suffered with the death of her first husband and couldn't begrudge her happiness. No, what Haik and Lu had, they shared, giving money when needed to both Haik's and Lu's folks. No one could justify threatening their world.

During a lull in the celebration, Mr. Meadows took Haik aside and led him out into the back yard.

"It's sure a fine place, 'a-yik."

He looked out into the cold woods and seemed content. It had not been easy for him since being let go, but he was managing, fixing a neighbor's car here and there, selling some of his beer, and making due on Junior's wages and help from Haik. It was more the principle of pride, though, than the need for money that hurt him. Haik glanced over at Mr. Meadows. Why had he helped him? What did he get out of taking a neighborhood misfit, a dark-skinned pug who ran the streets and railyards, under his wing and doing a kindness for him? Now he was seeing some reward, his daughter was safe and loved and by this man, he received help with some extra cash for food each week, but then, when he agreed to take Haik to the Rouge with him and see about a job, what made him do what he did?

"I couldn't of done it without you, Mr. Meadows. You give me the chance."

"I just done what anybody'd a done, no more, no less. You, 'a-yik, y'done more for me by doing for Lu. When you get yer own wee ones and they get to be the age you is now, you'll unnerstan' what I mean. Lu, she's in good hands w'yeh, son. She's 'appy. That's all a father really wants. I just wanted to say those things."

Mr. Meadows looked at Haik, then off into the woods. They walked back to the house together in silence.

It was a good time, and everyone was thankful. At the end of the day came the bombshell: Orlin proposed to Arkina. There was a moment of silence, incredulous looks from Haik's parents as events were explained to them, and then all beers were raised to the ceiling. Arkina told her father that she loved Orlin and her decision was set, and, being a man of few if any words, he simply nodded and took a swallow of beer. Later, they worked it out—after the marriage, Orlin and Arkina would move in with Haik and Lu and Charlie. Out in the country they would run into few people at all let alone anyone who didn't like the idea of a black man married to an olive skinned girl, and if they did run into such a person, Haik would have his gun handy.

It worked. Haik would drive in with Orlin each day and home with him again. If he had a late night run, there was another guy in the glass house who lived out in Utica who gave Orlin a ride. The space, the sheer *room* that the house possessed, was life itself. Lu and Arkina could cook and wash and clean and, most of all, talk all day until Charlie came home from school. They had all they needed to be happy.

But then came Lister's orders, the last set he would give to Haik directly. There was trouble brewing in town, some commies getting together on Saturday at Grand Circus Park, a little semi-circle of land off Adams Avenue.

"Same old, same old. Lazy piece of shit union boys crying about work," Lister informed him. Haik despised Lister's bluster. He didn't know what Lister was talking about and he didn't think Lister did either. The only person who mattered, though, was Harry Bennett—don't piss him off, don't do anything that caused him a headache or put yourself in a spotlight too hot to stand in. If Bennett put Lister up to the shake down in the barn, then Haik would just have to take it. If not, then there was a score to settle, but the time and place had to be right.

The protest was supposed to start at noon, so the SD boys would gather up near Woodward and Grand River Avenue about an hour before and make the trek up to the park in force. The cops, they were told, would arrive on the scene at the same time, marching down Woodward, Park Avenue and Witherell Street to greet the enemy, and they'd push forward and squeeze the unionizers right out of sight, sending them scurrying off with their tails between their legs down Bagley and Madison and the hell out of sight, half of them west to Corktown and the other half east to Black Bottom.

Haik would go—he had orders—but he resolved to stay toward the back and pretty much mind his own business. He had nothing against the union boys. As far as he could tell, they were just men who wanted to keep their jobs and not get fired for growing old or being sick. They had families and were in the same position as Mr. Meadows and tens of thousands of others; they had done nothing wrong to anyone and now they were stuck, left out in the cold with no chance to make an honest dollar no matter how hard they were willing to work. So what if they protested? What difference did it make to Harry Bennett or Henry Ford or hard guys like Cam Lister? If you don't like what they were saying, don't listen—unless, of course, you were afraid of what these jobless men were saying.

No, Haik had nothing against them. Lister and some of the others, though, wanted to be front and center for the show.

It was cold Saturday. Orlin was off work, so he stayed home with the women and worked about the house, focusing his attention on fixing a wobbly stairway banister and trying to get Mrs. Branch's old truck in the barn running. The truck hadn't been used for so long mice had eaten all the wiring inside, but they could use the extra vehicle for the women in an emergency, and Orlin could fix anything. With everyone at home busy, Haik set out. He had his pistol, but he had also been commanded to bring a set of brass knuckles and his billy club, which was to be concealed up a coat sleeve and unleashed at Lister's command. Lister was first in charge for this one, and he wanted his troops ready. If he pulled this off with the right results, he could sit at Harry Bennett's feet in the office and not have to run around town and keep track of a pack of small change stooges like Haik. Lister knew all about Bennett's private castle outside Ann Arbor and all his "summer cottages" on Grosse Isle and dotted all over the state, all courtesy of Henry Ford's money—Bennett had the life, and Lister saw himself grabbing a share of it for himself.

"Okay, boys, lissen up, lissen up, here's the plan," he shouted from the roof of a car, fashioning himself as some sort of Blackjack Pershing or Teddy Roosevelt at San Juan Hill. "We're gonna take us a little walk up the street here in about ten minutes. These sons-a-bitches in the park, well, they're what we're here for. Everything we stand for and believe in, everything that puts money in our pockets, these bastards is trying to take from us. Mr. Henry Ford called Mr. Bennett special for this, and Mr. Bennett is asking us to do a little favor for him and we're gonna do it. And the cops're gonna be helping us out, so don't worry about gettin' pinched. Now, we're gonna get right up close to these shits, and there's gonna be a lot of yellin' and hootin'. We'll let that go on a little while, put some fear in their bellies, and then you're gonna hear a pistol go off. When you's hear that, the billies come out and it's time to take it to town. We ready to toe the line, boys?"

A hoot went up from the troops, a rogue's battalion of smashed nosed toughs, wild-eyed hard guys, and oversized bimbos who probably could give the Chicago Cardinals or the Portsmouth Spartans a fair run for their money on the football field. Haik remembered what had happened back in '30 on Woodward when the men were busted up for protesting—warfare. He milled around with the rest of Lister's army and tried to lose himself in the crush of bodies, covertly squeezing his way to the back. It was a promised day's pay, five more dollars for showing up, money he would put toward gas in the Whippet for the coming week, but he didn't have the stomach for what Lister had just said. He'd go along, play the game, but he wasn't going to hit anyone or even shove or shout at anyone. That would be on someone else's conscience, not his. If anything, if it got too wild, maybe he could even sneak a crack in on Lister himself, a quick phantom billyclub blow to the back of his head. Yes, that was worth playing soldier for.

Somewhere in the front the signal must have been given to move out because Haik suddenly felt himself carried along in the pack of men. They moved at a slow, deliberately belligerent pace, and somehow he was pushed to the front of their formation. As strong as he was, the force of the mob, the crunching of arms and churning legs and shifting bodies, was stronger. When they reached the edge of the park, the protesters were already there, overcoated against the cold, signs in their gloved hands, *Ford Unfair to Workers*, *We Want Work*, *Strength in Unity*, *Workers Unite*, *Ford Must Listen*, like hundreds of battle flags raised to the sky. They looked as if they expected Lister's army, firing back with defiant looks.

"Fuck you lazy reds!" came the first volley from one of Lister's men.

A hail of insults showered back, and so it began, two dogs salivating on strained leashes, their frothing jaws snapping, gums flared and teeth flashing. Haik was at the lead of Lister's ranks, but he could not push back into the crowd. He looked into the opposing faces, seeing if he recognized anyone. They were all decent looking men, like most the men he had worked with when he was still on the line, not an enemy, not a mob of villains threatening anyone's way of life. Somewhere behind him, though, Lister was at his back and he could not turn around. A bullet from Lister's Walther could plant into the back of his skull and he would never have a chance to defend himself or return fire. He couldn't stay here.

As he turned to look back over his shoulder, his eyes caught an unmistakable sight on the opposing battleline—Mr. Meadows. Tall and hard-featured, he looked lost as he held a sign but did not join the deafening chorus of insults barked back and forth between the armies. Haik sank inside. Why were they here? Shame crept in him. He did not want to be seen, but he could not let Mr. Meadows get hurt once that pistol went off and the belligerence turned ugly. He had to act.

At any minute Lister's gun would go off. He steadied himself. No, no one here was going to touch Mr. Meadows. No one would lay a hand or a club on him. Piss all, he needed to move.

Haik elbowed free from his line. He strode directly toward Mr. Meadows, who turned and caught sight of Haik. Once eye to eye, Haik gripped him hard by the arms.

"Mr. Meadows, for the love of Jesus, you gotta get outta here. They're gonna start shootin'...."

"'ay-ik," Mr. Meadows shouted over the din, more of a question than a statement or greeting.

"Mr. Meadows, right now, we got to get..."

Shouts and screams and taunts shot from all sides, *That's it, clock the geezer...Get your paws off him, Ford bastard...Hit him! Hit him! Hit him!...Leave the old man be...Bust the commie one...Mind your own damn bee's wax you piker...Take your filthy hands off the man...Torpedo the old fool...How much Ford payin' ya to hurt an old man, Mr. Tough Guy...That how you earn your money, hero....*

"...the hell outta here, Mr. Meadows, please, we got..."

"'ay-ik, what're yeh doin' here?" Mr. Meadows shouted, his bright blue eyes flaring and his cragged face creasing in confusion.

A gunshot split the March sky. Before Haik could react he was plowed forward into Mr. Meadows and he tumbled to the snowy ground on top of him, his billy club clattering from his sleeve. Legs and feet crashed into him from every direction. He covered Mr. Meadows, then searched for the club with his right hand, which was stomped, pain jolting from his fingers all the way into his shoulder. Pummeled from above, he absorbed blows ricocheting off his back and head and the backs of his trampled legs—no one would touch Mr. Meadows.

Above the shouting he could hear more gunshots and then something like a cannon going off. Packs of legs brushed him as legions of men from both sides rambled to his left, and then seconds later another group careened into him on the right. Haik looked up and could make out the blue uniformed police swarming across Adams, weapons drawn and obviously working in unison with Lister. The cops wore gas masks, the same kind Haik had seen in pictures of the Great War. The goggle-eyed invaders made their way forward, their masked faces revealing nothing and everything about their purpose. In the next second, a haze filtered everywhere, tear gas spreading like morning fog. The thick vapor burned, setting Haik's eyes and nose and lungs on fire. It was his last arson run with Vahram all over again.

He had to move. He pulled the collars of his jacket up about his face to provide some protection from the gas.

"Lemme help you up. We gotta move."

But Mr. Meadows didn't respond—maybe he had been knocked senseless in the rush. Haik found his feet and, blinded, he gathered up Mr. Meadows and lifted him under his near arm and leg, and then lifted him in a fireman's carry.

"I'll get you outta here, Mr. Meadows. Don't worry."

He began to run, where he didn't know, but away from here, somewhere to escape the madness. He lumbered ahead, the uneven ground tripping at him, almost causing him to tumble to the earth. Squinting, he could make out blurred bodies in front of him, racing here and there while police whistles blew. The shouting and lethal pops continued and he ran, unable to breathe or see.

He cracked his eyes and searing tears flooded out and mucous streamed from his nose. He could make out an alley just ahead, and he staggered forward until he was behind some garbage cans and large bins. He fell against the brick wall, sinking to the alley floor with Mr. Meadows falling from his arms. He sucked the somewhat untainted air into his lungs.

"Mr. Meadows…," he panted, his throat on fire.

He wiped at the particles of gas that flamed and torched his eyeballs. His tear ducts flooded and he struggled to catch his breath. He wiped again, and laid his eyes upon his father-in-law, whose head slumped forward onto his chest.

"…Mr. Meadows…"

His eyes began to clear. Mr. Meadows' coat was soaked through in blood, and when Haik tore open the coat to find the source he found more blood, his father-in-law's white linen shirt now saturated red.

Haik propped Mr. Meadows up and looked into the silent face before him. His crystal eyes were wide open but sightless. His mouth was slightly cracked, almost in a peaceful grin, and Haik waited for him to say something, to laugh it off like being let go from the Rouge or giving his car away, to make some joke about joining the bootleggers or beer barons.

"…Mr. Meadows…."

The old man's mouth did not move and the lips would make no words of reply.

Part Two

He had done all he could and he'd done nothing at all. He did exactly the right thing and he committed the most shameful wrong a man could commit. He had tried to save his father-in-law, warned him, pleaded with him, shielded him with his own body, and at the same time he might as well have been the one who pulled the trigger. The anger he faced was understandable. Unless you were there, unless you really knew what went down at the park, you would think that something, anything, could have been done to avoid what happened. Because you were there, because you looked right into his pale blue eyes, though, *you* were responsible, and nothing said in your defense could change that belief.

When he finally admitted that Mr. Meadows was not getting up, Haik gathered up his body again in a fireman's carry and stepped from the alley. The tear gas was no longer as strong as it had been, and he looked about, finding his bearings. The park was carnage. Signs littered the ground, some spiked like spears into the cold dirt. Coats and jackets and hats were strewn about and, yes, bodies, motionless bodies, slumped here and there. The air was full of drifting smoke, either from guns or the tear gas or both, and blue uniforms raced here and there, some leading men away in irons, others chatting amiably with laughing members of the Service Department. Haik wanted no contact with anyone. He determined an outside path to his car and began jogging, Mr. Meadows' body bobbing heavily on his shoulders.

He could see the Whippet at the curb just ahead when he was blindsided by a shove or a fist or shoulder, sending him and Mr. Meadows' body to the sidewalk.

"Not so fast, union boy."

Haik looked up to see a blue uniformed cop above him brandishing a club.

"Fuck you."

The cop looked at Haik, unaccustomed to defiance.

"Excuse me? You say something, commie?" the cop continued, tapping his nightstick in his free hand.

"I got no time for you, shithead. Get the hell outta my way. I'm takin' this man home."

Haik rose. He didn't have time to unbutton his coat and reach for his pistol, but the brass knuckles in his pocket slipped easily around his fingers. The cop smiled at what he assumed was easy prey, and then went at Haik with his stick, cocking it back into position. Haik lowered and went directly at the man's legs in a wrestler's tackle to avoid the arc of the blow, plowing into his lower body and driving him back against a car parked at the curb. Rage was all he needed, not guns, not clubs, not brass knuckles, not blackjacks. The cop's hat flew off and he slid down the side of the car, unable to land a blow with his stick, and Haik would not let him come anywhere near finding his pistol. Two quick shots with the metal knuckles rendered his enemy useless, a gash opened across the bridge of his nose and another streaming blood over his left eye. He wanted to keep hammering him, to keep inflicting misery, but he had no time to waste, so he left the moaning cop leaning against the car.

As he returned to tend to Mr. Meadows, a squad of blue bellies, some still hiding behind their gas masks, sprinted at him, nightsticks and pistols drawn. He let the brass knuckles fall from his hand to the sidewalk. He unbuttoned his coat and began to reach inside to his shoulder holster. His life meant nothing now. Vahram dead. Mr. Meadows dead. He might as well join them.

"Wait, wait, wait a minute here," a voice commanded. "Danny, Stew, take care of Lenny. Get him back to a wagon and over to the doc…."

Haik looked toward the new voice, and then froze as a police issue sidearm pointed directly into his face. Haik followed the barrel of the gun up to his adversary's eyes. He knew the wiry curl to the hair beneath the police cap, the seagull wing curve to the eyebrows, the sharp point of the nose. Luigi Leoni, the boxcar busting compatriot of his youth, was holding a gun on him.

"…and watch who you're nabbing. This guy I'm pointing my gun at, he was with us today. Now I'm going to take care of this one and the rest of you get back to work. For the love of God, make damn sure who you're going after."

The squad eyed Haik for a moment, gathered up their fallen comrade, and went back toward the park and further adventures. Luigi kept the gun on Haik, whose right hand was frozen in the process of reaching to his holster.

"Haik," Luigi said, lowering his gun.

Haik let his trigger hand drift to his side.

"Haik, you need to get outta here, the faster the better," Luigi counseled as he holstered his weapon.

"My father, my father-in-law," Haik began, pointing behind him to Mr. Meadows' body. "They, they killed him."

"I know," Luigi said. "Here, let's get him to your ride."

The two men scooped up the lifeless body and walked in unison back to Haik's car. Haik opened the passenger side door, and they lay Mr. Meadows inside.

As Haik propped him up, his hands rested on Mr. Meadows' chest—it couldn't be. Lister said he'd draw his gun as a signal, nothing more. No one was supposed to get shot. No one should be dead. Mr. Meadows should be talking to him right now, telling him to go home to Lu, to look after what was most important, no more getting involved in marches and protests.

Haik looked into the lifeless face. For the second time, he was right there when someone close to him was on the wrong end of a gun. For the second time, he did nothing to prevent it. For the second time, he'd have to make a drive, alone in his own thoughts and guilt. This time, though, he had even less of an explanation for what happened and why. And now another ghost from his past had arisen and walked into his life, Gee-Gee Leoni, one he was not certain was real or not.

"How, how'd you find me? How'd you know I'd be here?"

"I don't have time to explain everything now, Haik. We've had our eyes on a lot of people. Not everybody in blue has his nose up Harry Bennett's ass. I've done a little looking around, and I saw you with Bennett's men down at Blossom Heath Park one night doing a drop. I, I didn't want anything to happen to you today, Haik."

Haik looked down at the pavement.

"What the hell was this today? Why you helping these pricks, Gee? You're supposed to be the law, you're supposed to...."

"I could ask you the same thing. Haik, I know what it must look like, I know it looks like we were working with Bennett today, but this wasn't supposed to happen. We were told no guns, no shooting, just a lot of shouting and noise. We got double crossed. Trust me, this isn't going to stand."

He looked at Luigi.

Trust him.

Was Gee full of shit? His whole life, cops had never done anything to help him or protect him or anyone he cared about, so why should he trust a cop now? The past they shared was over, long gone and buried. He and Orlin rediscovered their friendship, but they had something in common, the Rouge plant at first and now family. Luigi didn't have that, and Haik would be stupid to believe anyone involved in what just happened at the protest.

"Hey, you got to get your father home. I'm sorry, Haik. I'm really am. Let me tell you this, though, I'm gonna meet up with you later. There's some people we got to bring down, people you know and work with, some people I work with, too, people that planned what happened today. Not every cop's bent. Some of us believe in the law. But I'm gonna need your help, Haik."

Haik looked at Mr. Meadows' body.

"If you help me get who done this, you'll get all the help I got. I promise you. But I can't rest till I get who done this."

Haik sized up Luigi. He was no longer the terrified boy racing his father's rusted flatbed from the railyard at Greeley Street as Varham's blood froze into the hair on the back of his head. He was now a man. His uniform fit like a soldier's and he had a kind of authority about him. And as long as Cam Lister was on Harry Bennett's good side, Haik would need Luigi's help to get him.

He climbed into the driver's side, slammed the door, nodded to Luigi, and was gone.

What would he do now? Where would he go? Home to Lu in Utica? His old home to his parents and sisters? To the Meadows home? What would he say to Mrs. Meadows? The hospital was senseless. They could do nothing but take Mr. Meadows' body and ask questions and call the police while they made him fill out papers. He'd be arrested because of his dark skin, and then Mr. Bennett would be called, and that was trouble—rule number one, never bring the Service Department into any trouble. He had to go home, Utica, his parents, the Meadows, somewhere with family. He looked out his front windshield, where packs of people were striding up the sidewalks, anxious to see what had actually just happened at Grand Circus Park. What should he do? There was really only one place he could go now, only one decent thing he could do—he had to bring Mr. Meadows back to his wife and family.

The drive to the old Meadows home was too quick. What would he say? How would he say it? Who could really explain what had happened? He was just there to watch things, not cause any problems, and then the place went mad, fists and bullets and shouts and signs everywhere, and it was impossible to tell who did exactly what or started things. But that wasn't true. The bullets had come from Lister's side. Was it that first shot that hit Mr. Meadows? If so, then the man who killed him was clear. There was no need for any guns at the park. The tear gas was bad enough, and who could expect anything different from the cops, who might as well have been wearing Ford badges like tightass

Mr. Hoarseman back at the Rouge. But guns. You want to get a piece out to scare someone off, fine, but to use it on a man carrying a sign?

The Meadows' driveway was family, the rough cement cracked from years of exposure, uneven in spots, but familiar and solid. Was there any way to tell what happened and sound believable? To sound not guilty? He looked to his right, to Mr. Meadows' body, but he could not look at his face. Somehow it was like a stranger had let himself into the car and fallen asleep and refused to wake up—he did not know this person and yet this was the most important person in his life.

He slid out of the car and made his way up the steps to the front door. He wouldn't wait to knock—he was family and this was serious. Once he cracked the door, he was met by Liam, Jr., who was on his one day off for the week.

"Hey, there, Hai…."

"Junior…you, you gotta, you need to come quick."

"What?" asked Liam, feeling the seriousness in Haik's voice.

"Your father. He…just come."

His face told Liam not to ask any more questions.

"They, they got him, Junior. They got him."

He exhaled. Haik wanted his words to tell the whole story, to be his explanation and his alibi and his declaration of innocence. Liam broke away and ran to the car. Haik followed, ready to explain or console Liam or do something, whatever that might be he didn't know.

"Oh my, oh my, damn, no, no, no…."

Liam peered in the passenger side door. He opened the door and looked down at his father's body, his hands falling to his sides, seemingly afraid to touch it, as if placing a hand on his father would make his deadness more real. The front door of the house flung open and Mrs. Meadows rushed out. Haik sank. He was useless, with no power to change or shape what would now unfold. His time to act had been at the protest—now he could do no more than face his sentence.

"Haik, Liam, what is it?"

She ran to the car, and the sound of her voice cut Haik in half.

"Good God, no, oh my good Lord…."

"The protest," Haik began. "They started shooting…."

"My good Lord," she cried.

She pushed past Liam and gripped tightly onto her husband's body.

"Oh Christ, who? Who? Who done this?" demanded Liam.

"The police, they, they went crazy. The protest turned bad, and then people started shooting, and then tear gas went off. Nobody could see nothing. It was like a war."

Haik did not even believe his own revised version of what had happened. It wasn't a war—one side didn't have any weapons and never had a chance.

"My God, my God," repeated Mrs. Meadows, now joined by her son in holding the lifeless body.

"He's gone, mum. Goddamn gone. He just went to speak his mind. Don't no man deserve to die for speaking his own mind. My father...."

Haik had never seen Liam angry like this and he could feel the rage growing in his young brother-in-law.

"So what happen, Haik? Tell us what the hell happen. Where were you? Were you there?" asked Liam, and Haik stood mute.

Yes, he was there. Yes, he was right there. He was so close he held Mr. Meadows by the arms and could still see the confusion in his eyes before the shot went off.

"Yeah, I was there. I was trying to get your father out, away from everything."

"Well you done a hell of a job. So? So what happen? Did you see who done this?"

"I don't know who fired the shot. There was lots of shots. I seen dad there. I had him in my arms. I was moving him out and then somebody, somebody started shooting. It was a riot, Junior. And when the tear gas come, I couldn't see nothing."

"So you was right there..."

"That's what I said, Liam..."

Mrs. Meadows was brushing her hands through her husband's hair.

"Shut it, both of you, shut it."

"No, mum, let him tell us. What were you there for, Haik? Or is it Hank? Huh, tell us. Whose side was you on, anyways? Tell us, Mr. SD man with the pistol and fancy car and house."

Haik was cornered. He had always been friendly with Liam, but now the boy was jabbing him, shoving him to an edge.

"Liam, you wasn't there...."

"No, I wasn't there, you're right, but you was, and now my father's dead."

"Boys, please...."

Liam's sisters Emily and Cassie and Cassie's husband Donald came running and the front yard filled with wailing. It was Vahram all over. There could be no consolation, no words, no explanations. Haik looked at Liam, who glared at him. The showdown would have to stop.

"Here."

Haik put a hand on Mrs. Meadows' shoulder. She heaved, and when she released her husband's body, the front of her dress was stained with his blood. She moved aside and Haik gathered Mr. Meadows from the car, straining to cradle his sagging weight. Junior made a motion to help, but Haik looked him off, and then carried Mr. Meadows into the house, where he laid him on the couch in the front room. When the wailing heightened, Haik knew he could not stay. He had to go, home, anywhere, but not stay here.

"Mrs. Meadows, everyone, I got to go tell Lu. I got to tell her. But we'll be back."

Haik stood sheepishly in the doorway. He wanted to embrace someone, hold Mrs. Meadows or shake someone's hand, but there was a wall between him and everyone else present. They stared at him in silence. So this is what they really thought of him. SD man. Strongarm. Stooge. Shtarker. As good as he was to Lu, as much money as he sent their way to help them through these times, this is all he really was.

Haik turned and quietly paced out the door. As he went down the wooden steps he heard the door open behind him. It was Junior. His eyes were lit with fire.

"I'm sorry, Junior. I talked to the police," Haik broke in. "They said they're gonna find who done this."

"The police? What the hell the police gonna do? Didn't you say they were the ones who done this? They gonna finger one a their own? They all work for Henry Ford anyways. Ain't no one gonna do a damn thing about this and you damn well know it, you black-ass cocksucker."

Haik was penned in the open air. He had been found guilty. His story, his words, meant nothing but he had to say something as Junior skipped down the stairs.

"I got a friend in the force who's gonna…"

"You got a friend in the force, does ya? So where was yer friend when the guns gone off? He do anything to stop things? Huh?"

Liam strode forward and stood nose to nose with Haik. Haik wanted out, back into his car, back on the road to Utica but he wasn't going to take the accusations. He had no answers for anyone here, nothing they would believe or listen to, but he wasn't going to sit back and take being called a murderer. He was now the enemy, not the son-in-law or brother-in-law. Soon, Donald followed the noise outside onto the porch. Maybe he would listen to some sense.

"Donald, I don't want no trouble. I got to get home to Lu. Junior, you wasn't there. There wasn't nothing I could do. If your father woulda just told me beforehand...."

"He didn't say nothing because he didn't want to get you in no trouble, Haik. That's the kinda man my father is, was, a man like you could never be with your goddamned pistol and Service Department bitch buggy."

"Liam, look...."

Liam pushed even closer to Haik, who backed up but raised his hands, a warning for Liam to back off.

"What? You gonna shoot me too?"

"Liam, I didn't shoot nobody...."

"No, you just stood there while somebody else did."

"I'm telling you, Liam, this ain't the time. Why you doing this?"

"Liam, let it go, man," yelled Donald from the porch, sensing the escalation. "Let him get home to your sister. He didn't do nothing. This don't help nothing. He's kin."

"Fucking my sister don't make this bastard no kin to me."

Haik's right hand caught Liam square on the jaw, dropping him hard to the ground. He grabbed a handful of Liam's hair and cocked his hand before he realized what he was doing. Donald leaped off the porch and wrestled between them, grabbing onto Haik's fist. Haik whipped his arm back and flung him to the ground. Donald recovered and Haik let him pry between himself and Liam again. What had he just done? Why? Liam's sisters ran out the front door, followed by Mrs. Meadows.

"My God, ain't there enough misery here? What in God's name you boys doing?" the old woman screamed.

Haik let go of Liam's hair and pushed Donald backwards. He lowered his head, unable to look Mrs. Meadows in the eye. He saw Liam still on the ground, then backed his way to his car.

"Why don't you shoot *me*, you bastard?" shouted Liam, regaining his feet. "Huh? Get out your gun and shoot me too, SD man. I'll even turn my back and make it easy."

Haik looked back at all of Lu's relatives, all of them strangers. Donald held onto Liam, who continued to curse. Mrs. Meadows was bawling, pleading with him to just shut up and go back inside. Haik had thought of these people as his own, but now, what could he think now?

He felt the darkness of his skin. Isn't that what Liam had called him, a black-ass? He heard the strange, alien accent of his voice even though it was barely noticeable anymore. He was not one of them. But just when had they cast him out? When he joined the Service Department? When he moved into his new house? Or had it just happened, not even a half hour ago? Maybe he never really had been one of them.

He climbed into the car and settled in the driver's seat, but before he turned the engine over he noticed Mr. Meadows' blood staining the fabric where Lu would sit. He looked one more time at the commotion on the front lawn of the Meadow's house and was gone.

As he made his way back to Utica, his mind churned. He replayed smashing the face of the cop who had knocked him to the ground. His hands gripped the wheel of the Whippet, but he felt his fist draw back and plow into the man's face. Again and again, he relived the sensation of his fist, clad in the brass knuckles, mashing the bastard's nose and then the eye, seeing the bright blood splatter and stream over the man's face. When the image of Mr. Meadows, his head resting in his lap, forced itself into his mind, he again redrew the picture of delivering those heavy blows. He also saw Luigi and heard his voice. There were some men they needed to "bring down." How they would do this, he didn't know. For now, he had to believe it would happen. But Lu? What would he tell Lu?

When he rolled into the dirt drive of his new home, he wished everything was already explained and all the impossible questions were answered and everyone understood and knew it wasn't his fault and things could go back to how they were. He could just sit out in the car and wait for the sun to go down and everything would blow over or right itself. As he looked up at the front door, he admitted that could never happen.

Haik stepped inside and Charlie came rushing over to hug him. He patted the boy's head and crouched down to gather him in his arms.

"Ah, there you are. How was work?" sang Lu as she emerged from the kitchen. Haik's face must have said it all. Her mood turned stone serious. "Are you okay, darling? What is it?"

"Let's go outside, Lu. Charlie, find Orlin and see if he needs some help."

Charlie looked for a second, and then did as told. Lu got her coat before joining Haik out on the porch. Something bad was coming, but she couldn't have ever guessed the secret Haik now held.

"My God, Haik, look at you, more blood…"

"It's not about me, Lu…"

"You told me no more, no more problems, no more gettin' cut and punched and kicked.…"

"Lu, I'm not hurt. Listen to me…it's, it's your father."

Lu's clear eyes blazed.

"Haik, what? Tell me, what is it? What about my father?"

"Lu, there was a protest today…your father, he was in the protest," Haik fumbled, trying to find a way to a destination he did not want to visit. "Guns started going off.…"

"Haik, is he hurt? Is he…"

"Lu, he's gone. He's gone, Lu," he said, pulling her into him.

Her body stiffened. Arkina came out onto the porch.

"Haik, Lu, what is it?"

"Just take care of Charlie," Haik said, holding Lu tightly.

"Can I help?"

"No. Nothing yet. We got to go into town. Just you and Orlin, please, take care of him. We got to go."

Lu quaked in his arms, and then punched into his chest.

"What happened, Haik? What are you telling me? What happened?"

He searched for the right words. What he had said at the Meadows home did nothing but weld his guilt.

"Lu, dad was there with some other men who lost their jobs. Hundreds of them. And then the police were there. And I.…"

"And where were you? Were you there? I thought you had to go into the plant today."

"I did, but, then I was supposed to go to the protest to watch over it with some other guys from the SD. We went down to the protest, just to keep things in order.…"

She punched hard into his chest again, and he accepted the blow. His talking was done. Words just misrepresented what he knew to be true, what he wanted to believe to be true. He wasn't a good talker, he knew that, and more than ever he needed to keep silent to protect himself and those he loved.

"I want to go. Now, I want to go. I need to go to him."

"Can I.…"

"No, you can't do anything except drive the car. I want to go. Right now. Where, where is he?"

"Your house."

She looked away, her eyes streaming tears. He walked Lu to the car, his arm around her, and once inside the car the silence was more brutal than any blow he had ever taken. He kept both hands on the wheel. He tried to explain what had happened, but the events and the pictures that went through his mind scrambled and mixed and intertwined until he was not even sure what he was saying. Did he sound like a liar? Like he was hiding something? Like he could have prevented any of this from happening and didn't? Like he was a coward who couldn't stand up for the one good man he knew in his life? Lu's silence tore at him. He could change nothing, but how would he make up for what had happened? Was Luigi serious about bringing people down? Was revenge even worth it now?

Without revenge, Haik's life had no worth and he knew it.

The Meadows' house was painful. They had taken off Mr. Meadows bloody clothes, washed the blood away, dressed him in his Sunday suit, combed his hair, and closed his eyes to let him rest. Candles were lit all around his body, and tobacco and pipes laid out on an end table beside him. Those who came in brought whiskey and poteen and they smoked and told stories of Liam Meadows. Laughter could often be found at an Irish wake, but none here. Haik stood alone while Lu gathered with her mother and brothers and sisters. Junior ignored him, not even making eye contact, and Haik was grateful—being invisible was better than being openly despised. No one slept, and by the next morning, the pine casket was set out in the front room and black drapes hung in all the windows. Chairs were placed on the lawn to hold the casket before the trip to the cemetery. Haik could only stand by and watch, a ghost in the home he had once felt was his own.

He was never more relieved to see his own family than when they showed up at the front door. At least now someone could be on his side. Mrs. Meadows was gracious to them. Haik looked at his father, his face weathered and his spine starting to hunch, and he was ashamed he had ever looked down at this man. Maybe he was quiet and maybe he barely made a living, but he was honest and gentle and had probably never felt the guilt that Haik was feeling now.

Haik walked out into the yard. He had to change his life. No question, he couldn't keep living like two people, a decent, honest family man part of the day and crooked ape the rest of the time. But how would he change things? Quit the SD? No, the job gave him a house for his wife and a car and more than enough money to feed his family. And you just didn't "quit" the SD. It would look suspicious, and making Harry

Bennett suspicious was not smart. He went back inside. He didn't want to look at anyone but Lu. He found her sitting in the parlor looking white and weightless. She did not look at him but he put his hand on her shoulder and she reached up and covered it with her own. Relief. How could Lu cope with this? First a husband and now her father? Admiration for her strength and disgust over his own guilt mixed uneasily inside him.

On the ride home Sunday evening, more silence. Charlie rode with Orlin and Arkina, and Haik's car never felt so empty. He let the silence grip the space between them, hold it hostage, its hands bound and mouth gagged.

"I want you to leave Fords," Lu finally said without emotion, but a very clear determination in her voice.

Haik drove, looking straight ahead.

"How? How can I do that, Lu?"

There was argument in his voice, his tone saying that it wasn't possible, it couldn't be done.

"Easy. You go in and tell the murdering bastards you're done."

"And then what? What do we pay the bills with?" he asked softly.

He had already thought that through—he could not just leave the SD. Yes, she needed to vent her rage but at the same time not lose her reason. The Depression was wicked and it was killing people every day, starving them to death, freezing them in unheated homes and out in the snow frosted alleys, foreclosing on them and pushing them into the streets, lining them up like animals at the factory gates begging for a day's work, forcing them to scavenge through trash bins for food, stealing their work and their pride and their dignity and killing their souls long before it took their flesh. Those lucky enough to have kind landlords only had all the door and windows in their homes removed and were given a choice—pay, freeze, or move. Haik didn't want to be a SD man, but what was the alternative? At Fords, you didn't go from line worker to SD man and then back to the line. That just didn't happen.

"Go to GM. Maybe Junior can set you up…"

"Lu, GM ain't hiring. Ain't nobody hiring. And I'm the last man Junior would ever help. Right now, me and Orlin are working and we bring home good money to keep everyone alive. Charlie got more than any other kid you'll find. Lu, we got a big house and land and a car and…"

"I can live without a big house and a car, Haik. I can't live without a husband and Charlie can't live without a father."

Silence. He kept his hands firmly on the steering wheel, and his mouth clamped as if it had been slapped shut.

"Lu, I'll make you this promise. Gee-Gee Leoni's a cop now, you know that. He promised me he'd fix this. He'll find the man who done this and he'll punish him. I won't rest until that happens. I can't. And that means I got to stay on until he can pinch the sons-a-bitches. He needs me to stay on, whether I like it or not, or the bastard that hurt dad will never be punished. There's no other way we're gonna find this guy and get justice for your father. No other way."

He glanced over at her. She looked off into the distance in resignation, her jaw set, eyes rimmed red, her face locked forward.

"It's a little late for justice for my father. Do as you will," she murmured, and turned to look out the passenger side window.

They said nothing. A few times Lu would begin to cry but catch herself and stop. Haik put his hand on her near forearm, afraid she might brush it away, but she neither brushed it away nor took hold of it with her other hand. Every thunk in the road and rotation of the tires sounded in his head. Why couldn't she at least try to understand? He couldn't ignore the money he was making now. It kept the family alive. It made the payment to Emma Branch. It bought food for the Pehlivanian and Meadows families. Granted, the job was ugly, he wouldn't question that, and it made him feel filthy, but he could deal with it to keep his family away from the brutality of the city and all its misery. Once this Depression thing passed, he could go to GM or Chrysler or Packard or anywhere else, but now wasn't that time and they all had to ride this out. Just a little longer, that was all, just a little longer, then he was free.

"You need to know something," Lu said as they pulled into their drive and the engine cut off, finally breaking the strained silence, her voice drained of emotion. He steeled himself for more hatred, more guilt, more deserved punishment. "I was waiting for a good time to tell you, but, but there's no chance for that now. Haik…you're going to be a father."

The Service Department was in good spirits on Monday. A meeting was held in the Reclamation Garage with at least several hundred men present, talking, regaling each other with tales of what they were now calling the Ford Massacre. A few smacked Haik on the arm and said they'd seen him cross the line first and go right after the union pansies. Haik stood silently among them, one of the crowd but not one of them, nodding his head but unable to pretend he wasn't ashamed of being there. Bennett finally arrived in his '32 Ford Victoria, glossy red and black, plenty of chrome, but what really got the men's attention was Bennett's entrance. When he stepped out of the passenger side, he was holding a leash, which he tugged, and out sauntered…a lion. Yes, a lion, like what you saw in a damn Tarzan movie. Who could believe this? They had all heard about Bennett owning lions and tigers, but here it was, a big-headed, wild maned beast walking right past them like it was nothing more than an oversized showdog.

They quieted down when Bennett strode past, now flanked by Cutty, Gellinger, Franks, Zabriskie, and, new to the cast of toadies, a smiling Cam Lister. Bennett, his pet, and his entourage climbed a metal stairway that led to a small balcony and then on up into the catwalks above the garage floor. They stopped on the balcony, a kind of politician's podium overlooking the mass of muscle and ignorance assembled below, with Bennett's strongarms keeping a safe distance from the beast.

"Don't worry, gents, I just fed old Babe here a couple of Negroes and a union man this morning and he's calm as a kitten," Bennett blurted out to laughter, his voice echoing through the cavernous garage.

Don Marshall, a former city cop, was the only black man in Bennett's army, hired especially to keep an eye on black workers, who were mainly in the dirtiest jobs at the Rouge, the paint shop and the iron foundry and the clean up crews, and he wasn't here, so Bennett could get away with a crack like that. Even if Marshall was it wouldn't matter— Harry Bennett did as Harry Bennett pleased with no regard to anyone but Mr. Henry Ford, who would not have batted an eye at such a comment. Bennett raised his hands to silence the crowd.

"Okay, gentlemen, let's make this quick. Everyone have a nice weekend?"

Again, the crowd below erupted in laughter and hoots and an onslaught of smalltalk and war stories ensued. Bennett smiled and raised his arms, his message unmistakable, and they all knew to shut up quick. The lion looked on in lazy perplexion, its tail flicking every now and then, reminding the assembly that it was indeed a real lion.

"Things went well. I don't think there's going to be any more protests for a while thanks to the Service Department and its staff. You gotta break some eggs to make an omelet, and, well, some of these commie protesters, they took a permanent retirement, didn't they? Where was their union? Huh? Anybody tell me? The union save anyone's hide? What was a union going to do when we're on the scene? You saw exactly what happens when you try to stand up to Mr. Henry Ford and the men at the SD. We don't do things half way here, boys, no siree, and when we're given a job, we get it done with bang up results. So, I want to let you all know you did good and Mr. Ford is proud of each and every man who defended the company."

Bennett stood back for a second and began to clap and the crowd followed his lead with hoots and whistles thrown in for victorious effect. He raised his hands again, and the throng settled.

"We had some real heroes out there at the park. I hear tell Mr. Hank Pelini wanted some union ass so bad he couldn't wait for the signal. Ha-ha, that's the spirit I'm looking for, gents. And a little tear gas mighta burned the old peepers, but the job got done and the good guys won."

"Tear gas? I t'ought dat was Lister's breat'!" came a shout from the crowd, and the thugs erupted in laughter.

Haik had hid his face in shame at being singled out—they had no idea what he was really doing when he ran to Mr. Meadows. Haik wanted to contact Luigi right now and tell him he could solve half the city's problems if he just got six men with Tommy guns here at the garage and didn't stop shooting until no one was left standing, himself and the lion included. Haik looked at Lister. At the comment that came from the crowd and all the laughter that followed, the cocky grin disappeared and was replaced by a curling of his upper lip. His black eyes scanned. He had no humor, only a code of survival that put himself and what he wanted at the center of the universe. To see Lister embarrassed in front of a couple hundred men he felt smugly superior to was some sort of small consolation for all that had been destroyed over the weekend.

"Okay, men, that's all for this morning. Let's hit the trails and keep this operaton running ship shape. And, yes, Pelini, where are you, you stick around," commanded Bennett, and with that the crowd came alive and began to disperse, some pointing and gawking at the lion.

Haik waited, bumped and shouldered by the departing SD men. Bennett descended his overlook with Babe, followed by Cutty and Lister and the other hard guys. Haik made his way to him, but stopped cautiously just outside the range of the leash.

"Pelini," beamed the bow tied Bennett. "Every time I think you're an empty gas tank and forget about you, you go and do something.

I like how you took the lead this weekend. That's my boy. Way it's shaking out, you're gonna be in charge of some big doings in the future. Now, I told you a week ago or so about this job coming up. You remember?"

"Yes, sir," Haik replied with a nod.

He looked down at the lion, who appeared bored or drunk, his sparkling yellow-green eyes large and beautiful but ignorant and menacing. What if he drew his gun now? Everyone off guard, he could pop Bennett and Lister before anyone else drew, take out two maggots and let the others have him. Would it be worth it? No, he had to be patient. Gee-Gee had promised to bring people down. He would have to wait.

"Well, the gig starts bright and early in two weeks, confirmed through Mr. Ford himself. You go down to the Detroit Institute of Art at 8 a.m. sharp. You're gonna be met by some eggheads and a painter. Some big Mexican fella from what I hear. The thinking is, you look more like a spic than anyone else around here, so he'll feel comfortable, and you know your way around the city. What do you think, boys, should we have old Pelini here go by the name Pancho Villa Pelini for this gig?"

They all laughed on cue, but Babe the lion probably had a better idea of who this Pancho Vee-yah guy was than any of Bennett's hard guys.

"Now, your orders are simple. Whatever this Mexican joe wants, you get it. He needs a ride somewheres, you give him a ride. He wants something to eat, you take him to eat. He shits, you wipe his ass and powder his behind. He wants to play hide the salami, well, you know what to do. But, and here let me emphasize, *he is not to get too close to the workers*. Word is this spic is some kind of commie, red as red in the undershorts, and Mr. Ford doesn't need him putting ideas in the workers' heads. He can come in, paint, draw, play patty cake, whatever, but he keeps his distance from Mr. Ford's property, understand? Here, Cutty, give him fifty, here's fifty dollars advance toward expenses, get yourself some presentable clothes, you know, a shirt and tie and shoes and then swing by the office the Friday before the gig starts. Mr. Ford is really none too excited about this, but he wants his boy Edsel to quit whining about this artist guy and focus on making cars, so there's a lot on your shoulders, son. We can't have any problems or distractions, no red son-of-a-bitch shoveling his bull at the plant. You need a break in the evening, go over to Building B and find Nowitzki and he'll spell you, but you're the man we're countin' on. We copacetic?"

"Yes, sir, Mr. Bennett," Haik replied, pocketing the money and glancing over at Lister, who did not seem to like all this attention being lavished on an underling. If it made Lister jealous or uncomfortable, then Haik was all for it. Bennett then tugged at the lion's leash.

"So, what you think of my pussy, Pelini?" asked Bennett. Haik cocked his head in puzzlement. "My little kitty here, Babe? You wanna pet my little baby?"

Haik glanced down at the beast, which looked off distractedly. No, he didn't want to touch the lion. He wanted nothing to do with the beast, and even being in the same building with the lion made him uneasy.

"No offense, Mr. Bennett, but he looks like he might still be a little hungry," offered Haik, and Bennett let out a loud laugh, followed by his toadies.

"This dago slays me! You know that, Pelini, you're a real card! Now, seriously, go ahead and pet Babe. He wants you to pet him," said Bennett, which Haik heard as more of a command than an invitation.

Haik looked at Babe. He was big, his head reaching up well past Bennett's waist. He would take Haik's arm off in one snap of his jaws. Haik liked dogs, he tolerated cats, and that was about it for him with animals. Lions, they were a whole different story and best in a zoo or in the movie pictures wrestling with that new Tarzan guy, not Elmo Lincoln, the one in the new movie just out, Johnny Weissmuller, the big rig swimming champ.

"Go on, Pelini, pet Babe. I'm waiting," taunted Bennett, and Haik could detect a kind of evil amusement in Bennett's voice.

Haik looked at Babe, who was now staring at him with those golden green, entrancing eyes, his mouth slightly open.

"Go on, Pelini, let's see it," challenged Lister, throwing some gasoline onto the fire.

Haik wanted to chop Lister up and feed him piece by piece to Babe, but he had to focus on the situation at hand. No question, he would have to pet Babe; this had become a kind of test, one he could not back down from, and he'd have to pass. From what Haik knew of dangerous animals, the basics were simple. Move slow. Don't reach around behind the animal because it might think you're trying to put one over on it. Don't act scared even if you're scared shitless. He looked up again, and Bennett had him in his bullseye, waiting, waiting for Haik to answer the challenge.

"Hello Babe," Haik whispered softly, and then he began a half whisper, half childish attempt at song. "That's a nice lion. You want me to pet you? Huh? You want me to pet the pretty lion?"

Haik held out his hand, which fully extended was still about three feet away from Babe's disinterested face. He continued with his sing-songy supplication.

"...That's a pretty lion, Babe. Oh, my, you're a pretty lion. You want me to pet you? Huh? Babe want me to pet him?...."

Haik could feel that he was now the source of great amusement for everyone witnessing this spectacle. Even so, he was committed to following through. He could not back away, not with all these eyes on him. He did not like Babe—this was no pet but a toy to show off like a new car or a diamond ring, but this toy was born to maim and maul and not care a less. The more he hated Babe, the more Haik steeled himself to move forward, slowly, cautiously, but forward, closer to the beast. He extended his arm to its fullest length and his fingertips were now within sniffing distance of the lion. In some sense, it was not Babe's fault that he had an asshole like Bennett for an owner. It was less fair to judge the animal than the one who held his leash, and Babe probably didn't want to be in an oily car garage anymore than Haik wanted to be petting him. The lion regarded him with a cat's superiority, granting him the honor of his minute attention. Babe's head was three, maybe four or five times the size of a German Shepherd's, and he gave off a sweaty, hot animal's smell that repulsed Haik and made him want to piss himself right then and there.

"Go on, Pelini, we're all waiting. Babe's got a busy day ahead of him and ain't got time to be pussy-footin' around," teased Bennett.

Haik extended one more time and made contact with the top of Babe's long, flat snout. The hair was coarse and stiff. Haik made as gentle a scratching motion as he could, his eyes still locked tightly with the animal's.

"...that's a pretty baby. Oh, such a pretty lion. Babe likes Haik to pet him, don't he? Yeah, that's nice petting, isn't it? See, he's not afraid to touch the pretty lion..."

With that last line, Haik broke contact and stepped back, exhaled, flexed his hand once or twice, and immediately found the eyes of Lister. Did they catch the slip on his name? He surveyed the goon squad. Lister still wore his smirk, but his mouth was shut and that in itself was a small victory.

"Well, what'd ya think? Babe's not so scary, is he?" asked Bennett, beaming away and basking in the power afforded him by having a real live lion tethered at this side.

"No, not at all, Mr. Bennett. He's a real champ. A sweetheart," assured Haik. "Maybe Lister or one of the boys wants to give old Babe a little sugar. Go on boys, give it a go. Your turn."

Bennett enjoyed Haik's challenge, but the others did not seem too comfortable with it. Babe was a bundle of laughs when it was Haik's bloody stump of an arm they could see dangling from his mouth. Haik looked directly at Lister, who tried his best to evoke an aura of cool, maneuvering a toothpick in his smirking mouth, but nonetheless did not accept the offer.

"No, that's it, showtime's over, I've got work to do," chimed Bennett, breaking the stand-off before looking at Lister and the rest of Haik's audience. "Looks like Babe's not the only pussy here. Nice work, Pelini, and start gettin' yourself ready for the painter. Boys, let's get a wiggle on."

Bennett and his posse moved on, and Lister gave Haik a look of contempt that made Haik feel good inside. Haik watched Bennett and Babe disappear into his Victoria, heard the engines of the entourage flare, and gave one more cautious glance at the lion visible in Bennett's rear window. He couldn't wait to get to the glass house and away from this craziness. Would Orlin believe him when he told him that he had just scratched the nose of a real live Negro eating lion? At this point, anything that took his mind off of his misery was a welcome distraction.

Later that night after work, though, mourning still hung over their house. The funeral and all its emotions had become a smothering guest. Lu was distant, answering him in one and two word responses, and she hurt him, hurt him in a way only a woman could. Yes, Mr. Meadows was her father by blood, but he felt like a father to Haik as well. And underneath that tension, a new sense of mystery entered his world, and it unsettled him. He would be a father—what did that mean? A boy, a girl? What was it like to touch and hold a real baby? The care of his sisters had been left to his mother—it was tradition. But his own child, he wanted to be there for the child, holding it, dressing it, feeding it. He wanted to be a real father, but what that meant, he had no idea.

Most unsettling, though, was what Lu thought. Was she happy to become a mother again? Sure, she had to grieve for her father, but didn't the thought of a child, Haik's child, in some way help her to deal with her pain? Would it help her forgive him for whatever she thought he had done? From what Haik could gather, she was a month or more pregnant, although she wasn't showing a bit. He worried—he didn't want a child growing inside Lu when she was so filled with hate and anger and might somehow transfer those poisonous feelings to the unborn baby, but he had to tread lightly. He couldn't just command her to stop feeling what she felt. And she hadn't told anyone else, not even her mother, so Haik decided to follow suit—he would wait until *she* was ready to let others know. At home, she betrayed him no emotions. He would come into the house at night and find her there in the kitchen, setting food out to begin the evening meal. He washed up, and when he went to kiss her she would turn and offer him a cheek and no more. If his guilt ate at him in the days after Mr. Meadows died, Lu did nothing to slow this ravenous self-consumption.

The day before he was to meet the painter, Haik was issued a brand spanking new '32 Ford V-8 Sedan breezer complete with rear suicide doors. He was allowed to take it home and leave the Whippet at the garage, and he took Charlie for a long ride in the country with the top down even though it was freezing. The next morning he was to meet the painter, so he and Orlin drove in separately; who knew what this new job would entail or when he would be home. Before he took off, they spoke in the driveway.

"Good luck, Haik."

"Yeah, thanks."

"So who exactly is this guy you goin' to be rollin' around?"

"I dunno. They say he's a painter. A Mexican."

"What's he painting?"

"Dunno. I guess some of the buildings. Maybe he paints cars. I try not to ask too much, you know."

"Yeah, I know. Hey, this stuff here at home, with Lu, give it time, man. Ain't nothing you can do now but what you doin'. Be kind to Charlie, help her out, and she'll come around."

Haik looked off across the road to the stand of birches.

"Yeah, I guess. I just wish, I wish I didn't feel like every time I walked through that damn door, I wish I didn't feel like she thought I was the one who killed her father. It's killin' me, Orlin. I loved her father, too, you know, more than my own. I…"

"Haik, man, we all hurt. You're a good man. You couldn't a done nothin'. Just be strong. She'll come around. I'll make sure Kina talks to her."

Haik looked out again across the road. She'd come around. He'd done all he could. It wasn't his fault. Just keep doing what he was doing. Did he really believe any of that? Orlin was being a friend, but he doubted every last word.

"Thanks, O. I'll see you when I see you."

They both got in their rigs and were off. They rolled their way down Mound until Haik jaunted his way southwest, turning onto Caniff, taking it to Oakland, turning again at Holbrook until it intersected with Woodward. It was a drive that brought back memories: on Caniff, he passed Greeley, where Vahram caught his bullet at the Grand Trunk rail yard; on Oakland, he thought of the Bernsteins and Mr. Goldberg and their summers on the high seas of the Detroit River; and on Woodward, he thought of how it led on south to Grand Circus Park—you could map Haik's whole history in America on just a few of these streets. Down Woodward, the museum loomed large and solid off to his left, and once just past it he turned left onto Farnsworth and parked against the far curb.

It was April now, but it was Detroit, and the bright downtown sun was tempered with a brisk spring breeze. Haik left his car and hit the two long, shallow sets of steps that led to three enormous stone archways into the museum. The building was impressive, and here he was, Haik Pehlivanian, walking into a place of culture. He pulled on the massive center door and entered into another new world, a world as fantastic and as mystifying as River Rouge had been when he first laid eyes on it.

Inside, he thought he might be in some sort of castle where a king could live. Everything was stone and the ceilings reached up overhead like a church's. Long hallways opened up to the left and the right, and he could make out statues of naked people doing different things and even suits of armor with big long swords. Haik felt like he should kneel and cross himself before these important objects. As he gazed about in wonder, a small, sharply dressed woman approached him.

"Can I help you?" she inquired, and Haik could hear years of education in her voice.

"Ah, yeah, I'm here, to, to meet the painter. Mr. Ford sent me over."

"Oh splendid! Mr. Ford just arrived himself and the orientation has already commenced. I'm Miss Flora Parks. So, you'll be chaperoning Mr. Rivera then. Delightful. Follow me, they're just over here in the garden court."

Boy, the words she used—they were supposed to be English, but Haik had never heard some of them before, "orpilation" and what was the other one, "shappertoning." He was under strict orders to not screw this assignment up, but what was he supposed to do if people didn't use understandable language? All he could think as he followed the woman past big colorful paintings and more statues was that this Mexican fellow better speak English or he'd have to ask Bennett for a replacement.

They finally entered an immense room and for a moment Haik thought he was outdoors; he looked up to discover the ceiling was a grid of criss-crossed rectangular windows that allowed sunlight to pour into the giant room. The floor itself shined like it was coated in ice, with all kinds of fancy inlaid designs—just the floor had to be worth a fortune. There was also a fountain in the very center burbling with real running water—incredible. On the walls the carved heads of bearded men frowned down at Haik next to fancy pillars and dolled up inset windows. It was pretty, but the stone walls were so white that nothing stood out but the floor and burbling fountain. Just ahead, four men and a tiny woman that Haik thought might be a clown, dressed in a wildly colored costume, bright ribbons in her hair, all stood talking. Their speech moved at such a lightning pace and over so many strange subjects that Haik could only stand dumb and bear witness.

"...Miss Bloch and Mr. Dimitroff are already hard at work, as are Mr. Niendorf and Mr. Sanchez Flores, and we actually have too many people who want to assist in the process. Mr. Pablo Davis is here from Philadelphia to help as well. We also have some talented individuals from Detroit who are here at your service, Miss Winifred Grindley, Mr. Frank Stone, and Mr. Bob Rugovina. As you can see, Mr. Wight has already applied the first two coats of plaster..."

"Quite good. Mr. Halberstadt and Lord Hastings have arrived with me and my darling Frida, so my comrades are all present. We will be quite ready to begin our labors. I find no reason the scaffolding cannot begin to be constructed, yet I think we should hold off until I've done my preparatory sketches. Yes, no scaffolding yet. Halberstadt is the craftsman on scaffolding—he knows my specifications for what is needed."

"And we have three tons of dry lime packed in rubber bags ready and waiting for your go ahead..."

"Yes, splendid, but I must have time for sketching. Meticulous sketching. I must learn everything about my subject. I must delve into the heart of the machine, no? The machine, as I envision it, is not an enemy of the worker and the worker is not its slave. No, the relationship is symbiotic and mutually sustaining. One liberates the other as the other brings it to life. And steel, nothing in this city happens without steel. But I must experience this firsthand before I can convey it. The machine and the man who works it will become one on these walls. They will point to a future where common men are delivered from crippling slavery to the dirt they toil in."

"You did say 'walls,' Mr. Rivera. Ah, I would just like to remind you that we have only enough funds to compensate you for portions of the north and south walls, roughly $100 American dollars per square yard for a total of $10,000. This was clearly stipulated in the contract we sent to you. I only wish we had the funds to fill every bit of all four walls. What an honor that would be, but, well, unfortunately, financially, it simply isn't feasible for us. Is this, ah, agreeable?"

"Actually, no, this is not agreeable. No, not at all. This garden court must be brought to life—it cannot live with but a few portions of wall breathing. I will do all the walls, all that is paintable."

"But Mr. Rivera…"

"Don't worry, my friend, I'm not petitioning for more money. You have generously agreed to pay for supplies and for the work of my assistants. Quite honestly, I have always had to pay them myself from my own remuneration. I must paint all the walls and you do what you must with your money."

"Well, might I say, Mr. Rivera, this is a generous offer. But I simply cannot allow you to work without fair and proper compensation. My father will probably give me a tongue-lashing, no doubt, but, on my own conscience, I can't allow you to work unrewarded. What you are about to do for this city and its people is simply far too important. They need beauty, Mr. Rivera, they need hope. I will look into securing further funding if you choose to expand the project."

"No, there is no 'if,' Mr. Ford. These walls will live and breathe and speak, all of them. I cannot allow anything less than a complete vision. You haven't brought me here from San Francisco to merely whisper a few idle thoughts. No, you have brought me here to declare a truth, a new truth heralding a future in which the machine is subsumed in the creative spirit of men, their intellect, their imaginative power. My gravest concern, Mr. Ford, is the walls. Do as you will with finances."

"Oh, I'm sure you'll find plenty of space for creation. This north wall, for instance, offers tremendous possibilities…"

"Dr. Valentiner, my good friend, gross space is not the issue. I have covered walls in Mexico that have ten-fold the surface I propose to toil on here. Look—look about you. What do you see here? All about, Italian baroque. Why have you tinseled your walls with such, such, what shall I say, *horrorosa*? What does the elaborate, superfluous snobbery of baroque Italy have to do with the industrial age of a mighty city such as Detroit? These pilasters, windows, air grates, these abominable satyrs, this ridiculous fountain—everywhere I am to create, a break here, something to jump around there. I am not a sportsman leaping about. I am not here to compete with grocery store Italian imitation. But more than these nuisances of architecture is this stylistic confrontation I face. These ornaments, these outdated relics, they do not speak the truth of what I know of your city, and yet there they are, rearing their foolish baroque faces everywhere I turn."

"Well, Mr. Rivera, when the museum was built we didn't anticipate being able to secure the talents of an artist of you eminence to create frescos on these walls. When Mr. Cret designed the building, it was originally envisioned..."

"Dr. Valentiner, I am a modest artisan, a craftsman, much like the workers of your city who build these magnificent automobiles. I am not an 'artist,' a creature enamored of these redundant exaggerations. Look at this, this spiraling silliness all about the walls, it belongs in an Italian bordello, not here in your city's museum. Could a working man from one of your factories, Mr. Ford, come into this grand room and feel the least bit comfort or sense of place or welcome in this setting?"

"Well..."

"You, you there, my good man, come join us for an instant."

Haik was now aware of being directly addressed by the mountain of a man leading the discussion, a dark skinned giant with large, oddly spaced eyes who wore work clothes stained with dust and splattered paint. He looked like he could have stepped from Building B at River Rouge, dressed in worn workman's pants and coat, but the way he spoke, the expressions he used, the musical nature of his accented voice, all put Haik into a kind of trance.

"Ah, me, sir?"

"Exactly, my friend, you. Come here. We need to talk to you. Your name?"

"Ah, Hank. Hank Pelini."

"Ah, *salve, fratello*."

"Um, no, my name is Pelini, not Frateldo."

"Ha, my apologies, good friend, are you not Italian?"

"Well, yeah, I guess I am, but I'm, I'm not exactly from Italy. Ah, my parents, they came from Italy."

"And you retain none of your mother tongue?"

"Ah, my mother, sir? Her, her tongue, it's fine."

Everyone in the group smiled.

"He means, you don't speak Italian."

"Oh. No, no, I don't speak no Italian. My parents, they, ah, they didn't let me and my brothers and sisters speak no Italian. They, ah, they wanted us to learn American."

"Ah, so it is—how America wholly consumes all it takes into its swollen belly. Now, let me guess, you have worked in the auto industry, have you not?"

"Uh, yes, yes sir, I have."

"Actually, this gentleman is here to act as Mr. Rivera's chaperone," offered the smartly dressed woman who had brought Haik to this baffling meeting.

The contingent looked Haik over before the man the big one had called Mr. Ford, a kindly looking man in a tailored double breasted suit, chimed in again. Haik was dressed nicely, sporting a new suitcoat and tie and spiffy wingtips.

"Ah, yes, thank you, Miss Parks. I told Mr. Bennett to send only the most agreeable chap to chaperone Mr. Rivera," he said in a gentle, thoughtful voice. "Perhaps we can all introduce ourselves. In addition to Miss Parks, I'm Edsel Ford, this is Dr. William Valentiner, the director of the Institute, Mr. Edgar Whitcomb, director of the Detroit News and a magnanimous supporter of the arts, and Mr. Albert Kahn, the most prodigious architect building in the city today and, might I say, a brilliant artist in his own right, and, of course, our honored guests, Mr. Diego Rivera, who will soon be transforming the garden court here, and his gifted wife, Mrs. Frida Kahlo de Rivera. And your name again?"

"Pelini, Hank Pelini."

Haik made a point of shaking each man's hand. The American men's hands were soft and unthreatening in Haik's thick, muscled paws. He was amazed to find that Rivera's hand, despite being connected to such a massive man, was chubby but his fingers were tiny, delicate even, while the clown woman's hand was so dainty Haik thought of it as a child's or even a small bird's claw.

"As I was saying earlier, my good man Hank, please tell me. You have worked in the factories of Mr. Ford, yes?" continued the brown giant.

"Yes, I have, Mr. Rivera. Disassembly, a little spell in stamping, all different stuff."

"Very well. As I can tell from simply grasping your hand, you are a true member of the proletariat. Indeed, only a worker could possess such a grip. Now, look about you. All around, the walls, the windows, the doors, the fountain, everything. What affinity if any do you feel for your present surroundings?"

Haik was stumped. He did not know what the word "afinny" meant—to him, it sounded like "funny," so he decided to play along and not sound stupid.

"Yes, I guess it is quite funny. How it looks. All these different things."

"Ah, you see!" bellowed the giant. "Can a true proletarian find the least connection to this ornate foppery? This fraudulent *feismo*? No, of course not, not in the least. You see, we must make this a place where my good man Hank can come with his wife—you are married, no?—and his friends of the working class and their children and find sanctuary and peace and an expression of who they are and how they live. This is *public* space, not the inner sanctum of some Florentine lord who hoards and shelters his gifts from the world. Pah! This will be a place for the *people* of this physical city, not the privileged. These walls will be here for the people or they will not be at all."

"Oh, my darling *carasapo*! How you lecture! All this time you could be sketching. I say, *maestro*, a big shit on you for talking so much," shot the tiny woman, who, Haik could not help but notice, sported a set of eyebrows that met smack in the middle of her forehead.

All stood stunned at her bold vulgarity. Had this little elf really said what they just heard her say? Her clothing blazed, and her neck was surrounded in large, colorful wooden beads, which also hung from her earrings. For someone so small, she spoke *large*, Haik thought. He did not understand all she said, but he could understand that she was not a person to be brushed aside or taken lightly.

"Ah, *mi amor*, such a tongue, but you are always right! You see, gentlemen, such is the curse of being married to *un demonio oculto*—a hidden little devil who does not know how to be right and at the same time quiet! My Frida, *mi palomita*, is absolutely correct. I must get to work while my mind is alive with ideas. My friend Hank, are you ready to take me?"

"Absolutely, Mr. Rivera," Haik shot in on cue, careful not to let his mind wander in all this foreign talk. He had to sense his cues until he could learn to decipher some of what these people were saying.

"Allow me to gather my sketchbook and drawing utensils. I won't be but a moment. Gentlemen, you must excuse my sudden brusqueness, but the muse is calling. My *chiquita*, will you join me on this first excursion?" he asked Frida, addressing the sparrow of a woman.

"Ah, *Dieguito*, I am feeling a need to rest. It was a long trip. I will accompany you tomorrow."

"Are you feeling under the weather, madam?" inquired Edsel Ford, deep concern in his voice.

"Thank you, Mr. Ford, but I am with child and, some days, exhaustion comes quickly. I am fine."

Haik could see no evidence that this woman was pregnant—she appeared barely able to carry the weight of her jewelry and brightly trimmed blouse and long skirt and nothing more.

"I will make sure Mrs. Rivera is taken to her quarters and food brought to her," Dr. Valentiner, a genial, balding man, assured Rivera.

"Most excellent. Mr. Pelini, I will join you in short order. Gentlemen, it has been my honor and I am flattered by your kind generosity thus far. I trust that our joint labor will yield something that captures the true spirit of the people of your city," said Rivera, and they all shook hands and exchanged final pleasantries.

"Mr. Pelini, I'll have a word with you while Mr. Rivera readies himself," said Ford politely.

They waited for all the assembled dignitaries to move on their way before Mr. Edsel Ford took Haik aside for a private chat.

"Pelini," Ford began, an earnest look on his face, "I can't impress upon you how important your job is right now. To the point, my father doesn't care for Mr. Rivera. He's been made aware of a none-too-flattering portrait Mr. Rivera did of him in the Education Building in Mexico. My father has insisted that Harry Bennett provide the chaperone, and, despite my reservations, I have had no choice but to comply. He doesn't want Mr. Rivera to get too many ideas about the workers, what they really think and feel about the work they do. It may not seem like it, but my father has many fears, and this painter, Mr. Rivera, he may say some things with his paintings that my father doesn't necessarily agree with. He doesn't think much of this whole project or painting in general, unless it's finding a cheaper or stronger or faster drying paint for an automobile, and he will never endorse what is happening and will happen here at the museum. With that said, though, I am personally counting on you to make sure Mr. Rivera is treated with the utmost attention and courtesy, and anything he wants to see or hear or witness, you must gain him unfettered access and at all junctures intercede on his behalf regardless of my father or Mr. Bennett. My gravest fear was that there wasn't a man amongst Bennett's army that possessed the sense of courtesy and decorum required of this situation."

Ford's hand was at his chin as he paused to look directly at Haik. Again, Haik did not know what all he was being told, "the core numb" and "inner seeds" and "feathered cysts" and "uckmosses" in particular. He could gather that, basically, what Mr. Ford wanted was Haik to not be an asshole and treat Mr. Rivera right, and Haik had every intention of living up to that.

"Mr. Ford, sir, I'll treat Mr. Rivera like my own father. I think I understand what you're worried about, but, well, I'm not like the usual guy in the Service Department. I never been in jail, I don't gamble, I never pointed a gun at nobody, and, well, to tell you the God's honest truth, I actually didn't really want to be in the SD in the first place, it just, it just kind of happened. Whatever Mr. Rivera needs, he'll get and he'll never leave my sight," assured Haik, hoping he had said the right things in the right way.

"Very well," said Ford, still pondering the whole situation. "You seem a decent enough man. Let's leave it at this: I'm counting on you. And if there's anything you need or if any situation arises that you have questions about, you see me before you see Harry Bennett or my father. Understood? Here, here is my card with my direct phone line. If you need anything, anything at all, contact me immediately."

"Understood, Mr. Ford. That's a promise."

Ford handed Haik an envelope with what he called "expense money" inside. Haik grinned and bowed slightly—he was starting to like this job and this painter already.

Within moments, Rivera had returned, smiling and sad eyed at the same time, a man who in his largeness seemed to engulf the museum itself. They both shook hands with Mr. Ford and bid him good-bye, and Haik was again struck at what a kind man Edsel Ford seemed, not the weakminded fool his father had made him out to be when he talked to Harry Bennett at Bennett's office. Haik took Rivera's wooden box and led him out to the car and opened the trunk for him to put the rest of his artist materials, then opened his door for him. His parents had taught him well in the customs of politeness even if his life now gave him little opportunity to actually practice them.

"Now, the journey begins," declared Rivera, and they were off to River Rouge. On the way, the painter pointed out various buildings whose architecture appealed to him and others that appalled him. They talked about their wives, both of them sharing the status of early pregnancy. Rivera said that both he and Haik were filled with "infanticipation," and Haik smiled as if he know what the painter was talking about. Rivera was fascinated that Lu had a son when Haik married her and was actually older than he was. The mixing of the ethnicities, Irish and Italian, intrigued him, and he informed Haik that he himself had fathered a daughter with a Russian woman. Rivera jovially commented that they shared a great deal in common despite their obvious surface differences.

Something about this painter made Haik want to tell him the truth, that he was not Italian but Armenian, a fact that burned in his gut, that his name was Haik Pelivanian and not Hank Pelini, but the time was not right—too much was uncertain. Had he said too much to Edsel Ford at the museum? Should he have admitted to a total stranger that he didn't actually want to be a SD man? Would Edsel tell his father who would then tell Bennett? Haik had the definite impression that Edsel did not care for Bennett, and Bennett had done nothing to stand up to Edsel's father the morning Haik met the elder Ford. He was probably safe, but the past two months had taught him to trust nothing and no one.

"So, how much of the plant are you going to paint, Mr. Rivera?" Haik asked, more out of politeness than actual curiosity.

He was fairly certain at some point he'd be handed a paint brush and be forced into helping Rivera. Maybe he'd get to build the scaffolding Rivera was talking about or maybe he'd be the one that had to haul cans of paint to the factory. And the kind of money they were talking—$10,000—was this guy going to paint the plant in pure gold?

"Ah, my good Hank!" Rivera laughed, but Haik was unaware of having told a joke. "You think I am to be painting the River Rouge? The factories?"

"Well, I guess that's what I was thinking," Haik returned, unaware why that idea was so hilarious.

"Oh, no, no, no, I not that type of painter. I will be painting frescos," Rivera said, and he must have detected a look of nonrecognition on Haik's face. "You know, how do you say, murals, large pictures, great cartoons. And they will be at the Institute, in the garden court, not at the River Rouge."

It still made no sense to Haik. Why go to River Rouge if he was going to be painting at the museum? Why not just start right at the museum? He must be some kind of fancy artist painter, Haik deduced. But still, why not just start drawing the flowers and rainbows and apples and fruit bowls and kings in their capes on fancy horses right there on the spot instead of going off to a place where they made cars? Whatever. He was a driver and a host and his orders were to do whatever Rivera wanted and that's what he was going to do no matter how little sense it made.

Once inside the compound, Rivera explained that he had already been on a brief overview tour with the honchos the day before, and there were specific sites he wanted to see and become more acquainted with.

"This structure of glass, I would like a closer look. You know, Mr. Kahn, the man we met at the museum, I respect him a great deal. Much of this is his work. These buildings, they are his canvas. I've seen many factories, great rectangles of lifeless cinderblocks, but Mr. Kahn, he truly is an artist. *This* is what I must show the world, the possibilities of human intellect and creativity to transform, to deliver…"

Haik was lost in a barrage of words and ideas he could not follow on his best day. What the painter was talking about seemed to have absolutely nothing to do with sprucing up the walls at the museum. Despite this, he was glad Rivera had chosen the glass house; he would make a point of introducing him to Orlin. They parked and Haik helped Rivera retrieve his drawing materials from the trunk. He didn't have the heart to break it to Rivera, but he wouldn't find any flowers or fruit trees in the glass house—he hoped he wouldn't be too disappointed once he entered.

Once inside, though, Rivera looked about, smiling, wide-eyed, taking in all before him. Without a word, he readied his materials and began to draw. He moved slowly, like some great dinosaur, but before Haik knew it he was off, inspecting some kilns and the ribbon conveyer.

"Amazing," Rivera finally said. "Truly an accomplishment. And this glass, this is not typical sheet glass, no?"

"No," said Haik, confused by what Rivera was doing and welcoming the opportunity to sound smart for once. "My brother in law, he works here. They laminate this stuff now. Laminate. That means they, like, do stuff to the glass. They put on this like stuff between two layers of glass and laminate it, you know, stick it together. You can't even see the stuff is there, but it is. That way, it's not like back in the old days. Back then, the glass breaks and you're looking at a face full of slivers. They say a pal of Mr. Ford's, old Mr. Ford, Henry Ford, he was in an accident and he got all chopped up by the glass that broke and that's why Mr. Ford invented this new stuff. This way, you get in a crack up and the windshield or side glass stays together and you're safe. You put a rubber gasket all around this new kind of glass and put it in the frame, you're good to go. You couldn't be safer if you was sitting on your living room sofa."

"Yes, truly a wonder. Amazing what can be accomplished with a spirited application of science," gasped Rivera. "But, this building itself, it is mostly glass. No incongruity here, making glass in a house made of glass. This is the unity of conception that marvels me. Yes, a marvel."

Rivera appeared to be speaking English but Haik couldn't make heads or tails of what he was saying—maybe it was a kind of special Mexican English. He watched as Rivera went off into his world again, sketching and looking and sketching some more. Haik excused himself so he could find Orlin, who might be able to explain things better. He was nowhere to be seen, and when Haik inquired he was told that he had been shipped over to the foundry. What was going on with Orlin? He was a stand up worker, never missed no matter how sick he might be or tired he was. Like Haik, he was a big six and could outwork a crew of men. That was one thing they had all learned about Ford's $5 a day—you only got the full $5 if you met your daily "quota," whether it was doors bolted to a car, windshields cut and packed, radiators attached, crankshafts balanced, whatever, and Orlin was a man who made sure he maxed every payday. What Haik and Orlin had learned about working at Fords was that there was always a catch to every deal you ever made and little if anything was what people said it was on the surface.

After more than an hour at glass, Rivera wanted to go directly to Building B where the main assembly line flowed. Outside, he was struck by the immenseness of the structure. How many of Mexico's or Russia's largest factories could all be tucked snugly inside this one incredible building? Yes, it was truly a marvel, and you could almost see his mind swirling with possibilities. Again, no flowers or fruit, but if it didn't bother the painter it wasn't going to bother Haik.

"You see," said Haik inside, pointing to the flow of parts and pieces all around them, shouting over the din of construction, "nothing ever stops here. Right when you need to put on doors, there they are, right there, the worker just has to pluck one off the belt there and rig it to the body. The worker don't even got to walk nowhere or hardly move his feet. Over there, further down, when they need an engine, it's all ready to go and they swing it down on them chains and set it onto the frame and secure it down. Exactly when you need something, there it is, ready to be added, belt high, grab it and stash it, bolt it down. When all the insides are ready, then the chassis are lowered over everything and it starts to look like a car you could drive. In the old days, back in Highland Park, the workers would all be in a group and put together their own cars one at a time, and it took, I don't know, my father-in-law told me about 12 hours to do just one, which they thought was pretty quick. Hell, today, it don't even take hardly an eyeblink and you got yourself a whole car."

"I must spend many days here," Rivera mused, enraptured as he walked here and there, bent, peeked, mused, smiled, drew and drew and drew.

Haik was tempted to look over his shoulder to see what exactly he was doing, but he was too short and thought it might be rude, like sneaking a taste of something a cook was working on before it was all the way done. After several hours, Rivera seemed to be just getting started. Instead of growing tired, he was energized by what he was seeing, and Haik took him where he wanted to go and explained as best he could how things worked. They ended up staying about ten hours, and only decided to leave after Haik reminded Rivera of the time.

"Now, my eyes feed my hands. When I actually begin the frescos, the hand will feed the eye," he explained as they drove from the Rouge, smiling, somewhere in his mind a picture of the future he would soon create.

Orlin, Haik, Charlie, Arkina, and Lu sat at the dinner table, sharing a picnic ham, boiled potatoes, and spiced rice and tomatoes.

"It ain't right."

Haik pondered Orlin's words and thought of the future. Now that it was April, they had begun the process of starting their garden, digging and turning over the ground, soon to be followed by planting, weeding, growing their own tomatoes, peppers, watermelons, and cucumbers. This is what Haik had envisioned, a place where they depended on no one. Once he got everything squared away, he would raise pigs and chickens and keep some cows for milk—they would not need anyone to survive. Surrounded by trees, they had plenty of firewood for their stove and fireplace, and water from the well and down at the river. What more did they need? There might just come a day when Haik could tell Fords to get bent, to take their paychecks and assembly line and Service Department and guns and clubs and stuff it, good riddance, nice knowing you. Now was not that time.

"Who told you this?" asked Haik, addressing his brother-in-law.

"Who you think? Hoarseman. Hidin' behind his badge. 'We got to make some changes,' he say. 'We made a mistake sending you to the glass house. Besides, you were just filling in anyways until we could hire some wh...uh, more qualified workers. Now we get you where you need to be.' I say, 'Something wrong with my work? I ain't fast enough? Something don't get done right?' And he just get that damn smile on his face and say, 'When your people run a complex like this, boy, you can work any job you please, but from here on out, you are working in the foundry. After the visit from Sociology, you're lucky you got a job at all, darky'."

Orlin perfectly imitated Hoarseman's fussy, impatient delivery, but his anger came through.

"He really say that? What the hell that fool from the Sociology Department got to do with nothing?" asked Haik.

"Plenty. Sociology got plenty to do with me gettin' the bum's rush outta the glass house. 'Your people,' he say. Who the hell 'my people?' Ain't we all Americans? Hell, everything gone wrong for me since that sonna-bitch Billingsly come over."

"It's okay, O," Arkina said, patting his hand.

He was right, though. The week before Orlin was moved out of the glass house, they had a visit scheduled with a member of Ford's Sociology Department, Mr. Ward Billingsly. This was the new trend—someone from this mysterious department, more secretive than the Service Department, would call on all the workers to do some type of information gathering right at their home. Statistics, they were told, statistics and data needed by Mr. Ford. What this had to do with making cars, Haik couldn't guess, but it was required and it was just best to play along. Billingsly came into their house, wearing his shiny star badge, telling everyone he was on the "Star Roll," a boot-licker like Hoarseman who earned a straight up salary and didn't have to make a quota with stoolies looking over his shoulder all the time ready to bust him like all the common workers on the line. Billingsly arrived before Orlin got home from the plant, and immediately he went about asking questions, writing things down in a leather-bound notebook.

"I don't sense the odor of cigarettes about. Does anyone in the household use tobacco products?" he inquired, pushing his wire-rimmed spectacles up on his long, thin red nose.

Haik and Lu sat across from him at the kitchen table. They looked at each other before Haik answered.

"No, we don't got no money for extras like cigs," said Haik, cooperating but not really understanding what business it was of anyone if he smoked or not.

Back when Vahram was alive, they smoked when they could to kill the cravings for food in their bellies, but Haik only smoked now if offered a butt from someone else's stash at a speakeasy. There was no smoking on the premises at the Rouge anyways, so it was best just to leave that habit alone.

"Very good, very good indeed," commented Billingsly, recording his findings in his book.

Haik again looked at Lu, unsure of what to make of this odd man.

"Now, let's look at diet. Diet is the foundation of your ability to work. A poor or lacking diet, and your work efficiency will suffer," lectured Billingsly, seemingly to himself.

Haik looked at him intently. No way in the world Billingsly could even lift a monkey wrench, so whatever he was eating obviously wasn't worth a damn.

"Let's see, in the morning, Mrs. Pelini, what do you serve this hard-working man?"

Billingsly smiled, and there was a noticeable gap in between his two top front teeth. Haik wanted to laugh and just throw this bird out of their house, but he was on the Star Roll and that would be big trouble. No, they'd answer his questions and put up with whatever comments and faces he made.

"Well," said Lu, looking over at Haik with uncertainly, not quite sure if what she said might be taken the wrong way. "Well, I make Haik, ah, Hank, I make him some toast and eggs and if we have any bacon I make him some of that too."

She peered deeply into Billingsly, who took a handkerchief from his coat pocket and blew his nose violently before writing more in his notebook.

"Any oatmeal?" he finally said.

"Well..." Lu began.

"She makes me what I like. I only like oatmeal if we got some honey or maple syrup, and we don't got that too often," said Haik, trying to rescue his wife from whatever Billingsly was implying.

"Ha-ha, you may like those foods, friend, but hearty whole grains are the coal that fire the human stove," chirped Billingsly, and Haik did not care for his superior tone.

What kind of idiot would eat coal? This guy was an odd duck, to say the least, and so it went, question after question until he got onto a subject that truly puzzled Haik.

"So, let me just check my data here, yes, let's see, hmmm, there we go," mumbled Billlingsly, off in his world of numbers. "Now, let me clarify here, you have one child, a son, named Charles, aged eight, is that correct?"

"Yes," Haik and Lu said in unison.

"No other children?"

"No. I'm with child now, though," offered Lu, hoping the answer was one that reflected well on Haik and her.

"Pregnant, yes, let's see," mused Billingsly, writing furiously in his little book. "Hmmm, eight years since your last child...."

"Well, you see...," began Lu, but Haik would not tolerate such prying. He raised his arm up and across, as if to shield Lu from the question.

"Yes, eight years, that's right, so what of it?" asked Haik.

Billingsly smiled again, as if this were not just his job but also his ultimate form of amusement.

"Oh, nothing, nothing at all. But, with such a lengthy gap between children, I must say, I must delve further into this situation. Can you tell me, have your, your, ah, shall we say, 'relations' been, ah, 'normal' throughout this eight year period?"

Haik winced at Billingsly. What exactly was he getting at?

"Our 'relations?' We're still married, ain't we? Our relations been fine," assured Haik, and Billingsly once more smiled, nudging the spectacles back up onto the bridge of his nose.

"Indeed, you've been married. That's exactly my point. Perhaps you've been employing some method of preventing the expansion of the size of your family," Billingsly retorted.

"I work at Fords, I don't employ nobody, and we're all the size we need to be," explained Haik, trying to make some sense of what Billingsly was getting at.

Before Billingsly could answer, Orlin's car could be heard pulling into the drive.

"Oh, expecting guests?" asked the inquisitor, trying to sound cordial.

"No, that's Arkina's husband, Orlin," explained Lu.

"Arkina?"

"Haik's, ah, Hank's sister. She lives with us with her husband, Orlin. We're all family," said Lu, and Billingsly looked down into his book and consulted some papers he had folded up inside.

"Yes, yes indeed, here it is, that's what they meant when they said I'd be doing a double tonight," murmured Billingsly, off in his own world. "Yes, by Jove, I've got it. Orlin Cutright, right here, works in glass, yes, I'll be doing his survey tonight as well. Very good, very good indeed."

The front door cracked open and Orlin entered. He knew they would be having a visitor, but, like Haik, he was not exactly sure what the purpose of this visit was about.

"Boy howdy, I'd bet dollars to doughnuts he works with coal!" chuckled Billingsly.

Orlin looked at Billingsly quizzically before taking off his work boots at the door.

"Orlin, this is Mr. Ward Billingsly here from the Sociology Department," said Lu, a slight coolness in her voice, introducing their unwanted guest.

Billingsly arose, and Orlin stepped forward to shake his hand.

"Pleased to meet you, but my word, my good man, go wash up first and then we'll get down to the business of our meeting," smiled Billingsly.

Orlin pulled back his hand and looked over at Haik and Lu. Arkina entered the kitchen from the back door, coming in from hanging some laundry out on the line in the back yard. She kissed Orlin and then noticed the stranger.

"Kina, this is Mr. Billingsly from Fords," Lu explained. "He's here to ask us some questions."

"Oh," said Arkina, a sweet person of few words.

Orlin washed up at the sink, scrubbing his face and hands and forearms and drying off with a hand towel before rejoining the others at the dinner table. Billingsly gave him the most peculiar look, his mouth slightly agape in a pose somewhere between disbelief and indignation.

"You, you're Orlin Cutright?" he asked, an odd uneasiness in his voice.

"Yes, pleased to meet you," offered Orlin, extending his hand, which Billingsly grasped with a hand similar in consistency to a dead fish from Eastern Market.

"You, you're married to Mr. Pelini's sister?" Billingsly ventured, incredulous.

"Yes, this is my wife right here," Orlin responded, taking Arkina's hand. Billingsly began scribbling away furiously in his book.

"And, you, you all live here together, under the same roof, all of you here together?" continued Billingsly, his pencil poised to continue the assault on the pages before him.

"That's right, all of us, here, together, under one roof. Look up there, at the roof, there's only one," Haik interjected, laying it all out plain and clear for their guest.

Billingsly sat dumbfounded before he made some last notations.

"Very well then, very good, very good, I must be getting on," he replied, and began assembling all his papers and collecting his overcoat and hat.

"Don't you wanna know what Orlin eat for breakfast? Huh, Mr. Billingsly? Well I'll tell you. When Lu makes me eggs and toast, she makes Orlin eggs and toast too. We eat together. Off the same plates. Drink coffee out the same cups. Use the same knives and forks and spoons."

The gap-toothed smile had disappeared from his face and his feigned friendliness was gone.

"None of that information is necessary. Trust me, I have all the information I need to make a full report of what I've seen here."

At the door, he bowed slightly, gave a fearful look at both Haik and Orlin, turned the handle, and was gone. They could hear his engine start and his wheels roll away, and they were all relieved to be rid of this foolish man.

"Ain't nothing been right at the Rouge for me since that pencil neck come here," said Orlin as he picked at his dinner. "It's like they punishing me for something they seen here."

"It's okay, O," Arkina tried to soothe.

"No, it ain't okay. I had me a good job I was good at and now every time I blow my damn nose it's like I blowing out a mountain a coal dust out my lungs. And I'm pushing a damn broom, like I'm some kind a slave. Now we down to $4 a day. 'Depression hit everyone,' say

Hoarseman. 'Even a great man like Henry Ford.' Shit, you bet he ain't missin' no meals or wearin' last year's shoes. Shit, he talk about 'your people.'"

"Your people right here," said Haik. "Everybody right here at this table. We're our people. We're our own people. Hoarseman and everybody else can get bent."

"You know what about the foundry? Everybody else there black too. Hoarseman say, 'Your skin is more suited to these conditions.' I says, 'What conditions those?' 'The heat, of course,' he say, like I'm suppose to understand exactly what he mean. Why don't he just say it: 'You niggers belong in the jungle.' I suppose he want me to carry a spear around, too. Bullshit…"

"Language," suggested Arkina, taking Orlin's hand.

"Huh? Oh, I'm sorry. Charlie, I shouldn't a said that. Lu, I'm sorry."

"You're upset, Orlin. No harm done," responded Lu, looking down at her plate.

She was her distant self, as if she were here in the house with everyone and at the same time somewhere else. To cope with his wife's absence, Haik had taken to going out behind the barn after dinner and chopping wood. He'd pull some dead trees out of the woods and drag them in, then go to work busting them up. Where else could he channel his isolation? He brought the ax down without break, stacking close to two full cords of wood for the house. He missed the physicality of disassembly and stamping. He missed being so exhausted that his mind was clear and he could just focus on simple pleasures, warm tea, fresh bread, the sensation of Lu's skin. Now, his mind was always too full, full of things he wished were not there and could not get rid of.

"My grand daddy was a slave and my pop come north and left me and my momma and my brothers and sisters to fend on our own. Right when I make it, now I'm just a slave again. Got me moppin' the floors down and sweepin' up dirt. Foreman say, 'We do more'n 6,000 tons a iron a day, boy, we got to keep things spic and span.' Like I'm supposed to think what I'm doin' important, pushin' a damn broom. I cut glass better'n any man at the Rouge. No reason to put me out and stick me behind a mop. At least let me run a furnace."

Haik's mind worked. He could not sit around any longer while the world took whatever it wanted from him and his loved ones.

"Tomorrow, I'm talking to some people. I can't say you'll go back to glass, but you ain't gonna be pushin' no broom. Not long as I'm at Fords. I know Mr. Marshall at the SD and Father Daniel, and Mr. Price, too, for that matter, he's on the Star Roll. They all black and every one of 'em all big cheeses. They'll have your back, O."

They all went about eating in silence. Orlin had been at the foundry for three weeks now and he was miserable, but why was he even sent there in the first place? It wasn't a matter of pay, but rather of respect, something that didn't seem to exist anymore. After five years with Fords he was sent to the back of the line to an unskilled position on a clean-up crew.

It was Mr. Meadows all over again. Some policy, some belief, some whim and you had no power to speak up or stand up. Try to bring your voice together with others, and you were on the wrong end of a club or pipe or bullet. "Accidents" happened all the time. Men who were thought to be union sympathizers suddenly "fell" down some stairs, breaking both their legs, and they never returned to the Rouge again. Funny how SD men men were always the first ones present after such "accidents" took place.

Haik wanted to chop wood now. He wanted to take the ax and splinter a tree and bash it into little tiny pieces, to do something, anything but sit around here and feel useless. He got up from the table and turned on the Philco cathedral radio, hoping for music or anything to take his mind off things. They had food and shelter. A lot of people didn't have that. He sent money to his parents and sister Ovsannah and Lu's mother each week. Was he any better than anyone else? Despite what Liam had said about him, he knew he wasn't, but he didn't want to act like it or have anyone think he believed it. He just wanted things to be the way they should be, the way they were before Mr. Meadows' death. You work hard, you do your job, you should be left alone. You don't hurt anybody, nobody should hurt you. It seemed simple, like any decent person would follow along with those rules, but it wasn't even close to how the world worked.

Haik found his coat and trekked outside. Behind the barn, he set up log after log of thin pine on a wide oak stump and he split them in half, chunk, chunk, chunk. He was mad about Orlin. He was mad about Lu and Mr. Meadows and Vahram. He was mad at how Lu's family suddenly thought of him as a criminal. How could Haik explain what he did each day, just following around a big whale of a man drawing pictures, while at the same time there was Orlin, making the same money, no, less money, getting pushed around and shoved into the molten belly of the foundry. Haik bashed at the wood. When he could feel the blood pumping his forearms to the point it became hard to grip the ax handle, he piled up the kindling next to the barn. He repeated the process until there was nothing left to split, and made his way back to the house. Inside, he cleaned up at the basin while Lu and Arkina washed dishes. Charlie and Orlin were off drawing pictures at the kitchen table. It was peaceful. He looked over the members of his family. If he was an artist like Rivera, this is the painting he would make, everybody quietly and contentedly going about their life. Nothing fancy. Just what he saw right here before himself at this moment, this was his art.

That night, as Haik and Lu sat on the bed, Haik took her hand.

"How you feeling?"

"I'm…I'm doing." He thought he could detect a hint of thaw in her voice.

"How's the baby?"

"The baby's fine. Makes me a little sick in the morning, but it's nothing."

"Lu, I know…I know you're angry at me.…"

"Haik, I'm not angry with you.…"

"No, please, let me finish. I don't blame you. I blame myself, so I understand why you're angry and I don't blame you for feeling how you feel. Not a day goes by I don't think of your father."

She looked away, off to the darkened window.

"Haik, it's just, just that I'm out here and I like it, I do, you've given us a nice home, but, I don't know, I just think of going with my mother to Eastern Market and wandering down Russell Street and Adelaide and Division, buying fish and whatever come in from the country. I, I miss a lot of things right now."

Haik put his arm around her. He deserved whatever punishment she gave him. He knew how bad she must be hurting, and would continue to hurt for who knows how long. Hell, it still hurt to think of Vahram. So he would take the punishment for as long as it took Lu to heal and come back to him, which, more than ever, he wanted, no, *needed* her to do.

"Me too," he said, and kissed her on the shoulder. "Let's do this. Tomorrow you and Charlie come with me into the city. I'll drop you off at your mother's before I head in to get the painter. You spend all day doing whatever you want, shop, go to the market, visit, whatever. I'll get you whenever the painter is done with me."

"Haik, Charlie's got school…"

"To hell with school. School is bunk. He can add and he can spell, hell, he's already smarter than kids two years older than him. Christ, he's smarter than me, that's for sure. He don't need no school. People today, they get ahead with dreams and muscle, not sitting in a damn classroom all day with a pencil your hand. You need a day away from here."

She did not argue. The next day, he piled Lu, Charlie and Arkina into the Whippet and dropped them off at Lu's old house. Lu's face brightened, and Charlie couldn't have been happier playing hooky from school. For the first time since Mr. Meadows died, Haik felt hope warm him inside.

Rivera and Miss Frida were staying in an apartment at the Wardell Hotel on Kirby right across from the museum. When he arrived to pick Rivera up, this time his tiny wife was with him. She had been coming with him as often as she could, when she wasn't feeling sick, but lately she stayed with Miss Lucienne their assistant back at the apartment and Haik could tell that she was not well. Rivera had told Haik of her physical woes, how but for some miracle she was even alive after a terrible accident in Mexico. As if battling polio as a child wasn't enough, Miss Frida nearly had the life crushed out of her after some horrible crash involving a bus and a trolley car. *Everything was broken*, Rivera told Haik, *everything but her spirit, and now nothing can break it, not even I.*

Haik opened the door for his guests, and they emerged, bickering and consumed in some sort of debate. Rivera, as usual, looked like a gargantuan hobo, but Frida was dressed in men's trousers and linen workshirt, her hair pulled back tightly and wound into braids at the back of her head. They got in the car, with Frida crawling in to sit between Haik and Rivera, so small she took up less space than a child. Haik shut the door after Rivera had lowered himself in. They had agreed, out of politeness, that in Haik's presence they would speak English, even if they argued, so as not to leave him, a noble worker, out of anything they said to one another. He would have preferred if they spoke Mexican because he did not want to know their personal business, and much of the time they seemed to speak an English that was anything but English.

"…cannot explain why you insist on worshipping this, this bourgeoisie devil. Do you see any joy in these workers? Do you…"

"They are paid quite handsomely, better than anyone in the world, my dear."

"Oh, they are paid, yes, but are they happy? Do you understand that there is a difference? Do they have *souls*? They are paid to be slaves and give their bodies as parts of a machine, nothing more."

"Ah, here you misinterpret. These machines have the power to liberate the worker. No longer does he have to dig and scratch at the soil in a drought or beg the sun during floods. The machines give the power to recognize a long dormant soul. These machines, *mi ninita chiquitita*, have the potential to make the worker *more* human."

"Potential, you say *potential*, but are they really more human *now*? Right now, at this very minute? Can you say they are any more fulfilled than a penniless peasant in Coyoacan? Eh? These men, they cannot even shit without being told. Ah, *Panzas*, you can't see what is right in front of you."

"And what I see before me now, my dear Hank, is what you Americans call, what, a *bearcat*? Yes, they sometimes call Frida and me the Elephant and the Dove, for most obvious reasons, but let me assure you, this tiny woman is more bearcat than dove! I have no chance against her!"

Frida pushed him with a devious smile and climbed up to kiss his cheek.

"Ah!" she sounded as she settled back into her place between them, a panicked, wounded sound.

"My dear?" shot Rivera.

"Miss Frida, you okay?"

Haik knew she was hurt. It was his job to make sure there were no problems, and this sounded like a serious problem.

"Oh...yes...I think so. Thank you, yes, I am now okay. I tell you, this baby, it hurts me sometimes," she whispered.

"My wife's struggling now, too. Sick every morning. Can I take you to the hospital? Mr. Ford has his own hospital, you know," Haik offered.

"No, no hospital for me. My *Dieguito* has sketching to do. I am fine. A little Hennessy will help. Drive on," she commanded, removing a small flask from her pants pocket.

Haik shot a look across her to Rivera, hoping for some direction, but the painter just looked out his passenger side window taking in the scenery. The message was clear—no hospital. He drove on.

Today, they were scheduled to see the ore docks and foundry, which was good because Haik would follow up on his promise to Orlin. They parked at the docks before the 300 foot tankers and towering cranes, whose scoops reached into the bowels of the ships like titanic mechanical jaws chomping down into the carcass of their prey. No doubt, even for someone who had seen it a million times, it was impressive.

"This is how Mr. Ford does it," Haik explained. "He don't need nobody for nothing. He owns the mountains up north in the upper peninsula where he digs out the ore. These ships bring it across the lakes down the river to the docks, and them cranes there, they take it out. All that rock you see there? In just over a day it'll be a car—from rock to roadster in a day."

Rivera and Frida looked on as Haik spoke and Rivera sketched, glancing up and then feverishly returning to his pad.

"That ore gets sent to the foundry. Mr. Ford takes his coal from Kentucky and cokes them blast furnaces hotter'n Hades. They throw in some limestone and smelt off the slag and all you got left is just iron. He don't even let things cool off—takes too much time and money. He sends the metal while it's still hot off for casting. He don't waste no time or a cent for nothing. Boom-boom-boom, step one, step two, you got a car, as good and as cheap as it can be made."

Haik could not always tell if Rivera was listening. He might say *Yes* or *Aha* or *Precisely* every now and then, but all that mattered to him were the images that were filling his head and more and more entire sketch books each day. Haik had always thought of painters as kind of girlish people with their thoughts in the clouds, wearing beanies on their heads and smoking cigarettes and drinking wine and talking about flowers and feelings all day. He had always thought like Mr. Ford, old man Ford, wondering what good art did when the whole world was starving and dying. What could a picture do for you when your belly was aching with hunger? Could it keep you warm in winter when your clothes were worn to threads and your shoe soles were full of holes? Could it spoon oatmeal into a kid's belly or fill a cup with milk?

But as he watched Rivera draw, his ideas began to change. This man *worked*. Some days, he didn't even eat from the time Haik picked him up at the Wardell until he took him home in the evening. He even saw how Rivera himself had started to grow smaller—the more he filled up his books with images, he himself became less. Rivera was conscious he was losing weight and had joked that the Elephant was now a mere Rhinoceros, but there was no denying how much labor he poured into what he was doing. What all these sketch books were supposed to do or what made them so special, Haik had no idea, but if Rivera could get $10,000 for some books full of drawings, well, the more power to him.

Haik took to mirroring him—if Rivera fasted, he fasted; if Rivera ate fruit, he ate only fruit; if Rivera ate raw vegetables, he followed suit. By the end of the day, Haik was ravenous, baffled at how a man twice his size like Rivera could eat like he did and stay alive, and he made sure he ate a good meal as soon as he arrived home in Utica, but in the morning he was off to Eastern Market to gather more grapefruit, lemons, and oranges (no grapes or bananas) and the freshest vegetables for his master's table. Miss Frida, though, all she seemed to want was hard candies, and based on how small she was, she wasn't eating anywhere near enough of them.

After more than an hour of drawing, Diego was pelted by pebbles flying from Miss Frida's hand.

"My darling, not now," he pleaded. She only tossed more stones his way, the mischevious smile again crossing her face, a cigarette dangling from her lips.

"Please, ten more minutes. Don't exert yourself, *chiquita*," he counseled, never wavering from his sketches. An hour later, he declared himself finished and decided they would all walk to the foundry. They trekked on in pleasant silence. Once they entered onto the work floor, they were struck by the intense heat. The workers below looked like moles, goggled for protection against the blinding light inside the blast furnaces. They were to a man black, their dark skin glistening with sweat from the heat belching from the furnaces. The air was stained thick with the oppressive odor of dust, coal, sulphur, and other unidentifiable gasses. It was like Lucifer's workshop, with the molten iron gathered in vats and siphoned off to be processed and formed into the steel skin of automobiles.

"Maybe this ain't the best place for Miss Frida," shouted Haik over the straining sound of the furnaces. Here and there sparks of fire blasted forth from the bowels of the workfloor. The place was hell, a gigantic coal snorting oven that never shut down, its workers glistening in sweat, their clothes soaked through, their goggled faces always peering into a fiery abyss. The metal flowed like lava, beautifully alive, bubbling and glowing and thoroughly entrancing.

"Nonsense, I'm not a child," shot Frida defiantly, her bird voice barely audible, but her body language making it clear she would do as she saw fit.

"Your concern is very appreciated, my good Hank," Rivera shouted, "but I am afraid it is of no use. My little dove flies where she pleases, when she pleases."

Rivera poured himself into his work, and Haik could see him tracing the outline of valves and ducts and pipes and flames in the air before returning his hand to the sketchpad. Hank excused himself and ran onto the floor, the choking heat causing him to remove his coat. He spied Orlin and then found the shift foreman, bringing the two of them together for a meeting off to the side where they would not have to shout as loud to be heard.

"This man here, he don't push a broom no more," shouted Haik, pointing to Orlin.

"Says who?" the smudge-faced white foreman demanded.

"Says Mr. Harry Bennett and the Service Department, that's who."

"I didn't get no message from Mr. Bennett."

"Well, you got one now. You want me to have Mr. Bennett pay you a personal visit, smart guy? I can arrange it," said Haik pointedly.

"You don't have to get all huffy, I just asked a question," the foreman retorted, worry shading his face.

"I don't like your fucking question and you keep it up and I'm not gonna like you, understand."

Haik placed his index finger directly into the foreman's sweating chest.

"I understand," he surrendered. "So what am I supposed to do? Where's he supposed to go?"

"He don't go nowhere," directed Haik. "You take his broom and you give it to someone else. You put him on a smelter or a vat, but he ain't gonna clean up no more. He's a skilled worker, not no broom humper. You got it?"

The foreman nodded, and Haik shot a quick wink at Orlin. It was the first time he had ever used his position as a Serviceman to order someone about without being ordered to do so. He couldn't say he liked it, and it made him feel more like a heel than someone important, but he would not have Orlin treated like a dog. Maybe it wasn't fair to the guy who had to take up Orlin's broom, but Haik had learned that all the way around life wasn't fair, and it could be unfair in a lot worse ways than having to push a broom. He looked back and saw the foreman pointing and shifting Orlin with another worker and felt a small rush of relief and guilt.

When he returned to Rivera and Frida, he could tell that she was beginning to wilt but that her pride would not let her budge. He could not stand to let her suffer.

"Miss Frida, this place kinda makes me sick. You want to step out for a minute?"

Haik was careful not to betray the least hint of condescension or his true motivation. Frida looked faint, her tomboyish vitality sapped by the satanic heat.

"Yes, I think I will join you."

She reached up on tippy toes and kissed Rivera on a sweat coated cheek and then joined Haik back outside the foundry, where the air was cool and clean.

"Uh, it is unbearable in there," Frida commented. "Do you think Diego will be okay? Look, look how thin he is becoming. Too much work."

Haik looked at her with surprise. If anyone was in danger inside the foundry, it was Miss Frida and not the mammoth Rivera.

"No, I think he's okay. He's a strong man."

"Yes, yes he is," Frida said, a distance in her voice. "Hank, I must confide something in you. Diego, he does not want this child. He had a son die during the war, and he has three daughters, one he doesn't even acknowledge in public. He only wants art now, not children. I want art, as well, and most of all I want *his* art, but there is room for this child. He doesn't believe it, but there is room enough."

"Maybe he's just busy now," Haik said, trying to set her at ease, not really knowing what else to say. "Maybe, I don't know, maybe he kind of feels pressure to get his painting going, so he just wants to think about that for a while. When he gets some painting done, I bet he'll come around to the kid."

Miss Frida looked out towards the ore ships.

"No, his painting will never be finished. His pressure comes from within himself. There will always be another project, another wall. Always, with Diego, another wall."

Her voice trailed off at the end and disappeared somewhere into a place only she could see.

"Well, you still got to be careful, Miss Frida. Mr. Rivera needs you to be healthy and fit," said Haik, trying to cheer her.

Who was he kidding? He didn't even know how to cheer his own wife, although he was hoping the day with her family would start to bring Lu around. Miss Frida and Haik stood together outside the blast house and he kept a careful eye on her. She didn't seem well, as if at any moment she might scatter in the wind like the thin, soft pieces of a cottonweed. He studied her. Was she pretty? He couldn't really say. Maybe not in her looks, but more in how she was, how she carried herself, a bearcat, Rivera said, and that was pretty accurate. It was over an hour before Diego appeared outside, drenched in sweat but still wearing the genial smile on his face.

"Friends, I am ready," he announced.

"My goodness, Diego, look at you. When is the last time you cleaned yourself? Huh? *Oh, que hediondo estas!* You smell! You *will* bathe tonight if I have to bathe you myself."

Rivera laughed heartily and they were off to the car, as odd a threesome as had set foot on the premises.

"So, what was your business at the foundry?" inquired Rivera as they drove home to the apartment.

"Business?"

"I saw you conversing with some gentlemen there. It looked, pardon the pun, rather heated."

"Oh, damn, forgive me, I should have introduced you. That one guy, he's married to my sister."

"The bossman?"

"No, the other guy."

"The black one?" asked Rivera, incredulous, seeming to be pleasantly amused.

"Yeah, the black one. His name's Orlin. Orlin Cutright. We been friends since we been small. Long history, me and Orlin. Man, I could tell you some stories, Mr. Rivera. A *lot* of stories. We're like this," signaled Haik, crossing his index and middle fingers.

"Again, the mixing of races, the bringing together of bloods. Very important, a truly American theme," reflected Rivera.

"Many of us are a mixture of bloods," interjected Frida. "It is a strength."

"Indeed," agreed Rivera. He drifted off into thought. "So, this man, Orlin, he is, how you say it, your brother-in-law?"

"Oh yeah. He needed my help down there. He used to work at glass but they stuck him behind a broom in the blast house. He's been miserable. He don't deserve being treated like that. He needs to do real work."

"But pushing a broom..." began Rivera.

"Pushing a broom? This is your great Henry Ford. Just say it, Hank, your brother-in-law is a nee-gger in Henry Ford's eyes and all he deserves is a broom in the filthiest place on his land," shot Miss Frida.

"Well, him being black, yeah, that had something to do with him ending up in the foundry."

Haik did not want to get himself in the middle of an argument, so he said as little as he could and did not try to take a side.

"My darling...."

"Nonsense, this is the great 'dignity' given to these workers by their owner. Enough. Industry as the great liberator. Ha!"

Frida would not give one inch to Rivera. The conversation stopped.

In no time they were at the Riveras' quarters, a long day behind them. Haik looked forward to walking into the Meadows' home and finding Lu and Charlie there and embracing them. More than anything, he hoped Lu had a good day and would be in fine spirits and closer to her old self. Junior might still have a burr up his ass, but if Mrs. Meadows treated him civilly that would be enough. Haik got out of the car and opened Rivera's door and helped him gather his materials.

"My friend, Hank, I think I would like to hear some of the stories you mention. I've seen a great deal, drawn a great deal, but I must *hear* and *feel* more. I am drawing machines, learning the process, but, ultimately, my subject is the people...the *people*. Would it be too much of an imposition if, one day, we might make an excursion into the city to experience what life is like for the men who inhabit this great workplace? I'd like to get to know these men, see how they live, hear how they speak, watch how they move and eat and drink and breathe and live away from the Rouge. Would this be possible?"

"Mr. Rivera, I'm here to do whatever I can so you can make the best pictures you can for Mr. Edsel Ford. It would be my pleasure to show you what the workers do away from the plant. We got a whole other life you don't see in them pipes and smokestacks and engine blocks. I'll show you whatever you need to see."

With a handshake they agreed to take Rivera's studies to a more personal level.

He headed off to pick up Lu and Charlie, unsure exactly what Rivera had in mind.

As he pulled into the Meadows' driveway, he saw Charlie part the front curtain and peer out at him. In a second, he was bolting out the front door to greet Haik at the car.

"So how's hooky treatin' ya?"

"Fine!" smiled Charlie.

"Good. How's your mother?" He exited the car and took the boy in a warm embrace.

"She's good. She bought lots of things at the market. Good things to eat."

"Oh yeah? Good, 'cause I'm hungry. Long day at work today, son."

They walked together up the porch stairs, Haik's arm around Charlie's shoulders. Lu appeared at the door. Her smile was quiet and real. She held the door open to him and Charlie, and reached up to kiss him lightly on the mouth as he entered. He felt a steamy, humid comfort coming from the kitchen and smelled fresh chicken soup cooking and homemade bread. He could not wait to eat with his wife and son.

Hastings Street burned. Haik liked a good time as much as the next guy, but Rivera, he was a whole different story. He said he wanted to see and experience and feel the spirit of the people he was going to capture with his paint brush, but from Haik's observation it was Rivera who became the spirit of things wherever he went. Just the Sunday before, Haik and Orlin hosted Diego and Miss Frida out at their place and they enjoyed quite a feast. Rivera was his charming self, and Lu and Arkina complemented Frida on her festive Mexican clothing and jewelry. Lu and Frida talked of their pregnancies, and Diego sketched some quick portraits for Charlie. They ate fried chicken and ham hocks and sauerkraut and corn on the cob and spiced Armenian rice and bread and drank beer and whiskey. Frida had lamented how bland and tasteless American food was, potatoes and more potatoes and boiled unseasoned meat, so Haik was glad to have them at their home and show them not all Americans were so dull. Oddly, she ate very little, politely picking like a sparrow, but Diego proclaimed that he would take one day's respite from his strict eating regimen and partake of the culinary pleasures about him. Maybe they didn't eat prime rib and lobster and caviar and drink champagne, but they could turn what they did have into something lively.

Haik dropped the painter and his wife off late that night, and before escorting Frida inside Rivera confided to Haik that he still had a great deal of research he must still conduct into the spirit of the workers before he was ready to begin his actual paintings. No problem, Haik assured him, and the next night the first of many lengthy after hours excursions began.

Hastings Street in the Black Bottom was as spirited a place as one could find amid so much desolation and poverty. By day, jobless men and children wandered the streets rummaging through trash cans, selling pencils or apples, and begging pennies and nickels. At night, though, the area transformed. The blind pigs and speakeasies opened their doors and sounded their trumpets and cops paid to look the other way did as their benefactors requested. Haik and Orlin took Rivera out, and then he took over, a magnet for laughter and good times. At the Barrel House, the band rolled through "Tiger Rag" and "Minnie the Moocher" and "Happy Days Are Here Again" while the dance floor gyrated with women in silk slip dresses slit into low V's, swinging wildly to the Lindy Hop, the Collegiate Shag, and, for old times' sake, the Charleston. Men in double-breasted suits and spit shined shoes kicked it up and let the beer and Seven Crown flow. If Haik's time with the Service Department taught him anything, it was where every good time in the city was located.

And there was Rivera, smiling, for some reason drawing the flappers to him like moths to a blow torch. There were a good number of these dames who played for pay, but for Rivera all bets were off and the cash register shut down. That night at the Barrel House, Carlita, whom Haik knew from some of his business drops at various establishments downtown, cornered Haik near the bar and inquired about his rotund companion.

"He's a famous painter. You know, like an art type painter. A Mexican," he explained, buying Carlita a drink with Bennett's expense money. "C'mon, hon, I'll introduce you."

They walked over to Rivera, who sat jovially with Orlin and two other women Haik had never seen before.

"Mr. Rivera, this is Carlita, an old friend from way back. She wanted to meet a famous painter, and I said I just happened to know where to find one."

Haik smiled, glad to fulfill his role as gracious host.

"Ah, Carlita, such an exquisite name."

Rivera took Carlita's hand and placed a soft kiss upon the back of it.

"Why thank you," beamed Carlita. She was short and buxom, her shimmering silk outfit accentuating all her most positive attributes. "So, what brings you here to our fair city, Mr. Rivers?"

"Please, sit down, my beautiful, and I will explain my purpose here," suggested Rivera.

Haik lifted his glass of beer to the painter as if to say *Bon Appetit*, and Rivera's glass was raised in return. Haik was here to do whatever Rivera needed him to do. He had hosted him in his own house and taken him to his parents for home cooked meals. They even took a trip to Mexican Town down on Bagley, but Miss Frida said it only made her homesick. She went on very few of the trips as the strain of her pregnancy was beginning to take its toll and she did not have the strength to go out. However, this did not stop Rivera. In the mornings, he worked at completing the last of his preliminary sketches and visited a few final unseen corners of the Rouge plant and had Haik take him to see Chrylser, Detroit Edison Electric, Michigan Alkali, and the Park-Davis chemical facility, investigating laboratories as well as workshops, nosing in and out of every nook and cranny. What more he could want to know about Detroit and its industry Haik couldn't guess, but he did as Rivera requested. After a full day of visits and drawings and observations, Rivera wanted to walk the avenues, talk to street vendors and the homeless and the panhandlers and drugstore cowboys hanging out on the corners.

At night, he did not stop. He was an inexhaustible engine of adventure, and Haik was often tempted to fetch a tag team partner so he might get some sleep before starting over in the morning, but he fought through. The past week Haik had convinced Orlin to help him entertain this unstoppable dynamo, but even now Orlin was showing signs of wear and tear. *Eshu bes gakhame*, Haik's father would say about a man like Rivera, a wild man, one of insatiable appetites. They were common men who were used to doing what was commonly required of them to survive and protect their families. This, this nightly whirlwind of stimulation and wildness, was too much and they could only hope that Rivera would soon decide it was time to actually begin painting.

"…the automobile and its aerodynamic qualities, not much unlike the graceful curves of a seductive woman, a woman such as yourself, my darling Carlita…."

Haik watched and listened to the master at work, and already he was holding Carlita's hand as he spoke. No question, this man was straight up ugly—no way around it, he just wasn't any William Powell or Clark Gable. Even as he lost weight, and he had already lost a great deal since the first time Haik laid eyes on him at the museum, he was still puffed and saggy. On top of the cake, it seemed that bathing was more important to Miss Frida than it was to him, and his clothing, well, he had no identifiable sense of style. He was balding, and what hair he had was uncombed and scrambled beneath his Stetson hat. But make no mistake, women loved him. He had a charm, a way, a magnetism that outweighed everything negative that could be said about him. He could simple turn his widely spaced, baleful eyes toward the most beautiful woman in any joint, smile at her tenderly, and she was his.

"...would be most honored if you would allow me to show you a magnificent automobile. My dear Hank, would you be so kind as to allow me to take this lovely woman for a ride?"

Amidst all the swirling music and dancers and general merriment, Haik became aware he was being spoken to. He was about done, ready to spread out on the floor and nod off to sleep.

"Sorry, Mr. Rivera?"

"The car keys, my good Hank. The enchanting Carlita is most in need of a drive at this very moment."

"Oh, right away, sir. You need me to drive you someplace?"

It was common knowledge that Rivera didn't drive—he never took the time to learn for himself and preferred being driven.

"My good man, no, I could not trouble you. This will be a very, ahem, short ride."

Haik produced the key, placed it in Rivera's soft, diminutive hand, and smiled in admiration. Here we go again, he thought, marvelling at the master's undeniable skills.

"We shall return in due course. Ladies, Orlin, please excuse us for a few short moments."

Like a wooly mammoth, Rivera arose, helped Carlita push her chair back from the table, took her hand and winked at Haik and Orlin before leading his conquest toward the back stairwell.

"How's he do that?" asked Orlin, his brows wrinkled in bewilderment.

"You find out, let me know, brother," Haik replied.

While Haik worked in this wild and lawless circle, he did not indulge—too much risk, and he had all he could ever want in Lu if she would ever forgive him. She was still cold and they had not been together as man and woman since Mr. Meadows' death, but she was coming around lately he thought, showing him affection, smiling, embracing him when he came through the door at night after leaving the painter. The temptations, though, had begun to sparkle, particularly with Lu's continued distance. He watched a man like Rivera work the skirts, a man with a huge name and a famous wife, yet he showed no sign of feeling bad about escorting every Carlita he ran into. Was it so bad? So wrong? Haik began to survey the club around him, dames shimmying and laughing. Was it really so wrong?

"Why you say that? You palooks jealous?" chimed in one of the girls at the table, a redhead. "Diego, he's a sweetie. A real peacherino lovin' daddy."

"You're kiddin', right?" Orlin shot, his eyes half closed, the strain of having to keep pace with Rivera showing.

"Ab-so-lute-ly," her friend, a brunette, added. "I'd carry a torch for that one. He's, I don't know, he looks like he'd be cuddly. You know, like you could take care of him and snuggle on him and he could make you feel warm the rest of your life."

"If you say so," Orlin responded, the effects of whiskey and exhaustion making him short with the ladies.

"What?" demanded the first girl. "You big toughs with your big strong muscles, that's not what all dames want. Walkin' around all tough isn't everything, you know."

"Maybe so, ladies. But let me tell you, I been taking that fellow around for weeks on end now, and I gotta admit, whatever it is that makes his engine spark, that's one amazing man. I don't really know if he can paint, but he sure as hell can carouse with the best of them. Let's toast to Mr. Diego Rivera."

Haik lifted his glass in salute and all joined him in a long swill. The girls were heavily made up and, while not ugly, they were not overly attractive, and they appeared more interested in the prospect of free drinks than establishing any meaningful relationships in their lives, which was fine. Haik looked at them over the rim of his lifted beer glass. He and Orlin were married; these nights out were a kind of hazard duty they had to fulfill, not the chance to run loose in the hen house. Sure, Rivera was married too, but what he did with his life was his call and Haik was not about to judge him one way or another. No denying, the man had fun, but Haik would fight the impulse to be like him. He would do his job. If Rivera wanted to go to Belle Isle every day and watch the boats out on the Detroit River, he would have just as gladly done that for him as take him down Hastings Street to burn down Detroit's wild, free-swinging clubs. He killed the thought of emulating his master. The last thing he needed to do was add to his sins when he was far from atoning for the ones he'd already committed.

"So Hanky, what say you go get us another drinky-winky?" sighed the brunette.

Haik looked at his watch. How long would Rivera take? Was he really going to try to drive the car?

"Yeah, sure, whatever you dames want. Just stick around in case, you know, the painter is still, you know, still wanting a little entertainment."

Both girls gave him a disinterested glance as he went to the bar. Orlin was baked—he didn't need another. But Haik could use one. He took a healthy double shot at the bar and brought back three tall rye and gingers, setting them on the table without any acknowledgment or thank-yous. He felt good now and a second wind was lifting his mood. The music roared on and the lights became drowsing. How much longer for Rivera? Before he could process that thought, he felt a hand on his leg. He glanced over and the brunette was giving him a drowsy eyed smile.

"As long as we got to sit here, we might as well dance, huh?"

Haik glanced over at Orlin, who shrugged as if to say, Go ahead, who cares. The woman took Haik by the hand and led him out onto the floor. Dancing—the only person Haik had ever danced with was Lu. He watched everyone else and they made it seem so easy, so free and fun and effortless, but he really had no clue where to begin. Luckily, the band dropped down into a slow waltzy number, slow enough that Haik could keep step. He placed one hand around the brunette's waist and clasped her hand with the other.

"Don't dance much, do you, Hanky?"

He looked in the brunette's face and she smiled. The whiskey swirled his head and her smile warmed him.

"No, not really. That bad, huh?"

"Don't worry. It's cute. Strong tough like you gets all fouled up on a dance floor. That's cute."

They continued their paces, the music and whiskey hypnotizing him, taking him back to his early courtship of Lu. To the riverside and the beer gardens and summer nights that lasted for days on end. With Lu, in a light summer dress, the light catching her eyes.

"Well, what have we here?"

Haik returned to the Barrel House and found that the brunette had ahold of his crowbar through his trousers. She looked up at him, a wide lipstick smile. She had suddenly become beautiful. He pulled her close to him and let her continue.

Then he removed her hand.

"What's wrong, Hanky? You don't like a little strokin'?"

The brunette whispered in his ear, her tongue gliding along the rim. God, she felt good.

"Yeah, yeah I like it, but...."

"But what?"

But what? A good question. He let go of her hand and let her continue. Her fingers moved lightly and rubbed tenderly as their bodies swayed. The whiskey flowed and sparked in his veins. It *did* feel good. She, whatever her name, the brunette, she wasn't bad looking. Not great, but getting better by the minute. Who would know? Had Orlin seen? He looked over at the table—Orlin was face down in his own forearms, asleep. These places, there were rooms, upstairs one floor, Haik could slip off for a few minutes, no harm done. How long had it been since he had been able to, you know, let the lightning fly? Hell, Rivera was probably in one of the upstairs rooms right now with Carlita.

"But what, sugar daddy?" she cooed as she licked around the inside of his ear, her moist breath flowing all the way into his groin.

But what? It was a fair question. He pulled his head back and looked in the brunette's eyes and she was still smiling, glassy eyed and willing. He smiled back. He took her hand and turned her around toward the upstairs exit.

When he looked up, though, there was Rivera with Carlita in tow. Both seemed pleased with their car ride. Haik sobered up, stopped dead in his tracks, and led the brunette to their table, where Rivera beamed with pleasure.

"Now, my most beautiful acquaintances, it is time for me to retire for the evening. Please accept my apologies for such an early departure. Until we meet again," Rivera announced, and kissed Carlita very tenderly on the cheek.

"I'm coming to see that paintin' a yours soon as it's done," Carlita sang. "You know that, girls? Diego here's gonna be paintin' up the whole museum down on Woodward. Real important stuff. The *Fords* are payin' him."

The brunette let go of Haik's hand. The trio of girls gazed at Rivera in admiration, and he returned a humble smile.

"You will all be welcome as my special guests as soon as my work is complete. But now, *adieu, mes belles femmes*. Haik, if you please, I am afraid I must repair to my quarters. A grueling day awaits."

Haik stepped over to Orlin and shook him. He was startled, his eyes punished by the club's glaring lights, and he seemed to find himself in a new world naked. He looked to Haik and registered relief. Now, finally, they could begin to call it a night. Haik looked to the brunette, who formed a mock pout.

"Not tonight, honey."

Haik gently placed his hand to the side of her made up face. Damn, how close had he come to losing himself? What if Rivera had not shown up when he did?

He did not want answers those questions.

On the drive to Rivera's quarters, he thanked Orlin and Haik for being such attentive hosts. They could barely nod their heads in acknowledgement.

"But now, my true work must begin. Tomorrow, we construct the scaffolding. The garden court will become a place of industry. I have never felt more ready to create," Rivera declared. "In a few short days, the transformation will begin. Tomorrow, please meet me directly at the museum. I'll walk over myself."

Tomorrow. It was well after midnight, so Rivera was actually going to begin painting *today*. Haik could not even begin to think about getting up in the morning to drive in and get to work, and poor Orlin, looking ahead to a day wed to the blast furnaces, he would need to summon all his strength and cash in all his favors from God to make it through the day.

On the way home to Utica, Orlin and Haik, delirious with booze and exhaustion, could not be more grateful to hear that Rivera was going to finally begin painting.

"Tonight was it for me, brother," confessed Orlin. "I know you my brother-in-law and all, and you know I do anything for you, but I couldn't go out one more night with that man and live to talk about it. I'm done, man. I don't know how you been keepin' up with him. He something else."

Orlin reclined his head back against the seat.

"And how. I ain't never met nobody like that man. He's...I don't know. I can't really explain him. I just hope these paintings are what everybody is expecting out of him."

And what were these paintings going to be? Haik couldn't even venture a guess. And one more night and he might not be the man, the husband, he knew he needed to be if he was ever going to get Lu back. They drove home in the wee hours, and by the time their heads hit the pillow it was nearly time to wake up again for a full day of work.

This painting was not really a painting. And it wasn't even *a* painting, it was a bunch of paintings. Before he saw Rivera work, the way Haik understood art was way off the mark. He thought of Rivera throwing down a big canvas drop cloth on the beautiful floor of the garden court, assembling some cans of paint and stir sticks and turpentine and rags and, finally, some brushes, and there you had it, he'd start painting on the walls, shaping whatever pictures he wanted, roses and angels and George Washington over here, Honest Abe Lincoln over there, some horses, whatever, until he reached the end of a wall and ran out of space. But he was wrong. Rivera was doing something he called *buon fresco*, some kind of painting done by "the master," whoever that was. The paints didn't come in cans but were made right on the spot on the second floor by Rivera's assistants, Mr. Sanchez Flores or Mr. Dimitroff, who were often helped by Miss Frida, taking blocks of color and grinding them up into a powder before mixing them with distilled water, only distilled water, nothing out of the tap.

But before they even mixed the paint, though, they had to put this gooey, pasty plaster crap all over the walls. They put two coats of paste on the walls before Rivera even got to Detroit, and every time he painted a section they applied three more fresh coats. At three in the morning down in the basement of the museum, Mr. Niendorf and Mr. Halberstadt and sometimes another assistant would start mixing the lime from the rubber sacks with marble dust to make the plaster goo, which had to be perfect, not too runny and no unbroken chunks floating around. Mr. Wight and Miss Lucienne were best at spreading the plaster, and they covered the specific areas Rivera wanted to paint for that day. The last batch was real important, and they smoothed it carefully, making sure it was the right consistency, something only they knew how to judge. Right after the sun had been up a good while, about 9 a.m., they would alert Haik to fetch Rivera so the day's images could be brought to life.

Once the plaster was spread, the squad of assistants, including Mr. Wight, Mr. Pablo, Miss Lucienne, Lord Hastings (Haik called him Lord John), and Mr. Albert, who kind of mostly gave advice now and then, went to work, their main job tracing the outlines of the drawings Rivera had made onto the wet plaster. Rivera called these huge drawings "cartoons," but they weren't like Krazy Kat, Plainclothes Dick Tracy, or, Haik's personal favorite, Popeye. No, these were giant pictures they would kind of puncture and then hold up to the wall, and then they traced over it with this red stuff, *sinopia* they called it, and when they pulled the big drawing away an outline of what Rivera was going to paint was up on the wall.

By the time Haik got Rivera to the court, it was around 10 or so and he went right to it. He had about six to 12 hours max to work on a section before the plaster dried—once that happened, that was it, the colors were sealed into the plaster and the plaster hardened solid as granite, permanent, forever. The only way to correct a mistake was to hammer it off, which Rivera did whenever he felt something wasn't perfect, even giving Haik, the *caudillo* he called him, the honor of smashing off offending sections. Rivera first covered the outlines he was focusing on in a black paint, and then began adding in the color he wanted for the final product. And once he started, he was gone. He loved the skylights above him. He would not allow electric lighting as it might distort his perception of the colors he was applying. And the colors, oh, man, the colors. They were like sections of Frida's elaborate skirts ground up and mixed into a paint that was not paint but earth, water, wind, skin, fire, steel, rubber, steam and sky itself. Haik could look at Diego's pictures for hours.

And there was Frida, always doting, always checking on her Diego, bringing him water or juice, prodding him to eat his fruit and raw vegetables while she herself would only eat the hard candies she carried with her. She, too, was losing weight, but unlike her husband, she had nothing to lose. Her beauty, if it existed, was a mystery—if being around Rivera had taught Haik anything, it was that he actually understood very little about beauty, and that physical beauty did not always count for very much. If there was something about Frida that Haik admired, something that made him not think about her eyebrows, it was her commitment, her undying devotion to this man they both had come to serve. She, too, was an artist, supposedly pretty good, but everything she did now revolved around Rivera. Not that she was a mere fan or cheerleader; no, she would tell Diego directly if something was "working" or not. Rivera, for the most part, was quiet, completely absorbed in the process of bringing the barren walls to life, but when Frida spoke about art he listened raptly as if she had the final say.

Haik occasionally checked in at the glass house a few times a week to see how his turf was operating, and gave Harry Bennett frequent updates on what the painter was up to and received more expense money. Haik liked that he could now stop into Bennett's office, shoot the bull with him, take a few moments in the basement and appear at ease just like all the men he had first seen surrounding Bennett so long ago. He had Bennett's trust, and he had earned a measure of status. His life was solid and the beatings were a thing of the past, but not his memory of Mr. Meadows' death and the man who had caused it. No, that wound would never go away.

One day as he left the museum, Haik saw Cam Lister's Deuce Coupe parked directly behind him.

"Hey, pal, thought I might find you here," shouted Lister, toothpick in his mouth, walking up behind Haik.

He knew Lister well enough to know that he didn't just stop by on a lark hoping he might run into Haik to chat about old times. No, Lister had been following him and knew exactly when Haik would be leaving. Whatever you wanted to say about Lister, he was a planner. He scouted his mission, calculated his potential gains and losses, and he knew Haik would be here right at this place at this time. Haik thought of how easy it would be to draw his gun and take him out right there, but not in broad daylight on one of the city's busiest streets. Besides, there was something about Lister, his open coat, the set of his hands at his side, that said he knew exactly what Haik was thinking and was ready for him. Haik had not learned how to outsmart or get the drop on a man like Lister. Not yet.

"Evening," Haik said warily.

The thought of revenge had never left his mind, but his time with Rivera chewed up his schedule and being around the painter was what he needed, a complete removal from the world of everyday Service Department activities. Even though he was gone from home so often, Lu had started to brighten up as the child in her belly grew. The thaw was taking place—the guilt no longer rested on his shoulders like the cement ball Vahram had carried through the city of Detroit. Only Lu could free him from his guilt, and lately she seemed to draw closer to him and understand his situation. Haik had not killed her father, and he loved her, loved her enough to devote all he had to making her happy, and she would now greet him with a smile and a kiss on the mouth when he came through the door at night. Just the week before, she had allowed him to, well, be inside her. He didn't know what to think—was there room with the baby inside? Yet she was willing to have him, she had to know if it was okay or not, and the months of isolation built until he tremored everything he had pent up in him inside her. He was relieved and grateful. It was over.

"So how's the art world doin'? Create any masterpieces yet?"

Lister's attempt at humor and camaraderie annoyed Haik.

"Can't say I created none, but I think that man in there is working on a couple," returned Haik, trying to determine exactly what Lister was up to.

"Art, some a that stuff today, I tell ya, just plain garbage from what I can see, splashing paint here and there. Don't even look like nothing."

Haik decided not to answer to make Lister get to a point. Lister didn't know anything about art, but like any subject, that wouldn't stop him from piping up and Haik wasn't in the mood.

"So, you havin' fun baby sittin' the spic?" he asked, still trying to find some common ground. It wasn't working and Lister probably knew it. Rivera was no spic, and Haik would take his company over Lister's any day.

"Rivera is aces. He's a good joe. I got no complaints."

"That's good. Real good. Hey, while I got you here," Lister said, looking off into the summer traffic on Woodward, finally coming to the purpose of his visit. "I got myself a little thing going now, a little side action, you might say. I can use some good men, men I can count on, men who wanna make some real money. You think you might be up for it, old sport?"

Lister sized Haik up, scanning him as he spoke, trying to detect the least sign of success in his pitch.

"I'm listening."

"Well, I got me a little action goin' on the river. Got some product coming in across from Fightin' Island just north of Grassy. Set myself up a little operation on a small little isle off of Ecorse Park, teensy little drop a ground, like Paul Bunyan took himself a good shit in the drink and it stuck there. Don't no cops bother with it. Purples don't know it's there, so no harm on that front. Piece a cake, not one bit of risk involved."

Lister turned Haik's stomach and he had no interest, but he could not let his hatred for the man standing before him deprive him of a chance to pick up some information on him, maybe the kind of information Luigi Leone could use. He would keep the conversation going.

"What kinda product?"

"Oh, same-old, same-old. Some Canadian hooch. But I'm also branchin' out. Got me hold a something called hair-o-ween. Great stuff. Made it illegal back in '24, but a lot of folks still think it's the berries. You can snort it, you can smoke it, you can cook it up and shoot it with a nail. Once you're onto this stuff, boy, you can't get enough of it. Got yourself a customer for life. Hell, hear tell there's a Depression goin' on but I can't keep up with the demand. I'm working with an old pal named Goldberg. He's handling my on-site work and he needs me to find a drop man on the shore while he drives the truck. All we need is a good man on the land to make sure what goes where like it should and handle the money without no sticky fingers. Somebody who can keep his head straight so I can, you know, tend to the big picture."

Lister fashioned himself a real tycoon. The deal was simple, though. Lister wanted a chump down on the beach to take a fall if there was a bust or a bullet if the Purples showed up, a sap who was dumb enough to not steal whose life didn't mean anything if everything went south. He could stick it, but maybe this was an opening. Why Lister would approach him made Haik wary—somewhere Haik felt that deep inside Lister really knew how much he hated him. If he was down to asking Haik, he must have hit a lot of rejections or there was something not on the level about his proposal. And who was this guy Lister was partnering with—the name, Goldberg, sounded familiar, but Haik couldn't place it. He needed to know more.

"Well, I'm kinda busy here with the painter, doin' stuff for him. Mr. Bennett's big on me keepin' him happy…"

"Oh, I know you been keepin' him happy. Trust me, brother, you get a A+ on that count. I been hearin' lots of stories."

Haik didn't like Lister's tone. There was a tinge of jealousy, but also, as always with Lister, a whisp of threat. Did he know something about the brunette at the Barrel House, how she, she grabbed him there? Or was he talking about all the carousing Rivera was doing, the personal socializing with folks from the Rouge? Haik was supposed to keep Rivera away from workers, especially in their off hours, where Rivera could learn what they really thought of working at the Rouge and where a communist might have a chance to fill their heads with crazy ideas about unions and uniting their voices. To Haik, that was all a bunch of bullshit, but what was Lister trying to say? Was he snitching on what Haik and Rivera were doing and where they were going?

"So what's the when and how? I can't make no promises, Cam, because I can't leave the painter hanging. I do that, I'm fried. I'm not just answering to Mr. Bennett, I got Edsel Ford keeping tabs on me too. Lots a masters to serve."

"I hear ya. We all got our obligations. Now, brass tacks here, the when part is this coming Monday at around one in the morning. I suppose that would actually be Tuesday, technically speakin'. I'm guessin' the painter ain't gonna need you at that time, unless a course he's makin' a poontang run in Paradise Valley. As for the where part a things, meet in Ecorse where West Jefferson crosses White Street and Goldberg will have a truck there. If you're in, let me know so we can get you two acquainted real quick like. You show up, let him give you the drop money, then go a little ways to the water's edge and wait with a lantern. You hear the boat engine, you give a little signal that everything's clear. You wait for the boat to hit shore, you get the boys in the truck to load up and not break nothing, you pay the navy and that's pretty much it. Goldberg'll know where to drop the supplies. Simple stuff, no risk, just a nice payday if you take it."

No risk—anything you did with Cam Lister was risky. If there was no risk, he'd be leading the truck there himself and save paying a sap like Haik. Too much of what he was saying didn't make any sense. No, Haik took what Lister said with a few grains of salt, but he wanted to hear more.

"What kinda payday?"

"Oh, $20 for the first run. A lot more in the future if you can show me my investment's good."

It was chump change in Lister's book, but it was still $20, half a month's payment on the house for a couple hours of work. Orlin had this crazy idea of actually putting a toilet inside their house, a toilet that flushed, never have to freeze your ballbearings off again out in the Michigan winter every time you had to drop a deuce. It was a good idea, but money, always money, supporting the Meadows and the Pehlivanians and their own brood as well, keeping everyone fed and clothed and reasonably comfortable, paying the $40 a month on the land. As dirty as Lister was, the thought of an extra $20 was tempting, but not tempting enough to put a pebble of trust in him.

"Let me check what the painter has in store for me. You know I'd help you any way I can, Cam, but I got to make sure everything's copacetic here first. Sounds like a winner, though, really does."

Haik hoped his lie was not too apparent.

"Okay, you think it over. I'll be by."

Lister rolled his toothpick one more time and drifted off to his car and was gone. So what to do? Maybe Lister had something on him he could use against him with Bennett, but Haik now had something on him with…with whom?

As he walked to his car, it came to him. He headed off to Beaubien Street in Greektown, home of the police headquarters. The building dominated the block, and Haik approached with a sense of uneasiness. Since his youth, the police were always the enemy, the ones who would take the food out of your mouth or put you away for life for the crime of survival. Once he joined Fords, the police were just an attachment of Harry Bennett's army, the same thugs just with fancy blue uniforms. Luigi had told him two weeks after Mr. Meadows' murder that they knew who did it but for several reasons they couldn't link a murder to a Ford employee when he was doing Ford work, especially a SD man. They'd have to get the guy on something else, something not connected to the Ford name, and once they did they would put the screws to him.

Inside, he was told that Luigi was out and probably wouldn't be back for a half hour. This couldn't wait another day, so he walked out to the sidewalk and leaned against the outside wall to wait. The coppers gave him a bad feeling, so he didn't want to stay inside where they could keep an eye on him and maybe memorize his face and features. He watched the traffic of blue coats and drunks and painted ladies and toughs parade in and out. Lister made a mistake—or had he? Why did he come to Haik? Did he know Haik wanted to bring him down? Or was he desperate? A rat like Lister ran through friends like a whore through dirty underwear; maybe he was down to trusting a man who made no special effort to show any semblance of love for him and more than likely downright hated him. Haik thought back to the evening he was kidnapped and roughed up and the smell of Lister's putrid breath. He had passed the allegiance test in the barn that night, so this had been in the works for quite some time; no matter how many kicks, slaps, and punches he absorbed, he didn't give Lister up. The whole episode now made some kind of sense.

Haik waited for more than an hour before he spotted Luigi pacing to the front entrance, his uniform impeccable, his face all business. When he spotted Haik, though, the boyhood friend in him emerged.

"Hey, there's the man! How goes it, brother?"

"It's going. Need a minute of your time."

"Always. What brings you here?"

"Ah, is there someplace we can talk?"

"Of course, yes, let me just check in here with the deskman."

They stepped inside and Luigi exchanged some words with the copper at the desk and then rejoined Haik.

Haik didn't want anyone else to hear anything he was about to say. No, any one of these cops could have a line right into Harry Bennett's office and that wouldn't go. Had he made a mistake even showing up?

"Yeah, sure, enough said. Follow me, sir. We'll find that dog of yours in no time."

Luigi winked, and Haik followed him up some back stairs to the fourth floor where a few blues milled about. He took him to a back room, an interrogation room he guessed, and closed the door behind them.

"First thing, Haik. You can't be seen around here. You don't know who's talking in this building, and half the guys in blue are taking money from Bennett and other parties on the wrong side. Unless it's an emergency, if you need to see me, leave a message for me at the front desk. Tell them, 'I got a lead on Killer Burke.' When I hear that, I'll meet you at Dolgovich's at 8 p.m. and we'll talk there. So, what you got for me?"

"Well," Haik began, "I don't know if this is total bullshit, and maybe somebody's trying to set *me* up, but Lister came to me with a business idea today. He's going solo running some goods from Canada, but he's operating down in Ecorse. Right where Jefferson meets White Street, in Ecorse Park. He's bringing in more than booze, though— he's got something going with, what, what's he call it, hare-o-in. I guess he's working with someone named Goldberg. He wants me to be the pay-off man and handle the delivery. Anything with this guy stinks, but maybe this is where you can put the hammer on him."

Luigi frowned. He knew some of what Lister was up to, but this could be the break he needed. The fact that Lister didn't want to be near the pick-up indicated he was jumpy, which wasn't good. If he felt the pinch was on, he would be heavily armed and start blazing.

"You remember Goldberg, right?"

Haik searched his memory bur found nothing.

"Our old ship captain from our river runs. Pinchas Goldberg."

Haik's mind lit—sure he remembered, old gold-toothed Goldberg.

"Still a small timer. Got on the bad side of the Purples and is laying low doing solo work. Lister and Goldberg used to run together but I don't know what Lister's doing messing with him now. Doesn't sound right. What time's this coming off?"

"One in the morning on Monday. I guess it would actually be Tuesday morning."

Luigi again fell into thought, considering his options. They had time. They could set up a ring around the drop zone, stay invisible in the bush and wait for the goods to arrive. If Haik went, that meant Lister wouldn't be there—no good. Lister could always claim he didn't know anything about any booze or drugs and all the truckers they picked up at the drop were lying, trying to set up an innocent and honorable Ford employee like himself. Even if they followed the truck to wherever Lister was hiding his goods, he could still claim he didn't invite the truckers there and he was being framed. If they followed the goods all the way to Lister's hide-out, the advantage would be his and if guns popped they would be hit hard. The only way that route worked is if they just used Monday as a stake out and followed the truck and then investigated the hide-out later and determined the best way to hit it with the king rat inside. But that might take weeks, and if Lister was mixing up his drop days, which he probably was, they might never get a chance like this again.

"I tell you what, Haik. When Lister checks back with you, tell him you can't do it this time, something came up with the painter, but you're in for the next drop. He won't reschedule this one, it's too late, and if you don't cover for him, he's gonna be short manpower and it increases the chances he's gonna have to go there himself. A guy like him, he's not gonna trust anybody he doesn't know or doesn't think he can hunt down if he's crossed. It'll be tough for him to find a sap this late in the game. We want him there at the drop."

Luigi was smart. Haik wanted to be there when they finally got Lister, but what he said made sense. Justice—maybe there was such a thing. If all went well, Cam Lister would be getting his early next Tuesday morning.

Luigi lied to Orlin. Antonio, his little brother Toe, hadn't joined the Purples. But the real story, the whole story, was filled with too many questions, questions Luigi did not have answers to, questions he himself found it difficult to ask let alone answer. All the way home from the trainyard all those years ago, Toe cried and screamed. Luigi didn't know what to do, even if he should touch his little brother. As they neared their house, Toe pleaded with Luigi to not say anything to their parents. Luigi gave him his word, but struggled to comprehend what had just happened. What *did* the bulls do to him? He helped Toe clean off the blood but he nearly passed out when he saw the damage. Down there, where his parts should be, was nothing but a gaping gash.

He took Toe to the neighborhood doctor. Nothing could be done, even if they did have the parts. He placed chloroform over Toe's mouth and nose and then went to work stitching and applying salves and bandages. Keep an eye on him, the doctor said, keep the salves on and the bandages clean, but there was only so much that could be done: Toe was a boy, but he would never be a man.

And today Luigi could say honestly that if he knew then what he now knew, he would have done everything differently. He would have made Toe go with them on every boxcar bust and kept him in his sight at all times. He wouldn't give in to fear and humiliation. But he did. He decided that Toe should stay home while they went scavenging the city, picking through its trash and worksites and scoping out the railyards for their next bust. And what did Toe do? That's what Luigi would always regret. He thought he was protecting Toe by leaving him behind, but he was wrong. With their father at work and mother home taking care of the other kids and cooking and cleaning and sewing for the neighbors for a few extra dimes, Toe went out on his own, alone, into the streets. What he was looking for, Luigi would never know, but what Toe found, what he ended up with, was something worse than what happened to him in that trainyard so many summers ago.

Toe spent his days wandering up and down Jefferson, from Gabriel Richard Park to Owen Park to Henderson Park all the way to Waterworks Park. These were not places for a nine year old kid by himself in the middle of a Depression. There were too many spots where no one could see you, small culverts, out of the way spots. Here, the dregs of the city congregated, to sleep or beg or drink wine or do other things. And where there was misery, there were those who knew that misery bred desperation, the kind of desperation that knew no right or wrong. Odd men would circulate amongst the panhandlers and vagrants and, yes, kids, and offer a nickel or dime for favors, the kinds of favors that required secrecy. Some of the men had kindly faces and dressed well—they could not be bad men. They smiled and talked in soothing tones, and all they wanted in return for a nickel or dime was friendship, the kind that would take place in a stand of trees or in the back of a parked car. What did Toe have to lose? By the end of the day, he could earn a pocketful of change and buy his own Peter's and Cross potato chips and a Faygo soda pop in the new 12 ounce bottle and not trouble his family a bit. If Gee-Gee was ashamed of him and wouldn't let him go on the runs, he would take care of himself. Often when Luigi got home at night, Toe was still out on the streets, but Luigi let it go, let it go and put it out of his mind.

And that's what Luigi Leoni could not live down. When Griff Slater came by the house and got Luigi and told him to come quick, he had found something in the alley around the corner, Luigi could sense darkness. It was Toe. Lying in the rotting trash. Not Toe, but Toe's body, what used to be his little brother. He touched Toe's skin—cold. Like Vahram, he would not come back. He told Griff not to mention anything about this to anyone, not even his parents or the guys from the Rouge, nobody. Griff was a simple man—he was good for his word. He and Griff drove the body down to the river, wrapped it in some tarp Griff had in his trunk, tied off the bundle and laid it into the river, watching it bob and drift and eventually slide below the surface. And that was it.

As Luigi watched Haik leave the station, he reminded himself that every Cam Lister he brought down was another chance to make up for what he did not do for his little brother. It was a chance to exact revenge on whomever it was that took Toe's life and dumped what was left of him in the filth. There were compromises—yes, he knew Cam Lister fired the gun that killed Liam Meadows, but the politics of the time smothered justice. But not in the case he was now working on. This was not Cam Lister, Service Department lieutenant for the Ford Motor Company, who was being tracked, but Cam Lister bootlegger and dope smuggler acting out of his own personal greed and defiance of the law. This was who he would bring down, this version of Cam Lister, with no mention of or connection to the Ford name. And every time he did this, it was putting his arm around his brother Toe and taking him in the truck with him on another boxcar bust and never letting him out of his sight.

Luigi took a team of men down to Ecorse Park and scouted the areas around White Street. He walked to the shore and looked out and saw Cam Lister's island, a non-descript clump of earth littered with scrub brush and deformed trees. The Canadians would like this; they could transfer a boat to the island and not have to come too far into U.S. water and let the Yanks worry about what happened with the people on the land. If they had to come to the shore, they could charge more and they would likely tow a rowboat—if the cops intercepted them, they would just cut the rope to the rowboat and that was it, technically they were not in possession of anything illegal, just some friendly boaters out on a late night cruise who got a little lost, that's all. Sure, the cops would recover the goods, but not the men who brought them or those who intended to sell them.

That wasn't good enough for Luigi. They would have to be patient, stay on land, let the products up onto the shore and let the people on shore physically touch the goods, load them, and that was it, possession of contraband, dead to rights. And the payoff was Lister being there front and center, unable to hire out a patsy, overseeing the drop himself at the scene of the crime. Then the coppers could move, weapons drawn, ready to take out tires or men, depending on what direction the hoods chose to go.

And so they went ahead. Three hours before the party, they parked their vehicles south of White Road behind a cluster of trees—if Lister or his boys got a glimpse of any rides they didn't recognize, the show might be cancelled. Three men stayed behind with the wheels, ready for the sight of a flare or the bark of Tommyguns, at which point they were to fly down Jefferson and take out the first truck they saw, Lister's well-known coupe, or any vehicle looking like it had a hot date somewhere in the city. Luigi and the rest of his squad hiked up to the area surrounding the park.

He found his look-out base. Armed with a chopper and a flare gun, he lay down on a brush covered rise that gave him a clear view of the sandy shore and the trail that led down to it. Once he was sure the drop was made and Lister was present, he'd let them load all their stock and then they'd be on him. He'd shoot the flare, and one of his teams would bee-line for the truck, and the others would round up anyone trying to make a run for it. They were ready, but everything really depended on whether or not Lister himself made an appearance.

Time drifted. Light seeped from the moon overhead in the black sky and an occasional passing freighter. There were the sounds of nocturnal animals moving about, but the only sound Luigi cared about was a truck engine and Lister's voice. At about a quarter to one, Luigi made out a truck engine coming down White Street. Its headlights were off—he expected that. The engine was cut maybe only twenty yards from his vantage point, and he could hear voices. Some men chatted quietly and then he made out their black silhouettes trekking down to the shore. Once there, a lantern was lit and hung off one of the scrub branches near the water. It was a go. There was going to be some kind of drop, but would it include the main prize? Twenty minutes later, Luigi made out a distant light from the island—the Canucks were ready to make their cruise. The sound of a boat motor was heard chuffing off in the distance and soon the boat itself was seen in the moonlight reflecting off the water. Sure enough, the craft was towing a rowboat just in case the bellbottom blues were around. The motor boat scraped up to the shore and a man jumped out while two of the men from the shore ran to the rowboat and pulled it in.

"Let's make this quick, aye," came an unmistakably Canadian voice.

"My pleasure," said one of the men from the truck.

Luigi could make out the drop going down and the Canadian jump back onto the motorboat. The shoremen unloaded the rowboat at a serious clip, piling their goods on the narrow strip of beach. Once they had all they had paid for, they dimmed the lantern and the motorboat was already disappearing into the blackness, the empty rowboat in tow.

The shoremen moved the cases of product up from the shore and shoved them into the back of their truck. If Lister was here, he was in the truck, but that wasn't likely—he wouldn't put himself in with the goods no matter how desperate he was. Luigi let out an inaudible sigh. A bust. No Lister. When the truck was on the road, he'd set off the flare and his lead vehicle would follow the truck and hope they could locate Lister's warehouse. That would be good, but it would take more time before they could actually get Lister with something that could stick.

He heard the truck engine start, and he readied the flare gun. He then heard vehicles approaching and the truck grind to a halt. Doors opened and slammed shut and then, out of nowhere, the shredding rattle of Tommy guns. What the hell was going on? Had his men jumped the gun? Were they gunning it out with the truckers? Luigi let the flare rip and then scrambled through the underbrush, pointing his own chopper to where the truck had stopped just short of Jefferson. There was company. Bodies lay on the ground on either side of the truck and darkened figures leaped into the cab. There were two cars in the road, but they weren't cops. On instinct, Luigi uncorked his own trench sweeper and let the rounds rip into the back tires of the truck.

A confused lull fell over the scene, and then fire opened up from within the two waiting cars. They were way off the mark, but Luigi's men on the shore had now joined the battle and peppered the cars. They just had to pin them there until the rest of the force rolled in from down the road.

Luigi emptied a stick into the car nearest him and then rolled to his side, expecting a return of fire, and loaded a fresh clip. More shots came from the darkened cars, but the engines revved—they were going to make a break for it. Off to his left, Luigi could see the headlights of his cruisers gunning down toward them. He let another barrage of lead fly into the darkened vehicle, spraying at front tires, engine, and driver's seat. It rolled to a stop and died, engine still idling.

The second car backed up onto Jefferson and shifted into drive. Luigi let off the last of his stick and drew his revolver, chasing after the car on foot. He emptied the cylinder into the passenger side door, holstered his pistol, and fumbled for another clip for his Tommy. His cruisers were now barreling in, and he flagged the second one down and jumped in. They could not let the remaining car out of sight.

"What the hell happen?" asked his driver.

"Ambush," Luigi shouted. "This wasn't a drop, this was a pirate job. Lister's hijacking this load, not picking up."

This was an old trick mastered by the Purple Gang itself years before. Why import your own booze or dope? Just find out who was running the river, let them pay off the Canucks, and then hold them up for all the product they're worth. No investment except in bullets, then water down the liquor and sell it at a handsome profit. The Purples were all fighting within their own ranks now, taking care of police work by gunning each other down, so a hood like Lister thought he could jump into the game without being noticed. They gained on the fleeing car, which had to have taken some hits. Luigi hollered at the driver to nose his bumper right on their tail and he leaned out of his side window and let the Tommy gun flare, metal popping and glass shattering.

He reloaded, but he could spot someone in the back seat of the car ahead and make out the barrel of a weapon, maybe a shot gun.

"Get ready to veer," he shouted to his driver, and put a hand to the wheel.

When he saw the barrel leveled through the blasted out rear windshield, he ducked over onto his partner and jerked at the wheel as a muzzle blast flashed. The glass on Luigi's passenger side of the front windshield shattered, but he was up again and leaning out the side window, ready to return the favor.

"Go! Go! GO!"

They were now side by side with the pirates. This one had to count. From front to back to front again, Luigi laid in with his Tommy—nothing in that car could have escaped a hit. Sure enough, the car made an erratic carom toward them and then away again before spinning and tipping wildly. It began to slide along the road on its side, spark and dirt bubbling up in its wake. Luigi's driver locked the breaks, about sending Luigi through the front windshield.

They came to a rest. Dazed, they all froze before Luigi roused them into action.

"Let's go, let's go, weapons out! Nobody leaves that car."

He was out his door and off to the smoking hulk just ahead of them. If anyone was alive in there, they were still dangerous. If they could think and recognize, they knew they were had and, with nothing to lose, they were going to fire. The trick was to get to them before they could recover their senses and locate their weapons, which, if luck was with the police, they had lost during the wreck.

The car sprawled on its side, the undercarriage facing the police. Luigi signaled two men to the rear to check if anyone was moving in the back seat. He readied his Tommy and, taking one more good breath, rushed to the front.

The windshield was gone, and in the moonlight he could see two bodies crammed against the passenger side door, one pinning the other to the ground. The top body, which must have been the driver, was not moving, but the bottom man, he was nodding his head and struggling to free himself from under the dead weight of the other man. Luigi stepped forward without hesitation and placed the nose of the machine gun between the bottom man's eyes.

"Stop moving or you're done," Luigi ordered. As he crouched down to have a closer look, he locked eyes with Cam Lister.

There was an eerie emotionlessness about Harry Bennett's anger that paralyzed his victims. He never lost his composure, yet he always seemed to be one split hair from uncontrollable rage. Haik sat in his office on Tuesday morning, having been summoned from his duties with Rivera by a Bennett foot soldier, Gittens, who would not let on to Haik what he was in for, which was not a good sign. Had something actually happened with Lister? Some kind of trouble at the river? Was Luigi okay? Haik told himself he was square. He had been with Rivera until well after midnight. They were developing a bond and for some reason the painter found Haik good company during his marathon creative sessions.

When Rivera painted, his endurance was inhuman. The plasterers and tracers showed the extreme fatigue that enveloped them as they tried to keep safely ahead of the master, grinding his paints, testing and then applying the necessary layers of paste, sweating, their hair drooping, their eyelids sagging. Rivera, though, like some great bear, barely seemed to move, and yet he covered immense chunks of wall, his hand nimbly transferring vibrant colors to the once indistinct surface and making life-filled art where mere outlines had been only moments before. Like Henry Ford, he was a magician, but he was a wizard of sight and color and imagination, not steel and glass and rubber and gasoline.

Haik entered Bennett's office and he had his wingmen present, Cutty and some others sporting impassive looks that threatened extreme discomfort if provoked. Had Haik now become one of them? Did others see him the same way he now viewed these goons? Bennett put short work to Haik's musing.

"Lemme cut to the chase here, Pelini. Some shit went down early this morning, and your name has come up. I'm gonna ask you some questions and I want nothing but the straight dope from you. You with me?"

"Yes, sir."

"Good. Now, Cam Lister was involved in some, some events shall we say, and he's in some pretty hot water right now. What concerns me, Pelini, is that he appears to be mentioning your name quite a bit. Yes, several others, too, but he did mention you as being perhaps somewhat involved. Straight up, no bullshit, you tell me everything you know about what came off last night."

Bennett's bowtie blazed red and he pointed a stubby finger directly between Haik's eyes. Haik swallowed. Part of him was ecstatic that Lister was in some kind of trouble, but part of him feared what Bennett might actually know. Had someone tailed him to the station? Luigi told him it was stupid to visit him there, but it was too late to undo that mistake. Was there a cop on the take who ratted that he had a private conversation with Luigi? Damn, how could he be so stupid. He should have met Luigi somewhere else, anywhere else but police headquarters. Dumb, dumb, dumb.

"I was with Mr. Rivera last night, Mr. Bennett. You can ask him."

Bennett's lips pursed, and evil rose in his face.

"I didn't ask where the fuck you were last night, now did I? I asked what you *knew* about last night. Now, let's start again, and this time no bullshit. What exactly do you know about last night?"

The message was loud and clear. Haik would stick to answering the question and not cementing an alibi.

"Well, I don't wanna get nobody in trouble…"

"Fuck trouble, Pelini, we're way past trouble. In fact, you're gonna find yourself in a whole heap a trouble if you don't cut the bullshit."

Bennett had reached his limit. The next step was pain—Haik had to quit dancing.

"Right. I'm sorry, Mr. Bennett. All I know is what Lister told me. He wanted me to be his patsy on some kind of run from Canada. I was suppose to meet up with some guy named Goldberg down in Ecorse and handle the money on the drop. I told Lister I was busy with the painter. Mr. Bennett, I really didn't want no part of it, so I begged off. It didn't sound right. That's the God's honest truth of it."

Haik told the truth—most of it. He wasn't going to offer up the fact that he had a childhood friend in the police department and that he dropped a nickel on Lister—no, that detail was between him and Luigi and Lister. Bennett looked him over. Whatever you could say about Bennett, he had a way of sizing you up, from soles to crown and back again, like an x-ray machine of the soul.

"Tell me something. Would you say, Pelini, that you and Lister are…friends?"

Bennett sat back in his chair, now acting relaxed, his voice calm but threatening in a totally unthreatening way.

"No, sir."

Had he answered too quickly? He didn't want his hatred for Lister to become common knowledge. He swallowed hard. He'd have to slow down a bit.

"Why not? Something happen between you two? Some kind of problem I should know about?"

Haik thought of the night in the barn, tied to the chair, the punches and kicks, and being locked in the trunk of a car. Yes, something had happened, but this wasn't the time or place to drag it out.

"No, no real problems. I…I just, I don't know, Mr. Bennett. There's something about the guy, something that makes me not really trust him, his, I don't know…his teeth."

Bennett leaned forward and looked Haik straight in the eyes.

"His teeth! Goddammit, you just don't stop breaking my ribs, Pelini! Yeah, Lister does have himself a sewer for a mouth, don't he? Christ, them chompers would scare a crocodile! Makes you, I don't know, wanna scrub out his yapper with Ajax cleanser and a wire brush."

Bennett cackled and his toadies followed suit. Haik felt enough at ease to crack a slight smile. Bennett, however, was not finished.

"Let me ask you this, Pelini, and again, I want it straight. You wouldn't mind seein' Lister pinched, would ya?"

Bennett's manner was sly and disarming. Haik thought it over. He'd have to tread lightly here. He could feel Bennett's eyes boring into him.

"Whatever happens to Lister happens, Mr. Bennett, and I don't make it my business one way or the other. I don't like trouble I don't need, and I don't go looking for it. But to be honest, 100% on the level, seeing Lister pinched wouldn't break my heart, long as it didn't come back on you and the SD."

Haik couldn't have thought of a better answer if he had all night to think it over. Be straight up about your hatred, but more important show you're a company man. Kiss a little ass, lick some boot, but stay on the level.

Bennett smiled with approval.

"So, how's our painter doin'?"

It was over. Haik had passed. He eased back silently into idle.

"He's doing fine, I guess. Just making a lot of paintings now, up and down the scaffolding, putting colors all over the place."

"So what exactly is this guy painting, anyways?"

"Oh, near as I can tell, some naked ladies and these big hands, and some airplanes and cars. I don't really understand it, but there's all kinds of different stuff."

"Sounds like a crock of bullshit to me, but there ain't been no complaints, no reports a problems, and that's good to hear, Pelini. So far, everybody's pleased. Mr. Ford has no beefs, but he's keepin' his eye out from a distance. His son Edsel, well, he's got his head up his own asshole with this whole painting adventure. Basically, everybody's pleased with how you're takin' care of him and keeping everything nice and quiet. That's what Mr. Ford likes, and what Mr. Ford likes, I like. You okay for money? Shit, don't answer. Here, take some more. Buy the painter some tequila and tomato pie."

Cutty and the wingmen laughed and Bennett handed Haik some additional cash. He never counted money in Bennett's presence. That would be impolite, and maybe Bennett would get the idea Haik didn't trust him, which he didn't, or that Haik was hungry for money, which he was, but displaying distrust was a sure way to the doghouse, so he just took the bills and slipped them into his front pants pocket.

"Thank you, Mr. Bennett. You need me to do anything else?"

"No, we're done here. Gittens, before you take Pelini back to check on the painter, swing by the glass house. See if anyone's piking. We're square here, though. You're straight up, Pelini. I like that. Now beat it."

Haik got up, gave Bennett a slight courtesy bow, and walked out of the office feeling a sense of deep relief. He didn't have anything to do with whatever happened with Lister in Ecorse. Well, at least as far as being physically present—what Luigi decided to do with the information Haik passed along was Luigi's call, not his. But what exactly did happen? He had to find out something from Gittens on their ride to the glass house and then his trip back to the museum. How bad did Lister ball up? What the hell came off?

"Git, man, you gotta level with me here. What the hell happened with Lister last night?" asked Haik once outside.

"You really don't know nothin' from nothin', does you?"

Gittens was a palooka, a small guy, a former bantamweight with a nose that covered most of his face. He'd taken several severe beatings in the ring before signing on with Bennett. His scrapper's toughness and quarrelsome nature couldn't be underestimated, but he was mostly an honest guy who was straight with anyone who treated him the same way.

"You think I'd be dumb enough to lie to Mr. Bennett? C'mon, Git, you can't leave me blind here."

"No, I suppose you wouldn't lie to Mr. Bennett. That wouldn't be too smart, would it?"

Gittens was no college professor, and he was no jack rabbit at answering questions. They got in his car and headed off to check on the glass house.

"Christ Git, you heard what was going on in there. If Lister's trying to finger me for something I didn't do, I at least need to know what happened."

He'd rather get the story from Gittens than have to hear it from Luigi who knows when—right now, it just wasn't safe to be seen with a cop. And being dumb was good—if and when Gittens reported back to Bennett, Haik's sincere, desperate ignorance would play well.

"Okay, I'll tell you what I knows. From what I hears, seems Lister was doin' some double time. They says he was hijackin' a drop on the river. He shoots up the bootleggers, kills 'em dead, and was takin' their treasure for hisself when all the sudden the cops come round. Him and some of his boys tries to make a run for it, but the cops track 'em down and that was that. Two a the guys was killed, but Lister makes it out with just some scratches. Lucky guy. But he's unlucky, too. He gets pinched, so Mr. Bennett seen a judge and gets him out on bail but he ain't none too happy. Lister done laid a egg on this one, but he was sayin' that it wasn't his fault, he been set up. Leastwise that's what he's been sayin'."

So something did happen, lots of men down, no question, Luigi definitely had sprung the trap. But Lister was still alive, and now out on the street. What was he really thinking now? He mentioned Haik's name, but Bennett said he mentioned others too—probably everybody he tried to sham into getting involved in the ambush. Finally, Lister balled up so big he couldn't skate away, and worse than his trouble with the police was his trouble with Harry Bennett. The situation wasn't perfect, Lister was alive, but it was still sounding pretty damn good.

What Haik didn't know was that while he was on his way back to the museum Lister was being brought in to see Bennett face to face. Once he was escorted down the steps to the basement, he was shoved into Bennett's office and pushed down into a chair. This would be no friendly chat. Lister was bruised and cut from the car roll over, limping and a bit stiff from being smashed about, but miraculously he hadn't been touched by one bullet. Even so, being in a hospital with a couple bullets would have been better than having to face Bennett.

"I'm gonna cut to the chase, Lister, you puke-faced fuck. I have no fucking idea what you were thinking…"

"I know, I know, Mr. Bennett, I'm sorry…"

"Shut the fuck up when I'm talking," Bennett snarled, and he was out from behind his desk to backhand Lister across the face. Lister took the blow and lowered his gaze, defeated and knowing it.

"Don't I pay you enough?" Bennett questioned. "Don't I send you enough side jobs? Didn't I trust you at the massacre? Ain't you been compensated enough? Huh? I'm asking you a damn question."

He clubbed Lister again, this time with his fist closed, and blood popped from Lister's upper lip.

"Yes, yes Mr. Bennett. Yes sir."

"And this is how you repay me? Goin' solo? Christ, you got some nerve, Lister, I tell you. Some goddamned nerve."

Bennett looked at Lister with total disgust, but Lister would not dare return his gaze.

"I'm sorry, Mr. Bennett. It's just, I listened to Pelini. I shoulda never done that. He set me up good on this one, Mr. Bennett."

Lister looked up to see if Bennett was taking. He wasn't. Another backhand crossed his reddened face.

"Set you up, huh? Held a gun to your head, I suppose? How the hell this dumbfuck dago nobody set up a big cheese like you? Huh? Pelini don't know his ass from a hole in the ground, so how exactly did he set you up? Huh? Answer me."

"I, I don't know."

"Oh, bullshit. Everybody knows you used to run with Goldberg back in your Purple days. You doubled him down, plain and simple, catching an old Purple boy in his own game. Didn't nobody shit in your britches, Lister. 'Set me up.' Geez, you must really think I'm stupid. I don't know why I bothered to post your bail. Some reason, you got Cutty on your side on this one. By the books, you should be rotting in a cell until trial comes, but I burned a favor and now I got to listen to your bullshit. I'm regrettin' helpin' you already. My number one rule is don't bring unwanted attention to my door, and you just broke that rule a thousand different ways, pal. Right now, you used up strikes one and two. One more and you're out, not just at the plate, but outta the game, off the team, outta the league, the whole fucking business. Christ, I don't know why I don't just have you taken out and cut into little pieces for fish bait, you slag-mouthed shit. You went behind my back and now you're on a short leash. You so much as get mentioned anywhere near a problem, well, let's just say for your sake, I hope that don't happen. For some dumb reason, I'm givin' you one last chance, but I just might take that chance back. Are we square?"

"Yes, Mr. Bennett," Lister answered, castrated.

"Get this piece of monkey shit outta my office. You so much as breathe funny, you better just keep swimmin' to Canada. Now beat it before I change my mind about keeping you on the grid."

Lister rose, head down, and turned like a man headed to the gallows. What were his options? Solo operations were done, period, at least until this blew over, but that was going to take a good long time. He'd probably be a strong arm at the Rouge now, nothing more, just another fleecer breathing down the necks of lowlife assembly liners.

That was no life. He was bigger than that. But he wouldn't sit down long. He'd work his way back into Bennett's good graces, or, or he'd move it along, pick up and head to Chicago or maybe to Buffalo, he heard things were jumping there.

But he'd settle some scores first. He had to find out exactly who it was that fingered him. He had talked to, what, how many different saps about the gig? He'd retrace his steps and he'd find the snitch. The original plan, though, it was a good one, nice and simple. Goldberg had talked to him about needing a trusty to handle the drop. Goldberg, the washed up dummy Purple gang member, trusted too much and he gave up too much of the plan—it was too easy. All Lister had to do was show up at the drop site and let the lead fly. He'd have the truck, all the goods, and no one to cut in on the profit. If any of the chumps he recommended took Goldberg up on his offer of a night's pay, he'd be just as dead as Goldberg and the rest of his crew and no witnesses. It was almost funny.

But someone squawked. Who was it? He had only approached saps—he wanted to make sure Goldberg had enough bodies on hand to not run chicken and make certain the deal went down. Which son-of-a-bitch ratted him out?

Miles away at the museum, Haik's mind worked just as feverishly. If Lister was onto him, he needed to be ready. Any time he was alone or out in the open, he was a target. Lister would give no warning. Just as he had done to the men in the truck at Ecorse Park, he'd take him out without warning or a chance for retaliation. He had let Haik survive before because he thought he might be able to use him and he wanted to test his allegiance—Haik passed. Now, though, he had to be ready.

Haik found Rivera in good spirits. Frida was there with him as well as Miss Lucienne and Mr. Stephen. Rivera had come to recognize Haik's entrance without even looking up from his work. Now, he was up at the top of the scaffolding, the blazing Michigan summer sun pouring in on him.

"Good day, my young man," shouted the painter.

"Good morning, Mr. Rivera. Mrs. Frida, everyone."

"And everything is good, no?"

"Yeah, I suppose. Why?"

"Oh, I thought I might have detected some discomfort in your voice. Perhaps I am wrong. My sincere apologies," Rivera sang from high above the garden court, suspended like some giant spider above the marble floor.

He was smart. Yes, plenty was bothering Haik right now, but he couldn't just start beating his gums. He needed to talk to Luigi, to Orlin, to Lu and anyone else Lister might be a threat to.

"Ohhh, this heat, it's something," Miss Lucienne said, changing the subject.

"I did not realize your city could be so, so scalding," commented Frida, herself looking completely worn.

The natural darkness of her complexion had begun to wane and she looked almost as if she was the consistency of the plaster being applied to the walls.

"Oh, yeah, we get up over 100 degrees in the summer." Haik was glad to talk about something as harmless as the weather. "Isn't it like this down in Mexico, too? I thought Mexico was a hot place."

"Mexico is a large country, too, Hank," said Frida. "Not so large as United States, but large enough. I live in the *mesa central*, higher up. It is not so unbearable as this. Oh, this heat, we have nothing like this in my home."

"My dear, we're fine here," Diego advised, "but you need to rest. I'll meet you back in our quarters. Please, go back with Hank to the hotel."

"I'm fine," she countered unconvincingly.

She labored another hour or so, commenting on the application of the plaster and advising the assistants on the outlines they traced with the large cartoons before the master followed with the definitive strokes and colors. After everything was in order, she could no longer deny her exhaustion and Haik agreed to walk her across the street to their chambers at the Wardell Hotel. Once at their door, Haik could detect Frida shudder slightly.

"Are you okay?"

He was ready to catch her if she began to fall. He wanted her to stay on her feet because he was afraid to touch her—she was so fragile he might break her. She held onto the door latch and placed her other hand to her temple.

"Yes, okay. I'm just a little, a little dizzy. The heat," she explained, but she looked worse than a little dizzy.

"Here, let's get you inside."

Haik opened the door and led her by one leaflike hand to the living room couch. He found the kitchen and drew her a cold glass of water. When he returned, Frida was laying down, her eyes cast off into the distance.

"Here, try some water."

"Ah, *gracias*, but water will do nothing for me," she whispered.

Haik watched her, then set the glass down on an end table. He felt as helpless as he had not long ago with Lu. Pregnant women. They were tough, tough to do what they did by carrying a baby, but tough to figure out, too.

"You know, Hank, Diego has now been offered a total of $25,000 by Mr. Ford, Edsel that is," Frida began, slowly, purposefully. "Not $10,000, but $25,000. A great sum, no? And you know what he'll do with the money? I'll tell you. He'll give most of it away, trying to buy his way into the international communist party. He's done more for workers all over the world to give them hope and dignity and to tell their story than any of those prostitutes, but he is going to pay them for approval they'll never give him. No, as long as he keeps filling their pockets with his money, they'll keep denying him. These, these fools, Russians, Germans, Mexicans, Americans, they'll spend his money on suits and cars and trips here and there and mistresses and not one worker will benefit. But I tell you, what you are witnessing in that garden, that creation, that world he is creating right on those walls, that will last forever. What will Kurella, Pedreros, Britos, Toledano, even bullet-headed Stalin, what will they leave the world? *Nada*. But Diego, workers until the end of time will be able to stand before one of Diego's frescos and feel pride in who they are and they will be able to know where they came from. Diego is giving that to them, forever. I, I will die, this baby, it will die...but Diego, he will live forever."

Her voice trailed off. Haik did not know what to say. It seemed like odd talk for a woman about to give birth in several months. He looked at her but her eyes continued to fix on something beyond the room.

"So, my friend, how is your wife? Healthy, I hope."

For the first time, she looked over at Haik. He was thankful for a change in subject.

"Yeah, yeah, thank you for asking, she's doing good. Getting to where, you know, you can see she's got something in the oven, you know."

Haik was trying to make light here, but somehow speaking of his wife's good health made him feel guilty. Frida could not look less pregnant. The only thing she could be carrying inside her was an acorn.

"And her tits, they're getting big, no?"

Haik about fell out of the chair. Frida smiled devilishly. She had hit her bullseye.

"My good man, you don't need to answer that. Your wife, she is a good woman. I will never forget her opening her home to us. This is what Diego does with his art. His creations are his world, his home, his place. His gift, his food he shares with the world, all of that is found at the end of his brush. He...."

Before she could finish, there was a knock at the door. Miss Lucienne entered.

"Hank, there's someone to see you at the museum. Frida, honey, are you okay?"

Miss Lucienne went to Frida on the couch. Maybe a woman's touch was needed because Haik felt like he was just making things worse. He was not equipped for where this conversation had been or might be going.

"Okay, I hope you're feeling well, Miss Frida. You need something, you let me know. Good bye, ladies."

Haik quickly exited. My God, Lu's tits? Where did Miss Frida get that? He could only get in trouble back at the apartment alone with such a woman, such a bearcat, and he was glad to escape.

And who was at the museum? Lister? Haik put his hand to his holster—he was ready. Before he left the Wardell, he scoped the street for Lister's coupe or any other car that looked like trouble. It was clear. He walked briskly, looking in all directions at once, listening for wheels squealing on the pavement, the metallic click of a trigger being cocked, anything. He entered the museum's back entrance and looked left and right. Lister was not beneath ambushing him here. Haik strode to the garden court, and when he entered he was relieved to see Luigi, who looked fit and unharmed after his encounter with Lister.

"Man, this is really something," Luigi called, looking around him at Rivera's work. "Mr. Rivera, how do you stand it? It's got to be 105 degrees up there."

"Actually," Mr. Stephen, an assistant, chimed in, "we put a thermometer on the top of the scaffold and it's 119 with no breeze. A bit toasty."

"Oh, you flatterers," laughed Rivera.

He was a marvel. Just standing down on the floor of the court, Luigi was sweating. How could a man of Rivera's size work so slavishly under such inhuman conditions and not falter, misapply a brush stoke, pass out or simply give up until the heat abated?

"I can't imagine what this is gonna look like in another couple months. Incredible," gushed Luigi, but Haik was anxious for the lowdown on Lister.

"Please excuse us for a second, Mr. Rivera," Haik shouted up to him.

There was too much to discuss to sit here and small talk. Polite or not, Haik had to have some answers about what happened in Ecorse.

"By all means," the painter replied, never breaking stride in his work.

Haik and Luigi went to the men's room and locked the door behind them.

"C'mon, Gee, I'm dying. What what came off?"

Luigi smiled.

"Oh, your man Lister, he's in deep. He was setting you up, Haik. He wasn't working with Goldberg. Goldberg musta hit him up for help and Lister was planning on hijacking that deal from the get go. He rubbed out Goldberg and his crew. Now, unbelievable, but he's out on the street. Only in Detroit. But the good thing is he's in the shitter with Bennett. This wasn't part of the package with the Service Department— I'm gettin' word he's ready to pull the plug on Lister, which helps us. We just need to get him to trial before a clean judge."

Haik tried to understand what he was hearing. How could Cam Lister be a free man? He killed Mr. Meadows and now he killed Goldberg and his boys. Did he have to kill Henry Ford himself in broad daylight at Navin Field before someone put him behind bars?

"So, so what do we do?"

"Right now, hope he's scared shitless until the trial. I don't like him loose, but there's nothing anyone can do about it."

"I don't get it. How is this guy free, Gee? How many people he got to kill? I'm telling you, he's the kinda guy to come after Lu and Charlie. I don't give a damn about me. He wants me, I'm right here, I got a piece too. But Lu and Charlie, I can't have that. I don't like this, Gee."

What would happen if Lister took a trip out to Utica while Haik was in with Rivera and Orlin was at work at the Rouge? He needed some kind of protection, not for himself, but for everybody back at the house.

"He's free for right now. I'm gonna see if we can speed things up, get his ass into the courtroom. I know you're uptight and I don't blame you. Just give me some time, Haik. We got this far—we're close."

Luigi was trying to be reassuring, but too much was uncertain and far too much could still go wrong. Haik needed more than words.

"Yeah, I guess so. But I need a shotgun. A couple of 'em. One for home and one to keep on me. You got to hook me up. Lu and Charlie need something, Gee. That bastard come around…"

Haik couldn't finish his thought.

"Okay, I'll set you up. Shotguns, some boxes of shells, no problem. Least I can do for helping me clamp Lister. But you can't go looking for him, Haik. You gotta promise me that. Bad as you want it, it's not your deal, brother."

Haik looked at Luigi.

"Yeah, sure, you got it. Just get me the guns."

Lu learned fast. The little switch on the side, that was the safety. Click it this way, the gun won't go off, the triggers were locked. Click it the other way, the triggers were free. It was a double barrel shotgun, sawed off, so don't worry about being an expert with the aim. It was made for short distances and it sprayed a good wide area. Don't try to use it for someone across the road. If they're close enough to hurt you, then they're close enough for you to use this on them. And if you miss with the first trigger, you always had a second shot to finish the job. And it kicked like a mule, so use two hands and don't put the stock near your belly, not in your present condition.

"Haik, do you realize what you're training me to do?"

He was somewhat resentful of her tone. What was he supposed to do? He couldn't be everywhere at once. This was for her good and Charlie and Arkina.

"Yeah, yeah I do. Lu, I'm trying to teach you something to protect you and Charlie and Arkina when me and Orlin ain't here."

"Yes, but why? Why do we need to live like this, afraid and carrying guns?"

He didn't know where she was going with this. Instead of being grateful that he was protecting her, she sounded angry.

"We need to live like this because this is how the world works, Lu. I didn't ask for things to be like this. My brother Vahram didn't ask for this. Your father didn't ask for this. Luigi didn't ask for bullets whizzin' under his nose. I didn't ask someone to sucker punch me every time I turn around. But that's what everybody got. That's what it is. And now, we're gonna do something. We ain't gonna just sit back and let that happen to us."

Lu would not relent.

"When did we have to start protecting ourselves, though? We never had to do this when you worked on the line."

"Yeah, that's true, and when I worked on the line we ate potato soup and a slice of bread every day and me and you and Charlie shared a room and didn't own a pot to piss in or a window to throw it out of."

He had raised his voice, which wasn't his way, but he was tired of his guilt, the feeling that moving out to the house was the cause of everything bad that happened to them. He was not the cause of all their misery. No, they could still be sharing a room back in the Pehlivanian house and Mr. Meadows would still be dead. That wouldn't have changed, and they wouldn't have a car and a house and enough money to eat three times a day and travel to town on Sunday and see a picture show. Wasn't that worth something?

"We were happy, Haik."

Her looked off toward the barn. Was it true? Were they really happy living on top of one another, alternating between a few changes of worn clothes, their space filled only with themselves, the sounds of their own breaths as they drifted off to sleep, the windy fragrance of clothes fresh off the backyard line? Her words were too direct and true for Haik to comprehend or give in. And would Mr. Meadows really be dead if he had never joined the SD? Would someone else have run to the front of the protest line, alerting Cam Lister where to aim his pistol? Was Cam Lister really aiming at him and not Mr. Meadows? If so, he *was* guilty in Mr. Meadows' death.

Her eyes were wide and clear, her mouth slightly open, as if about to speak again.

"Lu, darling, please believe me, we're almost through with this. I know I'm spending a lot of time running the painter around, but it's the safest I ever been in a long time, and it's the safest you ever been until Lister come into the picture. Luigi's working every minute to put him away. Once he does that, we're home free. We got it then. We live out here, we plant our food, we breathe fresh air, we raise our kids to play in the woods, they grow up not hungry and not hating nobody and being safe. That's what we want, ain't it?"

Was he the only one who wanted the life they could live here in this house, out here on this land, away from the city? Was it only *his* dream?

"Haik, I know what you're trying to do for us. Bless you, I know, but don't you think there are more Cam Listers out there? You think once Luigi puts him in jail or somebody just as evil kills him no one will step in and take his place?"

He'd already thought about that himself. If Lister went down, Bennett would just move another bimbo up, someone else who would turn your stomach. Where exactly did it stop? Even worse, would Haik take Lister's place and become just like him? Deep down, was Haik really any better than Lister?

"So what do we do, Lu?"

She looked into him. Her eyes were never more clear or beautiful.

"Honey, I don't know," she whispered and looked off. He latched the safety and put the gun down and drew her near. She was now seven months along, showing and glowing, round as a mound and healthy. No one would harm her. No one.

"Lu, I got lots of pressures on me. I'm keeping this house going, I'm supporting my family, your family, I got a lot of people counting on me and I ain't gonna let 'em down. There ain't no money or work nowhere—this is it for now until somebody can fix this Depression. Just let me do what I gotta do for a little while longer. Please. It's just gonna to be a little bit more. I promise."

He didn't like what he was doing any more than she did. Right now, working for Rivera, yes, but overall, being a SD man, no. If he could choose, he'd rather be the right hand man for the painter than a SD slappy, but Rivera was gone from Detroit as soon as the walls were covered. If he wasn't with the SD, what would he do? Go back to the line? It was good enough money, but once you crossed over to SD man, you either stayed or you left Fords altogether—there was no going back. Go to Chrysler, General Motors, any of the thousand machine shops in the city? Yeah, but who was hiring? Who was really living now except the big cheeses and the crooks on their payrolls?

"Okay, a little bit more. I'll stand for a little bit more. I just worry. Charlie, he's happy here. He can play in the woods or fish and just be a boy. He has plenty to eat. It's good for him, and I want it to be good for this baby, too. Darling, I'm just sick of worrying every time you leave here what's going to happen to you, who's waiting for you, who has a beef with you and would hurt you to get even."

She leaned her head against Haik's chest.

Haik kissed her hair. Lu was right, but being right didn't make any of them safer. He double checked his own shotgun and then headed off to work. He stopped in at the glass house before driving to the museum. True, he didn't spend as much time there as he did before Rivera's arrival, but he had started some changes. He redid the whole lottery. Now, only the men who wanted to play put in a dollar, and Haik no longer took any cut. Maybe that was stupid, but these guys were hurting and he was doing fine with Bennett's spending money. Most guys still played, especially now that the kitty was bigger, and Haik felt less like a heel for orchestrating the game. When he arrived, there was some kind of dispute going one between the guys on the line and one of the belt operators. It appeared that the belt operator was told to speed up the belt by two seconds and the guys were beat trying to keep up and wanted a piece of the beltman. The foreman was trying to get the workers to just go along, alternating between pleading and threatening, but he was getting nowhere. Haik got both sides of the situation and made his decision.

"Slow it down by a second."

"Mr. Higgins said Mr. Bricker..." started the beltman.

"That's right, Higgins said..." added the foreman.

"I don't care what Higgins or Mead Fucking Bricker said. Slow it down by a second. That's final till we see how things are running."

What did these jackasses want, a total shutdown? For the linemen to kill them? All because they were afraid of a limp dick like Higgins? While they were standing around arguing, no cars were being made—that was a recipe for disaster for all of them.

"We got to speed...," the foreman started, exasperation in his voice.

"You are speeding things up, but by a second, not two. And who's the 'we'? You work down on that floor? You used to. You used to know what it was like. But you ain't down there no more, they are, and they say it's too fast. One second speed up, final."

Haik pointed at the linemen, but his eyes were zeroed on the foreman.

"Yeah, I used to be on the floor, I know damn well...." the foreman began.

"You worked on the floor when it was 30 seconds slower than what these guys are working at, so don't give me that shit. You slow that fucking belt down or I'm gonna have one of those men come up here and run it and you'll take his place on the floor. You want that? Huh? You think you can keep up with the belt running this fast?"

The foreman looked away and then nodded, fearing the idea of having to do what he forced on the others.

"Higgins isn't….."

Haik grabbed the man by the shirt collar.

"Higgins has a problem, you have him see me. If I hear from these men you sped the belt up on them again, we're gonna tangle. Now set the belt back a second and get to fucking work."

He released the man's shirt and went back to the floor and said the belt would be slowed and if it wasn't to see him the next morning when he stopped in on his rounds. He also told them that another increase might come, so strap it on tight and get ready to work, no complaining and no more stopping. They nodded, thanked Haik, and he was on his way to rejoin Rivera.

The museum was a welcome refuge from the noise and stupidity in the glass house. Management drove the men to move faster and faster and at the same time their pay went down. Increases were going to come, always, but at least let them come slowly so the men could adjust. There was nothing worse than somebody with his head in a book somewhere who thought he could tell the men on the floor who actually did the work what they should be doing and how fast they should move. They knew. They sweated, they worked, they were there. Haik was no engineer, but he would stand with the guys who were actually doing the grunting and not some tightass with a stopwatch in one hand and a whip in the other.

And what if Higgins confronted him tomorrow? Worse, what if old man Ford was behind the two second speed up? No question, Haik would be in deep muck. He couldn't win this battle. Do what was right and back up the guys on the line, and he faced a beating or worse. Strongarm everyone like a SD man should, and he was a heel who couldn't stomach himself. Either way, he would eventually pay a price.

The garden court, though, took his mind from everything. Once inside, he was again amazed to see how much ground Rivera had covered. The assistants, who had been in since three in the morning when Mr. Art and Halberstadt started preparing the paste, strained to keep pace. Rivera would go through two crews of plasterers and tracers and not skip a beat. The assistants could stop and rest—the master could not. He would pause briefly for some fruit or juice or his raw vegetable salad or a cigar, but the work continued.

"Well, my dear friend, what do you think?"

Rivera sat atop the scaffold eating some grapefruit sections.

"Mr. Rivera, it's, I don't know, it's, it's amazing to me."

Haik felt stupid that he couldn't discuss art and sound like he knew what he was talking about. But he *was* amazed. The colors and the sheer size of what Rivera was doing confounded him. There were giant women in the upper portions of the room, bigger than any drawings he had ever seen, and everything was filling in around them, images of diamonds and birds and tires and other things. The walls were about more than making a car. What Rivera was doing wouldn't break down on a road full of potholes. It wouldn't run out of gas. It wouldn't need new tires in a year. Its paint wouldn't scratch at a kicked up stone. Rivera's creation was completely foreign to Haik but something he could understand the value of without being able to explain what exactly it was.

"Allow me to tell you something about what I am saying with these figures and colors. Yes, it is true, all I am doing is telling a story, using these earthen materials and my hand and eye to offer my perspective on what I see and know and feel. Look there, and there, you see these female figures? Strong, no? Great earth mothers, yellow, red, black and white who provide to their sons and daughters. Black, like your brother Orlin, they are the coal that runs the ovens that power all, the carbon and combustible power that all rely upon. And red, like the first peoples of this land and my homeland, they are the fire that comes from the burning coal, the fire that will harden the steel that makes your city and all its inventions. And yellow, the most common color of skin on the earth, it is the color of sand, which is made into the glass that protects all and allows us to see both out and inside with clarity. And white, like lime, like the lime needed to prepare these very walls, it completes the steel, not the largest ingredient in the steel, but an agent without which nothing else would be possible. All are needed. All necessary—less one, less all. If the world is to prosper, each of these women must be allowed to grant her gifts, and we must accept them."

Rivera scrutinized his work. Haik looked on at the upper levels of the room, trying to fit together all the painter had just explained to him. As far as he could understand, the painting meant that everyone had to work together and all colors were important for one reason or another. It wasn't so complex after all. It was a good message, one he was glad Rivera was trying to put into his painting. How could old Mr. Ford or Edsel object to that?

"Are you feeling okay, my friend?" inquired Rivera, snapping Haik from his perusal of the court walls.

"Me? Yeah, I'm fine."

"You seem, I don't know, somehow, hmmm, worried, my friend."

Of course, Haik *had* been worried. Worried about Lu and Charlie and everyone at home. Worried about Lister waiting for him behind every corner and shadow he passed. Worried about Luigi and his family and Lu's family. Worried about the conflicts at work and finding himself in the middle of new violence. It must be showing, but what could he do with so much bottled up inside?

"Well, Mr. Rivera, maybe a little. Lately, I don't know, I, I got lots of worries. It's a long, long story."

"If you are in the mood for talking, I certainly have time to listen. Today is July 4th, your day of independence, yes. A great day of celebration for your nation. You see, I have exhausted all my crew and I still have wet wall to cover, a full *giornata*. Tomorrow, I have told them to rest. For now, though, I must keep myself alert. The plaster will not wait. Will you join me? Let this be your day of independence. Come, let your story free."

Haik could not tell this man no, no matter how much he wished he could head home or to sit quietly and just watch him paint. Rivera had made a request, to hear his story, so he would stay and maybe he could get some things off his chest.

"My pleasure, Mr. Rivera. I can tell you some things. Man, where the heck do I start?"

Haik laughed, but he knew there was nothing funny in what was on his mind. He had to be careful, and he felt almost as if Bennett or Lister or old man Ford might be listening in on what he was about to say.

"Why not with your friend? The one who was here the other day—the policeman."

Haik stopped to think. How did Rivera know Luigi was a policeman? He wasn't in uniform at the time. Well, Luigi probably told him before Haik arrived. But what exactly did Luigi tell Rivera? And how much should he tell Rivera now? He really had no one to talk to about anything. In his youth, Vahram was the one he could go to when anything bothered him. Vahram, Atlas himself, who could carry the world and Haik on his shoulders with ease. After Vahram, though, there was no one. Perhaps Orlin, but they ran in different circles now and even though they lived in the same house they were miles apart. And sure, there was Lu, but that was different. He was the person who was there for her to voice her fears to—she was not that person for him. He had to reassure her at all times and he could not be weak in her presence. But whom could he admit his fears to? Who would listen to him and not use his weakness against him in some way?

"Oh, Luigi. Yeah, he's an old friend. We been through a lot together."

Rivera had already resumed painting. Haik sat down on the edge of the fountain and placed his hat next to him. He was tired. He was ready to get rid of some of his burden.

"He seemed to have urgent information for you. All is okay?"

"Yeah, for the most part. It's kind of complicated."

"I have several hours. Please, be my guest," Rivera assured him.

Haik thought. Rivera didn't actually work for the Fords. They had hired him, but he didn't owe his whole future to them and they sure as hell didn't own this man. Nobody did, not even Miss Frida. He wasn't even American, so no laws really applied to him and nobody could arrest him for coloring up the walls in a big building. As soon as the painting was done, Rivera was onto his next adventure. Out of Detroit, probably out of the country. If there was anyone Haik could talk to right now, it was the painter.

"Mr. Rivera, I want to be honest with you. I, I ain't been able to tell nobody many things, things about me, my life, the things that have happened to me. Anything, really, my story, my whole true story. Some things, some things I told you about me, they ain't true."

"My good Hank, we all have our hidden truths. My job as artisan is to use my hands to bring certain truths to the people, the worker, those who labor to make the world what it is and what it can be. To bring a truth to light, to release what is hidden, it is a natural impulse. No, my friend, you need not feel bad for that. Please, proceed."

Rivera worked methodically with his brushes over the areas his assistants had outlined for him. So, here he was, alone with a great artist, a large man so much larger than life, a man who made things that were bigger than a whole house and worth ten times as much. Where should Haik begin? What could he tell this man?

"You know, my name, it's, it's not Hank Pelini. I ain't no Italian."

Rivera burst out in hearty laughter.

"This is no secret, friend! When Frida and I visited your lovely home, we met your parents and your sisters. I lived in Europe during the war. They were most certainly not speaking in the tongue of the master. No, not at all, we knew right away you were not Italian."

Haik felt foolish. To an educated person, he must be so easy to see through.

"I hate that name, really. Hank Pelini. It ain't me, Mr. Rivera. My name, my real name, is Haik. Haik Pehlivanian."

"Ah, *mi querido camrada*, an Armenian! I should have known. Your people are now part of mother Russia, protected from the Turk. Yes, I know your man Gorky. His name is actually Adoyan, quite a talent, although my own interest in cubism as such is long past. For me, the mythic cultural figure is most essential. Your people, though, they have known suffering, yes, like our own natives in Mexico, the Aztec, the Mayan, who suffered at the hands of Cortez and the others. Yes, Armenian, I see it very clearly now. Please, please continue."

Haik composed himself. He didn't know this Cortez guy or Porky, but he would keep going.

"Yeah, Armenian, right from the old country. You're exactly right. We know suffering, Mr. Rivera. Everyone I knew back in Armenia, they're dead now. My whole family except who came here. No one left. All of 'em dead."

Confession felt good, and Haik was eager to continue.

"But why change your name? You are in America, free now. For the Armenians I have known, their name is a great source of pride."

"No, trust me, my name is something I'm proud of, Mr. Rivera, it really is. But, well, I was hungry, my family was starving, my brother, he just got shot and killed and the only way I could get a job was to have a name that didn't sound too, I don't know, weird I guess, like something that made you think the person was weird, a foreigner, so my neighbor, he ended up being my father-in-law, Lu's father, he thought up a name that would help me get a job...."

Haik talked, unable to stop the words. Rivera did not miss a beat with his work, stopping only to load more paint onto his palette. Haik continued. Bishop School. The Purple Gang days. Vahram's death. Meeting Lu. Being drafted into the Service Department. Harry Bennett. The death of Mr. Meadows. The whole Cam Lister situation. The beatings, the threats, the danger, how he now feared for his family. Speaking was cleansing, like he was scrubbing himself with strong soap and a horsehair brush in a hard downpour. He talked until sunlight had disappeared from the overhead windows and Rivera became a shadowy god suspended above, still painting, still laboring.

"...Mr. Rivera, I'm sorry. I can't believe it. I'm sorry I talked so long. My God, look at it. It's dark. I shoulda been home. You should be home too."

"No, no, no, *amigo*, it is I who must apologize. I'm sorry, but I have been transfixed by your tale. You have family awaiting you, but I have kept you here selfishly as I work. It is I who am sorry."

"No, you ain't got nothing to apologize for. I needed to talk. I ain't never told nobody my whole story. Ever. My parents, my sisters, Lu, Orlin, they're the only ones who know who I am, but I ain't really never talked about it to nobody. Even to family. And you're gonna have a family yourself soon enough."

At this comment, Rivera paused.

"Haik, allow me to make some confession as well. Frida, as you have no doubt noticed, she is not well. This child, she wants this child so badly that she does not even think of her own survival. Haik, there will be no baby. I had visions of this when she first told me she was with child—from the beginning, I knew this child would never taste one breath of life. And later, when we arrived here, the doctors confirmed what I had already suspected. I have not told Frida—she would be crushed, but it is for the best. Her pelvis, her spine, they had been so damaged in her accident in Mexico she could never hope to survive nine months of hell with a baby. No, I cannot lose her to an unborn child."

"I'm sorry, Mr. Rivera," Haik offered.

"No, please, do not be saddened. I think she herself knows this as well—she's begun drinking quinine. Somewhere, she knows, too, I am sure, but she will not give up the thought of giving me a baby. I have children already, and I've lost a child—I need no more. But sadness, no, please, no sadness for this circumstance. This is life. Nothing to grieve over. Not in the least."

Rivera went back to his work. Now, the only light coming through the ceiling windows was from the moon. Rivera did not tolerate artificial light, which he said perverted his work, but how on earth could he even tell what he was doing in almost total darkness, even with his face nearly pressed into the drying plaster?

"Mr. Rivera, I can't really understand it, but how are you even painting right now? I mean, I can barely see you, but there you are, you're painting away. How can you even tell what color you're using or if it matches?"

Rivera laughed heartily again, dabbing away at the wall and reloading his brush as if he'd just started at the beginning of the day.

"Haik, to truly know the colors in the daylight, one must know them in complete blackness. If I have but a few rays of moonlight, my eye can still see as if the world were bathed in full sunlight. You know, my Frida, she calls me *carasapo*. In English, you would say 'frogface.' It is a pet name of great affection, but, I must tell you, I believe perhaps my wide eyes, they give me some power others do not possess. The great master had some such power. Michelangelo, he lay on his back, torches illuminating his world, but he knew color so well that a ceiling, a wall, curved surface or flat, he knew how every shadow created by the architectural trim and every angle of light from the upper windows affected his composition. How? How, lying on his back, paint falling back into his eyes, suspended so high above the ground, four years with his arms outstretched from his body, how could he know what he was creating would look like to a peasant over in the far corner of the chapel? But he did. This was his brilliance. And his work, all public. Any man, woman or child who wished could stand before this great majesty and behold. This is what any true artist seeks. Yes, I have been blessed with my vision."

"Well, for whatever it's worth, Mr. Rivera, I think you do pretty damn good pictures. I can't say I understand everything you're doing, at least until you explain it, and I learn something new every time I'm here. I never seen what that Michael guy did, but you gotta be up there with him."

Rivera laughed. They sat in silence for a while, Haik unable to see what Rivera was doing and the painter continuing to dab away.

"You know, Haik, the more I consider your circumstance, I have some ideas. First matters first, but I would like to do a little sketching of you and Orlin back at the Rouge. And then, something else, something to help you and your policeman friend with this man, Lister, this man who threatens you."

At that moment, the doors to the court burst open and Haik made out the form of Miss Lucienne, whom Rivera and Frida shared their quarters with.

"Mr. Rivera, it's urgent. Frida, she's bleeding. Badly."

Without hesitation, Rivera placed his palette down and descended the scaffolding with the ease of some great orangutan. In the dark, he gestured to Haik.

"Haik, please, come, we must go to her."

He followed them out the back entrance of the museum and across Kirby Street to the Wardell. Rivera had never moved with such speed.

"The bleeding's bad, not like before," said Lucienne, panic in her voice.

"Haik, you know Mr. Ford's hospital?" asked Rivera.

"Yeah, I do. I'll pull the car around and meet you inside," he said, running off to his car on the sidestreet.

He wheeled up to the curb next to the Wardell's entrance and ran inside, past the twin opposing wall fountains with the lions' heads streaming with water. At the Rivera quarters, he found the painter crouched over Frida, who lay on the couch, pale death on her face. Rivera talked to her in Spanish, comforting her, brushing her hair, but the fear on her face did not abate.

"Lucienne, please, stay here and alert the hospital we are coming and ask for Doctor Lam," Rivera commanded. "Also, call Mr. Edsel and let him know what has happened, and Mr. Valentiner as well. If they need me, they can reach me at the hospital."

"I'll call for an ambulance…"

"*El nino, me duele, el bebe me esta matando…*"

"No, there is no time. Haik, can you help me? We must get her to the car."

Rivera stood up, pleading on his face. Frida lay there, bone white, wounded, blood soaked through the front of her skirt. Haik scooped her up and was at the door before Rivera could open it. They made their way downstairs to the car, where Haik placed her as gently as he could in the front seat. Her agony was apparent—her breathing was labored and every few moments she shrieked at some striking phantom. Rivera met them at the car, out of breath, sweating, and once he was inside they took off north on Woodward. Haik did not want to wait until they got all the way to West Grand before he headed west—he took a short cut, left on Antoinette, crossing over 3rd Street, merging onto Holden, rolling over the railroad tracks and then heading back north on Trumbull, finally racing across West Grand to the emergency entrance of the hospital.

At the curb, Haik was up and helping Rivera out before Rivera had fully opened the door. He then slid in and worked his arms under Frida and lifted her from the car. His son Charlie weighed more than Frida, and he rushed past the painter and into the hospital. Doctors and nurses were already waiting and Rivera finally ambled in, completely winded.

"It is…as expected…," Rivera panted to the doctor.

"How long has she been bleeding like this?"

The doctor examined Frida as she lay on the gurney sheets, which were already deeply stained in blood.

"I, I think Lucienne said an hour. She…she is so stubborn," Rivera gasped, placing a hand to Frida's forehead.

"Shut up, *Dieguito, elefante gordo!*" Frida spat, before a spasm of fresh pain seized her, forcing her to cry out.

"*Por favor, mi paloma, descansa, descansa, yo estoy aqui,*" said Rivera soothingly, brushing back her hair with his hand.

"Please, Mrs. Rivera, you're going to be fine, just try to rest," said the doctor, but his face betrayed the direness of the situation.

Haik tried to imagine how a woman so small could lose so much blood. Rivera had said the baby would die, but Frida, what of her?

"We're going to take her directly to the operating room." The doctor gave commands to various nurses to make ready. "The main thing, at this point, is to control the hemorrhaging."

Frida looked up at the ceiling, her head moving slightly back and forth, wild-eyed, one hand clinging to Rivera's arm.

"My friend, *gracias*. I must go," Rivera called to Haik, and Haik nodded dumbly in return.

"The colors…" Frida murmured, still glancing wildly about and now completely caught in the delirium of pain. "*…que precioso!*"

Haik watched the clutter of doctors and nurses and patient and painter rumble noisily around a corner and out of sight. He stood dazed, trying to comprehend all that had just happened. He looked down at his shoes and then to his hands and forearms, which were covered in Miss Frida's warm blood.

Rivera's prophecy was correct. The baby did not live, and Frida herself was lucky to survive. Haik and Lu both visited her at the hospital, where Frida and Rivera greeted them warmly. The whole time, Rivera did not leave her side. A few days after Frida's admission, Haik visited to bring her some of her painting materials she had requested, her sketch book and some paints Miss Lucienne had put together for her, and she began to work immediately despite being incredibly weak. She lay in bed recovering, but an easel was set up next to her bed by the room's windows and Haik could tell just from the early outlines she made she was a different artist than Rivera but still, at least to his untrained eye, a good one.

The painting he looked at was being done on a thin sheet of tin and the different parts of the painting both entranced and repulsed him, so much so that he could not stop looking. In the center was a woman who looked like Frida herself lying in the same cast iron bed she was now in, except in the picture she was naked and the sheets were covered in blood. The image made Haik uncomfortable—he checked to see if Miss Frida or Rivera noticed how he stared. Was it polite to look at the painting of a nude woman when the nude woman and her husband were right in front of you?

The painting was strange. From out of the bed in the painting there were these different things that seemed to hang in the air but were connected to the woman in the bed by red ropes, and in the background he could make out the outline of various buildings from the Rouge Plant. How did all this fit together? The one thing that stood out to Haik was the baby who floated right above her, a baby but it was as big as the woman in the bed. She called the baby in her painting "little Dagueito," and Haik could feel her pain when she spoke of this child.

"This is what I now know," she remarked tiredly, "everything I have, right there. You know, I met Diego when I was just a schoolgirl at the *Prepatoria*, 15 years old, and I said to myself at that time, 'Frida, you will bear this man a son one day.' Do you believe that? Ah, then, then I believed so many things. *Que tonto*. You know of my accident? Actually, I have had two great accidents in my life—one with the streetcar, and the other, the other is this man here with us, my Dieguito. They say I will never have a child, but they are wrong. They are very wrong. Look here, do you recognize the background of my painting, your Rouge factory? 'Rouge' they call it, but nothing red allowed inside. Funny, no?"

Haik did not know of any rule barring anything red from the Rouge, but he nodded.

"My dear, this is Haik Pehlivanian, not Mr. Henry Ford, destroyer of unions and *insurrectos*."

Frida looked away, out the window of her room.

"Yes, I am sorry, Haik. I like this new name, which is really your old name. It must be nice to be someone else when you need to be. Did you know, I am actually half Hungarian Jew? Good thing Mr. Henry Ford thinks I am some Mayan princess and not a Jew or he'd have me sent back to Mexico."

The tired corners of Frida's mouth curled into a mischievious smirk, but Rivera frowned.

"You think so?" ask Rivera. "Mr. Ford, darling, he has no ill will toward Jews. Look at Mr. Kahn, the maker of his buildings. Ford trusts no one but Kahn in the realm of architecture. Why work with Mr. Kahn if he did not like Jews?"

"Why? Ha! *Panzas*, you can see like no other painter who has ever lived and yet you are blind as a mole. *Tu cegura is increible.* Ford tolerates Mr. Kahn because he can build a building that Ford could never dream of doing himself. Do you really think if Mr. Ford had one ounce of architectural power in his puny brain he would even give Mr. Kahn the steering wheel from one of his glorious cars? Look, look at the buildings Kahn did not design and you have your answer—gray, gray, and more gray. Look at what he eats—all gray. Look how he dresses—more gray, everything gray. Thank goodness for Edsel, and, I hope you have at least noticed this, the old capitalist son-of-a-bitch doesn't even like his own son, the only one in the family who would spend a peso on art. And look, look at how he treats Haik's brother Orlin and all the other blacks—clean up the messes of the other workers or take the jobs no one else wants, breathing in toxic paint fumes and eating coal dust all day. *Oh, como me enfadas*, you fat old man!"

Despite the scolding, Rivera laughed mightily, and Haik looked on in polite confusion.

"You see, she attacks me like a lion and I could not happier! Despite her weakened condition, she paints and, most important, she challenges me at every turn! Truly, I am blessed. She will be fine again in no time."

Rivera caressed the tiny woman's hair and adjusted the sheet that covered her. Haik thought of Lu at home, baking bread, cleaning clothes, doing everything as she carried their child. There in Utica, he had all he needed. The mere birth of one healthy baby was a miracle, and soon, God willing, he was about to experience that miracle himself. Frida was frail, and the doctors had warned that she could never have a child, but Lu, she was healthy and strong and had already brought a strong son into the world. Maybe Lister was a threat looming off in the distance, but what really mattered in his life was good. No, he was not a great artist like Rivera or Miss Frida or a millionaire inventor like Henry Ford, but the core to his world was solid and good.

Haik looked again at Frida's painting, taking in all the floating images, the small woman in a bloody bed that sat outside in the middle of nowhere with the Rouge plant miles away in the background, the dead baby, a slumping flower, pieces of human bodies, some kind of snail or something, some medical tools. It was not a happy painting, not even the flower part, and as Haik thought of Miss Frida the painting brought his mind to pictures of Vahram and Mister Meadows and he felt a kind of sadness.

"Well, I got to get back to the plant. You take care, Miss Frida. And you know, I like your painting."

"You do? What exactly do you like about it?"

Haik fumbled. She was a hellcat, and she had just pounced. He was trying to be nice but she had him here, and obviously her old fire was returning. He didn't know how to talk about art—he should have said nothing.

"My dear, Haik was trying to cheer you. No need to dangle him over a fire."

Haik appreciated the save, but he would not give in. He was learning, every day, learning something new, and if he was not smart he was at least smarter than he was before Rivera came to Detroit.

"Well, Miss Frida, I do like your painting. That don't mean, you know, that I understand it or can talk real clear about it. But what I get from it, it's, it's just sadness. All around. Everywhere. And even though there's all them things floating, you, ah, that lady in the bed, she's, it's like she's, she's all alone. And that's sad."

Frida looked at him, admiring, scrutinizing.

"Bravo, maestro. Here is a true critic. 'Since feeling is first.' Yes, you must feel before you understand. You pass my test, Haik."

Rivera offered to walk him out, and he nodded to Frida as he left. She looked so small in the bed, so distant from where she was, like *she* was floating off in space except there was no red rope connecting her to anything. Despite Rivera's presence, she *was* alone.

"In some way, this tragedy is a blessing," confided Rivera quietly as they walked down the hallway away from Frida's room. "I could not have watched her suffer any longer. Still, she talks of children, but there will be no children. Now, though, her mind is on painting, and you can see the power of what she is doing. No other woman has had the courage to paint with such cruel honesty and truth. She has *duende*, a spirit that speaks what no one else is willing to say. Now she is released for her true calling, to create art, not babies."

"What about *your* painting, Mr. Rivera?"

"Oh, there is time. If anything, I am far ahead of what anyone expected. This brief respite is nothing. Now, Frida needs me and she will have my attention. I will tell you this, my friend. As soon as Frida can return to our quarters, I have a favor to ask and a favor to grant, but we will discuss that in due time."

The painter smiled, and the two men shook hands before Haik took off to the glass house.

What were these "favors" Rivera mentioned? Haik had asked for nothing, and he was content with the expense money being funneled his way. As Haik walked to his car, the thought of patrolling around the glass house made him uneasy. What was he really doing there? He had no real function, and the most useful thing he had done was making the line slow down by a second, but technically that wasn't anything even close to his job. When he arrived, Gittens was waiting for him outside and it could only mean one thing—they would be making a visit to Mr. Bennett's office. Gittens would tell him nothing, and after a silent ride, they shuffled down to Bennett's sanctuary. When they entered, Bennett was at his desk, admiring a pistol Haik had never seen before.

"Whattaya think a this baby?" Bennett asked, siting down the barrel of a pistol that had a clip like a machine gun.

"I ain't seen nothing like it," Haik said, more concerned about the reason for his visit than Bennett's latest deadly toy.

"Krauts make it. C-96 Mauser nine millimeter, fully automatic. Twenty round clip on a pistol. You believe that? See this little switch on the side? Can shoot rapid fire or one at a time, just flick this baby right here. Nifty little do-dad, you think?"

"I like it," agreed Haik, giving as safe and noncommittal an answer as he could.

"Mr. Ford likes some a what he's sees goin' on over in Germany. We totally kicked the shit of 'em in the war and now they're showin' signs of comin' around. Got some little guy over there really makin' some noise, gettin' things movin'. Mr. Ford likes a go-getter. Yes sir, he's impressed with this little German guy," he mused, still not getting to a point.

Haik didn't know anything about Germany or the little guy and he didn't really care—he had enough problems right here in Detroit.

Bennett kept siting down the barrel, lining up imaginary targets here and there. He then turned the gun directly at Haik and held him in his sites. Haik stayed still, not wanting to betray any fear. Then Bennett's finger tightened around the trigger.

Click.

Haik flinched and Bennett smiled before placing the pistol on his desk.

"Any troubles with Lister?" he asked, and Haik composed himself before answering.

"Ah, no. I ain't seen him, Mr. Bennett."

Haik's voice was a bit quavery. He had to pull it together.

"Good. I told the slag-mouthed son-of-a-bitch to keep his space from you. He's full of shit. No good lying bastard screwed up and he tried to take down other people with him. I got no respect for that, Pelini. No sir, you know your role and you stick to it, no more, no less. Now, since we're at it, let's talk about roles. What's this I hear about you startin' some fuss at glass?"

Bennett looked Haik directly in the eye. Here was the point, the reason he was here and had a gun pointed at him and a trigger clacked in his face.

"Well, Mr. Bennett, I, ah, I went in and things were balled up when I got there. The guys, they were sore with the feedman and they were gonna fight over the speed of the belt. There wasn't nothing getting done."

Haik was bumbling and he knew it. Sure, he was telling the truth, but was it a truth Bennett wanted to hear?

"Yeah, so? Go on."

"Well, I told the foreman to slow it down a bit and the guys went back to work. No more problem. Everybody started working again."

That was as simple as he could tell it and, in his mind, exactly what had happened. Haik looked at Bennett to gauge his reaction but saw nothing usable.

"So, lemme see, are you now in charge of operations over there?"

The message was clear: Haik had overstepped his bounds as a strongarm.

"No sir."

"So why the hell did you slow the belt down? Do you think you know more about how to run the Ford Motor Company than Mr. Henry Ford?"

"No, ah, no, Mr. Bennett. Mr. Ford knows way more than me."

"So, again, why the hell did you give the slowdown order?"

Haik could not say directly what he was thinking, that the feedman was a gutless son-of-a-bitch who hid behind his orders and liked throwing his weight around with the people who were actually doing the work while he sat on his candy ass and moved a lever.

"Mr. Bennett, when I went in, there wasn't nothing getting done, nothing getting made. And really, the guys were working faster, a full second faster than the day before. The feedman sped it up by two seconds, so I just split the difference. I thought it was best for Mr. Ford that some things got done instead of none. If what I done was wrong, I'm sorry, real sorry, but it seemed like it made sense at the time and got the line moving."

Bennett looked him over closely, his eyes narrowing, his mouth pursing. He sat like a stone for what seemed like a full minute before speaking.

"Well, I see your point, Pelini. But in the future, a problem like this, see if you can't be a little more persuasive on the side of speed. You got a billy and a blackjack—see if those can't help motivate the workers to put a little extra elbow grease on it and pick up the pace. Got it?"

"Yes, Mr. Bennett."

Haik was frozen. His eyes darted around Bennett's office, at the bull's eye target on the cabinet, the pictures of Bennett with all the important looking people, and his mind drifted. It was not Haik Pehlivanian who had just agreed to abuse innocent people. No, it was a sap named Hank Pelini, Service Department stooge, a toad who was so desperate for work he would do or say anything to shove a dollar into his pocket or drive a fancy car that really wasn't his. He thought of the painting Miss Frida had done, the one of the woman laying in the bloody bed. He could see another painting, one of a man that looked like him, laying naked on the frozen bloody ground at Grand Circus Park. From out of this man came a bunch of bloody ropes, all attached to different things. One was connected to a brand new Kolster radio, another to a shiny Ford V-8 Sedan, another to a snubnose police revolver. There were other ropes. One was connected to a picture of Mr. Meadows' body, a hole through its chest, and another to Vahram, the side of his head blasted off and caked with frozen blood and brain. The last image, it hovered in the air right above the man on the ground, it was the same baby he had seen in Miss Frida's painting, a large, reddish-skinned baby, its arms and legs curled close to its body, its eyes closed, unaware of all going on around it.

"And how's our painter doing? I heard about the little mishap with his old lady. A real shame."

There was not one breath of sincerity in Bennett's voice. Haik looked back at him, as if he were looking at one of the empty suits of armor he had seen standing along the walls at the museum.

"Yes, it was a shame. But I think he's going to be back painting real soon."

"I must say, Edsel was very grateful for all the help you gave the beaners and how you handled the situation, gettin' them to the hospital quick and all. That's good work, Pelini, a real positive reflection on the Service Department. You keep it up. Here, here's a little bonus for keeping everything on the level."

Bennett reached into his desk and then flipped an envelope to Haik, who automatically picked it up from Bennett's desk and placed it in his front trouser pocket. Bennett signaled them to leave and Haik thanked him before following Gittens out of the office and back up the stairs into the daylight.

Miss Frida stayed in the hospital for 13 days, and the entire time Rivera was with her. In some sense, Haik needed the respite too. He did some booze runs in the mornings for Bennett and kept things on task at the glass house. He was not going to butt into anything on the production line, not after the meeting with Bennett. God, how he wanted out. He'd rather run hooch than face the prospect of using a club on a worker, and he prayed they just shut up and did their jobs. He did catch one thief trying to make off with some tools under his jacket, and he had no problem busting that man, justifying getting him out of the plant because the man wasn't straight, but that was different. A thief was a bum in anybody's book. Somehow, though, he was going to have to come up with a solution for what his future was going to be after the baby was born.

That solution almost came early. In August, a decline in sales caused a slowdown at the plant that sent several sections of workers home, without pay, until demand for automobiles rose again. Haik and Orlin were kept on, although Haik was shifted on an irregular basis to various parts of the plant—the Servicemen had, in Bennett's words, "become too chummy" with their regular beats and were now moved on an unpredictable basis to look over the shoulders of workers all over River Rouge. Haik wasn't going to complain. In fact, he liked to move and not feel tied down to just one section or group of men. It was true, though, the closer he got to a group of workers, the harder it was to lay the law down if he had to.

One day he was making his rounds at the foundry when Bennett's lieutenant Cutty came in with an entourage of muscle. Unexpected visits were never good.

"Pelini," Cutty called, and Haik looked up obediently. Cutty was non-descript. He wasn't a thug and didn't scare Haik physically. Outside the Rouge, you could picture him smiling in a white pharmacist uniform handing out prescriptions at the counter of a drug store. He wasn't scarred and his nose wasn't flattened—just a normal looking joe. He was trusted and he was good with money, so there a need for a man like that amongst all the brainless goons and toughs. He was carrying a kind of megaphone with him like you would cheer into at a sports event.

"Yes, Mr. Cutty," Haik said, more as a question.

Cutty was smiling, another bad sign.

"We need to straighten some things out after the incident at the glass house. Mr. Bennett needs to be sure you can do your job when push comes to shove. So, we've been having a few dust-ups here at the foundry. Seems we got some pickaninnies meeting in their after hours and rumor is they're flapping their gums about starting a union. That will not happen. These darkies are lucky Mr. Ford even bothers to hire them, and this disloyalty is not acceptable. We've got to send a message that workers work, period, and they can leave other matters up to Mr. Ford. So, you're gonna go down onto the floor and pick out a man and send that message to everyone in this building. Understand?"

"Not really. So, what exactly do you do want me to do?"

Haik sensed the answer but wanted to make sure.

"Simple. At shift change, we're gonna go down there and I'm gonna use this bullhorn here to announce an end to any talk of unions. Then you're just gonna pick one sambo and play him a song on his chin with your knuckles. You follow through, or, Mr. Bennett assured me, there would be consequences for you."

Haik looked right at Cutty, who did not blink. He was supposed to go down and just pick someone out and start laying into him. What kind of deal was that? As far as he saw, no one in the foundry was piking it and the work was getting done, so who cared if the men wanted to get together after work and shoot the bull and talk about baseball or unions or dames or whatever. Two of Cutty's strongarms pushed him forward and they walked onto the main deck, where Cutty began to shout into the megaphone, barely audible above the rumble of foundry life and new workers filing in.

"Gentlemen, your attention up here, your attention. I will have one minute of your time. That's it, put down what you're doing, immediately. Immediately, that means right now. This is the Service Department, so pay attention. Now, you all have been warned about your illegal and disloyal discussions of forming a communist union, and you were told to stop all such activities. However, Mr. Ford is very disturbed to learn that these activities have continued. Anyone caught partaking in such activities in the future will meet with a very serious consequence. Today, you will understand the punishment that awaits anyone for this illegal activity."

Cutty looked at Haik, and one of the toughs shoved him forward. What was he supposed to do? Just go up to someone and swing at him? He looked around at all the workers, who were looking at him, their goggles in place, their black skin glistening with sweat. He looked for Orlin, who was supposed to be coming onto his shift. He knew many of these men from having a drink with them after they punched out before heading home. Who the hell was he supposed to pick? Bass or Washington? Old Freeman or Hez Duncan? These men were his friends. He looked back at Cutty, but Cutty signaled his stooges and they drew their handguns. This would play out, one way or another. Anyone he chose could be totally innocent, but that wasn't the issue here—it was sending a message, a live and bloody message to toe the line or else. Haik readied himself. Beat someone or be beaten himself. He'd make it quick. Pop pop, done. He'd explain later, but it had to be done. Once again, he had no choice.

As he scanned the crowd, one man stepped forward...Orlin. Haik's heart dropped—what the hell was he thinking? He was not going to tangle with Orlin, no way, no how. He'd take a beating from Cutty's men before he laid a paw on Orlin.

"You ready to play some fighting?" Orlin called out, and he put his hands up and circled so that his back was to Cutty and the henchmen.

Haik kept his hands at his side and circled opposite his foe, but Orlin winked at him.

"I ain't afraid a you, Hungy. Who you, Jack Johnson? Guess that would make me Jim Jeffries, wouldn't it? What, you afraid? I ain't gonna play fight with you, Hungy," challenged Orlin.

He winked again at Haik, and Haik put his hands up in complicity.

Play fighting—it was what they used to do as kids, roughhousing, recreating the fights they read about or heard on the radio or were told about by the oldtimers who saw them in person. Play fighting was rough fun. You had to know how to look like you were throwing a punch and taking one. Hell, movie stars made thousands of clams doing this stuff. The easiest to fake were body shots because no one expected any blood from a punch to the gut. Damn, Orlin was smart.

Haik bounced up on his toes and began the pugilistic dance with his friend. They would give Cutty his money's worth. Orlin began with a few slicing jabs that were intentionally just left or just right of the target, Haik bobbing his head in mock defense. Orlin then sent a wide loping right sailing over Haik's head. Just like in the old days, Haik lowered and ripped a stifled right to Orlin's gut, which sent Orlin doubling over in phantom pain. Haik then landed a powerful-appearing chop to the back of Orlin's head, which sent him staggering sideways.

"All you got, gray meat?" taunted Orlin, panting, applying a quick rub to the back of his neck.

Haik decided to have some fun. They would have to sell Cutty and the others—it would have to get a little vicious.

"Come and get it, nigger," he sneered, letting a word from his mouth he would never use outside this fantasy.

Orlin rushed him, bulling in and grabbing at Haik's shirt, swinging him this way and that, throwing a few blows not with his fist but the soft inside of his forearm to Haik's ears. Haik went again for the midsection, letting out a battle cry as he delivered the non-existent blow, and Orlin doubled over. The obligatory blow to the back of the neck sent Orlin to the ground, where Haik decided to throw in some Armenian wrestling. He leeched onto Orlin's back and applied a choke hold, rocking Orlin back on top of himself and straining to look as if he were really choking his opponent. Orlin, who was always the best fall guy back in their play fighting days, squirmed and flailed his arms, a bug-eyed look of pseudo strangulation seizing his face. Orlin was so good that some of his co-workers motioned to step in and help, but Cutty's men cocked the triggers of their heat.

"Cutty, you stop this or you got one dead nigger here."

The strongarms moved in and took control. Haik released the gasping Orlin. It had worked. Mission complete. No one hurt.

"Let's get him out of here," Cutty said to his aides.

"No," demanded an infuriated Haik. "Make the no-good nigger finish out his shift. And if he don't make his quota, tomorrow I finish the job. Permanant like."

He did his best to project rage, flaring his nostrils, clenching his teeth, pointing menacingly at Orlin, straining against one of Cutty's toadies to hold him back. Cutty looked at Haik with a degree of satisfaction. He took up the megaphone.

"Okay, good idea. Let the sambo go. He makes his quota or we pay another visit tomorrow. All a you hear that? Huh? You really think a union is worth your lives? Unless you want another visit from the Service Department tomorrow, I suggest you all shake a leg and get working."

The goons let go and Orlin fell to the floor in agonizing imagined pain, lolling about, holding his throat as if he might never breath normally again.

"Now, gentlemen, let this be a lesson." Cutty gave a wary glare to each and everyone on the floor. "Now get back to work. All quotas will be made today or you will suffer consequences. Your foreman will have an extra sharp eye on all of you."

Cutty approached Haik and gave him a nod of approval.

"That's what we were hoping to see. Good work, Pelini. Now keep these black-ass baboons on their toes."

Cutty summoned his two goons and they all strode out of the foundry. Haik had dodged a bullet. He looked about, though, and was met with menacing glares. Haik looked back to make sure Cutty was gone and grabbed Orlin up off the floor by his shirt and walked him roughly behind one of the giant ladles that held the molten steel once the furnace was tapped.

"Goddamn, you son-of-a-bitch!"

Orlin returned a grin. They embraced quickly, not wanting the foreman to catch their commiseration.

"Yeah, I still got it," Orlin beamed.

"Lucky for me. I was in real trouble there."

"No problem. But don't expect me to let your sorry ass ever win again. That was painful actin' like you could really whup me."

"Hey, let's put this to rest and we'll meet up at Dolgovich's later. And please, explain to the guys, Hez and everybody, I didn't mean nothing I said. Or what I'm gonna say," Haik confided, before walking Orlin out from behind the ladle, holding him by the back of his collar.

"You cross me again, you're gonna be one dead Negro!" shouted Haik, letting go of Orlin's shirt with a shove.

There it was, message sent. Haik looked up at the foreman and walked out of the foundry, anxious to get the hell out of the Rouge and up to the museum. He danced over thin ice, and if Orlin hadn't been around he would have taken a beating or had to live with himself after delivering one to an undeserving worker. It was no good. It would have to stop, but he'd have to get together with Orlin before any kind of plan could be made. He needed time to think, to clear his mind. There was no better place than the museum.

Rivera was at the hospital with Frida, so Haik laid low at the garden court. Rivera's assistants were chipping off some of the plaster that had dried before the master could finish applying paint the night of Miss Frida's accident. He watched them work a while, then headed out early to Dolgovich's and waited for Orlin, who arrived about an hour after Haik.

"Well, if it ain't Mr. Jim Jeffries, ex-heavyweight champion of the world," Haik beamed.

"Afternoon, Mr. Johnson. Lookin' kinda pale, champ," Orlin returned. "And let me tell you one thing, you Armenian bastard, that is the very last time in my life I'm playing Jim Jeffries. Hell, that was hard work bein' that clumsy and slow."

"Hell, O, you played it like a star. How the hell you think a that? You saved my ass and how." Haik motioned for the barmaid to bring Orlin a beer.

"Well, I seen them pistols come out and I knew you was in some deep doo-doo, brother. I wasn't about to explain to Lu why you come home this time with your head all beat in."

Once Orlin's beer arrived, they clinked bottles in relieved celebration.

"You tell the guys, you know, I didn't mean nothing I said?"

"Oh yeah, they ducky. Next time we need a white boy to lynch, they expect you to volunteer."

"You got it. O, serious now, I can't keep doin' this," Haik muttered. "One a these days, something bad gonna happen on top of everything bad that already happen. Bad, like forever bad. It's only a matter of time."

Orlin placed a hand on Haik's shoulder.

"So what can you do? You got a plan?"

Haik looked deeply into his beer bottle.

"No. That's the problem. I ain't got no plan, no back-up plan, nothing. No ideas. Vahram, he woulda knowed what to do. It's like I'm stuck in this place I can't stand to be. I don't like how it looks, I don't like how it smells, I don't like how it make me feel. I'm starting to hate even waking up in the morning. That ain't right, O."

He took a long drink.

"We could do something out at the house. We got a lot of land we could plant."

Haik had thought about farming, too, but he wasn't a farmer. He wanted to grow enough for them to eat and can and store for winter but he didn't want to till and plant and hoe for a living. No, he wasn't going to farm.

"I don't want to farm. No, too much work for not enough dough."

They sat in silence until Haik rapped the table with his knuckles.

"Sweet Jesus, are we about stupid or what?"

"You want me to try and argue that?"

"No, no, smart ass, listen to me. Where do we live?"

"Utica."

"Yeah, Utica, but what are we surrounded by?"

"Hicks and cornstalks."

"Exactly," Haik gushed, looking for the same sudden insight to flash in Orlin's eyes.

"Exactly what? You just said you didn't want to farm."

Orlin looked at Haik like maybe some of those fake punches at the foundry had really damaged his brain.

"No, not us farming, just everyone around us. C'mon, O, what do all those hicks own? Every last one of 'em? What's in all their barns that they can't do without?"

Orlin looked at Haik and put an index finger to his chin. He could sense a direction in Haik's punchiness.

"Uh-huh, yeah, I see it, they all got trucks and tractors."

"Damn straight. And who knows better how to fix an engine than you? And who knows better how to tear something apart than me?"

Orlin took another drink and mused over Haik's observations.

"These hucklebucks got a problem they can't fix themselves, they got to go into the city or have somebody from the city come to help them," Orlin added. "I see where you headed. We could start ourselves up a little something out home way and not have to swallow anybody's shit at the Rouge no more."

Their minds were firing, and they had one more beer and talked over their plan before heading back to Utica.

Within a week, Orlin got the old truck in the barn drivable and he and Haik set off after work and scoured the countryside for junked cars. Haik could tear a car down in a jiffy, and Orlin could build one back up. For days, they hunted junkers, any make and model, for usable parts, axles, carburetors, fenders, seats, anything. In two weeks, they had built up quite an inventory of stock in the barn, and Lu and Arkina wrote up little flyers that they put in all the roadside mailboxes. On the weekends after work at the Rouge was done, Orlin and Haik started to run a small time fix-it shop, mostly doing work for neighbors in Utica and Mount Clemens, with an occasional job out in Pontiac.

They did good work cheaper than anyone else around, and no one complained. No, there wasn't great money to be had, not yet at least, as long as the Depression continued, and they were tired working two jobs, but there was a volume of work that could keep them busy and paying their extra bills. Best of all, it *felt* right. This, Haik thought, was their future. They didn't need to answer to anyone and they didn't need to carry guns or worry about someone speeding up a lever on them. They did as they pleased on their own time at their own pace. As the first few weeks of business passed, the more Haik was at the Rouge during the day, the more he longed to be back in the old truck with Orlin taking jaunts over dirt roads through the wooded landscape hunting for junkers.

When Rivera finally resumed work, he asked Haik to come pick him up and to have Orlin meet with them at Building B after his shift at the power house was over. As requested, Haik met a joyous if not disheveled Rivera at his apartment after work, and he exchanged pleasantries with Miss Frida and Miss Lucienne before leaving to the plant. Miss Frida seemed better, a bit more color in her face, and Rivera seemed genuinely happy, his sketch book in hand. Once at the plant, they met up with Orlin, and Rivera looked about, searching for something in the noisy ocean and hubbub of the assembly line. He walked past welders and assemblers and balancers and handlers and all the tributaries of parts streaming from overhead conveyers, looking, assessing, calculating as the line drove each ever-growing car skeleton closer to completion. He wandered down the living canals of car parts and then retreated again, looking for something very particular.

"Here, yes, over here," he finally said, pointing to a flat cart of engine blocks ready to be hooked up to a conveyer. "You and Orlin, yes, your sleeves rolled up, if you would, please assist these gentlemen in rolling the cart to the conveyer. Yes, that's it. You just work, push the cart Orlin, yes, Haik pull the cart, and I'll draw. Nothing special, just help them as you normally would. Yes, perfect, like so...."

Rivera coached them, and Haik and Orlin complied, joining in with the station of workers assigned to load the blocks. The hollow blocks were heavy, but Haik enjoyed the strain of wheeling the flat cart to the conveyer. Here, he felt more useful than he had the past month. He and Orlin put their backs into their labor as if it were their regular job, and Rivera sketched away, his drawing hand moving feverishly over the pad. He flipped to a new page and did not seem to miss a beat or stop, his eyes carefully capturing every needed detail of the scene. After about 40 minutes, Rivera informed the men they could stop.

"Oh man, I was just gettin' into it," laughed Orlin.

The men at the station laughed and thanked their two visitors for the extra hand before they escorted the painter from the plant. What was the purpose of all this? Were they to be some part of the great paintings in the garden court?

"All I can tell you, gentlemen, is that I think you will be pleased when you see the end result."

Rivera smiled slyly, and both men wondered what he had in store for them.

September finally arrived with a hint of coolness in the air, and Haik was summoned to the Wardell for an emergency run. At the apartment, he met Rivera, Frida, and Miss Lucienne. Miss Lucienne let Haik in, and there was noticeable sullenness in her voice.

"Come in," she said softly. "Diego's helping Frida pack. Her mother's ill in Mexico and we have to leave today. We're flying out of Mr. Ford's airport in an hour."

Haik sat down on the couch in the living area and waited. Eventually, Rivera and the two women appeared from their sleeping chambers.

"Ah, Haik, so good of you to come on such short notice. Frida and Lucienne will be journeying back to Mexico on some unfortunate business. Frida's mother Mathilda is gravely ill. Mr. Ford has generously offered to fly them home to tend to this matter."

The fact that his wife would now suffer even more was etched in Rivera's face, and he was not his usual buoyant self. Frida was dressed brilliantly in her native garb, and more color was finding its way back into her skin.

"Yes, away from *Gringolandia*. Not for pleasantries, though," whispered Frida.

It was no secret that she did not like the United States—who could really blame her with all that had happened here. Haik gathered their cases and bags and made a trip to the car, then pulled up to the curb outside the main entrance. He returned to their apartment and gathered the rest of their luggage and they all walked in silence to the car. The drive out to Ford's airport in Dearborn was quiet. Down Warren Avenue, the vagrants were already forming lines for soup, unshaven, sunken faced men who glared as Haik drove past. As they neared the complex just north of Oakwood Boulevard at Rotunda, the sight of hangars and planes and a hotel and the concrete runways came into view.

In the middle of a Depression, how could one man have so much and others so little? Haik asked the question many times but never had a sensible answer.

They were met at the airport by blue uniformed men and all the baggage was taken directly to the plane. Rivera made sure Frida and Miss Lucienne were settled for their journey. He walked with them onto the runway to the rolling ramp so they could board the plane, where Rivera gave Frida a tender kiss, engulfing the elfin woman. Within minutes, the engines of the plane were fired and the propellers whirling, and they were gone. On the ride back, Rivera contemplated the future.

"You know, Haik, I was not created to be faithful. It is simply physiologically impossible for me," he mused. "But please make no mistake, there is no woman more important in the world to me than she. I have enjoyed the pleasures of the flesh with many a woman, ah yes, many, many women, and rest assured I will with many more, but Frida, she is truly all there is to me."

"I definitely think you're the most important thing to her, Mr. Rivera," Haik responded.

This was the painter's confession to Haik. Sure, Rivera had a funny way to show his devotion, but that was how he lived and Miss Frida seemed to accept it.

"I may be, indeed," Rivera continued. "But she is an artist, and I am hoping this time away will rejuvenate her. She really does not like this country, and I cannot say her feelings are without foundation, but this return, I am hopeful it will strengthen her spirit. I would welcome much more talk of painting than of babies."

When they returned to the museum, Rivera immediately prepared for work, but took a moment to address Haik.

"Haik, a moment please." The old smile was back on his face. "Here, look very carefully, this lower section of the north wall. What do you see?"

The wall was...a wall. Blank. Not like the upper sections Rivera had begun to tell his story on.

"Well, Mr. Rivera, it looks like it ain't got too much on it right about now."

"Yes, indeed, a veritable *tabula rasa*," grinned Rivera. "Some day in the not so distant future, I will ask you to examine this very spot again. I think you will be both surprised and pleased by what you see. And, my man, I may be needing some entertainment one of these evenings while my Frida is away. I will give you ample notice."

Rivera smiled in confidentiality and then returned to work, climbing the scaffolding and preparing his palette as his assistants busied themselves for the work to come.

The next day, though, all came to a head. When Haik arrived at the museum, he was given a message by Mr. Valentiner's secretary to report to the reclamation garage at the plant. There was no meeting scheduled for the SD boys and Haik had no regular business at the garage—what could it be? He parked outside and when he entered through the service door he was met by Cutty, Gellinger, Franks, and Zabriskie. There were no smiles of recognition or nods of acknowledgement, just dead, stone faced stares.

"Let's see your piece," Cutty said, and as Haik stood dumbfounded Gellinger and Zabriskie moved on him, taking both his arms so that Franks could reach inside his jacket and snag his pistol.

"What's the deal?"

"The deal is this, Pelini, you done fucked up. That was a pretty funny stunt you pulled at the foundry the other day. Really had us going. Come to find out, though, that nigger is a pal of yours, isn't he? Yeah, your boy Lister did a little diggin' and tipped us off. That's it, you're done. Give us the keys to the car and get the fuck off Ford property. Now."

Haik stood mute. So that was it, done? Finished...*free*? He wouldn't protest. No, the decision he should have made long ago was now made for him. In some sense, it was a relief—now he *had* to think about the future because it just landed in his lap. These assholes had just done him a favor. And the biggest asshole, Cam Lister, was the one he really had to thank.

"What about the black guy?" Haik asked.

"The nigger? He's joining the soup line like you. Always a new nigger to take his place." Cutty had a mathematician's coolness in his voice.

"I need my old car," said Haik, wanting to get off Ford property as quickly as he could.

"Car? You kiddin'? You don't own no car. Anything you think you owned's already been sliced and diced and disappeared," smirked Cutty, and with one nod of his head Franks cut into his stomach with a swift body shot.

Haik doubled over, held up only by Gellinger and Zabriskie, losing all his air, his lungs twisting shut in pain. They released his arms and he crumbled to the greasy floor. They then took the boots to him, one jackhammer kick after another. Without a gun, the best Haik could do was protect himself, try to cover his privates, his stomach, his temples, curling into a fetal kicking ball.

"That right there," said Cutty matter of factly, "that was a real beating, Pelini. Feel a little different than playing pattycake with Sambo? Here, we're even gonna do you one last favor. Guys, why don't you give Mr. Pelini a ride off the premises. And Pelini, anyone sees you around here again, you'll be shot, no questions asked. You should feel lucky you're leaving here alive. Mr. Bennett kind of liked you. Not like him to let a man walk like this."

Haik sputtered for air, unable to straighten up—yes, the blows he had just received were very real. Gellinger and Zabriskie grabbed him under the arms and dragged him to their car and tossed him in the back seat, with Zabriskie crowding in next to him. Franks took the wheel and soon they were speeding off toward the nearest gate. Haik righted himself on the seat, his insides cramped in electric pain, his breath still not recovered. Once outside the gates, Gellinger got out, opened Haik's rear door, and Zabriskie gave him a swift kick out onto the ground.

"You heard Mr. Cutty, we see you around here again you're dead," warned Gellinger as he slid back into the car. "Bennett's orders. You're a lucky man we didn't take you for a longer ride. You keep the fuck away."

And that was it—they tore off back into the plant and left Haik stranded outside the fence.

He lay on the ground for a while, still dazed, unable to bring enough air into his shrunken lungs. What had just happened? He was fired, very physically, very clearly, without a doubt fired. So what did he do now? First of all, he had to find Orlin—at least Orlin still had a set of wheels, and hopefully he wasn't in any worse shape than Haik right now. He picked himself up, knives of pain slicing through his gut, his ribs, his back, the side of his head, the ghosts of fists and shoes still lodged throughout his body. He dusted himself off with short, pain-cramped movements. He had about a half mile to walk to reach where Orlin parked each day. If things were as he suspected, Orlin had been shown the exit right about the same time he had been. Lord, how did this happen? What the hell did he tell Lu? In some sense, she would probably be happy—this is what she wanted, her husband free, and now she had it, no more Fords, no more dirty work, screw the filthy bastards.

He walked on, feeling a sense of euphoria, like a zoo animal suddenly set loose. So much to think about, so many matters to tend to now. Orlin would need work too. Damn, how many months could he hold out on the $40 a month payments? What would his parents do? Lu's mother? They all depended on him, and now what? He had nothing, not even the Fliv. Nothing, like that kid on Greeley Street waiting for a train to stop long enough to smash into its insides, praying there was something to eat or sell inside.

Once he reached the worker lot, still feeling Franks' punch securely lodged in his stomach, he surveyed the sea of vehicles. He tracked down Orlin's car and found him sitting there in the driver's seat, looking out at the bustle inside the plant fence.

"Guess we weren't as good at play fighting as we thought," Haik called through the passenger side window.

Orlin looked at him blankly.

"Glad you think it's funny."

"C'mon, I'll let you be Jack Johnson this time."

Haik opened the door and climbed carefully onto the seat. Orlin looked him over.

"I'd Jack Johnson all over your dumb white ass, but it look like someone beat me to it."

Haik looked at him, tired, hurting, but not totally defeated. He could laugh or he could cry about their plight right now, and he wasn't going to cry. He had cried enough over things far worse than this.

"Later on. Jim Jeffries has officially retired."

"Well, least we got our health," Orlin observed.

"Speak for yourself. I think my stomach's gonna fall out my ass."

Haik winced. Orlin looked at him and they both laughed, although laughing just magnified Haik's pain, and he held his midsection, trying to control the angry ache and push it back inside.

"Don't make me laugh, you black bastard. I think I got a couple a cracked ribs."

They sat in the car, staring out at the Rouge compound.

"Well, what we do now?" Orlin finally asked.

"I don't know. We'll do something. Maybe we start up our garage full time." Haik reflected for a moment. "Right now, though, let's go to the museum. I wanna tell the painter good-bye, give him the scoop. It's only right."

"Hell, it's on the way. Why not."

They pulled out of the lot, past the ocean of cars belonging to all the men still lucky enough to be employed, and made their way to the institute in silence. They entered the back door and paced to the garden court, where they found Rivera working on the scaffolding.

"Ah, my good friends, Haik and Orlin, welcome," beamed Rivera, and just being in his presence revived Haik's spirit. "Come in, come in."

"How do, Mr. Rivera," Haik said. "Well, I guess I better get right to the point. I'm here to say good-bye."

Rivera turned and looked down at him in amazement.

"Good-bye? How can this be? You have quit your job? What, look at you. What has happened? Who has done this to you?"

"No, no, I didn't quit. No sir, I like the job and being around you and all this art and stuff. It was Lister again. You remember when I told you about the little problem me and Orlin almost had at the foundry, the little fake fight thing? Lister ratted us out. And then, well, this. Boom. Out the door we go."

Rivera's immense eyes widened.

"You have no job now? What will you do?"

"We ain't sure. We'll figure it out."

"No, this cannot be. You two have done nothing to deserve this. How can Mr. Ford allow this to happen? No, I promise, I will not allow this to pass...."

"Don't get yourself in no trouble, Mr. Rivera," Haik cut in. "I don't know, I liked working for you, but all that other stuff, it was bound to catch up with me. Maybe this is for the best. In a way, I'm actually glad it happened. Not getting my ass kicked. No, I can do without that. I mean getting fired."

"Yes, perhaps, but you cannot be penalized for merely surviving." Rivera applied color to the wet plaster as he spoke. "No, I have not come here to see two working men treated this way. Absolutely not, I will not accept this."

Haik was heartened by Rivera's support and sense of conviction, but this wasn't his fight and he sure as hell didn't owe anybody anything, least of all a couple of scrubs like Orlin and himself. Whatever crazy things Rivera did on his free time behind his wife's back, he was still a good man. An unstoppable man of insatiable appetites, but a good man.

"I don't think there's nothing anybody can do, Mr. Rivera," Orlin offered.

"No, I believe you are wrong there, my good man. I have been giving some consideration to your situation with this Mr. Lister ever since you told me of your father-in-law's death. I have had a great deal on my mind of late, as surely you can understand, but I have had a plan that has been gestating in my head. Yes, I think it is time to enact this plan."

Haik had no idea what the painter had in mind. His situation with Lister was a done deal now—Lister had gotten the last laugh. The court proceedings were delayed, and once he was in court the judge would probably be bought off anyways and ask Lister's forgiveness for all the inconvenience. Who exactly was behind his defense? Who was making the pay-off on his behalf to keep him from justice? Bennett? Why would he waste a dime on Lister when he had a whole army of stooges, many of whom outranked and outproduced Lister? He should have been before a jury already and sitting behind bars in the Jackson State Penitentiary waiting for the electric chair or at least a lifetime behind an iron window frame, but he was out somewhere in the city doing who knows what.

Haik had to finally admit to himself that Lister may never come to justice. What had he told Lu? That's how the world works.

"For my plan to work, I will need both you and Orlin to participate. It is essential that you both be here tomorrow, at, let's say, a bit before five in the evening, absolutely no later. You will need to be out of sight. In fact, park on Brush Street at the very closest and walk over, just across the street but within clear view of the back main door. My signal will be this. I will come out onto the landing and quickly wave my handkerchief, see, like so. You must then run to the window outside the men's bathroom. I will give you instructions at that time."

What on earth was he talking about? They had just stopped by to politely say good-bye and now the painter was trying to get them involved in some kind of "plan" to get Lister. Luigi and the whole police department couldn't do anything to Lister, so how was an oversexed, frog-eyed Mexican artist going to suddenly make things right?

"But, Mr. Rivera, what exactly are you gonna do? What's this whole plan thing?"

"In this circumstance, the less you know will be to your advantage. I must keep you innocent to a degree. Do you not trust me?"

Rivera's eyes lit with mischief.

"No, I mean yes, Mr. Rivera, yes of course I trust you but I, I don't know. This guy, Lister, he's dangerous…."

"All the more reason to make sure he is put someplace where he cannot hurt you. He has already beaten you, no?

"Yes."

"If he had his way, he would have had you killed the night your friend arrested him, no?"

"Yes, he would have killed me."

"So, it is clear. My good man, please trust me. I cannot bear to watch you, an honorable worker, become the victim of this animal's violent chicanery. Right now, no one is helping you. Yes, your friend Luigi is trying, but he cannot fight an entire empire of corruption. I wholeheartedly endorse what Mr. Edsel Ford is trying to accomplish with his industry and I can only hope his vision for the future is realized, but this network of thuggery and intimidation of the workers, no, this must be stopped, at least in this one case. If you object, please tell me now and I will gladly withdraw my offer. Otherwise I will proceed. Objections? No? Very good. I think you will find the results quite satisfactory."

Haik looked at Orlin, who was equally speechless. What had they just gotten themselves into?

"One additional question. Orlin, what type of automobile would you prefer to own right now if you were allowed to choose?"

"Me? I can't afford no new car, Mr. Rivera," Orlin laughed.

"No, no, no, the question was, if you could possess any automobile, regardless of price, what would you choose?"

Rivera continued to work without looking up, but he was enjoying this game, like he was some photo negative Santa Claus. Orlin thought a good moment, considering the generosity of the offer.

"Hmmm, let's see, I guess I'd get me, I don't know, maybe a Model B Deuce Coupe roadster."

"What about a Phaeton? Or a nice '32 Sedan?" Haik interjected.

"He ain't askin' you, so get your crooked white nose out my business. No, I want me a Deuce roadster."

"Very good then," Rivera said. "Now, I have one final request. I will need you to bring my radio from my quarters here to the court. And while you are there, stop at the cigar stand, yes, here is a dollar fifty, please purchase for me three Garcia Grandes in the glass tubes. Here, here are my keys. Just bring the radio over and set it, I don't know, right over there. This will be essential for tomorrow's activities. If you will excuse me, I mean no rudeness, but I must return to my work. Remember, tomorrow at five in the evening."

Rivera continued to dab and punch color onto the wall with his brushes without breaking stride. And that was it. No explanation. No say in the matter, just a whole lot of trust that this big secret plan would work. Yes, Rivera seemed quite certain that he could bring Cam Lister down, but he was a painter, not a copper, and here he was assuring Haik to trust him. Trust, though, was vanishing from his nature.

During his next break, Rivera strolled to Dr. Valentiner's office and had the operator connect him directly to the office of Mr. Edsel Ford. His order, yes order, not request, was that Mr. Harry Bennett contact him within the next 15 minutes or there would be a very real problem, a problem of major consequence. No, he was not going to explain, what he had to discuss was beyond explanation or compromise, and Mr. Bennett must contact him at once to make this situation right. Within ten minutes, Bennett was on the phone with the artist.

"Yes, Senor Bennett, this is he, Diego Rivera. Yes, the famous painter—ah, you flatter me with your recognition. Mr. Bennett, I will be direct to the point with you. I have learned that my trusted man Hank Pelini will no longer be serving with me. Is this true? He was a fine, fine man, the best, a most loyal and obedient comrade. He is sick? That is quite a shame, I must contact him. Oh, he is highly contagious? This is indeed terrible. You will please pass along my wishes to him for a speedy recovery. No, no, I will not accept a new man, just any man, no, don't bother to send anyone over unless it is a very specific man. Yes, a specific man. Hank, many times he talked very admirably of a man named Cam Lister. Yes, indeed, he said he held this man in great esteem and that he owed him a great debt for helping him so often. Yes, Cam Lister, he must be a wonderful man the way Hank spoke of him. Only this man is fit to replace Hank. Yes, Cam Lister will come to me tomorrow. No, I will accept no other replacement. Never. Yes, he will come or I will be forced to speak directly to Senors Henry and Edsel Ford. Exactly, this is not negotiable, not in the least. I can only trust Cam Lister. Yes, and one more matter, I will need Senor Lister to bring a Ford Model B Deuce Coupe roadster to the museum here. Yes, I am in the middle of a most critical section of my painting and I cannot afford to travel to the Rouge to do any sketching. Yes, the car is to be used as a model only, no harm will come to it as long as Senor Lister is responsible for its security. Yes, very good, Senor Lister will be by tomorrow, no? You can tell him that he need not be here until 4 p.m., and have him park the car in the back, yes, on John R Street, yes, John R, in back of the museum. Exactly, 4 p.m., tell him we will be working late, yes, and to bring the car at that time. Yes, I will be expecting Senor Lister and the car at that time. I thank you, Senor Bennett. Yes, good day to you, my friend, *buenos dias*. Good-bye."

And that was it, the machine was set in motion. The next day, Lister happily picked up a brand new Deuce Coupe early just as it was being readied for loading onto a flatbed for delivery. He had the gas tank topped off and took it for a spin through the city, waving to any women he passed on the streets. He stopped by a speakeasy and had a few drinks and then picked up a load of whiskey he would deliver for Cutty later that night. He put it in the trunk before pulling up to the museum and parking along the curb on John R.

He was back in Bennett's good graces—not easy, but he had gotten himself out of plenty of jams in his life and always come back out on top. Give it a few months, clear up the mistake down in Ecorse, and then back to business as usual. This gig with the painter, it was vacation really, nothing to it, the berries. How hard could it be? A sap like Pelini was making it and everybody was kissing his ass saying how great he was like he was the cat's meow. Hell, he had him eliminated and took out a nigger in the process. The berries. It was better than killing them because now they had no work and they'd have to suffer like all the dumb Dora's walking the streets with a tin cup in their hands begging nickels. No, babysit the painter for, how long, how long could it take him to do a painting, a week or so, and then he'd be back on the street and making up for lost time.

Lister let himself in the back door and wandered around, ignoring the pictures on the walls and the different statues—middle of a Depression and people wasting their time on junk like this, like little kids with baseball card collections or bags full of marbles. He lit a cigarette and kept wandering. Finally, he could hear people talking so he followed the noise to the garden court. Inside, he looked around. A bunch of scaffolding, some butt-pilots walking around putting some kind of slime up on the walls, and yeah, over there, the big greaser who had requested him, old Pedro himself.

"My good man, you will extinguish that cigarette immediately," commanded Rivera, and Lister stopped for a moment to confirm that he was the one being addressed. "As you can see, I myself enjoy a good cigar, but I am the one exception I permit to my rule when I am painting."

"What's that?" hollered Lister.

"The cigarette. I need you to extinguish your cigarette."

"Oh, yeah, sorry, sir."

Lister dropped the cigarette to the ground and ground it into the floor with his shoe.

"Mr. Lister, I presume?" Rivera tended his palette, still not making eye contact with the stranger.

Lister put his hands in his pockets, completely out of his element and not starting out on the right foot.

"Ah, yes, sir, Cameron Lister, pleased to meet you. Please call me Cam. I'm here, ah, to do whatever needs done. You name it, Mr. Ri-veer-a."

"Very well, then. I have heard nothing but good about you. Mr. Hank Pelini gave you the highest recommendation. And you have the car?"

"Yes, I sure do, parked right out back like you asked."

"Very well. Can you please give me the key? I will go for a thorough examination as soon as I am able."

"Yes sir."

Lister looked over the scaffolding. Did the painter really expect him to climb up there and hand him the keys? Christ, this guy was going to be a real kick in the britches. He found a foothold and pulled himself up and climbed over to Rivera. What the hell was all this shit on the walls? And the smell, the pasty smell of the crap the fudgepackers were spreading all over everything. And they were paying this guy to make this mess?

"Thank you. Now, if you would, my compatriots are in need of their dinner. Would you please go to the Wardell and pick up their meals and bring them right back to us?"

Lister nodded and climbed down, and then tried to remember his way out. He wasn't going to take too much more of this being ordered about. Yeah, the quicker this painting was done the better.

Once Lister was out of sight, Rivera quietly slipped the keys in his pocket and continued painting. Lister walked the hallways and ended up at the front door and peeked into the office, where he spied Miss Flora Parks through an open door.

"Hello there, beautiful, ah, can you tell me where the Wardell is?"

Miss Parks looked out to spy Lister. She pushed back from her desk and approached him.

"Why yes, the Wardell is just across the street."

She pointed and Lister flashed his gangrenous smile. Of course he knew where the Wardell was—this was just part of his bottomless charm.

"Why thank you, darling. Cam Lister's the name. I'm Rivera's new right hand. I'll be stopping in quite often this week."

Lister approached her and shook her hand, holding it a second too long. Parks attempted a smile.

Lister exited and walked to the Wardell, smoking a cigarette along the way. Who did the painter think he was? *My good man, you will extinguish that cigarette immediately.* Like hell. Some fat fuck Mexican wasn't going to give him orders. He picked up the food and carried it back, checking in again to see Miss Parks, asking her if he could stop by later. She alerted him to the fact that she would be leaving shortly, 5 p.m., at museum's close, so she'd have to take a raincheck. Lister smiled and continued on his way to the court—he'd make time with her later. He delivered the food, and all took a break to eat but Rivera, who continued his labor. Lister helped himself to a sandwich. So what was he supposed to do all day? Sit around and watch the paint dry? Keep his nose up the painter's ass? Christ, this was a joke. Easy money—no wonder Pelini liked the gig so much.

Rivera checked his watch—exactly 5 o'clock. He smiled, excused himself to go to the bathroom, descended the scaffold and walked methodically to the back of the museum. He exited the back door, and saw Miss Parks walking home across John R. He called to her to wish her a pleasant evening and waved. Once she was out of sight, he removed his handkerchief, wiped his face, and then whirled it above his head three times, a jovial smile on his face. He retreated back within the confines of the museum and proceeded to the men's room. He relieved himself and then went to the window, opened it, and spied outside. In a matter of seconds, Haik and Orlin appeared below. Rivera smiled broadly.

"Good afternoon, or is it already evening? My good friends, I am giving you the key to your new car. I sincerely hope it is all you expected and more. However, keep it very safely out of sight for the next several days. Your part in this great mystery is now finished. Just keep the car hidden until we are all brought together again, which will be shortly, I assure you. Enjoy!"

He tossed the key down to them, and Orlin caught it with a puzzled look on his face. Haik was equally baffled, but Rivera pointed to the gleaming beauty parked at the curb on John R and smiled. Haik looked at Orlin, and when they both looked up at Rivera for an explanation he was gone. That was that. Off they went, briefly discussing their next step before Orlin took off toward the Deuce Coupe and Haik returned to their jalopy on Brush.

Rivera returned to the court, where his assistants were still eating.

"Comrades, I am in a working mood. I will just need one more section of wall covered, this portion here, right here, this exact area. Once the cartoons are applied, I shall be fine. When you have completed this, you may take the remainder of the day off and Mr. Lister and I will remain."

They finished their food and crumbled their wax wrappers and paper cups and placed them back in the food sack. They had their motivation—prepare one more small section of wall, and they earned a well-deserved break. Lister watched them work. How long would he have to do this? This was more of a punishment than going back to the clink for taking out Goldberg and his birds.

"If you like, you may turn on my radio for amusement. And please, turn it up loud, yes, that's it, even more," Rivera offered, and Lister cranked the volume to Rivera's request.

The assistants completed their assignments, carefully applying the fresh coats of plaster, checked with the master if they were needed any longer, and then left to clean up and ready themselves for the very next day. Lister asked if he was dismissed but Rivera assured him that he was not, that he would need him to make a run to the Wardell very shortly but to wait patiently. Lister was antsy—how long could this go on?

Finally, as the light from the overhead windows began to disappear, Rivera asked him to go to the Wardell and fetch him a half a flask of juice and some grapefruit sections, and he would be back at the front door in 45 minutes to let him in. Lister couldn't have been happier to get out. He sped to the front door, and looked behind him before exiting. He was not going directly to the Wardell. The Mexican Fatty Arbuckle would have to wait a bit for his damn juice. Just down from the museum there was a little hot spot Lister liked and he'd saunter on down for a quick one before snagging the juice, and, what was it, bananas? Whatever, he had a whole 45 minutes. He lit a cigarette and headed toward the speakeasy.

From the front window of the museum, Rivera watched and smiled. He locked the front door and used his keys to let himself into Mr. Valentiner's office. There, he had the operator connect him with the police department, and when she did he asked to speak to patrolman Luigi Leoni.

"Leoni here."

"Mr. Leoni, yes, Rivera here. It is as planned. He has left the museum but he has not gone to the Wardell as directed."

"Where'd he go?"

"He began walking in the opposite direction."

"Hmmm, if I know old slagtooth, he's headed for the Majestic. I'm heading down and we'll be very well concealed. We'll let him stop by the Wardell and then we'll wait for him. He'll try to bust the door down if I know him."

"Very well. Such a pity—Mr. Lister seems such a fine citizen. I will be painting and I will have my music playing very loudly. I will not have heard a thing."

"Absolutely, Mr. Rivera. You will have had no idea what's going on outside. You have a great evening and get some painting done. I'm telling all my friends they got to head down there once you finish. They can't wait."

"I am most honored. A very pleasant evening to you, Mr. Leoni. Good bye."

And that was it. Luigi and eight cops sped to the museum in unmarked cars and parked on Farnsworth, then took position to stake out both the front and back doors and wait for their man. It was more than an hour later before Lister came strolling down Woodward, a woman in tow. He took her to the Wardell, and it was another hour before he emerged, alone and carrying a sack, and walked up the steps of the museum to the front door. He yanked but the first door did not budge, so he tried all three. Nothing doing. He swore and proceeded to the back. The cops in the front kept out of sight but slid along behind him to the back of the building. There, Lister tried the doors but again found no luck. He swore once more, and began to walk back toward the front.

"Get your hands up in the air."

Luigi emerged from the shadows, his gun drawn.

"What?"

"You heard me. We got a report of someone trying to break into the museum. Now get your hands up."

Lister shook his head and smiled in irritation.

"You? Christ, you guys never quit, do you? Listen, blue, I'm working at the museum with Harry Bennett's blessing, and you're pretty close to signing your death papers. And if you're smart you'll put that peashooter away and…"

"Shut up and get your hands up," Luigi repeated, and the full squad of eight men began to close in on Lister.

"You chumps are really funny, you know. Really fu…."

Luigi wasn't in the mood. He flashed the butt of his pistol quickly against Lister's jaw and followed with another blow to the side of his head. The bag with the juice flipped into the air and then smashed to the pavement while Lister went down without another sound. They shackled his wrists and ankles and carried his half conscious body to the first vehicle, and tossed him into the back seat.

As this drama unfolded outside, Rivera placed a call directly to Edsel Ford himself.

"Mr. Ford, good evening. Yes, the painting is going fine. Yes, yes, I have talked to Frida and her mother's suffering is thankfully over and she looks forward to returning here to Detroit once all arrangements have been finalized. Yes, thank you, she should be back early next week, yes, thank you for asking. Please excuse my disturbance, but my reason for calling, sir, is that there seems to be something gravely wrong with my new liason, this man Cam Lister who was so highly recommended by Mr. Bennett. He is a strange man indeed. He came in today smelling of whiskey and insisted on smoking in my painting area. I had to reprimand him, and when I sent him on a simple errand for some juice over two hours ago he has not returned. Most upsetting, the Ford Deuce Coupe I requested as a model is nowhere to be found either. He said he had a key, but I have no idea where he has gone off to. No, I simply cannot understand what this man is doing—I think he may be *loco* in the brain. Yes, indeed, this is an embarrassement, I am sorry to trouble you, but I cannot paint with such disruption. I spoke directly with Mr. Bennett himself and was assured the Deuce Coupe would be here. No, agreed, something must be done. I cannot lose time with such interruption. Again, I am most sorry for the disturbance, but this Mr. Lister has cost me an entire evening of work. Yes, I am sure you will. A very fine evening to you as well. Thank you. Good night."

Refreshed and his mood lightened, Rivera paced slowly back to the garden. The night was still quite young, the radio was loud like he liked it, and he had painting to do.

Lu was happy, but she was not happy. Finally, Haik was free from the Fords and their dirty business, but what would they do now? She had become attached to their house, Arkina's company all day, the men coming home at night, Charlie's joy at racing through the woods and having his own room. But would they lose it? And what about Haik's parents and her mother and younger sister? How would they all manage now?

"I got some money tucked away," Haik reassued her as they lay in their bed that night.

His body still ached and he had to control his breaths to contain the pain in his ribs. He curled around her, careful both for himself in his present state of misery and for her, filled to the brim with their child. She was less than a month away and worry was not good for her. Yes, he had the Deuce, a case of whiskey in its trunk and yet another shotgun, but he had no job. There was still more to Rivera's plan, but he would have to travel into the city to speak in person with him to find out exactly what the next step was.

"There…did you feel it?"

Lu took Haik's hand and moved it on her belly. Haik waited, and then he felt the poke of the baby's foot kicking inside her.

"My God," he whispered.

The baby was alive and it was talking to him with its body, pushing and kicking and letting anyone who was listening know that it wanted out, out into the light. Was it a boy? A girl? He didn't care—just bring the child out safely. Sometimes at night he could see the red baby in Frida's painting and he would wake with a start, out of breath, running his hand over Lu's body to make sure she was still warm and breathing. So much could happen. He had seen it with his own eyes and felt Miss Frida's blood on his hands.

"The baby's strong," he said, and kissed the back of her neck, but he could sense her distance.

"Will we be okay?"

Haik pulled her close.

"We'll be okay. Orlin and me are gonna get going on the shop. We got plenty of parts we're stocking up and we got plenty of space to work on cars. We done okay only working in the evening and on weekends. Hell, now we can work all day, every day, nobody to take us away from business. We're gonna go out tomorrow and find us some more cars. It won't be the same kinda money as before, but it'll do. Henry Ford can't take back all his old junk."

He tried to fill his words with as much reassurance as he could. He had to comfort her, but there was still much he was unsure of himself. What exactly, though, happened to Lister after he and Orlin took off? He probably had a conniption fit when he realized the car was gone. Haik smiled. That would have been worth the price of admission to see. It wasn't putting a bullet between his eyes or taking a hammer to his skull, but it would have still been good.

The next day he awoke with a clear mind. He did not have to go into the city, and that felt good. Yes, he would miss Rivera but there would be no more slinking around the Rouge like a hired snake. He and Orlin would take the flatbed out and hunt for a junker or two. Sure, they could even take Charlie out with them, a day for the men of the house. Lu would not want him to miss school, but he would have fun and they could teach him some things about cars, useful things, not dead facts from smelly old books.

They awoke early like they normally did, the sun still far from up, ate some bread with honey and eggs and glasses of milk, and they were ready. Charlie got his work cap and they were off. Just like the people of the time, their cars met unkind fates, wrecks, breakdowns, lack of a dollar for a new part. It was no one's job to pick up abandoned vehicles, so you might find them anywhere, fields, roadsides, ditches. They drove along the Clinton River toward Lake St. Clair and off in a gully Haik spotted a '28 Chrysler Imperial seven-seater down on the bank. Orlin pulled over and they assessed their find.

"What kinda fool drive down into the river?" Haik asked, patting Charlie on the shoulder.

"He musta been drunk," said Charlie and all three laughed.

"Don't look like it's been here long," Haik commented. "It wasn't here when we come by last week."

Carrying a chain, some boards, and a shovel, they walked down and found the front grill and half the front tires submerged in the brown water. The hope was that the wheels had not settled into the muck, making the extraction more difficult. Haik shimmied beneath the backend of the car and cinched the chain to the rear axle while Orlin ran up to attach the other end to their truck. Haik had Charlie helped him wedge the boards beneath the exposed portion of the front tires, which they'd need for traction. Haik opened the driver's door and looked around for anything that might have been left behind before telling Charlie he could be the driver of the stranded jalopy.

Orlin revved the truck's engine and slowly applied tension to the chain. The Chrysler wasn't at a very steep angle, and after some artful steering on Orlin's part and some pushing and shoving from Haik, who had taken off his boots and socks and rolled up his pantlegs to enter the water, the submerged front wheels were freed from the river and the car was pulled fully up onto dry land like some trophy whale. Charlie beamed as the car was lugged up onto the dirt road, and with a few quick maneuvers the truck was pulling the captured beast by the front fender back to Utica. The ride was slow—it appeared that the Chrysler might have a cracked steering column—so they would have to take their time, which they had plenty of. Once in the drive, they unhitched their new prize and Orlin and Haik pushed it into the garage.

"Well, whattaya think?"

"Pop that hood and let's see what the problem is," Orlin answered, anxious to get to work.

If they got this car squared away and tightened up, washed it up real good, they could get $75 or maybe even $100 for it, enough for a month's house payment and groceries.

"Lemme get Charlie in and check on lunch," Haik said, and he and Charlie went in the house while Orlin readied for a look at the engine.

When Haik came out he found Orlin already buried under the hood.

"What you see, old man?" asked Haik.

"Well, she ain't in too bad a shape, really. We could have her up and going soon enough. Yeah, somebody buy her and get a heck of a deal."

"Maybe you gents could fix me up a nice deal on a brand new Deuce Coupe."

The voice came from the side door of the barn, and both Haik and Orlin turned to find Otto Franks pointing a pistol at them.

"Yeah," Franks continued, "decided to take me a little ride in the country today. Parked not far down the road, so beautiful out I decided to walk a piece. And look what I find here, two vagrants out hopping cars. Now, gents, show me where you got the Coupe."

Haik looked at Orlin and then back at Franks.

"We ain't got no Deuce Coupe here."

"Bullshit. You're up to something with that fat fuck Mexican. I'm not fooling with you two."

Franks leveled the gun at them and fired. The explosion caused Haik and Orlin's knees to buckle and a splintery divot was blasted into the wall of the barn behind them. The warning was well taken.

"I swear, we ain't got no car. Look, look around. Look anywhere's you want, we ain't got no Deuce. You see a car here?"

"No, I don't, and that's why you fucks ain't dead yet. Maybe it's not exactly in this barn, but maybe you got it out in the woods, maybe across the street covered up with some brush. I think we need to take a look around out there. I know you bastards got the wheels, so we're gonna quit playing games and we're gonna find that car right now or it's curtains time. Saw a cute little boy a while ago. Maybe I'll start with him. Now get your hands up above your heads. We're going for a little walk."

Franks was a killer. Even if they brought him to the car, he would take them out anyways, but Charlie, Kina, and Lu, he couldn't touch them. Haik looked at Orlin. The best they could do now was buy time, look for some kind of opening somewhere, and maybe at least one of them could get at Franks before he cut them both down. Maybe they could get him out behind the barn to the woodpile, where Haik could go for the axe he kept there, or maybe they could lead him out into the woods so Lu, Arkina, and Charlie could get into Orlin's car and get out, just get the hell out. They had to have heard the shot—it could only mean trouble, the kind of trouble Haik had warned Lu about.

"Okay, we'll take you out. You wouldn't never find it with a map. It's a walk aways."

Haik glanced again at Orlin and then slowly paced to the front doors of the barn. The slower he walked, the more time he had to think. Orlin followed behind him and Franks brought up the rear, far enough away that they couldn't make a lunge at him. Haik felt light and weak. He had a baby waiting, a wife, a son, a sister and her husband all counting on him. There was no clearcut answer to the riddle he now found himself in. Would he bow down like a flunkie just like he'd done as a good SD man, take his bullet without a word? His mind worked but found nothing.

He exited the barn and turned to his left, toward the woods and the the axe—in a few seconds, he would have to try something, no matter how desperate. If he went for the axe and drew Franks' attention, it might give Orlin time to hit him from the blindside. If he was lucky, maybe Orlin could keep him from getting off a clear shot, and they could work together to put Franks down. Maybe, maybe, maybe....

Thunder split the open yard.

Haik and Orlin's knees buckled a second time.

He whirled to see Franks lurch forward, and when he hit the deck, there stood Lu no more than eight feet behind him cradling the smoking sawed off shotgun, her mouth slightly open. Haik went right after Franks and wrestled the pistol from his hand. He rolled Franks over—the same guy who pummeled him the day he was fired, a big Bennett tough with his gun, wasn't quite so tough with his back full of buckshot. Franks was alive, his eyes open. Without thinking, Haik's hands were at his throat, squeezing, squeezing, his fingers digging for all they were worth.

"Haik," Orlin started, but he could not hear and he was not about to stop.

His hands made a vice that cinched off the air to Franks' lungs, and he could feel the windpipe collapse between his thumbs until it popped and Haik's thumbs were nearly touching. Franks looked up at him but there was no register in his eyes.

"Haik!"

Lu's voice brought Haik back to the yard, the barn, their truck parked by the house, the dead body beneath him. He arose, lightheaded, and went to Lu, who stood quivering, the gun in her hands.

"Lu, Lu girl, you okay?"

He placed his hands to the sides of her face and looked into her skyblue eyes. Her mouth was still open. Haik pulled her to him and held her, her bulging belly firm against him. He took the gun from her hands and set it on the ground, and then walked her back to the house, holding her hand and supporting her at the waist.

"C'mon, honey, we don't want Charlie to see," he soothed, but when they went in the front door Charlie was there at the window, witness to everything.

"Charlie, get your mother some water." Haik led his wife to her chair in the parlor.

"Haik...," she began, but she couldn't finish her sentence.

"Shhhhh, anushas, shhhhh," he whispered, and brushed the hair back from her forehead. She could not stop trembling.

"You okay, Lu?" asked Orlin, now by their side with Arkina. They each placed a hand on her shoulders.

"I'm, I'm, I'm okay."

She tried to gather her breathing. Haik kissed her forehead. What would he have done without her? What would any of them have done? There would be five bodies strewn about the property and Franks would now be safely on his way back into the city, without the Deuce but no worse off for killing five people.

"Haik."

Orlin motioned for Haik to meet him out on the porch. Once outside, he addressed what had to be done.

"We got to get that man outta here." Orlin nodded toward Franks' body in the yard. "Don't matter what he done or how he die, they gonna come after us if they know what happen."

He was right. They weren't going to Luigi. Working with the cops had done nothing with Mr. Meadows and it would do even less now. This was their business, and they would handle it.

They placed a broken axle shaft on top of Franks, draped his arms around it, and tied him to it with some thick copper wiring. They rolled the body and axle up into some tarp and tied that off with rope, lacing in some old cinderblocks. They both lifted Franks' large frame into the bed of Mrs. Branch's beaten truck and Orlin got some blankets before they headed off toward Lake St. Clair. Up this way, there were miles of shore and an ocean of lake. It was November and soon everything would freeze over. They went east until they hooked up onto Jefferson and drove north towards Anchor Bay. They rolled past the harbor and continued toward Brandenburg Park. Just short of the park, they took a side path right to the lakeshore. They looked long and hard—no one in sight, either on the land or out on the water.

"Best thing we do is walk the bastard far out as we can and sink'm. Ain't nobody come out here but fishermen, and they like to fish farther out. Once he out here, we don't know nothing."

Haik agreed. He had Franks' pistol with him—it would go too. They looked over the body one more time and found Franks' wallet, wrapped him back up, tied him extra tightly to the cinder blocks. They took off their shoes and socks, pants and coats, lifted their load, and trudged to the beach, the air cutting into them. The load was heavy but they were fueled with urgency. The water was freezing, stopping their breath, but they kept wading out until they were up to Haik's chin. They gave the body a shove out into the black water and waited a moment to make sure it did not surface, and worked their way back onto shore, soaked and freezing. They dressed quickly, stiffly, and then Haik took the pistol from his coat and cast it as far into the lake as he could just to the right of where they'd let Franks go.

Once back at the truck, they bundled into the blankets, their mouths chattering and bodies shaking on the journey home.

Franks' car tore down quickly. They found it hidden in some brush just south of their house and went to work on it as soon as they had it in the barn. Haik felt as if he was dismantling Franks himself and went at the metal beast with a vengeance. Whatever they could swap out with the Chrysler Imperial they did, and they stacked the rest of the parts in their growing arsenal of usable axles, tires, brake cables, tie rods, doors, transmissions, and engine blocks. Soon the only thing left was the empty chassis.

"We don't want nobody to know that son-of-a-bitch was anywhere near this place."

"Well, if we got to, we can load this skin up and dump it in the river," Orlin responded, pointing to Franks' hollow shell. "Ain't nobody gonna know he was ever here. Least they could never prove it."

They hefted the chassis onto the flatbed with an overhead winch and then drove to a narrow bridge over the Clinton River. They pushed the doorless hull overboard, heard a splash, and that was the last trace of Otto Franks anyone would ever see.

The next day Haik was supposed to see Rivera and find out what exactly had happened after he left the museum with the Deuce Coupe.

The ride in was familiar but haunting—he was returning completely as Haik Pehlivanian, not Hank Pelini the SD man. It felt good.

He knocked at the apartment door and was greeted with a hug by Miss Frida, who was back from Mexico. Despite the many hardships she had suffered, she now had color in her flesh, and her nails were painted a fire red that matched her lipstick. There were painting materials in the open main room of the apartment, canvases, brushes and various tubes of paint, and Haik recognized the work as Miss Frida's, the same style and coloring he remembered from her painting in the hospital. However, what stunned him was an image on one of the canvases. There was a woman, Miss Frida, and it was like she was opened up down the middle, and inside was this like broken up metal column, and her skin was pierced all over with nails. In the background was a house that you could see inside, and it was all bluish in color. To the side, and this is what caught Haik, was a nude man holding a baby, a man of strong stomach muscles, dark-hair, thick forearms.

The man was Haik.

Why on earth was he in the painting? He hadn't sat down for any sketches or posed as he had for Rivera at the Rouge. And naked…my God, Haik felt himself explode with sweat. His thing, his, you know, his man piece, it was right there looking at him, nothing covering it. And the baby, it wasn't the giant red, blind baby Haik had seen in the hospital painting. No, this child was normal sized and dark skinned but not bloody, and its eyes were open. What was the painting supposed to mean? When Rivera entered, Frida lit a cigarette, looked at Haik quizzically, as if to monitor his reaction to her creation, and then excused herself for a moment.

"My good friend, how are you?" Rivera asked, and Haik didn't know where to really begin.

"I'm, I'm okay. Some, some stuff been happening, that's for sure."

He looked to the floor and still felt embarrassed about his image in the painting. He sat down self-consciously and began to explain what had gone on in the past two days.

"You see, *panzas*, what this is really about? You see what they are willing to do to your noble worker? Welcome back to *Gringolandia*, home of the happy and benevolent capitalist liberator and his magical machines of freedom."

"Your family, they are okay?" asked Rivera, ignoring Miss Frida.

"Yeah, they're fine for now, they ain't stayin' at the house. I don't know who still might come out there. But me and Orlin, we're stayin', workin' on cars, got our shotguns on us every second."

In fact, his sawed off was wrapped in his overcoat next to him at this very moment. He had Lu sew a long pocket into the inside to hold the weapon where he could reach it quickly.

Cam Lister, Rivera explained, did get a nice little visit to city jail, and it seemed that his luck had run out with Bennett—losing the Deuce Coupe and having Edsel brought into the middle of it was too much. He was under strict orders to keep his nose clean and he hadn't, no two ways about it, so his ticket was punched. But who had sent Franks? They hadn't driven the Coupe since he and Orlin hid it in the Pehlivanian garage back in the old neighborhood—no one knew where Haik came from or what his real name was. No way anyone would look there, even if they got information from the Sociology Department. But would someone come looking for Franks or the Coupe again out in Utica? If they did, it wouldn't be one bimbo by himself, but a swarm armed with more than pistols.

"This is why you are best suited to serve the worker with your brush, not your mouth," snipped Frida, chiding Rivera without mercy, but he did not give way so easily.

"You think I am new to such intrigues? How does this differ from when Machado had Mella gunned down? Every fool knew who was behind the trigger, but whom did the honorable detective Quintana blame for the murder? Need I remind you? Our friend Tina Modotti, a completely absurd scenario, just a shameless attempt to silence an innocent comrade."

"Yes, *our* dear, dear friend Tina, whom you used as the model for your murals in Chapingo when you weren't fucking her. Yes, shameless, indeed."

Haik looked at Miss Frida—did she just say what he heard? A woman just didn't say something like that. He wanted to crawl under the couch and take Miss Frida's painting with him.

"My dear, let us address the issue at hand. No, this is but another step in a never-ending journey to justice. This is how revolution works, dialectical struggle, movement and counter movement, cycles until the world sees the true path to freedom. Nowhere is it said that the path is straight or without dangers."

Haik did not know any of these people Rivera was talking about or which person killed who, or what motorcycles had to do with anything, and to him it really made no difference because now his family was the one in danger, not all these strangers Rivera ranted about.

"But your painting…," Frida started.

"I have lost not one moment of painting helping Haik and Orlin," Rivera said in defense, careful not to counter the fiery woman before him too severely. "Indeed, this whole circumstance has only fused my commitment to continue the fight. This country, our country, Russia, all forged in revolution. But I am telling the truth. The good of Mr. Edsel Ford will be preserved on those walls. I truly believe he is an honorable man. The evil that is beyond his control, well, some of that will be settled shortly."

Rivera was still in for the battle, but he was not the one having guns shoved in his face. And how exactly were things going to be settled?

"But matters have gone too far now, *Dieguito*, people are in danger…"

"Danger? Do you forget that my early training was as a military man? Do you not remember the days of threat as I worked in the Ministry building in Mexico City? Did I not wear a pair of pistols as I worked? You forget so soon, my dear, that I am prepared to defend my proletarian brothers with more than a brush. If I have to walk into the institute brandishing *bandoliers*, I most certainly will."

Rivera splashed a dash of heroic flourish on all the right syllables.

"Mr. Rivera, how exactly, how are things going to get settled shortly?"

Haik did not want to appear impolite, but he needed to cut to the heart of things. Where was anything in Rivera's speech about Lu or Orlin or Charlie or Arkina? Talking was not good enough right now, not with so much unsettled. Rivera looked at him quizzically, then at Miss Frida.

"The road to justice is often paved in upheaval. Give me two days. Now, though, there is something I must share with you. Will you walk with us now to the garden court?" asked Rivera, mischievousness in his voice.

Haik agreed, put on his overcoat, feeling the sawed off shotgun dangling inside, and walked with the two artists to the museum.

On the outside, nothing seemed to change. It was November, and the arctic chill of winter was threatening—no wonder Miss Frida could not find her place here. Once at the garden court, though, there was a kind of radiance coming from inside that had not been there the last time Haik visited, and its power could be felt before even entering. When they stepped inside, Haik was overcome by all the colors. The east and west walls, which were interrupted by large doorways and the pillars and windows and grates that Rivera so detested, were finished, and Haik's eye was drawn to the east wall, where, below the two large nude women and above the entrance way that lead to the stairs to the second floor, there was an image of a baby huddled up inside some kind of circle thing—it was not Miss Frida's bloody red baby that was as large as a person, but one that was more alive and healthy looking, like it was asleep. The two women, who held grains and fruits or rocks or something, looked down peacefully at the baby, and to the side of the baby were two small paintings of more food, which looked like it could be plucked from the walls and eaten.

It was dazzling, and in this room Haik forgot the threats and violence that had enveloped his life over the last several days and months and how many years into his past. Behind him, the west wall was complete as well, with the airplanes still fixed on the uppermost portions of the wall above the entranceway they had just passed through, but now there were vents and ducts and pipes that looked like they could have been a part of the museum's own boiler room. The way the images flowed and wound around, they were like music, a music that did not lull your ears but your eyes, taking them from one image to the next and back again on pathways of color. Haik would be the first to admit he knew nothing about art, but he knew how the room made him *feel*, and he felt weightless and unproblemed and unthreatened as he turned and gazed about him.

"Here, see here, Haik. Do you recognize these men?" asked Rivera, an impish grin on his face.

Haik turned to the north wall, and before him was, oh sweet Lord... an image of himself and Orlin moving the cart of engine blocks!

"See, look at the strength in your forearms, how the muscle twines smoothly as you pull and Orlin pushes, like the precise innerworkings of a great and beautiful machine, but fully human, fully engaged, fully important."

Haik looked on in wonder. Yes, there they were, just as they were that day, and now they were melded into the wall like hardened steel, the only way to remove them a hammer. Oh, man, what would Lu and Charlie do if they could see him up there with Orlin! And how about Orlin and Arkina and Ovsanna and his parents, and Mrs. Meadows? This was beyond explaining. The only thing missing, Haik thought, was

Mr. Meadows and Vahram—somewhere, if he was the artist, he'd work them in. They were a part of this whole journey that had led Haik here, they were part of the story, the root of it, and there would be no story without them and they deserved a piece of the wall. Even so, what Haik stood before was spectacular.

"You said you were a sportsman at one time, Haik, a wrestler, which would account for the musculature of your arms. In Mexico, the ancient Maya played a game called *poc-te-poc*, quite a savage game, which always ended in a beheading—for the winner!" Rivera declared.

"Oh, don't bore us, *panzas*," quipped Miss Frida, her feistiness nearly at full strength.

"Mr. Rivera, I don't know what to say, it's, it's fine, as fine a thing as I ever seen."

Haik tried to in some way give thanks for something he could not even begin to guess the value of. He still couldn't get over it—there he was, right there, right there on the wall. He looked away at some of the other images, but his eyes always returned to that image, front and center, of Orlin and him, as if it might not be there if he stopped looking.

"Diego has given you this image. Now if he would only give me another chance at a child," Frida said, a sense of challenge in her voice but also a thread of pain.

"My dear, we have nothing to discuss on this front. Please, I will no longer allow you to harm yourself."

There was a rare sense of authority in his voice as he addressed his wife.

"I am fine now, I know this climate now, it will not drain me like before," she persisted. "*Ah, la vida es un gran relajo*. My goodness, perhaps I need to coax Haik into giving me a chance. He can give me a baby. I find that he would be most capable...."

Rivera gave her a look and then glanced quickly over at Haik. Haik stood mute. Where on earth did she come up with that? Haik looked at Rivera, who still eyed him—was his innocence as detectable as the other portions of his life Rivera had so easily deciphered? He had touched Miss Frida, yes, but only to hold her up from fainting, to scoop her up and carry her to the car when she was bleeding to death and again into the emergency room. He had been alone with her many times and absolutely nothing off the mark had taken place—never, not a chance. Sure, he had seen her naked in her painting, but that wasn't something he could help or could be held against him. That painting that was now in their apartment, and he had no idea where that came from or how

Miss Frida figured out how to paint his, his, well, his private parts—there was no way she had ever seen them.

"Haik, I am curious how a man with such little training in the fine arts has become such a focus of contemporary painting."

Rivera raised an eyebrow to him, and then glanced at Frida. Haik stammered. He had no answer. He never asked to be painted and, he would be the first to admit, he was nobody anybody should want to put in a painting. His faced balled up in confusion. Was Rivera angry with him? If so, why? Miss Frida was the one saying things, not him. He could find no words.

"What I do when you are preoccupied is my business and my business alone. Goodness knows, you have done as you liked on your own time, no?"

Frida was enjoying this verbal joust.

"Ah, so you have been, how do you Americans say, *screwing* my wife?"

Haik's eyes widened. What on earth was happening here?

"Mr. Rivera, I ain't...."

"Don't be cruel, *carasapo*," taunted Miss Frida, the redness of her skin intensifying.

"I am not being cruel, just observant. Haik, my *ninita chiquitita* appears to have taken a, ahem, very personal interest in you. And do not think I have not noticed how often you have accompanied her alone."

Haik fumbled inside, wanting to say something to clear up this whole matter.

"Mr. Rivera, I swear, I ain't...."

"My good man, you need explain nothing. If I were the jealous type, perhaps we would have a dilemma to resolve, but such is not the case. If you have given my little dove pleasure, I owe you thanks, not anger."

"Not the jealous type, huh? What if I tell you he fucks like a panther while you, you are nothing but a fat elephant?"

Miss Frida's dark eyes flared with a wicked defiance.

"Darling, you will get nowhere with this. I celebrate your affair with this fine man. I bless it. Please, continue if you like."

"But Mr. Rivera, I swear I, we, we didn't never...."

"Haik, please, do not fret so. She is a free woman, just as I am a free man. No one owns either of us, not even each other. The most serious sign of her deep interest in you can be found on the canvas back at our apartments. This is more alarming than a simple matter of the flesh."

How did this start? He couldn't explain how he ended up on a canvas. Frida was the artist, so if anyone could answer, she could.

"Mr. Rivera...."

"In two days," Rivera cut in, an unsettling lack of emotion in his voice, "be here with the automobile and we will bring this drama to its climax. For now, I have work to do. My comrade, please excuse me."

There was too much that could go wrong, and yet what else was there to do? Haik wanted to bring his loved ones back to the house in Utica without fear of unwanted visitors, but that was not possible now. What did the Service Department want with him? He was done with the Rouge, so why not just let him be? What would Bennett or anyone else have to gain by continuing to harass him? He would bring the Deuce Coupe back, fine, it was theirs, but there was nothing doing on Franks' car. The bastard came out and threatened his family—that was his mistake and he paid for it.

But what if Rivera was upset about Frida's painting and the comment she had made at the museum about Haik, you know, being close to her? Was he jealous, and would he use this final meeting as a way of getting rid of Haik for good, eliminating a possible rival? Haik had two fresh shells locked into the sawed off shotgun. He pulled on his overcoat, placed the weapon in the long inner pocket, and gathered up some back-up rounds. He had no idea where this was headed, but it was time to bring the ship to shore.

"Are you sure you're going to be okay?" Lu whispered.

How could she still be so strong after all she had been through? He was ashamed he had ever doubted her or ever given her less than all his love. He looked at her and smiled.

"Orlin's coming with me. I'm just gonna drop the car off and then Orlin will drive us back. No problems," he reassured her, but he knew he had made that promise before.

He hugged her softly—any day now, and the baby would come, probably sooner than later since the commotion in Utica had rattled her so deeply. Lu handled the incident like a warrior—she was more concerned about bringing the baby early than having shot a man. What more could Haik ask for in a wife? She did what she had to do to protect her loved ones. She had been through enough and now, finally, it was time for him to do his part.

"Don't be long," Lu whispered. "The baby's restless."

He looked into her eyes, kissed her, and was off.

Haik and Orlin drove separately to the museum. They parked in front on the far side of Woodward—they wanted everything out in the open. Orlin hid the shotgun they'd found in Franks' car under his own long coat and the two walked briskly across the street and up the front stairs of the institute, hands inside their coats, ready. As they approached the second bank of stairs, the center doors opened and out walked Cutty, flanked by Gellinger and Zabriskie.

"That's far enough, Pelini," called Cutty, but Haik and Orlin kept walking, meeting them face to face at the landing of the second row of steps. "You turn the car over and you just might have a chance to live."

Haik did not hesitate—this was no time for talk. His right hand was already on his weapon and he drew, as did Orlin, and Gellinger and Zabriskie, taken off guard, belatedly began to reach.

"Don't even try or I'll splatter you."

Part of Haik hoped they made a motion for their pistols so he could follow through on his warning. They froze, though, and Haik and Orlin kept their weapons leveled.

"You're crazy," muttered Cutty. "You just signed your execution papers, pal."

He was trying to smile, but he could tell Haik and Orlin were not playing.

"Maybe, but you're gonna be dead if you don't shut the hell up and unload. Hands up. Now, hands up. That's it. One at a time, starting with you, Zabriskie, you reach inside real slow and take out your piece by the handle and lay it on the ground, real slow, then lay down over there."

Zabriskie looked at Cutty, who nodded, and Zabriskie reached inside and withdrew his pistol, and, looking again at Cutty, placed it on the ground, where Orlin picked it up. He then looked at Haik before lying on the ground himself, giving the tough-guy's signature look of contempt.

"That's good. Now you, Gellinger," Haik commanded. Gellinger looked right at Haik, his face burning, then he slowly withdrew his gun and bent down, placing it on the pavement, where Orlin collected the second trophy and backed away.

"This is really gonna cost you…" Cutty started, but Haik closed the gap on him and, using the shotgun like a billy, delivered a swift club to the side of his head.

Gellinger made a motion to intervene but Orlin cocked his weapon and zeroed in on him. He motioned Gellinger to lie down, and he slowly lowered himself to the pavement.

Cutty lay on the ground, the side of his head bleeding, and Haik bent over, placing both barrels into the downed man's face just under his nose. It made sense now. Cutty was in with Lister and had been a part of the beating at the barn and the showdown on the river in Ecorse. He probably fronted Lister's bail, too, and pulled the strings to spring him.

"That's for the little gig at the barn with Lister. Now, you're next, you reach inside and take out your piece, real slow, and don't give me no reason to scatter your brains all over this sidewalk."

Cutty looked up at Haik in obedience. He carefully reached in his coat and then slowly placed his pistol on the ground. As his hand retreated along the sidewalk, Haik raised his booted foot and smashed down as hard as he could. The contact made a crunching noise, definitely some bones breaking in the process, and Cutty screamed. As he writhed on the ground, Haik returned the shotgun to his face. He scooped up Cutty's piece and kept the barrels in his victim's nostrils.

"That's for sending Franks out to my house, you piece a shit."

He picked up Cutty's piece and placed it in his coat. Both Zabriskie and Gellinger were on the ground looking up, and Haik thought that's where they all should be, on their bellies slithering along the earth.

"Now, we're going inside and you three mugs better stay on the ground until we get inside them doors. You go anywhere near that car, I'll break more than your fingers. Bennett and the Fords know the car is there, and if it's missing you're the ones they gonna look for."

"You're dead, Pelini," started Cutty.

As the last syllable left Cutty's mouth, Haik delivered a placekicker's boot right to his mouth, exploding it in blood. Gellinger started to rise and Orlin let loose a blast with his shotgun, ripping through Gellinger's pantleg, sending him back onto the cement. Zabriskie held his hands out in mercy.

"We told you fucks not to move. You wanna move again? Huh? And there ain't nobody here named Pelini. You assholes remember that."

Haik and Orlin took a wide berth around the prone figures to avoid any more contact and backed up the second flight of steps. They walked backward to the front doors, keeping their weapons trained on the three bodies below them. Orlin found the long handle and pulled the door open, backing in and holding the door for Haik, who followed right after him. Once inside, Orlin replaced his spent shell and they rushed quickly toward the garden court.

On the way, they looked left and right, distrustful of all they encountered. They were met in the hall by two cops, who were obviously responding to the gunshot.

"Outside," yelled Haik, "three a Lister's pals. Keep'm away from the Coupe."

Haik and Orlin moved together to the court. Once at the west entrance, they could hear voices inside, and when they entered they saw Henry and Edsel Ford, Bennett, Luigi, Lister, Rivera, and two more uniformed policemen all huddled together. All eyes turned to them.

"What on earth was that ungodly noise out there?" sputtered the elder Ford.

"Just sounded like a little thunder," smiled Luigi, a hint of relief in his voice as he saw that Haik and Orlin were okay.

"Well, here's your men. An easy open and shut arrest," said Bennett.

"Well, there it is, let's get them under arrest and be done with this," chimed old man Ford, as if he were judge, jury, and police chief.

"Not so fast. We're not arresting anyone until we get to the bottom of exactly what has happened," Luigi cut in.

"They stole a goddamned car," spat Lister. "They set me up."

As Lister spoke, Cutty staggered into the garden bleeding, flanked by one of the coppers.

"These pricks, they just assaulted me. They shot Gellinger," he gasped, holding his damaged hand, blood seeping from his forehead.

Haik looked about him—it had become a circus. He noticed that Rivera had a sly grin on his face. He could not be happier with all the chaos and drama.

"Hmmm, looks like someone's going to visit the pokey," Bennett grinned, looking directly at Haik.

Haik said nothing—yes, it was true, he did bash Cutty upside the head and, yes, he did stomp his hand. And Orlin did shoot Gellinger in the leg. So much for just leaving the car off and driving home a free man.

"Wasn't no assault," shot in Orlin, and one at a time he pulled out the pistols they collected moments before and handed them to Luigi's men. "Here, look at these. Trace 'em down, whatever you got to do, but that man right there and his two boys was ready to use these on us. We just defended ourselves. Law says we can do that."

Luigi didn't need much more of an opening.

"You carrying one of these weapons?" he said to Cutty.

"Yeah, so?"

"Nothing. Jenkins," he called to one of his men. "Cuff this man for assault and escort him out."

Jenkins went to Cutty, who looked at Bennett incredulously, slapped him with cuffs, and then began to lead him away.

"Wait, wait, wait a minute here. I'm the one who got assaulted. Look at me, for Christ's sake. Check him out, he's carrying a goddamned shotgun!" screamed Cutty, now being dragged.

Luigi approached Haik and held out his hand, signaling him to hand over his weapon. Haik complied. Luigi looked the weapon over.

"No problem here. Police issue. This man was deputized to help us in a longterm investigation of corruption in metropolitan Detroit, particularly bootlegging across the river. Good work, deputy."

Cutty could be heard screaming as he disappeared from the museum. What had just happened? What was Luigi talking about, being a deputy? Haik was no cop, but Cutty was on his way out in cuffs so he wasn't going to argue.

"Don't think you can come in here and start playing knight in shining armor here, copper," Bennett seethed.

"No, Mr. Bennett, you're right, but that man is being arrested for smuggling alcohol and narcotics onto United States' soil. We all know Mr. Ford's sterling reputation and dedication to proper health and clean living, and I'm sure that contraband whiskey and heroin are things he does not want his name associated with."

Luigi looked directly at Henry Ford.

"My word, no," gasped Ford with indignation, "absolutely not."

"And Mr. Bennett, I'm sure you don't know the half of what these men have been up to, including Mr. Lister here," Luigi continued before Bennett could speak.

Haik smiled—Luigi, he was smart. He just gave Bennett an honorable out, a way to save face in a potentially inflammatory situation. Now he could play along or get drawn into the net with Cutty and Lister, but the choice was his.

"If you got any proof of any involvement in those types of activities, then no, I have had no knowledge of that, and that's not the type of thing Mr. Ford would ever or will ever have connected to his name, or myself either, so help me God," Bennett said.

Old man Ford placed a birdlike hand on the diminutive brute's shoulder, showing their confederation.

"I was sure that's how Mr. Ford felt."

Luigi nodded in deference to the old hawk.

"I most certainly do. If that man, what's his name, Cutty? If he's involved in any such matters then neither I nor Mr. Bennett will tolerate his presence. Not on my life."

Ford was defiant, as if the mere thought he could be associated with anything the least bit vile or illegal was itself grossly unthinkable.

"Now we have the matter of the car," Luigi broke in.

"There's your men, right there. A nigger and a dago, nothing but thieves."

Lister pointed at Orlin and Haik.

"We ain't stole nothing," countered Haik.

"Then how's you got the car? Huh, smart guy? How'd you get here in that car if you didn't steal it?"

"That's a good question," Bennett added, liking the turn of momentum. "Let 'm explain that one, without big blue talkin' for 'em."

"If these two men have taken so much as a tire spoke, I will prosecute to the fullest extent of the law, make no mistake," old man Ford added, extending a bony finger in the direction of Haik and Orlin.

"Well, how exactly did you come into possession of the vehicle?" asked Edsel, not accusing like the others, but genuinely perplexed.

Haik looked at Orlin, who looked back at him. They had no story prepared, and, in fact, they knowingly did take something that didn't belong to them. Sure, Rivera put them up to it, and what else was that but stealing, just another variation of what they used to do in the railyards across the city? Straight up, there was no defense for what they had done—whether they were just doing what Rivera instructed or not, they stole.

Haik glanced to Rivera—was this the price he was to pay for Frida's interest in him and having his image captured unwittingly in a painting? Was this his plan in full operation? To eliminate a problem by having Haik pinched, getting him to walk into his own arrest like a blind man? Did he really think there was something between Haik and Frida? The damn painting, surely Rivera had to know it was just some kind of thing that happened in Frida's imagination, like the woman in the bed with all the bloody ropes coming out of her. And the comment on, on doing it like a panther, hell, Haik was no panther. How could an uneducated, low class rube like Haik exert any influence over a sophisticated bearcat like Frida?

"Might I interject here?" piped Rivera, a certain authority in his normally soft voice. "These two men, they have been my hosts, my dinner companions, my friends, my comrades. I have considered them brothers, and as brothers I would neither expect nor condone the least betrayal...."

Haik looked down. That was it, he was done. *Betrayal*, Rivera said. Well, if he was going down at Rivera's jealous hand, he would go down alone—no way would he let Orlin go down with him. This was Haik's mess, no one else's, and he would accept the punishment by himself. He'd tell them he shot Gellinger and admit to whatever else they wanted to throw at him, screwing Miss Frida or causing the stock market crash itself.

"...and this is why I was so stunned to learn of his termination as my escort. What could he have done to merit this ignominious fate? He had been such a complete gentleman...."

Haik wished Rivera would just get it over with—there was no need to call him ignorant on top of it all. So what if he didn't know things like books and paintings and the names of presidents. Let Luigi clamp the handcuffs on him and lead him to the paddy wagon to sit with Cutty and the other scum.

"...even having borne a thousand injustices at the hands of Mr. Lister still considered him a friend and recommended him as his replacement. Trusting this man, I requested no one but Mr. Lister...."

Rivera pointed to Lister, who seemed to puff his chest out at all the nice words directed at him. Cutty was going down, and Lister was already in tough for the fiasco in Ecorse, but he'd have to count on Rivera to get him out. Haik listened, but thought of Lu and Charlie—who would take care of them now? What would happen to the house? His parents and sister? Mrs. Meadows? He had blown it all the way around.

"...and this is why it was most difficult for this man you see before you to comply with my latest request, even though he no longer was under my employ, to go to the place, you say Ecorse, and retrieve the automobile in question for me. Mr. Cutty told me where it was located, at a park, and begged forgiveness for Mr. Lister's indiscretion, to have Hank get the car and all would be forgotten. I guess this is why Mr. Cutty was waiting for Hank, so ensnare him just before the meeting.

But I assure you, this is all that Mr. Hank Pelini was doing. The only guilty man present is this one."

Haik stood mesmerized, just as he had when Rivera painted, only now Rivera was painting in the words of a language that was not his own but was completely his own and he was pointing his finger at Cam Lister and not him. Henry and Edsel Ford, Harry Bennett, Cam Lister, Luigi Leone and Orlin stood mute, entranced in Rivera's explanation for Haik's possession of the Deuce Coupe.

"So, Mr. Pelini was just bringing back the car as you requested based on the information provided to you by Mr. Cutty regarding Mr. Lister's theft of the car?"

Luigi restated Rivera's explanation, making sure everyone in attendance got the condensed version of the tale.

"That is exactly what I'm saying."

"That fuckin' spic is lying," fumed Lister, making a move toward Rivera.

Bennett, though, his reflexes as a former boxer taking over, shot a right cross up at the taller man, blindsiding him and sending him reeling sideways to the museum floor. All stood in stunned rigidity at what was taking place except Rivera, who beamed in amusement at all the festivities. Luigi pounced on Lister, rolled him to his belly, placed a knee into his back, and twisted his arms roughly to apply his cuffs. Everyone looked at Bennett, who rubbed his knuckles.

"I'm sorry, Mr. Ford, but I won't listen to that slagmouth talk about our guest like that. And if he had anything to do with Cutty and any illegal activities he had it coming."

Harry Bennett adjusted his coat sleeves, and looked to his boss.

"Mr. Rivera, I am so sorry...." began Edsel, extending a hand in reconciliation.

"No, my good Edsel, you have nothing to apologize about. I knew this was a vile human being from first sight of him. He has been preying upon simple workers like a wolf among sheep and now he must pay for his crimes. How he is still walking the streets as a free man, well, sometimes I just cannot understand your country."

"This man," interjected old Ford, "most certainly does not represent our great country and he most certainly does not represent the Ford Motor Company. And as you will see, I will make personally sure he is punished to the full extent of the law."

The old man was trembling, looking directly at Rivera, seemingly more infuriated at Rivera's assessment of his country than Lister's trail of deceit and murder.

"Cam Lister," Luigi announced as he rolled Lister onto his back, "as Mr. Henry Ford requested, you are now under arrest for grand theft of a 1932 Ford Deuce Coupe. You are also under arrest for the murder of Liam Meadows, and you have officially broken the terms of your bail for the alleged murders of Pinchas Goldberg, Lem Rickolter, and Carl Showalter, as well as the alleged smuggling of alcohol and narcotics onto United States soil. That enough for you? On your feet. You're going for a nice trip downtown, and the only thing you can do to get out of your mess this time is attempt to resist me in any way at which point I will be forced to use the maximum power in my possession to neutralize you."

Luigi yanked Lister up to his feet, the beaten man still groggy from the blow Bennett had delivered. As Luigi walked Lister out, his eyes connected with Haik's. Haik wanted to say something Lister would remember to commemorate the last time they would ever look at one another, not as recruit and master but as free man and hopeless criminal, but no words could find their way into his mouth. The look he gave Lister would have to do, a look that said you killed Liam Meadows but now you're going to pay the price for the rest of your worthless life at the Jackson State Pen and no Cutty or Bennett can help you or will even bother pretending to know your name. It wasn't the blood and pain Haik had dreamed of, but it would have to do.

"I'm sorry for that little problem," Bennett said to Henry Ford, adjusting his bowtie, but beaming in satisfaction.

"You've nothing to apologize for, Harry. That foul-mouthed lout needed a good sock to the jaw," the old man assured Bennett. "Now that our business here is concluded, we can put an end to the ugly affair. I've seen and heard more than enough for one day."

"No," countered Rivera. "I am very sorry, Mr. Ford, but this business is not concluded yet. This man, he has lost his car, his job, his father-in-law, everything but his own hands and heart. We cannot just leave him to the wolves."

The remaining dignitaries looked at one another, unaware that they had any further obligation in this matter.

"What man do you speak of?" asked the old man.

"This one. The honorable Hank Pelini."

"What exactly do you propose?" asked Edsel.

"I propose that we do what is most just," commented Rivera, as if the answer were obvious. "There is a car outside with no owner. Here is a man with no car who has been robbed of his. I think...."

"Wait one God-fearing second," interrupted the elder Ford, his impatience bubbling over. "I was the one who was robbed, and if you are implying that this man is owed anything by the Ford Motor Company you are sadly mistaken, Mr. Rivera. You are a painter, and you are being fairly compensated for your work, but I'm the car maker here, let's not forget that. You need to stick to your painting and I'll...."

"I'm the president of Ford Motor Company," Edsel interjected, "and yes, father, we do have a moral if not financial obligation to make right by this man. Two criminals who, given a little more time, would have brought shame to our name are now in police custody thanks to this man. We *do* owe him something. Hank, you will keep the key to the Deuce Coupe. The car is yours. That is my final decision. Please accept this as a token of appreciation from the president of the Ford Motor Company."

Edsel looked his father directly in the eyes, and the old man returned the gaze before he let out a sigh of disgust and turned away. He motioned to Bennett to follow, and off the two headed.

"My goodness, Harry, sometimes I don't know if in ten years time there will even be a Ford Motor Company, the way that boy runs things," the aged man muttered, his back turned to everyone but his voice audible to all.

Bennett nodded to Edsel and Rivera and began to walk out, but stopped as he passed Haik, who stood in mute observance of all taking place before him.

"Pelini, you come by my office tomorrow morning and turn in that Deuce and we'll get you back on staff where you should be. Two men just went down today, and I got room for a big six like you, a position of authority, and, hell, bring the darky with you. I'll get you your old car back and, what the hay, I'll throw another ten dollars a week onto your salary. We got a deal?"

Bennett smiled, holding out his hand, confident that in one stroke he had gotten Mr. Ford his new car back from this immigrant fool and taken control of a situation he had up until this point been a mere player in and not the conductor. Haik took Bennett's hand and squeezed it firmly, exerting a pressure that only a man who had handled wrenches and pliers and hammers could apply, and then increased the pressure as he began to speak.

"My name is Haik Pehlivanian, and that car out there belongs to me, and me and my brother-in-law already got us jobs, clean, honest jobs. But thank you."

He released his grip. Bennett looked at him, narrowing his eyes, sizing him up, and then shook his head and followed after the older Ford, the sound of shoes on the museum floor fading off into the distance. Haik was now owner of the Deuce Coupe. He looked at Orlin, who smiled at him and winked.

"Mr. Ford," Haik began, addressing Edsel with deference. "You don't gotta do this, sir."

"True, I don't, but it's what's right. We owe you a debt of gratitude for working with Mr. Rivera and for what you've experienced. I know you've been through a great deal, and much of it I wish had never happened, but if you need a job anywhere at the Rouge, I will personally make sure you're brought on board."

Haik thought it over. He could go back, maybe even get Orlin in, take the best paycheck to be found in the country for a working man, maybe a place in Building B on the line, a safe 40 hour work week.

But he then thought of Lister and Cutty and Harry Bennett. The Service Department still existed. He and Orlin could take any job at the plant but the second a SD man came by, they would again be prisoners, breakable, expendible parts to be greased and oiled and thrown away or recycled when they wore out or were no longer needed. Haik looked to the mural on the north wall, to the images of himself and Orlin as they battled with the engine blocks, their arms and legs and backs straining against the weight of dead steel. Rivera made sure that he would always be a Ford man, forever, as long as there was a north wall to the garden court of the Detroit Institute of Arts, whether they ever actually worked there ever again.

"Thank you, Mr. Ford, but I think I got to stay closer to my family now. Me and Orlin, we got a little business we're just getting started. I'll have to pass on the job."

He shook Mr. Ford's small, soft hand. He looked at Rivera, who stood smiling, a look of satisfaction covering his face, the widely spaced eyes filled with triumph.

"My friends, Haik and Orlin, we must make one last stop at my chambers. We'll allow you to say good-bye to my Frida, and I have something for you to take home with you. Mr. Ford, I believe we are now concluded with today's drama, and I still have work to do."

With that, Haik and Orlin accompanied two of the most powerful men in Detroit at that moment out the doors of the garden court and onto Woodward Avenue.

Ararat is the holy mountain of the Armenian people. Some believe it is the site of the Bible's Garden of Eden, and others tell stories of the remnants of Noah's Ark being lodged somewhere on its snowy cliffs. Ararat is their identity, their symbol, their reassurance that no matter how low they are dragged, how crushed their spirits or bodies may become, how much they suffer with no sign of redemption or relief in sight, there is always a height that belongs to them, a cairn of rock that reaches up to heaven, a place where they rise above all else on earth and cannot be defeated. To name a child Ararat is to give that child the serene strength of a mountain, the solidity of something sacred that cannot be washed away, torn down, burned or erased from history.

On the afternoon Haik Pehlivanian legally took control of the Deuce Coupe, he also became a father. After visiting Rivera's apartment one last time and bidding him good-bye, he and Orlin drove to the old neighborhood to the Pehlivanian house, relieved, exhausted, and filled with a sense of freedom. Once inside, they found Lu had been moved to an upstairs bedroom, her water broken, her forehead dewed with perspiration, and pain, anticipation, and joy radiating from her face. Haik's mother and Arkina and Ovsanna were running up and down the stairs, tending to Lu, boiling hot water on the kitchen stove and readying clean towels for the delivery. Haik stood witness, holding Lu's hand until finally it was time, and with such effort and strength and concentration he had never before seen in a woman, Lu fought until the head of the baby breached, at which point Haik's mother took control, pulled as Lu pushed, and soon the entire baby, slathered in blood and fluid, was free.

Haik's mother bit the umbilical cord and tied it off, and Haik stood there, amazed, looking at the red-skinned, wailing little ball of flesh. Arkina and Ovsanna cleaned the newborn off and then wrapped him in fresh towels before handing him to Lu. Haik was speechless, touching the baby with his thick hands, almost afraid it might break, while Lu's eyes told the story of her pride, relief, and thanks to God for a healthy child.

And they named the boy Ararat Liam Pehlivanian, a name that could be Americanized to Art or Artie as the situation demanded, or shortened to Rat for a teasing father or uncle. They brought him home to Utica, where Lu rested and Haik and Orlin went to work on their new business. They nailed some planks together to form a sign on which they painted "H & O Garage" and hung it proudly above the doors of the barn. Year by year, the city crept north out toward where they lived and more cars and trucks and tractors broke down and needed fixing, and they never lacked for work no matter how heavily the Depression hung over everthing. No, they did not become rich, but they made their monthly payments to Mrs. Branch until the house and land were theirs free and clear, and they fed their clan, which grew after Orlin and Arkina brought their first child into the world, a world mired in strife and headed toward another World War.

On St. Patrick's Day in 1933, Diego Rivera's murals were finally unveiled to the public, and the reaction couldn't have been more mixed. Conservatives on the social right demonized Rivera as a sacrilegious devil and demanded the murals be destroyed. The President of Detroit's Marygrove College, Dr. George Hermann Derry, spoke for all who detested Rivera's work and declared, "Señor Rivera has perpetrated a heartless hoax on his capitalist employer, Edsel Ford. Rivera was engaged to interpret Detroit; he has foisted on Mr. Ford and the museum a Communist manifesto." An editorial in the *Detroit News* suggested that "the best thing to do would be to whitewash the entire work completely," while Monsignor Doyle, who did not even bother to look at the paintings, felt qualified enough as an art critic to condemn them as "an affront to millions of Catholics."

Taking the battle lines on the other side were those who championed art, the freedom of expression, and the mere enjoyment of what Rivera had created in a very dark and gray time in the city of Detroit. Edsel Ford himself was cautious. He knew that whatever he said would have implications on his ability to sell cars, which was his livelihood and legacy, and would only cryptically comment, "I admire Rivera's spirit. I really believe he was trying to express his idea of the spirit of Detroit." Whatever side one took, the raging battle was perhaps the ultimate endorsement of what Rivera had wrought on the walls of the garden court—great art inspires passionate response, whether in support or in condemnation, and his murals certainly achieved that. As Dr. Valentiner wrote Rivera several years after the painter left the city, "Your murals here are still the greatest attraction in Detroit."

And those same murals still exist today.

As for the last meeting with Rivera, Orlin and Haik said warm good-byes to the painter and Miss Frida, promising to see each other again although all were certain they never would. Rivera presented Haik with a large wrapped package he said was a parting gift for all the hospitality they had shown him. What could they say? He owed them nothing. Haik had been paid for his services, so Rivera should feel no sense of debt. Haik remembered all the nights at the speakeasies and the time he spent with Rivera and Miss Frida at the Rouge and later the lonely and mysterious sessions with the painter as light seeped out of the garden court. People would later ask him about those times, but he could not really explain. The only thing to do was to enter the garden court itself, and rotate slowly 360 degrees, allowing the kaleidoscope of color and action melded into the walls to engulf the senses.

Haik took Lu and Charlie to the museum not long after the paintings were unveiled, and they marveled at the workers and cars and airplanes and generators before them and the vibrant feast their eyes enjoyed. Yes, Haik answered Charlie, that was really him and Uncle Orlin there on the north wall, yes, it did look exactly like them. He hugged Charlie and Lu and looked forward to the day he could take Artie to see his father in all his glory there on the wall at a big fancy museum. Haik had heard eggheads say that you can look at a painting for hours, but for him that only held true for Rivera's whirlwind painting in the garden court.

The Purple Gang members, almost to a man, died violently. The Siamese Twins, Axler and Fletcher, were executed and their bodies later found next to each other in a car, their faces blown away but their hands posed holding onto each other in grim humor. Harry Millman was gunned down bellied up to a bar at the age of 26 after he survived a car bombing, and Sam Davis disappeared after escaping from a prison for the criminally insane, apparently assassinated and disposed of without a trace. Harry Altman died in prison, his liver destroyed.

As for Rivera and Miss Frida, their tempestuous relationship is the stuff of legend, a legend of its own with all its own fascinating twists and turns, triumphs and tragedies. Miss Frida never bore Rivera a child, and they woud divorce and remarry, fight, reconcile, love and battle, infuriate, betray, and inspire one another until her death and beyond. Henry Ford actually outlived his son Edsel, who died during the second great war. After Edsel's death, Harry Bennett was sure he would be named President of the Ford Motor Company, but Edsel's son Henry

Ford II took the job and promptly fired an infuriated Bennett, ending his dubious reign of terror.

Regarding the Deuce Coupe, it really belonged to neither Haik nor Orlin individually. Rivera had made the choice of model Orlin's, and Edsel Ford awarded the keys to Haik. Whomever needed the car drove it; most often, it was members of both families aboard at any given time. If something needed fixed, they swapped out a part they had reclaimed or bought the part from the till of the garage's profits. If their experiences had taught them anything, it was that a car or anything else that could be bought was not worth fighting over.

And the package Rivera gave to Haik? When he and Orlin got back to the house in Utica, Haik placed the package on a work bench in the barn. Later, he and Orlin went out and tore off the brown wrapping paper, and inside were two paintings. One was the painting Miss Frida had been working on that seemed to cause Rivera so much jealousy. Orlin laughed at the nude image of Haik and was simply puzzled by the odd image of Miss Frida. Haik got Orlin's word not to mention the painting, and he scaled the ladder to the barn's hay loft and hung it there safely out of Lu's reach, hiding it under an old tarp. He could not explain why he was there on a canvas in all his glory. It was best to keep that canvas silent.

The other painting was a small replica of Haik and Orlin's images that stood in the museum. Haik and Orlin were both proud of this picture, and hung it in the parlor of the house they shared in Utica, each of them often looking at it long into the night after everyone else was asleep.

ALSO BY JOHN JEFFIRE:
MOTOWN BURNING
- 2005 Mount Arrowsmith Novel Competition Winner
- 2007 Independent Publishing Awards Gold Medal for Regional Fiction

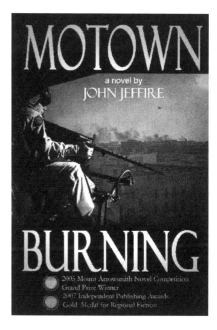

Late July of 1967, and Detroit boils over. For Aram Pehlivanian, known as Motown, the Grande Ballroom and the music of the MC5 and Iggy Pop and The Temptations no longer provide a haven as destruction engulfs his city. However, escaping death in the streets during the '67 Detroit Riots only leads him to the jungles of Vietnam and away from Katie, the girl who might be his salvation. Beaten on the streets of Detroit, hunted in the jungles of Vietnam, and fueled to survive by the music of the Motor City, Aram burns with one goal...to see Katie again.

"John Jeffire's novel Motown Burning *breathes life into an all too familiar battered and bruised Detroit, reminding me of John Dos Passos's* Manhattan Transfer, *how 200-plus characters as a collective group define New York City, where the setting 'becomes' the main character with a steady flow of immigrants coming and going, searching for opportunity, for a place to call home."*
—**James Tomlinson**, *winner of the Judith Siegel Pearson Prize*

"It works. I don't often say that, but it has a drive and integrity that gives it credible life....I find a novel with heart."
—**Philip F. O'Connor**, *former chair of the Pulitzer jury*

*"*Motown Burning *is raw, the emotions, powerful, and the images, brutal. The dialogue is coarse and gritty and paints an uncompromising portrait of war. It is through this language and Jeffire's rich imagination that history comes to life."*
—**Holly Smith**, *thedetroiter.com*

Stone + Fist + Brick + Bone

John Jeffire's debut collection of poems, nominated for the Michigan Notable Book award.

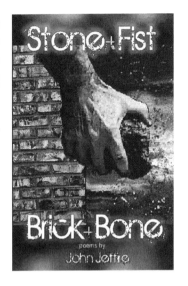

"John Jeffire's tight, unflinching poems pack a real wallop. He knows these people, and he knows these streets. He can be tough, and he can be tender—and funny too. There's nothing unearned in these deeply felt, authentic poems. Like the people in his poems, he works hard, and he plays hard, and it all pays off in this moving, memorable collection."

—**Jim Daniels**, author of *Eight Mile High* and *Trigger Man*

"...a terrific one for our city."

—**Philip Levine**, former U.S. Poet Laureate and Pulitzer Prize Winner

"John Jeffire's poems are perfectly urban: gritty and beautiful, tragic and comic, tough and tender, profane and sacred. He finds the lyricism of the polluted River Rouge, of the piss smell behind the dumpsters, of the child home from rehab, of the lionfish. He knows that 'we learned our commandments/ by breaking them' and he offers us, through these poems our penance, our forgiveness, our Detroit psalms."

—**Gerry LaFemina**, author of *Zarathustra in Love*

"The poems of John Jeffire are first magical and then harsh. They are never sentimental. The poet re-creates a boyhood in the streets and alleys of an earlier Dearborn, but the poet is not a tour guide. There is pain here and sorrow, but there is never self-pity. These are manly poems that took my breath away."

—**Rhoda Stamell**, author of *Detroit Stories*

"Travel with Jeffire through his street level poems of pool halls, whiskey nights at the K of C, hunger and talking old soldiers. John Jeffire is the real deal. You will be moved to a new awareness about the world we all live, work and die in, and you'll be a stronger person for having traveled these paths through his poetry."

—**M.L. Liebler**, author of *Breaking the Voodoo*